THE
TRAPPED
WIFE

BOOKS BY SAMANTHA HAYES

The Reunion
Tell Me a Secret
The Liar's Wife
Date Night
The Happy Couple
Single Mother

THE TRAPPED WIFE

SAMANTHA HAYES

bookouture

Published by Bookouture in 2021

An imprint of Storyfire Ltd.
Carmelite House
50 Victoria Embankment
London EC4Y 0DZ

www.bookouture.com

ISBN: 978-1-80019-759-6
eBook ISBN: 978-1-80019-758-9

For my family with love…
The whole amazing lot of you
Xxx

PROLOGUE

Then

The boy sits on the tarmac, knees drawn up to his chin, his feet crammed into scuffed black school shoes as he stares at the ground between them. Across the playground he hears the whoops and cries of the other kids at break time – charging about inanely as they shriek and scream in a steam-releasing chorus.

He doesn't need to let off steam. What a waste that would be. He likes to let it build up, to simmer inside until he feels his brain swell and his nerves jump. Nothing gives him more pleasure than feeling the twist in his guts, the pressure behind his eyes as his body builds and tenses. Why, he's not sure, but he knows, as certain as those two insects scuttling between his feet, that he's not going to play tag or football or swap trading cards like the others. That's for babies. And he's not a baby. No way.

He hates this school; wants to burn it down. The other kids have barely spoken to him since he started a few weeks ago. Things were fine when it was just him and his mum at their old place, their old life, without Griff or his new baby sister.

He wipes the back of his hand under one eye. Something is making it water, making his vision blurry as he stares at the iridescent beetle waddling one way then back the other. He puts out a grubby finger, stopping the bug in his tracks, wanting it to meet the ladybird. He doesn't know if beetles eat ladybirds for lunch, but he hopes so.

A thud resonates through his head as a football hits the wall next to him. He hates that he flinches – he can't help it – and also doesn't like that the fat kid from two classes above him lumbers over to fetch the ball, panting, sweating through his pale-blue shirt. His tie is knotted short, his trousers hanging low on bulging hips.

'Idiot,' the older kid spits down at him, laughing. Picking up the ball, he draws back his foot as if he's about to launch it at his thigh but thinks better of it at the sound of the teacher's voice. Instead, the big kid flobs on the ground, narrowly missing him, before striding off with the ball tucked under his arm.

Fat fucker, the boy yells back in his head, imagining his foot sticking out to trip the other kid up, his nose bloody when he hits the ground, everyone laughing at him. But that's not real life, not how it goes for him. He wipes his eye again as the feeling grows. Steam. *More* steam building as he turns his attention back to the insects.

Not real life. Not *yet*, he thinks, fighting the tears, clamping his teeth together.

'Go on, don't be afraid,' he whispers to the ladybird as she spreads her wings, showing a petticoat of wonder beneath her black and red coat. He had no idea. Didn't realise she had so many delicate layers – each one vulnerable and fragile. Not like the beetle, he thinks, marvelling at the shiny green and blue of his armour plating, making him appear metallic. Invincible – just how *he* wants to be.

He uses a twig to coax his new pets closer together. They're a good distraction from his thoughts – the thoughts that pound the inside of his head from the moment he wakes up until the moment he struggles for sleep, trying to block out the noises coming from his mum and Griff's room.

'Maybe you'll be my friends,' he says under his breath, rummaging in his pocket in case that old Tic Tac container is still there to put them in. "'Cos I haven't got no others,' he whispers, his shoulders slumping forward.

Something in his eye again.

And that's when he's aware of a shadow – a presence looming over him, blocking out the sun from his private corner of the playground. He sees two tatty trainers on the ground in front of him, the grimy laces thickly knotted with no hope of ever being undone, and the once-white plastic a muddy brown. Hanging down over the trainers are grey school trousers, their hems frayed and crusted with mud.

Before he knows what's happening, one of the feet lifts up and stamps down hard on the tarmac where the insects have just met. He feels the involuntary gasp in his throat, shuddering as his nerves fire jolts through his body. He's never felt pressure like it.

Then the foot lifts up again and he can hardly believe that the flattened ladybird and beetle had so much stuff inside them. So much *ugly* stuff. It feels as if his brain is letting off fireworks.

Slowly, his eyes track up the skinny legs – a hole in one of the knees exposing grazed and scabby skin beneath. One side of the boy's pale-blue school shirt hangs untucked from the waistband, a button missing, and two arms dangle within a navy-blue padded anorak with the stuffing coming out of one elbow.

The face belonging to the bug-squasher is smaller and paler than he'd imagined and, when their eyes meet, the feeling inside him is unlike anything he's ever experienced before. It's like a thousand happy playtimes all rolled into one. He feels like he might explode. A *release*.

And then, as he stares up in awe, the boy above him smiles. Slowly at first but his own mouth soon follows suit, returning the grin as his cracked lips stretch wide – each of them unaware of what is yet to come.

CHAPTER ONE

Now

Jen

I stare at the pregnancy test strip, waiting for the results. My cheeks still smart from the dank February air outside, even though it's warm in my office. *Too warm*, I think, making a mental note to ask Peggy to turn the heating down. I glance at my watch. Fifteen minutes until clinic starts – my first day back at work since... since the accident six weeks ago. Since I lost Jeremy, my husband. And only three minutes to find out what the rest of my life holds.

My hands are shaking, so I close my eyes and take a few deep breaths. It does little to ease the ache in my heart, the fear flowing through my veins. I miss him so much.

Somehow, I have to pull myself together, get a grip, focus and block out everything churning inside me – at least while I'm at the surgery. Half a dozen patients were already queuing up outside when I arrived, some of them greeting me, offering their condolences, though I didn't stop to talk – just nodding a small smile as I rushed past. Peggy will unlock the doors on the dot of eight thirty, allowing them all to file in, wait their turn for their allotted ten minutes with me or one of the other GPs here at Waverly Medical Practice.

A precisely planned day lies ahead, filled with patients, meetings, reviewing test results, phone calls and occasionally a home visit, because I refuse to give them up entirely. Waverly is a community practice and our patients rely on us – on *me* – and our personal service, the relationships we've built through generations of families. Though, try as we might to run a tight ship, nothing ever goes to plan. Life gets in the way. Besides, I couldn't stay off work any longer. I was drowning in the whirlpool of my own thoughts, bubbling under my grief just sitting at home alone. Kieran has already gone back to school, only missing the first week of term after the Christmas holidays – needing his friends, routine, some kind of normality. And now it's time for me to do the same. Get back into some kind of life again. A life that will now always have a hole carved in it.

I place the test strip down on my desk next to the sample I took on my way in, having dashed into the toilets without any of our three receptionists noticing me as I arrived. After I'd finished throwing up, I'd filled the little container and gone straight to my office with my head down. Apart from a vase of fresh flowers on the windowsill and a 'thinking of you' card from my colleagues (and the room having been cleaned), everything is just as I'd left it the day before New Year's Eve – a time capsule from when my life was normal. When I'd *forced* it to be normal, even though I'd had my suspicions it wasn't.

'Please, please, *please*,' I whisper, biting my lip and watching the liquid seep slowly up the strip, creeping ever closer to the control line, and then onwards to the second marker. 'Human chorionic gonadotrophin,' I say, unwinding the pale-blue scarf from around my neck, not taking my eyes off the strip. Three words with the power to turn a night of… of… I shake my head, shuddering and daring to take my eyes off the strip as I slip off my overcoat, hanging it and my scarf on the back of the door. Into a terrible *mistake*, I think, staring down at the test strip again.

Another minute to go.

None of this seems real.

The phone on my desk rings.

'Welcome back, Dr Miller,' Peggy says through a swallow. She always brings breakfast in to work. The staff have been kind and understanding since it happened – not least Tim Blake, my fellow partner at Waverly. 'Dr Blake wants to know if you can change the partners' meeting to three o'clock instead of two.'

'Change the meeting…?' I say, distracted, not taking my eyes off the strip. If I could change anything right now, it would be that one stupid, reckless night a couple of months ago – a night I can barely even remember. Barely remember except when I wake from the terror-filled dreams, sweat pouring off me, fragments of it still stuck behind my eyelids – a bar, alcohol, a man. A warm hand on my shoulder – breaking through a psychological barrier that I'd convinced myself needed breaking. *Payback*. How could I have been so *stupid*, so reckless?

Except I'm neither of those things; they're so very far from who I am. And I didn't want revenge, either. I would *never* have done anything to hurt Jeremy on purpose, to betray him – not even taking into account what I'd suspected about him for some time. But then how is this even *possible*, I think, still staring at the test strip?

My head is filled with missing time, a feeling that something's not right, a deep sense of fear about what happened that night. And whatever it is, I know I can't tell a soul.

'You're not thinking ahead,' I hear Jeremy say, the memory of his voice soothing as I picture him leaning over the chequerboard, a cut-glass tumbler of whisky in one hand, the fire crackling beside us as he waits patiently for me to make my move. 'See the game as if you were me, as if you were in my shoes…'

Then I'd be dead, I think, only realising I've whispered it out loud when Peggy says, 'Sorry? You OK, Jen?'

'Yes, yes, I'm fine,' I reply, touching my head. I blink several times, trying to refocus on the strip. It's as though a camera flash has gone off in my face, and the residual image is in stark negative. My mouth hangs open.

'The meeting?' Peggy repeats.

Bodies squashed close, rounds of shots, more wine, laughter, bright lights, loud music – the thud of the bass hammering my skull. A face close... a man's face, his hand in the small of my back...

I suck in a breath, closing my eyes. 'Yes, yes, that's fine, Peggy. Move the meeting,' I say before quickly hanging up.

When I open my eyes again, I look at the strip.

Two blue lines.

I blink hard. Still two lines.

Pregnant.

Slowly, I pick it up, struggling to convince myself it's even real as I hold it.

'Christ,' I whisper, my hand shaking as I stare at the result. I can't deny that things had been tense between Jeremy and me in the months before he died, with him either sleeping in the spare room or us lying with our backs to each other. It breaks my heart that I can't remember when we last made love, when my husband held me, the shape of our spent bodies curled into each other. But I know I've had a period since we last slept together.

If the test is accurate and I am pregnant, it can only have been that one night at the medical conference in Oxford, early last December. But I don't understand it; I simply don't remember what happened. The only things I know for certain are the sense of dread I've been left with ever since, and that I woke up in my hotel room alone.

Though you *hadn't* been alone, had you, Jen? I think, dropping down into my chair, my inner voice both ferocious and fearful. What the *hell* had happened that night?

I remember the two half-finished glasses of wine on the dressing table that morning – a crescent of lipstick on one. My underwear discarded on the floor, my new dress flung across the room, one shoe in the bathroom, the other under the bed (how did I even dance in those heels?). No other evidence – apart from the gentle thrum low down in my body, the embers of a fire reignited. Warm blood finally flowing through my veins. It had been a long time since I'd felt it. Yet it could easily have been a fantasy, a dream. An escape.

I chuck the test strip down onto my desk and cover my face, my shoulders jumping in time with my silent sobs as I try to think back. All I know for sure is that something must have happened – something that my mind is intent on hiding from me. And after the couple of days away at the conference, I'd returned home to my husband without an inkling that in less than a month, he'd be dead.

'I wasn't thinking ahead,' I say out loud, mainly for Jeremy's benefit. If anyone is able to hear or communicate beyond the grave, it'll be him. I reach across my desk for the photo frame – a picture of him and Kieran, shoulder to shoulder in the fishing boat we hired a couple of years ago on Loch Lomond. I find myself smiling. An unfamiliar act these last few weeks. They didn't catch anything on the loch, of course. My boys. But we ate fresh fish at a local restaurant that night by way of compensation, Jeremy chatting to anyone and everyone, as he always did, that trademark smile of his with his dark eyes sitting beneath a mop of messy curls, winning over even the most closed-off locals. He always had a tale to tell, an adventure to share, which was why he'd started writing the book in the first place. The book that never got finished.

I run my finger gently over his face before opening my desk drawer and slipping the photo inside. News will have travelled fast in the village, and I don't want patients asking questions that I can't answer or offering sympathy I don't want. They come here for me to help them, not the other way around. Getting back to work is meant to help me move on, to resume as normal a life as possible – for Kieran's sake, too – and I don't want to be reminded of what's happened every day. Jeremy would have insisted on it. 'Don't bloody well sit around pining for me, you silly woman,' he'd say in that gruff but amiable way of his. 'Just get on with your life.' I loved him for his straight talking, his no-nonsense honesty.

I open my desk diary to today's date, drawing a line through the partners' meeting and rewriting it in the 3 p.m. slot. Then I turn a few pages, stopping when I get to Friday. My half day. Well, my three-quarter day in reality, but it meant I'd always be home by 4 p.m., maybe stopping at the butcher on the way back to pick up some steaks. That, plus a bottle of something red from Jeremy's prized collection, some art-house movie he'd been hankering to see, and our night would be made. Kieran would usually be in his room or out with a friend. At sixteen, he rarely sat with us in the evenings now.

I turn the page to Saturday – that was all about chores and errands in the Miller household, with Jeremy trundling about the paddock on the quad bike at this time of year, checking the fences were secure, the hedges clipped, the ditches clear and the pond dredged of weed.

'Man's work,' he'd say, knowing how much that annoyed me, that I'd happily tackle the tasks myself if I had the time. I'd always been happier in wellies, jeans and a baggy sweater, and getting covered in mud and scratches never bothered me. Afterwards, Jeremy would come inside and grab me, his cheeks glowing and his skin flavoured with the outdoors as I kissed him.

Sundays were quiet days – filled with lazy brunches, the newspapers, coffee and sometimes chess. It was a ritual for Jeremy to beat me at the game. But I didn't mind. It somehow kept my mind fresh and allowed me a couple of hours to unwind with my husband before the craziness of the week began again, or he took off on another of his so-called research trips.

But that was before things went sour. Before I suspected there was someone else.

'I don't think I've *ever* beaten you, have I?' I remember saying to him during one of the last games of chess we ever played. It was a particularly foul Sunday – the rain sheeting sideways, hammering the big expanse of glass in the side of our old barn. He'd stoked the wood burner with a fresh supply of logs, and I'd put a joint of beef in the Aga. Kieran was meant to be studying in his room, though I could hear him strumming a tune on his guitar. He was never going to be any good but he loved practising. It was the most clichéd Sunday afternoon ever. And, despite everything that had been brewing, my suspicions, it was the most perfect one, too. I didn't want it to end, didn't want *anything* to end – apart from my paranoia.

'Checkmate, mate,' Jeremy had said with a laugh, his grey eyes sparkling as he leant back in the battered leather armchair. *His* armchair, the one he always sat in, giving anyone who dared settle in it one of his looks. He'd swept back his almost-black curls that were beginning to be flecked with silver, the firelight reflecting in his eyes as though it was the fire inside him bursting out.

'Say, *whaat*?' I'd said, wide-eyed and incredulous at yet another defeat. 'It's only been about eight moves.'

'Six,' Jeremy corrected.

I laughed, shaking my head. It was hopeless. *I* was hopeless. He'd been trying to teach me the game for years, and it wasn't my lack of knowledge of where the pieces could move or, indeed, the aim of the game. It was my complete inability to see ahead. To *plan* ahead. To me, it was like trying to read a book with one page out of every three missing. None of it made sense. None of it was logical and relied solely upon the other person's thoughts and moves. And as it turned out, I certainly wasn't a mind reader.

'My record was four moves, remember?' he'd said in a deep voice, winking at me.

I shook my head, smiling as I got up to check on the beef.

'Fool's mate,' he'd called out after me as I went through to the kitchen.

'*Fool's mate*,' I whisper now, wrapping the test strip in a tissue and pushing it into my bag. Was that me, the fool? I cover my face again, screwing up my eyes as another fragmented memory from *that* night in Oxford flashes through my mind.

*

'Come in,' I trill as my first patient knocks on the door. I check the intercom is switched off after having summoned her through from the waiting room, putting on my 'welcoming doctor' smile as the young woman enters backwards, her elbow propping open the door as she struggles in with a pram and a toddler in tow. I leap up, holding the door wider for her.

'Hello, Sally,' I say. 'You've got your hands full there.' Three bags of shopping, the toddler and a nappy bag hang off her wrists as she manoeuvres the pram, getting the front wheel caught against the door frame as she reverses in. 'Have a seat,' I say as she finally gets inside and I close the door. 'What can I do for you?'

'Mum-*my*...' the toddler whines, pulling at his mother's sleeve. Sally is only twenty-four but looks tired, drained, as if she's having the life sucked out of her. Literally, it transpires, when she reveals why she's come to see me.

'OK, well, let's take a look at you, then,' I say. 'Danny, why don't you see what toys I've got in my special box?' I point to the tub of brightly coloured plastic things in the corner. The toddler releases his mother and coyly walks over to the toys, his thumb shoved in his mouth, his eyes big and round.

I draw the curtain around the examination couch, asking Sally to take off her top and bra, having a peek into her pram while she undresses. The baby is asleep, her bottom lip quivering as she sucks through her dreams, her fists clenched either side of her head. A baby girl, I think, knowing the sex of the embryo growing inside me will already have been determined.

A wave of nausea surges through me. Adrenaline and shame rather than antenatal sickness this time. It was the early-morning vomiting during the last week or so, plus the realisation that I'd missed at least one, if not two, periods that convinced me to do the test. With everything that had happened, I was hoping my symptoms could be put down to stress.

'I'm ready,' Sally says from behind the curtain.

I duck into the cubicle, leaving the fabric slightly apart so she can keep an eye on her toddler. Sally is lying on her back, her engorged breasts splayed out either side and the top of her leggings cutting into her post-pregnancy belly. She only had the baby three weeks ago.

'It's this one,' she says, pointing to her left breast. 'It started in this area but it's all hot and swollen now. It's agony, especially when she feeds.'

'Sorry if my hands are a bit cold,' I say, gently examining her. It only takes a moment for me to diagnose mastitis. I take her temperature.

'Is it up?' she says, a concerned look on her face. 'Danny, stop it!' she calls out as her little boy chucks a wooden brick across the room. It skids under the couch.

'A little,' I tell her. 'I'll give you some antibiotics. They won't hurt baby. Feed her from your sore breast first, express between feeds if you can, and a warm flannel will ease the pain. Paracetamol is fine too. If it isn't any better in three or four days, come back and see me,' I add. 'I'll leave you to get dressed,' I say, forcing a smile that would normally come naturally.

At my desk, I type up the prescription and print it out for her, eyeing her toddler as he empties the entire contents of the toy box onto the floor. I close my eyes briefly, imagining myself on my hands and knees clearing up... night feeds, changing nappies a dozen times a day, childcare, tiredness, the expense, coping alone… not to mention what everyone will say. *Obviously a mistake… her husband's dead and she's forty-two!*

'Having a second baby isn't just twice the work,' Sally says with a sigh, coming out from behind the curtains and straightening her baggy top. 'It's like ten times as much work.' She tries to laugh, but I see through the exhaustion. 'And Steve is on nights, so it's hard to keep them both quiet in the day when he's sleeping.'

'Two under two is hard work,' I say, handing her the prescription. 'Look after Mummy,' I tell the toddler as he trots over to take his mother's hand, clutching a small plastic fire engine in the other, holding it against his chest as he stares up at me. He has dribble on his chin, his skin sore and cracked. 'It's fine, he can keep it,' I tell Sally, holding the door open as she leaves.

She stops, the pram half in, half out. 'Do you have children, Doctor?' she asks.

Her question catches me unawares. 'Yes… yes, I do,' I tell her, gripping the door handle hard. 'A son. He's sixteen.'

She smiles at me, pausing, giving a little nod.

'Don't worry,' I say as she heads off. 'It gets easier,' I add, knowing full well that it doesn't.

CHAPTER TWO

Jen

Sweat pours out of me – rivulets running down my face, seeping into my sports top, the breath burning in and out of my lungs as I pump harder. Pink and electric-blue lights flash in time with the music – a fast beat that my legs are supposed to follow. They don't.

'Ramp it up a notch now!' the instructor yells into the tiny wireless mic by his mouth. How can he even speak, let alone shout? I wonder, pedalling harder, feeling an unbearable burn in my quads. 'C'mon now, go for the final hit!'

He's been yelling encouragement for forty-five minutes so far. Like work, it's my first day back in the gym for a while. I was hoping exercise would take my mind off my pregnancy test results, but it hasn't. If anything, it's making me think about the little life growing inside me even more, conscious that I don't overexert myself. It might feel like the end of *my* life as I know it, but it's the start of this little baby's.

I glance across at Rhonda, who's on the spin bike next to me. She's standing up, her legs cycling hard and fast, her knuckles white as she grips the handlebars. She leans forward, her chin jutting and her eyes filled with determination and grit. Her wavy blonde hair is high in a ponytail with strands of it stuck to her sweaty face; her teeth are clenched and bared as she draws upon deep reserves of energy. A far cry from my weak performance.

While the others reach down with one hand to increase the resistance of their bikes, I tweak my knob to an even lighter setting, gradually feeling the ache in my muscles ease. Throughout the session, I've not been working out at my usual level.

'Final hill!' the instructor calls out, his pumped and toned body making light work of the class. There's a bright grin slashed across his face as if… as if he's *enjoying* this, I think, remembering that I once did too. Just not any more.

The music speeds up, the lights flashing faster, making me screw up my eyes. If we were actually cycling up a hill, I'd be way behind the others, probably getting off my bike and pushing it up the incline by now, breathless and fed up.

There's a baby growing inside me.

And then I'm back there – *that* night – for just a few seconds, my heart thundering at the recollection. Recalling the early part of the evening is easy, but as the night wore on, all I'm left with are fleeting memories, random snapshots that I can't control.

I was in some kind of bar or club… crowded and filled with groups from the conference letting their hair down after an intense few days, all of us standing squashed shoulder to shoulder: sweaty bodies, strobe lights, not dissimilar to the spin class studio now. Some of the faces I recognised from the medical talks, and I remember thinking that it was strange to see them out of their business clothes, knocking back shots or swigging from a bottle, laughing, relieved that the intensity of the three-day conference was done for another year.

Someone had knocked into me, jolting me forward and making me spill my drink.

'God, I'm so sorry,' I'd said to the man next to me, who took the brunt of the mess. My voice was barely audible above the loud music and din of the chatter. Shouting an apology somehow made it seem less genuine. He shook his head, grinned and told me not to worry. Then he asked my name and offered to buy me another drink. I'd seen him around, caught him glancing at me once or twice over the last couple of days. Not thought anything of it. He was friendly enough.

I keep pedalling, my eyes flicking to the clock on the wall. Cool-down in three minutes.

'Bit claustrophobic in here,' the man had gone on to say, handing me a fresh drink. I had no idea what it was – some kind of cocktail – and I wondered if he was about to ask if I wanted to go somewhere quieter, perhaps outside for a smoke. I remember the telltale shape of the packet of cigarettes in his shirt pocket. He had that expectant look about him – because he'd bought me a drink. I was in his debt now.

I was all set to tell him that I actually liked the thrum of the bass pounding through my head, bodies pressed close and people shouting to be heard above the music, but really, it was the anonymity I craved. Somewhere I didn't feel like me, where no one knew who I was; a place that was more dominating than my actual thoughts. An environment that used up all of my cognitive resources so I couldn't dwell on things. Couldn't dwell on *her*. But he got the message just from my expression, didn't push it further.

I nodded at him, flashed a quick smile after half shouting, 'Thanks for the drink,' before walking off, weaving through the crowd, shoulder first, glancing left and right in case there was a free seat. I'd wobbled a tipsy path through the groups of people as I'd tried to find somewhere to sit. Truth was, I'd just wanted to be alone with my thoughts and I figured the best place to do it was in a packed club.

It was just as I'd spotted the empty stool, set next to a tall aluminium bar table, that I felt the hand on my shoulder, the warm breath brush my neck from behind. Even without looking, even in my inebriated and exhausted state, I sensed trouble. Smelt danger. Felt the prickle of goosebumps rise on my skin, working their way down my body, making me freeze.

*

'Right, wind it back now!' the instructor calls out. 'Let's bring those heart rates down a notch,' he adds, sitting back on his saddle and taking a water bottle from its holder. He swigs, not caring that water runs down his chin and onto his neck, making his slick black skin even shinier.

I glance across at Rhonda, who, sensing my look, turns to me. She grins, wiping her brow with the back of one hand in an overstated gesture, making a silly face as she blows out.

'Knackered,' she says, dropping down onto her saddle, still keeping her legs moving. Whipping her towel off the handlebars, she wipes it over her face. I do the same, but only to make it look like I've worked up more of a sweat than I actually have.

Ten minutes later, after stretching out beside the bikes, I follow Rhonda out into the main gym area. The familiar clank and clunk of the weights machines surrounds us, with an assortment of men and women standing around chatting, spotting for their workout partner, or lifting weights on their own.

'Love Dale's classes,' Rhonda says breathily. Her pale skin glows pink on her cheeks and her blue eyes seem brighter than usual.

'His workouts are still bloody evil,' I say with a laugh, draping the towel around my neck.

After we've showered and changed, we head into the gym café and grab a couple of smoothies from the chiller cabinet, Rhonda insisting she pay. Since Jeremy's death, she's gone out of her way to be a good friend, whether it's helping me around the house, cooking and delivering meals, or ferrying Kieran about when I've not felt like getting out of bed. I'm so grateful to her, and don't know how I'll ever be able to repay her for her kindness.

'So,' Rhonda says once we're seated. 'How are you doing?' She asks this often, has done since I got the devastating news from Switzerland six weeks ago. Her concern began on a much higher level back then, of course – code red – and has dwindled slightly over the weeks to a paler shade of amber, though not because she doesn't care. It's as if she's taken on the management of my grief, carefully measuring my periods of anger, frustration and denial as I wind my way through the perilous stages. She's always asked how I am, of course, even before Jeremy was killed, but it's just that I didn't particularly notice – a casual 'How you doing?' as we hugged a greeting, neither of us ever expecting much more than a 'Good, thanks' in reply.

Now, Rhonda purposefully places the question during the middle of our meets, so it's not seen as throwaway chit-chat, but rather taken as a serious enquiry after assessing my mood. And if I'm evasive, she'll divert the conversation back to my well-being until she's satisfied that I'm not going to throw myself under a bus.

'Fine,' I say, taking a sip of smoothie, glancing at her. I feel a twinge low down in my belly. I want to tell her – *need* to tell her – but I don't know how. It would mean explaining everything… and how can I do that, when I don't have any answers myself? 'Busy first day back,' I add, knowing she won't settle for a single syllable. 'The new booking system has had a few teething problems but it was actually functioning pretty well today.' I look at her, hoping that's enough. 'How are things with you?'

'You look different,' she says, giving me a sideways look, her eyes narrowing.

'I do?' I reply, my voice tinged with guilt. 'Probably because I feel as though I'm about to have a heart attack after that bloody class.' I force a laugh, fighting back the words *I'm pregnant*. Because once it's out, there'll be questions I can't answer.

Rhonda shakes her head. 'It's not that.'

I pause, feeling my skin twitch under my right eye. 'It was just a bit… well, it was a bit overwhelming being back at work today,' I say, hoping that's enough for her to chew on. 'The thought of Jeremy not sitting in his study when I get home is… well, it still hasn't truly sunk in, if I'm honest.' At least that's the truth, I think, dreading my first return home from work with him not being there to greet me. 'I miss him so much, Ronnie.'

Rhonda nods, her eyes heavy. 'I know,' she says. 'I still can't believe it myself most days.' She puts a hand on my arm before glancing behind me. Her face lights up. 'Come for supper at ours tonight,' she says quickly, before finishing with a warm, 'Chris!' as she greets her husband. She tips her face up towards him as he bends down to give her a peck. Then he reaches across and gives me a brief hug.

'Sorry I'm a bit late, Ronnie. Traffic was horrendous,' he says. 'How was the class, ladies?'

I make a face and a groaning sound. All I can manage as I survey him standing next to our small table. At first glance, you'd never know he was a copper – a slightly rounded dad paunch visible through his sweatshirt, even though he doesn't have children of his own to earn that title. Despite that, he's fit, and goes running regularly, sometimes with Caitlin, Rhonda's teenage daughter, and he has a home gym set up in his garage. Mostly he's an unremarkable forty-something – unlike Jeremy, who was anything but unremarkable with his shock of wild hair, his intense eyes and planet-sized personality. I feel bad for making comparisons.

'Jen survived her first day back at work as well as a spin class, so I'd say she's winning at life today,' Rhonda tells him.

He glances down at me, pushing a hand through his light-brown hair – always neatly cropped. 'That must have been…' He trails off, not knowing what to say.

I nod. 'A little strange. But everyone was lovely. No big fanfares. They know how much I'd hate that.' I take a sip of my smoothie. 'Anyway, I wouldn't say I was exactly winning at life,' I add. Since the accident, I seem to be living in a time lag, a few minutes behind everyone else. It feels as though I'm on a permanent long-distance call that won't properly connect. 'More like muddling through somehow.'

I put my smoothie bottle down on the table, but can't help wanting to take a swipe at it, sending the green sludge flying as I yell and kick and scream out that nothing in my life feels right any more, that inside I'm burning up with... with *something*, though I have no idea what. But I don't, of course. I'm adept at keeping my cool, holding it together. Aside from anything, at least two of my patients are in the vicinity.

'I've asked Jen round for supper,' Rhonda tells Chris.

'Thanks, but I can't tonight.' I stand up, hooking my gym bag over my shoulder. 'Kieran is expecting me home. Anyway, it's my turn to cook for you next, to say thanks for everything you've done,' I add, as the pair of them arc their heads with what I perceive to be relieved expressions. No one really wants a grieving widow to come for supper on a weeknight. Besides, I want to spend time with my son. He's become so withdrawn since he lost his dad, as though a part of him is lost too. 'Thanks for dragging me here,' I say to Rhonda, giving her a peck on each cheek. 'I'm sure I'll sleep well now,' I add, knowing I won't.

And, as I walk off towards the turnstile, I imagine myself yelling out that I'm pregnant, my arms spread wide and my face red and demonic as I spin around, confessing to everyone that I don't know whose baby I'm carrying, that Jeremy and I hadn't had sex for at least three months before he died, and I'm pretty sure the father is a stranger I met in a bar.

In reality, I dash across the freezing car park and get into my car, leaning forward on the steering wheel, allowing the tears I've been holding back to flow.

CHAPTER THREE

Jen

The next morning, I reach for the button on my desk phone. 'Yes, Peggy,' I say into the speaker, taking off my coat and scarf and hanging them on the back of my consulting room door. I'm breathless – not from being later to work than I'd have liked, and rushing since the moment I got up (or rather, since the moment I hauled myself up from leaning over the toilet bowl), but rather from the resources being harvested from my body as the embryo's cells divide and multiply at a million miles an hour. I feel exhausted. Empty. And, despite the spin class wearing out my body last night, I didn't sleep at all.

'Just reminding you about your two house calls later,' she says, her mouth full of something as she chews.

'Don't worry, I haven't forgotten,' I say, managing to sound jovial as I sit down. 'And thanks, Peggy. It's appreciated.' I click the intercom off and sit back in my chair. She never used to remind me about my schedule. The room smells faintly of polish and disinfectant, soon to be filled by back-to-back patients in the morning's clinic – tainted by the smell of other people's lives, their collective histories, stories and ailments. I can't bear to think what scent I'd leave behind – regret, wretchedness, shame. Though it's the growing sense of dread that stinks the most.

Inside my bag, my phone beeps. I reach for it, reading the text from Kieran.

Home late. Football training.

I send a quick reply, asking what he wants for dinner, adding a couple of kisses. When nothing comes back straight away, I go into my photo stream, scrolling back to December. It won't take long to locate what I'm looking for as I haven't taken many pictures these last few weeks, not like I normally would – capturing innocent family moments just because I could. Jeremy hunched over his laptop, perhaps, working late by the glow of his desk lamp, unaware I was in the doorway of his study, fondly watching him work. Kieran coming in from school, his face fresh from saying goodbye to his mates yet hung with heaviness at the prospect of a night of studying. Maybe a close-up shot of the chessboard, a glass of red either side of it with Jeremy's hand reaching to move a piece, or a photo of the dinner I'd cooked, proud of a new recipe. Just these little reminders, like bookmarks in my memory, unravelling the hidden photo stream inside my head.

I keep scrolling back, stopping on one particular photo – an unflattering selfie, taken in the woods on one of my cross-country runs last autumn with the sunlight angling down between the trees. I didn't take it out of vanity, and nor was it to catch the pretty light behind me. No, I took it to check if there was someone following me, anyone lurking in the background, half hidden behind a tree, or the flash of a face, someone crouching in the cover of a bush. I'd sworn I'd heard noises – twigs cracking, a couple of spooked pheasants flapping out of a tree – and didn't want to keep turning round to check, didn't want to show my fear. It wasn't the first time it had happened either. I'd had the feeling I was being watched a couple of times by that point – and not just on my runs. I zoom in on the photo again but, as I'd already realised at the time, there was no one there. Not caught in my photo, at least.

And then there are the pictures I took at the medical conference in Oxford. I flick through them, my mind dragged back to what should have been a normal work weekend away – though I now know it was anything but that.

There are a few shots of the conference itself – several of the speakers, but mainly they're zoomed-in shots of the presentation slides on the big screen. It was the references I wanted, reading material to catch up on in my own time. Which, as yet, I hadn't done. There had been other things to contend with since – such as my husband dying.

I choke on the sob, breathe the tears back in. Just before clinic is not the time to get emotional. I glance at the clock on the wall. Seven minutes to go. Seven minutes to scan my list, review any test results, liaise with the practice nurses. I do none of these things. Instead, I keep thumbing through the pictures, unfurling the ribbon in my mind.

The first night of the three-day conference, a group of us went out to dinner. Nothing flash – just six or seven GPs (several of whom I knew from med school in Leeds) eating at an Italian bistro in the city centre. Seafood pasta and a glass of red, that's all I had. Some decent chats with the people sitting either side of me and then I retired to the hotel, as did most of the delegates, from what I'd gathered over breakfast the next day. Everyone had had an early night, drained from the previous day's input, perhaps saving themselves for a Saturday night blow-out.

I'd sat alone at breakfast that first morning, scrolling through the news on my phone as I'd sipped my coffee. On my phone now, there's a picture of my full English. I remember snapping it and sending it to Jeremy with a silly comment. He didn't reply, probably thinking me annoying for interrupting him with such a trivial thing as bacon and eggs. They'd been particularly good though – or perhaps it was just because I hadn't had to cook them. Plus my mind had been all over the place with thoughts of *her*, whoever she was – and if she was there with him, in my house while I was away. I couldn't stand the thought of it – another woman stealing my husband.

The second night of the conference, we went to a different place for dinner, and there was a bigger group of us, men and women. I didn't know most of them but everyone seemed amiable enough. The Indian restaurant was very accommodating and, after we'd finished, someone had suggested hitting a couple of bars in town.

'Coming, Jen?' one of the male GPs had asked as he'd stood, slipping on his jacket.

It had taken me less than a second to decide. 'Sure,' I'd replied, folding my starched napkin and placing it on the table. 'Why not?'

But in my head I'd been thinking, *Sure. Why not? Why not get wasted to the point of forgetting I even exist? Why not obliterate every single concern I have about my marriage with alcohol and hope I pass out in the gutter and get run over by a bus?* It had taken all my resolve not to say it out loud.

So I'd donned my coat and followed the others out into the street, my clothes smelling faintly of cumin as I brought up the rear of a long line of merry doctors letting their hair down after an intense day of presentations. That was all. Just letting our hair down. *My* hair down.

'First patient's here, Dr Miller,' our youngest receptionist, Chloe, says through the intercom. She's a new recruit and I'd not met her before starting back at work yesterday.

'Send him through,' I reply, not instantly realising that I'd instinctively said 'he'. I've not even checked the names on the list yet. Was it some kind of telepathy, I later wondered? A sixth sense kicking in, warning me?

It's as I'm switching off my phone, popping it in my handbag under my desk, when he strides into my office, following the single sharp knock on my door.

'Good morning, Mr...' I trail off, my head still half under my desk as I scoop a few belongings back into my bag that have fallen out.

Still the assumption he's a man, but by this time he's in the room, so perhaps I'm already picking up a man's cologne or unconsciously hear him clear his throat or sense the heaviness of his footsteps.

No, I'll tell myself later. *You always knew trouble was coming. Have* always *known it would come calling. You just didn't know when.*

'Take a...' I trail off again as I sit up.

He's already taken a seat and is right opposite me as relaxed as anything, facing me squarely with a slightly amused smile on his face. He's classically handsome – but in an exaggerated way, as though every feature has tried too hard to be perfect. Square jaw, high cheekbones, a broad forehead and bright-blue, symmetrical eyes. Sandy hair, a neat crop of similarly coloured stubble, a pale shirt undone at the collar with a navy jacket on top of dark jeans completes his effortless yet stylish look. Oh, and I can just make out the tip of a polished tan brogue poking round the corner of my desk. And his nails are well manicured – oddly white at the tips for a man – with his hands clasped loosely in his lap. *Strong* hands.

I swallow drily. My mind must be scooping up all the detail unconsciously, balling it into one big first impression: smug. No – *dangerous*.

'Right, Mr...' I glance at my computer screen, blinking, frantically clicking on my morning's list. But the mouse pointer freezes before it opens. 'Sorry,' I say with a smile, regaining some composure as I square up my shoulders, though I can't seem to iron out the frown that has set in between my brows. 'Computer's taking its time this morning.' I give him a glance, then turn back to the screen.

Do I know you? I want to say as I wait for the system to catch up with itself. But that would be ridiculous. Of course I'll have seen him before at some point, though admittedly some patients are more memorable than others. And surely he would have been one of them? I bat away the thought. Inappropriate.

'Ah, and hello to you finally, computer,' I say, rolling my eyes and forcing a laugh as the patient list opens at last. I click on the first name. 'What can I do for you, Mr Shaw?'

'Scott, please,' he says after a moment. 'Do you always talk to your computer?'

'Scott, then,' I say, having to consciously force my lips to form the most basic of syllables. 'And no, no I don't,' I add with a laugh, even though my frown gets deeper. I glance at the screen again, just as the shard of light flashes in front of my eyes, just as the pulse of a few beats bangs through my head – *the music, the alcohol, the dancing. The hand on my shoulder…*

I shudder, jumping back to the moment.

'Ah, right,' I mumble, clicking on his notes. 'I see you're a new patient,' I say, relieved because now I don't feel bad about not remembering his name. But it doesn't stop my heart thundering in my chest, as if it's trying to tell me something, as if I should be taking notice of some minor detail I've overlooked. Thing is, I'm just not listening. Not listening to myself at all – because if I've not seen him in surgery before, then why does he seem so familiar?

CHAPTER FOUR

Jen

'So when did the pain start?' I ask Scott, once I've introduced myself properly and taken a brief history. The system shows me that he registered at the practice about two weeks ago, while I was still off work.

Scott thinks, tapping his forefinger on his thigh. 'Maybe a week or ten days ago?' he says, almost as if he's asking me. His voice is deep and slow, resonating inside his chest. He doesn't take his eyes off me, and I don't take mine off his.

'And did it come on gradually or suddenly? Have you done anything extra-strenuous or out of the ordinary lately? Heavy weights, or some kind of lifting you wouldn't normally do?'

My patient shakes his head slowly, glancing at the ceiling. 'No, no I don't think so. I moved recently. I'm new to the area.'

'Heavy boxes and furniture the culprit, perhaps?' I ask, giving him a quick glance as I type up a couple of notes.

'No. I don't have much stuff. The few bits I have are in storage.'

'Right,' I say. 'OK, I'd better take a look.' I smile, trying to put him at ease, though I don't know why. It's me who needs her heart calming, her sweaty palms wiping on a towel. I have no idea why. 'If you want to slip behind the curtain and take off your top half, I'll come in and examine you. Let me know when you're ready.'

'Of course,' Scott says, waiting a beat before he rises and goes into the cubicle, dragging the curtain closed around him.

I turn back to my computer, taking a moment to look at his registered address. *Stuff in storage… New to the area…* I click on his personal details and see that he's registered at a temporary address. Beckley Park Inn, 74 Radley Road. Quickly, I google it. It appears to be a grim-looking, seventies-style concrete motel near an industrial estate on the outskirts of Shenbury, our nearest town. It also looks as though it should have been pulled down thirty years ago. So why didn't he register at a surgery nearer to the motel?

My eyes narrow, my fingers clasping my chin as I bridge the gap in my mind between what I already know about Scott Shaw – not much – and the type of person I imagine would relocate to a place like that, even if only temporarily. The two don't match up. His clothes and appearance don't make him look as though he's short of money, yet the place he's staying at reeks of that being the case. But then in my job I know only too well how people can be the opposite of what you think. I put aside my judgement.

'Ready?' I ask.

'As I'll ever be,' he replies.

I pull back the curtain and a second later, I'm gripping onto the fabric, as if it's going to somehow steady me. It's as though a camera flash has gone off at point-blank range in my face, as if someone's forced my head into a place where all my senses are overloading – my ears pounding from the noise, my skin sore, my nostrils flared and alert. Even my tongue tingles from the shock.

I suddenly have an overwhelming urge to run for my life.

Instead, I close my eyes, take a deep breath – though it feels as if a hand is around my throat. I cough, feeling choked and unsteady, terrified of what's going to happen next.

'Are you OK?'

'Sorry, yes,' I say, opening my eyes. 'I stood up too quickly, that's all.'

That's all it is, I tell myself, knowing my blood pressure is going to be doing all kinds of crazy things at the moment. Briefly, I put a hand on my stomach, reminding myself of the cause. That there's nothing else at play, nothing untoward. My baby and I are safe.

'Let's see what's going on with your shoulder, then,' I continue, trying not to stare too much at my patient's naked torso. He's fit-looking, muscular and in good shape – his broad shoulders in proportion with his flat, six-pack stomach. He sits on the side of the examination couch, staring at me as if I haven't got a clue what I'm doing. Right now, it feels as though I haven't. It may as well be my first day at medical school.

'Sorry if my hands are a bit chilly,' I say, approaching him. My stock phrase. But it's a lie, I think, feeling the heat radiate from my palms. I also feel the heat radiating from Scott as I lay my hands on his left shoulder. 'Tell me if it hurts anywhere in particular,' I say, gently pressing my fingertips into the firm muscle of his rotator cuff. And that's when I notice the jagged scar on his chest, slightly off to the right side, running diagonally through the sandy hairs. I can tell it's not a medical scar from an operation and, going by the pale colour, it looks a few years old.

'OK, elbows by your side and forearms out, palms facing inwards… That's right.' I guide him into position. 'Gently ease your hands apart, while keeping your elbows against your waist.'

'Like this?' he says, our faces closer than I'd realised.

'Mm-hmm. Any pain?'

He shakes his head.

'Try to get your hands as far apart as you can.' I nod. 'Good. OK, stand up and let me see how far up your back each hand can reach.' He completes the test adequately, me trying to focus on that rather than the muscles strapping across his back that show he clearly works out often.

'Now, lie down on the couch for me, if you could,' I instruct, clearing my throat as he gets on. It's as his shirt falls to the floor, as I bend down to pick it up for him, that I catch the scent of his cologne – a spicy sandalwood fragrance that can barely be called a fragrance, more an actual memory, it's so… so *reminiscent*. But of what, I have no idea.

I put a hand on Scott's shoulder and take a deep breath, feeling dizzy and light-headed again.

The music was so loud, it had battered my mind, my head, my entire body. I loved it. It made every fibre of me dance, even though I wasn't actually dancing at that point. It was more like I was *escaping* – just for that one evening. Being in the bar was like being in another universe – all-consuming, taking me out of myself, making me forget. It wasn't at all like me, but exactly what I needed at the time – to feel drunk and alive. Free of my own thoughts just for an evening.

I'd walked away from the previous guy who'd bought me a drink and had woven my way to the edge of the dance floor. Then I'd spotted the spare table… the stool… a place to sit and be alone… trying not to twist an ankle in my stupid heels.

And then the hand on my shoulder…

I'd stopped, dead still. It seemed as if my blood vessels had suddenly frozen, and I even wondered if my heart had actually stopped beating. There was an oasis of warmth where the man's hand had settled on my skin, trapping us both inside a perfectly still cocoon with everything around us dissolved. The strangest thing was, it felt like I'd been waiting for that moment my entire adult life.

'I don't think it's frozen,' I say, my own voice snapping me back to the present. 'Your shoulder. You have a full range of movement,' I add, lowering his arm down by his side again.

'Frozen?'

'Adhesive capsulitis. I wouldn't wish it on my worst enemy,' I say, for some reason raising my eyebrows.

'That's good to know,' he says with a smile, sitting up, his abdominal muscles tensing.

'It's incredibly painful and can last for several years. Treatments are fairly limited and include surgery.' I clear my throat. 'Do get dressed,' I say, going to the basin to wash my hands. For some reason, I wash them twice.

'So what *have* I got then, Dr Miller?' Scott says, standing outside the cubicle as he buttons his shirt.

I feel dizzy again, the paper towel between my hands as his shape morphs into someone else. No, some*where* else.

'Perhaps... perhaps a mild rotator cuff injury,' I explain, shaking my head. I sit down at my desk again, managing several deep, calming breaths, just like I had to do day in, day out to prevent the panic attacks after I lost Jeremy. It was the only way I could get through those early days of grief – a moment-to-moment lifeline that somehow, along with the diazepam, helped to numb reality.

'For now, I recommend ibuprofen for a few days and I'll print out a sheet of exercises to do daily. If there's no improvement within a week or if it gets worse, come back and see me and we'll look at a referral and a stronger painkiller.'

'Thank you,' Scott says slowly, tucking in his shirt and putting on his jacket. 'I'll do just that.' He gives me a smile – warm and familiar – before heading for the door. With his hand on the knob, he turns back and says, 'It was good to see you, Jennifer.' And then he leaves.

CHAPTER FIVE

Jen

'Hello?' I call out, after knocking on the front door and ringing the bell for the third time. 'Elsie, are you there?' Of course she's there, I convince myself, though that doesn't stop me being concerned for her. She's eighty-five, doesn't have a car, has limited access to public transport, and her only remaining family member is her daughter who lives two hundred miles away and refuses contact with her. I, plus a couple of other kindly souls from the village, are the only visitors Elsie has. She relies on us. Each time I pay a house call, I wonder if it will be my last. And each time I knock, I wonder if she's lying dead inside.

The thought makes me shudder.

I hear a noise and let out my breath. *Thank God*. I couldn't stand to think of her all alone, perhaps having had a fall or suffered a heart attack or stroke. Though, apart from her feet giving her trouble, medically there's not a lot wrong with Elsie Wheeler.

A key turns in the lock and, after a bit of rattling, she pulls the door open on its chain. She scowls up at me. Elsie is barely five feet tall and refuses to wear her glasses or her hearing aid. A pungent smell of stale urine and dog excrement escapes from the gap in the door, wafting out in a warm, fetid stink.

'Who's that?' she says, almost in a bark. Following which, there is an actual bark. Minty, her wiry old terrier who's anything but

minty, shuffles up to her ankles, letting out a croak of a yap, all
the ancient creature can manage. Like her owner, the dog can't
see well though doesn't have the opportunity of glasses. And the
poor thing regularly messes in the house.

'It's me, Elsie,' I say. 'Dr Miller.' I never call myself Jennifer.
Somehow, it doesn't seem right.

''Allo,' she says in that northern accent of hers, her tone brightening when she realises it's me. 'Come on in, duck.' Elsie shoves
the door shut and removes the chain before opening it wide and
beckoning me inside. I take a breath and step over the threshold.

'Has the new care agency not been in touch yet, Elsie?' I say
loudly, looking around as I head into her small sitting room. The
gas fire is on full blast with the heat from the flickering orange
and purple flames amplifying the smell. I sit down on the worn
beige velour sofa, knowing which bits to avoid.

'What? Nooo, we don't need none of that care rubbish,' she
chuckles. 'Do we, Mint?' She bends down with surprising ease for
a woman of her age and scoops up the dog, tucking it under her
arm. 'How are you then, duck?' she asks. Adding, 'Tea?' before
I can reply.

'Thanks, OK then,' I say. After I've checked up on Elsie I don't
have any other appointments and I can't quite face going home
yet, especially with Kieran not back until later. The emptiness of
my house would swallow me up.

Elsie shuffles off to put the kettle on so I follow her to the
kitchen, a ten-foot square room that wouldn't look out of place
in a nineteen-sixties museum. Dilapidated green and cream units
line one wall with chipped cross-hatched Formica on top. There's
an old wooden storage cupboard against the other wall and beside
it a small, boxy refrigerator with rust along the edges of the door.
Next to that is an ancient free-standing gas stove. Beneath the
window, which only appears frosted from the grimy splashes, is a
sink and drainer, dull from limescale.

'You need to get these tiles sorted,' I tell Elsie, pointing at the floor. 'They're dangerous,' I trample down the edges of the dark red linoleum squares.

'Stuff and nonsense,' Elsie says, filling the kettle. 'They've been that way for fifty years at least.' With a shaking hand, she turns on the gas on the old stove and presses down the knob, waiting for the spark. 'Takes bloody ages,' she says, glancing up at me.

The gas hisses out. 'Elsie, I don't think—'

'Where's me sodding matches?' she says, shuffling off to pull open a drawer. The gas stays stuck on so I quickly turn it off, lunging at Elsie as she finds the matches and goes to strike one.

'No, wait,' I say, placing a hand on her arm. 'Let's open the door first, eh? Get some air in. We don't want an accident.'

'Right, duck,' Elsie says, suddenly looking thoughtful. 'No, no, we don't want another one of those.' She nods and heads for the back door, giving the bottom of it a sharp kick with her foot to get it open.

'Tell me how you've been then, Elsie,' I say, checking the rim of my mug before I sip. While she was brewing the tea – for her, it's a ritual with loose leaves and a pot – I found a pair of rubber gloves and some kind of disinfectant spray and cleaned up the dog's mess in her living room, dumping it all in her overflowing dustbin outside. 'Do you feel you're coping OK?'

'That's kind of you to ask, Doctor,' she replies, rattling her cup on her saucer. 'You're about the only person who cares, but I've not been eighty-three years on this planet for nothing, you know. Everyone seems to think I'm not able to look after myself. First Cherry from number twelve, she pops in on me, you know, wretched girl, telling me I'm doing things wrong, and then that woman from some care place poking her nose in about sending someone regular, like. Surely not you too, Doctor?' Elsie shakes her head and slurps her tea. Her top lip and chin are covered in a fine mist of grey hairs. 'I thought you were on my side, of all people.'

Oh, I am, I want to tell her. *More than you know.*

'I'm not saying you can't cope, Elsie,' I say with a smile, admiring her feistiness. 'But sometimes, as we get older, it's nice to have a bit of help.'

Elsie makes a growling sound and shakes her head.

'And I hate to break it to you, but you're eighty-five,' I add with a laugh.

'Oh, get away with you now,' she replies, a glint in her eyes.

'And Cherry is only trying to help, Elsie. Between you and me, I think she likes to get out of the house. She's got her little toddler to cope with and he's hard—' I stop myself. Christ, how could I be so insensitive? I watch Elsie, but the expression on her face tells me she didn't hear properly, or if she did, she's not made the connection.

I mentioned to Cherry a while ago it was probably best she didn't bring little Tyler round when she visited Elsie, all things considered. At three years old, I was concerned about the trigger, about the impact it could have on Elsie's mental health. As her doctor, I've seen the signs of her PTSD getting more pronounced the older she's got but, Elsie being Elsie, she's consistently refused any help or counselling over the years. I don't suppose she'll change now.

'Some things are best not spoken of,' she kept telling me, always in a whisper. '*Ever.*'

'Are you still managing to cook for yourself, Elsie, or would you like me to see about getting some meals delivered? It might help.'

Elsie clacks her teeth and pulls a face. ''Course I'm managing to cook, duck. How else would I be alive?' She laughs, slurping more tea.

By cooking, Elsie means emptying half a tin of spaghetti hoops into a saucepan before spilling them, lukewarm, onto a piece of white bread. Dessert is always a mini chocolate roll. She eats cornflakes for breakfast and a ham sandwich for lunch. And she drinks copious amounts of tea. Somehow, she survives. But, as I already know, Elsie is a fighter. As stoic as they come, grinding from one day to the next. Nearly thirty years ago, she and her family experienced the unimaginable. The *unthinkable*. No mother, no grandmother, should have to suffer what they did. I shudder, forcing myself not to dwell on it.

Minty attempts to jump up onto Elsie's lap and, on the third go, the dog manages it.

'Hey up,' she half croaks, raising her cup and saucer until the dog settles. 'Mrs Popular, am I?'

'Minty is good company,' I say thoughtfully, wondering how a dog would fit into my lifestyle – or what's left of my lifestyle. The simple answer is, it wouldn't.

'You should get a pup,' Elsie says, giving me a sideways glance, as though she's read my mind. The thought of that makes me shudder again.

I laugh. 'It wouldn't be fair on the dog.'

'It would be company for you, duck,' Elsie says with a nod. 'I heard what happened to your husband. That Cherry can't keep her sodding trap shut. I'm so sorry for your loss.'

I suddenly feel like laughing and bursting into tears at the same time. There's no doubt news travels quickly in Harbrooke. After all, I'm doctor to many locals, and word would have spread about the reasons behind my temporary absence from the surgery. And it's not the first time I've heard Elsie swear. Rather, it's the matter-of-factness of what she said, as though my grief for Jeremy could be magically fixed by getting a pet, that makes me want to bury my face in a cushion and scream. But then if anyone knows about grief and loss, it's Elsie. In that sense, it makes us the same – we each blame ourselves, feeling we could have somehow prevented the deaths of our loved ones.

'Thank you, Elsie,' I say. 'I have Kieran for company, don't forget,' I add. Though he's often not home these days, I want to tell her but don't, and nor do I mention that the worry I have for my son right now is off the scale. I didn't come here to vent. The opposite, in fact. While I don't find it necessary to check out Elsie medically every time I visit, me popping in each week is a way to keep track of how she is in herself. Not *duty* visits as such, but close. I've done it for as long as I can remember.

'You'll learn,' Elsie says, peering at me over the rim of her cup as she slurps the dregs of her tea.

'Learn?' I say, loudly so she can hear.

'You'll learn about losing people, duck. That even though they're gone, they're never really gone,' she chuckles, petting Minty. She leans forward and nuzzles the dog on the nose.

I narrow my eyes, wondering what she means. Her grandson was brutally murdered, aged three. He's been dead nearly the same number of decades. 'That's some comfort,' I say, my words seeming to lose any empathy given that I have to almost shout them so she can hear.

Elsie freezes, making me wonder if she's suffering some kind of episode. She grips the teacup hard, her fingertips whitening, making me think she's going to snap off the china handle. Her eyes frost as though she has fast-forming cataracts and the loose skin under her jaw trembles, as though something is bubbling up inside her.

'Oh no. No, no, no. It's no comfort at all,' she whispers, barely moving her mouth.

CHAPTER SIX

Rhonda

Rhonda dumps her bag down on the kitchen table, pulls off her coat, hanging it on the back of a kitchen chair, and heads to the fridge – the glow from inside illuminating her tired face. She wipes a hand down one cheek, staring at the near-empty shelves, only wanting a snack – something to knock the edge of the burn in her stomach since she didn't get lunch, but nothing takes her fancy. She's not had time to go to the supermarket this week and, besides, anything decent usually gets hoovered up by Chris or Caitlin within a couple of hours of being bought, as if they have some kind of survival competition between them. She smiles – whatever it is, it's fine by her. Everything is better with Chris in their lives.

She pulls out a bottle of Beck's from the fridge door, checking to see it's not one of Chris's alcohol-free bottles. His dry January has smugly continued into February. Hers never made it past the third of the month. A Beck's Blue would not hit the spot that needs hitting, currently, and she doesn't want to get into the remaining spirits left over from Christmas. That's a slippery slope on a weeknight.

'Slippery bloody slope indeed,' she whispers under her breath, popping the top off the bottle and swigging directly from it. She shakes her head. She still can't believe it – that Jeremy is dead. And she still can't believe it, either, that Jen seems to be *coping* – even though she suspects she's not. She worries for her friend. Worries that she's burying her grief so deeply that it's gradually turning her insides to concrete. Worries that soon, she won't be able to move from the weight.

'Slippery slope,' she says again, slumping down at the kitchen table, bottle gripped in one hand and her forehead resting on her other arm. For a moment, she sees only white behind her eyes – perhaps what Jeremy saw during his last moments as the avalanche hit. She forces herself to tune out of that. She can't deal with those thoughts right now, not after such a bad day at work, hating that she has not one but *two* bottom sets to deal with this year. The staff meeting was the same old, same old, with Old Hairy, the deputy head, taking over as usual. As if anyone wants to hear his politically charged rants about—

'You all right, Ronnie?' a voice asks.

Rhonda whips up her head, her wavy blonde hair falling over her face, reminding her of something earlier.

Are they meant to be beach curls, Miss? She hears the girl's giggling voice echoing through her mind – Brittany, the pupil with the biggest mouth and grating personality to go with it. *No, you stupid, attention-seeking girl!* she'd wanted to yell back at her. *I was just born this bloody gorgeous.*

She knew the passive-aggressive teenager was being sardonic, always picking on and mocking every single item of clothing, jewellery or make-up she wore to work – Brittany and her gang. Sure, she felt intimidated by them. Intimidated by their privileged sixteen-year-old raging hormones and knowledge of all things cool in a world that she wasn't sure she understood any more.

Caitlin felt the same about that group in her year and sensibly gave them a wide berth, making herself almost invisible to them. It was out of necessity – she was the teacher's daughter, the scholarship kid in a fee-paying school, after all. But Caitlin didn't have to teach them three times a week, attempt to hold their attention while fielding their contempt. None of them were the slightest bit interested in classic literature. Girls that age could be so cruel.

'I *know* you were born gorgeous, sweetheart,' the voice says in a teasing way. Rhonda feels a hand on her shoulder. Something warm on her head briefly. A kiss. She must have been talking to herself.

'Hey,' she says, smiling up at her husband. 'You're back early.'

'No, I'm back on time for once,' he laughs, feeling the weight of the kettle. He flicks it on. 'Usually I'm just back late.'

'True,' Rhonda says, smiling, going up to him and slipping her arm around his waist. She leans her head against him, feeling safe.

'And I repeat, you *were* born this gorgeous,' Chris says, planting another kiss on her before sliding away to fetch a mug. He holds up a second one, but Rhonda shakes her head and points to the beer. 'Had a good day, then?' He rolls his eyes. He knows about Brittany and her group.

'Just the usual,' Rhonda replies. 'It's just this time of year, you know? I hate it. I can't bloody wait for the Easter holidays.'

'I do know.' Chris spoons some coffee granules into the mug and sloshes on boiling water.

'I was just thinking about… about Jeremy, actually.' She takes a deep breath. It hit Chris hard, losing his good friend. They'd been close for years and it was Rhonda who was the newcomer to their group. Well, her and Caitlin, ever since they'd walked hand in hand, mother and daughter, into Chris's bachelor life five years ago. None of them had ever looked back. Moving to the area was the best thing she'd ever done. No, she corrects in her mind. Swiping right on Chris in a last-ditch Tinder session before she resigned herself to being single for evermore was the best thing she'd ever done.

Chris flashes her a look. 'It's still hard to believe what happened.'

Rhonda clasps her hands around her beer, one finger picking at the slightly damp label. 'Do you think he suffered?'

'No,' Chris says immediately. 'Let's believe that. We have to.'

'It's what Jen believes,' Rhonda replies.

Chris nods sharply. 'I'm glad I didn't have to break the news to her,' he says, with Rhonda knowing that job is left to the uniforms. Even if he had been given the grim task of telling Jennifer that her husband had been killed, he'd have passed it on to a colleague. It wouldn't have been right, him knowing the news before she did.

Rhonda nods in agreement as she sips more beer. For some reason, she suddenly wants to bite through the glass – press her teeth so hard against the bottle that it shatters in her mouth. She imagines herself crunching, swallowing, her lips and tongue bloody.

'Does Caitlin say how Kieran's doing?'

'Not really,' Rhonda replies. 'I don't think he's spoken to her about it much.'

'It's hard for the poor lad.'

'Do you think they'll ever find Jeremy's body?' Rhonda says in a hushed voice, glancing at the door.

'Very unlikely,' Chris says, shaking his head. 'I haven't mentioned anything to her, but I did a bit of research online about… you know.' He makes a tumbling gesture with his hands. 'And this was a big one, apparently. The snow and ice can be tens of metres deep. There's no chance of anyone finding him now.'

Rhonda is silent for a moment, wondering what it would be like to see an avalanche approaching but knowing there wasn't a damn thing you could do to get out of the way in time. 'Jen says it's a small consolation that he was doing something he loved when he died, that if Jeremy had had to pick his own demise, then skiing would be it.'

'Hey,' says a voice across the room.

Rhonda's face lights up as her daughter comes into the kitchen. The three-bedroomed semi seemed a squeeze for them at first, but now it feels just the right size, as if they've moulded themselves perfectly into the shape of Chris's life. And Rhonda couldn't ask for a better stepdad for Caitlin. Attentive without being overbearing, Chris is also fiercely protective and equally involved with her daughter's well-being – worrying about what time she'll be home, who she's hanging out with, if she's got a boyfriend, if she's been secretly drinking or smoking or worse. Rhonda shudders. Between them, they form some kind of parenting team, with the gap left by Caitlin's absent biological father filled more than adequately.

'What's for tea? I'm starving,' Caitlin says, opening the fridge.

'OK. Time to whip up some pasta,' Rhonda says, forcing herself up from the table. 'I think there's a tin of tuna, too. I'll make a cheesy bake, if you like.'

'Cool,' Caitlin says, opening one of the cupboards and pulling out the last bag of crisps. 'I'm going upstairs to do some homework.'

Rhonda wants to ask her what subjects she's got, but she can't face any more school talk today. Most of the local kids from the surrounding villages and nearby town go to the academy in Shenbury – apart from a select few whose parents fork out the fees for St Quentin's, located just outside the market town. It's not a particularly prestigious or expensive private school, as they go, with its history not particularly salubrious either, going by the staffroom gossip that she's picked up on. But they have good and dedicated staff, and Caitlin is a diligent student, doesn't need to be chivvied along – which is why she won the full scholarship in the first place. There's no way she and Chris could have afforded the fees otherwise. While Caitlin might look a bit alternative, with her piercings and dyed black hair, Rhonda would take that any time over being slack at school. Or worse, if she was part of Brittany's clique. Caitlin has her sights set on a top university and there's every chance she'll make it.

*

Later that evening, Rhonda watches Chris from the bed as he leans over the basin in the tiny en suite, brushing his teeth. His back is broad and his shoulders still strong, though less defined these days. He splashes water on his face and reaches for the towel, making that noise he always makes when he dries his face – part shudder, part growl.

'Come to bed,' Rhonda says, pulling back the duvet on his side. 'It's warm.' She smiles as he turns, briefly pulling the covers off her too, exposing her naked body for a second. Chris's expression warms, his eyebrows rising briefly. He turns off the bathroom light and takes off his boxers before climbing in beside her. Only Rhonda's bedside lamp is on, softly illuminating the room that, when she moved in, only had a bed and a wonky chest of drawers in it. Gone are the drab grey walls and flat-pack furniture, replaced by calming neutral shades, soft rugs, matching oak wardrobes and a dressing table for all her stuff. For a nineteen-eighties, three-bedroomed bachelor pad, it had been an easy transformation. And Chris had seemed pleased, too. His job was too stressful for him to have bothered with homely touches before.

'You didn't tell me about your day,' Rhonda says, laying a hand on his chest.

Chris groans.

'That case still?'

'Mmhh,' he says, yawning. 'Had to release the suspect. CPS kicked it out due to lack of evidence. They weren't convinced by what we had to pin him at the scene. Three months surveillance and countless man hours down the drain.'

'Don't give up,' she says. 'You know you had him.'

'*Had*,' he says, rolling onto his side to face her. 'Exactly. But tomorrow's a new day.'

'Did you get that from Jeremy?' she asks. 'He always used to say that.'

'He did?' Chris pulls a face. 'Don't remember.'

'Do you… do you find that the memories are fading already? It hardly seems real that we used to see Jen and Jeremy at least once a week as couples. I mean, I used to see a lot more of Jen at the gym and stuff, but… I just can't believe it won't ever be the same again. The four of us. We'll never get to go on holiday with them again, cook for them, or—'

'Ron, don't,' Chris says, turning onto his back again. 'I don't want to think about all that. Not before sleep.'

'Sorry.'

Silence, but thoughts tumble around Rhonda's mind, making her feel neither tired nor aroused any more. 'Do you think the gathering that Jen held for Jeremy was enough? Doing something low-key at home like that?'

'The memorial?'

Rhonda nods.

'Christ, yes. Jeremy would have hated it as it was. No way would he have wanted a big fanfare in a chapel with maudlin music and everyone weeping.'

'It just seemed so weird without a coffin and a vicar. As if he might walk in through the door at any moment, drop down into his favourite armchair before telling everyone to get out.'

'I can imagine him doing that,' Chris laughs flatly. 'In his big, booming voice. "*Sod off, you bloody lot,*" he'd have growled.'

'Yeah, and then he'd have sloped off into his study before pouring a whisky and getting on with his book.'

The pair of them fall silent for a moment.

'That bloody book. He was never going to finish it, you realise,' Chris says, shaking his head against the pillow. 'Jen had the patience of a saint, if you ask me, supporting the family single-handedly like she did for so long.'

'You say that…' Rhonda stares at the ceiling, remembering Jeremy telling her about his novel, his face animated and excited. He was so sure he'd become famous, win prizes.

'I know *you'd* appreciate it, Rhonda,' Jeremy had said, leaning forward across the dinner table up at Swallow Barn when Jen was in the kitchen and Chris had gone to the loo. His voice was intense and low. 'You're like me. You think differently.' He'd stared at her for a beat then, the firelight glinting in his eyes as he'd touched her hand. Rhonda had said nothing, wondering where the conversation was leading. She'd felt uncomfortable and wished Jen would return from the kitchen. 'This book is going to be big, I can feel it. You understand that, don't you?'

'Sure,' Rhonda had replied cautiously. 'I'd like to read it someday,' she'd replied kindly, her fingers toying with her wine glass as she eased her hand away. 'What does Jen think of it?'

She hadn't really needed to ask. While Jennifer was tolerant of Jeremy's creative pursuits, she knew her friend was at, or at least nearing, breaking point – not that Jen would ever reveal that to Jeremy. Rhonda knew she worshipped the ground he walked on. But over the last couple of years, not only had Jen taken on most of the mental load of the family, but the financial one too. Jeremy's year off to pen a literary masterpiece had already turned into two, albeit with stints of research and documentary-making stitched in along the way to show willing, to try to contribute to family finances. *Or have an excuse for a holiday*, she'd wondered. Though neither of those pursuits brought in much cash. Rhonda had tried to hint to Jen that perhaps it wasn't fair, that maybe Jeremy should consider some lecturing work again, but it had fallen on deaf ears.

'What does Jen think?' Jeremy had said, repeating her question and sitting back in his chair. It creaked. He was a big man, though not overweight. At six foot five, he commanded a presence with his shock of wild curly hair, the black flecked with threads of silver, his intense dark eyes, and his big hands flailing as he spoke. His persona took up way more space than his physical form, drawing people to him like a magnet. 'She wouldn't understand. Not like you.'

'Just because I'm an English teacher...' Rhonda had replied with a tipsy smile, but Jeremy had silenced her with a finger over his own lips and a mischievous look in his eyes.

'No boring book talk allowed at the table,' Jen had said as she came back into the room carrying dessert. Rhonda had been glad of the reprieve.

Later that evening, Jeremy had whispered in Rhonda's ear that he'd put a copy of his half-finished manuscript in her car when he'd gone outside for a cigarette, that it was in a plastic bag on the passenger seat, and he looked forward to hearing her comments on the first draft. That was only a couple of weeks before he'd died and Rhonda still hadn't read a page of it. Couldn't steel herself to delve into the mind of a dead man – her best friend's husband. Perhaps one day she would.

'Goodnight, Chris,' Rhonda says now, leaning over and giving him a kiss. Their lips touch for a few seconds before she pulls away and rolls over, flicking off the bedside lamp. As she closes her eyes, she hears a barely perceptible sigh coming from somewhere deep inside her husband.

CHAPTER SEVEN

Jen

I sit on the stairs, tying up the laces of my trainers. I still don't feel much like exercising, but perhaps if I run fast enough, long enough, hard enough, it will make everything go away. Everything *inside* me go away. But I know this isn't true. A gentle jog, which is all I'm aiming for, isn't going to affect a single one of those cells inside me, multiplying at a rate faster than I can even think. And neither will it take me away from the nightmares that have started again – those, along with the flashbacks that are becoming more regular. If only I could remember exactly what happened that night.

'Kier?' I call out. 'You up yet? I'm off out for a run.'

Nothing. I hear my son's alarm go off, followed by a groan and then silence.

'Don't be late again,' I say loudly up the stairs.

'Yeah…' is all I get back a moment later.

I stand up, zipping up my running top and glancing in the mirror quickly before I leave. Drawn, tired, worried, stressed, anxious, not eating or sleeping properly, underweight… these are the initial impressions I would have if I'd come to see myself in surgery. *Let's run some blood tests, shall we?*

I tuck my phone inside my pocket, reaching for my earphones left tangled on the hall table. But I stop. I don't feel like music today. I want to be fully aware, to hear the sounds of nature around me, be present with my thoughts in the woods. Be able to hear any footsteps behind me.

I set off and turn right at the end of our drive, heading into the village. I flick a quick wave at a couple of people I know – mums with buggies, an older couple waiting at the bus stop. Cherry comes out of the village shop, her toddler wedged on her hip as I run past. When she spots me on the opposite pavement, shots of white breath coming out of my mouth, her expression changes expectantly and she raises her hand, flagging me down. I concede, slowing and crossing the road.

'Hi, Doctor,' she says, almost apologetically, tucking back a strand of her fiery red bob behind her ear. 'Have you got a moment?'

'Sure, Cherry,' I reply. 'Is it Elsie?'

She nods.

'I'm going to chase the care home, see if they can get someone out this week for a proper assessment. I'm concerned for her, too.' I try not to pant, even though I'm out of breath already.

'She's a stubborn old bat,' Cherry says, rolling her eyes. 'Got this for her. Gonna drop it round on the way home and see if she hasn't set fire to herself yet.' She holds up a chocolate Swiss roll.

Swiss… Switzerland… skiing… Jeremy. I can't take my eyes off it, imagining what must have been going through my poor husband's mind as he fell to his death. I've watched clips of the avalanche on the news websites over and over again, wondering if I might have spotted the dot of a body tumbling into the abyss.

'You OK, Doctor?' Cherry asks.

My face is gripped by a frown. 'Sorry, yes. I'm fine.' I smile, watching Cherry put the cake back in the bag hanging on the buggy. 'Well, you know where I am if there's a prob—'

'Elsie mentioned her grandson last time I saw her,' Cherry says unexpectedly. There's a waver in her voice. Everyone in the village and surrounding area knows the story. It may have happened a long while ago, but still no one local likes to talk about it – as if the very mention of it is bad luck. Lenny Taylor's murder casts an unseen layer of fear, an undercurrent of dread in the community, as if it could happen again. A warning. And even though little Lenny's killer is long since behind bars – a child himself when he did it – young mums like Cherry still keep an extra-sharp eye on their children.

'She did?' It's not like Elsie to open up.

'She was looking at old photos.' Cherry glances down at the pavement. 'Without thinking, I asked her about the little boy in the picture. She got quite upset and threw the album on the floor. Then she said, "It's God's punishment, allowing me to live this long." How can one little mistake end in such tragedy?' Cherry asks, shaking her head. 'She must really hate herself for letting Lenny out of her sight.' She shudders, hitching her child further up on her hip.

'It wasn't a mistake,' I say quickly in Elsie's defence. While Cherry's generation is one step removed from the event, I, like others my age and older in the area, still remember it well – recalling the police presence and the scummy reporters camped outside Elsie's house, waiting for the scoop and pictures of the broken family. 'I can't imagine how awful it must have been for her,' I add, thankful that Kieran is sixteen and able to look after himself now.

But then I remember, instinctively placing a hand low down on my belly. Still flat. Still no sign of the secret I hold in there.

'I'll have a word with Elsie,' I add, being careful not to break patient confidentiality. 'Right, better crack on,' I say, wanting to escape. 'Bye, Cherry,' I add before kicking off on my run again so she can't keep me talking.

Ten minutes or so later, I reach the edge of Bowman's Wood – half a mile outside the village and a gentle jog up the gradual incline.

Between the wood and Harbrooke lies the old quarry, and behind the village, the beginnings of the Westbourne estate. The disused quarry is a reservoir now and has been that way long before I can remember, with no obvious signs that the land had once been dug raw for sand and gravel. Bowman's Pool is now a blue-black expanse of water surrounded by scrubby trees, undergrowth and undulating land. It used to be a favourite spot for swimming when I was a kid, but the council put paid to that in the last decade. Red signs forbidding swimmers, warning of the dangers that lurk beneath the surface, are dotted about.

There's a path snaking around the perimeter of the reservoir, now that it's a country park, with picnic tables and benches set along the way, the pool at its centre. It's still a popular spot with fishermen and families, but no one's forgotten what happened there nearly thirty years ago when Lenny Taylor's waterlogged body was hauled from the water. He'd been missing for almost a week.

I shudder as I run, forcing my thoughts onto other things. What to have for dinner. The team meeting later to discuss the possibility of an over sixty-fives' well-being clinic. The fundraiser for the new portable ultrasound scanner… questions to ask at Kieran's parents' evening later in the term… finding a tree surgeon to take a look at the old oak down in the paddock at home. Anything is preferable to thinking about the reservoir.

I veer off the lane and climb over the gate, heading into the woods and slowing my pace as the track becomes less visible the deeper in I go. Each time I come, I take a different route between the trees – picking my way between the knotty trunks of beech, ash and silver birch. The undergrowth is thick, almost impenetrable in some areas, and I pick my way through hawthorn and elder bushes in a half-jog, half-walk, snagging my sweat top on a thorn.

'Damn,' I say under my breath, swinging round to unhook it. The fabric pulls, leaving a visible loop. I don't care. I've got loads of running tops – most of them ruined in the same way. I set off again, my eyes scanning around. Not much light gets into Bowman's Wood these days; it's grown up so much over the years, making it seem far more sinister than it really is. But I love it for the solitude, the fresh and earthy air, and the stunning view of the surrounding countryside. It's why I come up here.

Suddenly, I stop again. A crow claps out of a tree above followed by three pheasants flying vertically out of the bracken and ferns up ahead. I've disturbed their cover. I turn slowly, scanning behind me, my eyes tracking for the slightest movement, the tiniest hint of an unnatural colour – clothing, skin, the glint in an eye. Though surely if anyone was following me, they'd have the good sense to wear dark colours. The February sun has not long risen, with the street lights of the village still on, twinkling through the trees in the dip below.

There. A different light. Small and orange.

The tip of a cigarette?

My heart kicks up, pounding in my chest. I try to convince myself that it's just my imagination playing tricks, that I've been fuelled by adrenaline and anxiety since Jeremy's death. With my loss and what happened at the conference, I've not been myself.

Then I think about the baby growing inside me – that I must protect her at all costs, that I couldn't stand for anything to happen to her if someone is following me, trying to scare me. Or worse.

Her… I think instinctively. It was like that with Kieran. I knew instantly I was having a boy.

I swallow down my fear, convincing myself I'm being ridiculous, that no one wants to follow or harm me. Stress, grief and anxiety will do that – transform sense and logic into a bubbling pot of catastrophe. But even so, I walk briskly out of the undergrowth, back onto the rough track that loops through the woods, glancing over my shoulder a couple of times before cutting my run short and heading back home – the only place I feel truly safe.

CHAPTER EIGHT

Then

'Wanna play?' the pale-faced kid standing over him says.

'Yeah, all right,' he replies, putting down his hand and scuffing his feet on the tarmac as he gets up. No one's ever asked him that before. 'Er, yuk,' he says, staring at his palm. 'Bug blood.' He grimaces to make out he's tough, that he doesn't care about a bit of squashed insect on him.

'What's your name?' the other kid says, looming two or three inches taller now they're both standing face to face.

'Evan,' Evan says, still staring at the mess on his right palm. His mum'll kill him if he wipes it down his trousers. She's always moaning she has enough washing to do for Rosie, his new baby sister. Things turned bad after Griff, and then Rosie came along. 'What's yours?'

'Mac,' Mac says. 'Lick it off,' he adds, his face remaining deadpan.

Evan wrinkles his nose.

'Go on, lick your hand clean. What are you, a baby or something?'

'No,' Evan snaps back, scowling. He stares at his palm a moment before sticking out his tongue and running it over the heel of his hand. It tastes disgusting and bitter, but he doesn't say anything as he fights down a retch.

'Funny,' the other kid says with a laugh. 'C'mon.' He walks off and Evan follows. He's seen Mac around school, but they've never spoken before. They're in different classes and don't have any lessons together, though he knows they're the same year group.

'Where we going?' Evan asks, trotting along behind Mac. The other boy's blue anorak is grubby, torn and a bit too small. But that just makes him look cool. As if he doesn't care what people think of him.

'It's a secret,' Mac says, glancing over his shoulder.

He's not like the other boys, Evan thinks, feeling the pressure swelling inside him. Mac's skinnier and paler for a start. And his skin looks too soft and smooth and doesn't even have a single spot yet. Not like Evan's. He's constantly got a dot-to-dot of scabby zits around his mouth. His mum says it's 'cos he keeps licking and picking. Griff says it's because he's dirty.

'Here,' Mac says, drawing to a halt at the far end of the play-ground by the caretaker's old shed. He heads round the back and pulls one of the low planks aside. Behind it, there's a padlocked metal tin the size of a shoebox. He slides it out and puts it down on the mud.

'Wicked,' Evan says. 'What's in it?'

He watches as Mac takes a key from his pocket and undoes the lock.

'Ta-da!' Mac says. 'Impressed?'

'Ye-*ah*,' Evan says in awe. 'Like, all that stuff is yours?'

'My stash,' he says. 'You can pick something, if you like.'

Evan stares inside. There's every kind of chocolate bar imagin-able, plus a couple of packets of crisps. It might as well be buried treasure. 'Anything?'

Mac nods. His smile is kind, Evan thinks. Not like the other boys, whose faces are pinched and mean.

Evan pulls out a packet of Monster Munch. He's never had them before, though he's seen them in the shop when his mum buys Griff's fags. 'I can't pay you,' he adds, about to tear the packet open. He doesn't want to get a belting.

'Nah, they're free. I nicked them.' Mac takes out a Bounty Bar before locking the tin and hiding it away again. 'Mum'd go mental if I kept it at home.'

Evan bites into a crisp. 'I nick stuff too,' he says, his cheeks burning. Truth is, he's never stolen anything. Well, apart from a bit of loose change from Griff's pockets here and there. He'd got a steel toecap in the shin for it, and later found his piggy bank smashed beside his bed, all his savings gone. Four pounds eighty-three down the pub in Griff's pocket.

'Where d'you live?' Mac asks, licking the chocolate off one half of his Bounty bar.

'Westbourne estate,' Evan says in a way that's almost an admission. Or a confession.

'Tough luck,' Mac replies, shrugging. 'I'm in the village, down Stanley Close.'

Evan rarely goes into Harbrooke. He knows Westbourne has a bad reputation, sitting between the posh houses in the village and Shenbury, the local town, with the main road skirting around it, as though the rows and rows of council houses are being corralled, kept separate.

'I could come round to yours one day,' Mac says, licking his lips. 'I've got a bike.' His pale-blue eyes open wide, glinting with something Evan doesn't recognise – something that gives him a feeling in the pit of his tummy. Mac's messy dark hair hangs in waves around his face. He reckons he'll get spat at by the other boys if he doesn't get it cut soon.

'Yeah, all right,' Evan lies, knowing there's no way Griff will allow anyone round to theirs. 'But it's really hard to find,' he adds in the hope it might put him off.

Mac laughs. 'Mum's a community nurse and visits patients there. She'll tell me how to find it.'

All Evan knows is that Westbourne seems to go on forever. One identical street endlessly leading to another, with alleyways joining the tightly packed houses. Him and his mum used to live in a flat in another town – a drab grey low-rise block that had black stuff growing on the walls, especially in the bathroom, no matter how much his mum scrubbed it. It felt safe, just him and her – but when Griff and then Rosie came along after his dad died, they all got moved into an actual house with three whole bedrooms on Westbourne. It even has a garden, though he has to watch where he treads. Griff's Staffie poos all over it and no one ever clears it up. And there's always that crying noise coming from over the fence next door. The constant wailing does his mum's head in, she says. Gives her migraines. He loves his mum with all his heart, but since she's got with Griff and had Rosie, he isn't sure she loves him back quite as much any more.

'Want to make a gang, then?' Mac asks with a sideways look, snapping Evan out of his thoughts. He savours another Monster Munch, enjoying it as it melts on his tongue.

'Yeah, go on then.' Evan wipes his nose on the back of his hand. He can't believe his luck. Like, in one playtime he's made a new friend, got some crisps and he is now in a gang. 'Who's leader?'

'Both of us,' Mac says. 'Then it's fair.' Mac takes off his anorak, exposing his school shirt with the outline of what looks like a vest beneath.

'And it's a secret gang, right?' Evan says, getting that feeling inside again. 'We can catch more bugs to kill.' He sniffs his palm to make sure there isn't any insect smell.

'Yeah, a secret one,' Mac says back, popping the last of the Bounty Bar into his mouth. He laughs, tipping back his head to expose his neck. Evan thinks it looks thin and brittle. Snappable, almost.

'Way better than stupid football,' Evan says, staring across the playground to where the popular boys have formed two teams. On the other side of the playground are several groups of girls huddled together. Evan doesn't like the girls, either. They're mean, too. Sometimes worse than the boys. He catches sight of that girl from earlier, his stomach knotting when he sees her.

He's seen her around before, tries to keep out of her way. He doesn't know her name, though she's in his year group too. Long dark hair hangs in two bunches down her front and, coupled with the knee-high white socks she wears on her stick-thin legs, plus the short skirt she's hitched up at the waistband, she seems taller than she really is. Like a piece of string, Evan thinks.

'Oi, Fathead,' she'd called out as he'd gone to get something from his locker first thing that morning. The girl and her friends were loitering in the corridor, so he was going to keep on walking, but she'd stuck out her foot, making him stumble and fall to his knees. There was a ripple of giggles around him.

'Watch where you're going, loser,' the girl had said, sneering down at him.

Evan had frozen, looking up at her. He'd never been this close to her before and he reckoned he could even *smell* her – something floral and sickly. She had pale freckles on her nose that looked as though they'd wash off and, when she opened her mouth, her teeth were black from metal braces.

As he'd stood up, Evan suddenly felt a pain in his shin as she kicked him.

'Oww!' he'd cried, hopping about, rubbing the front of his leg.

'Get out of my way, stupid,' the girl had said, causing another raft of giggles. 'Can anyone else smell shit?' She'd leant forward, sniffing the air around Evan. More laughs, and then they'd sauntered off, pinching their noses as they went.

'What shall we call the club?' Evan says, shuddering at the memory as he looks up at Mac standing above him.

The other boy peers down, his hair suddenly seeming darker and his eyes blacker, and his skin looking as though all his blood has drained away.

'I know,' Mac says. 'Let's call it Kill Club.'

CHAPTER NINE

Jen

'Dr Miller?' a voice behind me says. Something touches my shoulder briefly. *A hand.*

I freeze, gripping the shopping trolley handle until my knuckles turn white. I'm almost waiting for the warm breath on my neck, the whisper in my ear. Bright lights, thumping music, free-flowing drinks… all of it flashing in front of my eyes as if I'm not really standing in the fresh produce aisle of the supermarket at all. Rather, I'm back at that club after the conference. The night when everything changed.

I snap myself back to the present and swing round, my training automatically kicking in – a hardwired skill to remain professional when bumping into patients outside the surgery.

'Hello, Mr Shaw,' I say, reaching for a packet of vine-ripened tomatoes and dropping them into my trolley. Head down again, I walk towards the peppers, not caring if I need them or not. I grab a pack of three – a traffic light of colours. It's the red one that screams out at me.

'I had a feeling I'd bump into you today,' Scott says, drawing up beside me with a lopsided smile. He has a basket in his left hand, nothing in it as yet. 'Must be fate,' he adds in a voice that conjures up much more than the words alone.

'I don't believe in fate,' I say, waving the peppers at him. 'Just science.' It's a small community and I bump into patients outside the surgery often. Yet for some reason, encountering Scott feels different – and it certainly doesn't feel like fate. Perhaps more like karma. I grab an avocado, pressing my fingers into it to gauge its softness.

'My shoulder's no better,' Scott continues, tracking beside me as I slowly browse the salad aisle. There's probably a bag of rotting leaves in the fridge at home. I should grab another.

'Sorry to hear that,' I say, glancing up before checking the date on a packet of rocket. I switch it for a newer bag. 'Make an appointment to come and see me again,' I finish, hoping that will be the end of it. 'I'll refer you on to a physio.' Anything to get rid of the strange sense of unease this man gives me.

But Scott positions himself right in front of my trolley, his free hand placed on the front of it. I can't go forward and, when I try to pull it backwards, he prevents it from moving.

'Excuse me,' I say through a surge of adrenaline, gently pushing against him with the trolley.

Scott stands firm, staring at me, those intense blue eyes boring into my soul. That's what it feels like, anyway. As though he's delving deep inside my mind.

'I just need to get to the sweet potatoes,' I say, adding a smile in the hope it appeases him.

'How very… middle-class,' he says. 'Sweet potatoes.'

I think it's a joke but can't be sure. 'My son likes them,' I say, trying to sound casual.

'You have a son?' Scott shifts his weight onto one foot, cocking his head. 'Who would have thought?'

'Sixteen,' I say, kicking myself for engaging with him, let alone giving out details about my personal life. And worse, about Kieran.

'You and your husband must be very proud,' Scott says. Anyone else listening to our stilted conversation wouldn't think it odd or sinister or unnerving or notice any of the heart-thundering feelings I'm experiencing right this moment. Yet there's a layer of… of *something* in this interaction that's not right. Something threatening I can't yet place.

A hand on my shoulder…

'Hello, Jennifer,' the voice had growled in my ear. I shouldn't have been able to hear it above the din of the music that night, but I did – almost as if his words were being beamed directly into my brain. His breath was warm and moist against my skin.

I'd turned, confronted by a man's face close to mine. I didn't recognise him, and it didn't even occur to me how he knew my name. I'd had a few drinks already and supposed he'd clocked my name badge at the conference. He was taller than me by a good six inches, which made him taller than most of the men in the club. And striking, too, with his piercing blue eyes that almost looked frozen they were so icy. Strobe lights flashed around us and, somehow, I found it in myself to continue my walk – my *stagger* – to the free table I'd spotted. The table with thankfully just one bar stool next to it.

'Mind if I join you?' he'd said, following me.

'Free country,' I'd replied, thinking I was being clever.

I took a glug of my drink and set it down, sliding onto the stool. I'd lost count of how many I'd had, didn't even care. I was off duty, away for the weekend and in dire need of forgetting. Already Jeremy, Kieran, work and home felt like a million miles away. Perhaps if they hadn't seemed so distant, perhaps if I'd phoned my husband or even bailed out of the evening meal earlier and driven home a day early, none of it would have happened.

'Normally, I'd say something like "How's your evening going?" or "You look stunning in that dress" or some other banal chat-up line,' the man had continued. 'But I'm not actually chatting you up.' He stood beside me, one elbow leaning on the bar-height table. 'Just for the record.'

'And normally I'd tell you to fuck off,' I'd replied, still believing I was being clever, in control, when actually I was neither.

'Spirited or just in a foul mood?' he'd asked, one corner of his mouth curling up.

'Both.'

'As I expected,' he replied, to which I turned up my nose and sipped on my drink, glancing around the bar as if I wasn't bothered. But I was. I remember my hackles were raised and my skin prickled with tension.

'You're with the medics?' the man had then asked, not giving up.

'Uh-huh,' I'd replied without looking at him.

'Actually, I already knew that.' He laughed – a confident laugh that somehow drained me of my power in this ridiculous play of what, at the time, I'd assumed to be flirting. I wasn't game for it. Not at all. There were other things on my mind. I'd swear he told me his name then, but I can't remember it. In fact, I don't remember much else about the evening at all.

'Watch my drink, will you?' I'd said in a slightly bored way. 'I need to pee.' I'd cringed inwardly at my choice of language, but had already decided I didn't care what he thought of me. I'd never see him again. I wanted to be alone with my thoughts, with my drink, and was hoping he'd be gone by the time I came back from the toilets.

He wasn't.

'No one else touched it,' he said, his hand hovering over whatever cocktail it was that other guy had bought for me. There were some more drinks on the table now, too. *Promise on my life,* he'd added, coming right up close and whispering it in my ear.

'We are… we are very proud of him,' I say now in the supermarket, forcing myself back to the present. 'Kieran's a good lad.' I kick myself for revealing his name. 'Can I…? Excuse me, I just need to get…' I attempt to swing the trolley to the side of him but he has it fixed in place. His foot is also wedged under a front wheel.

'And is your husband proud of *you*, Dr Miller?' Scott goes on, his eyes boring into me.

I stare at him, my eyes narrowing slightly.

A hand on my thigh… a finger slipping beneath the hem of my dress…

'Of course,' I manage to say, even though my throat is suddenly constricting from the broken memories.

'That's good to hear,' Scott says in a slow, drawn-out way. 'A wife supporting her husband.'

I feel the sweat break out on my back… my face… under my arms.

I'd finished my drink… then drank the shots… somehow found myself laughing with him… dancing… feeling dizzy, free, unreal… Something wasn't right, yet I couldn't do a damn thing about it. 'Let's get you up to bed…'

'Excuse me, Mr Shaw. I really have to go now.' And with that, I thrust my trolley hard at him, catching him unawares as the metal shoves him in the thigh, forcing him to step aside as he fights a look of shock.

'Hi, Ronnie,' I say down the line, glancing at the kitchen clock. 'You got a minute?'

'Sure,' she says back, the single drawn-out syllable indicating she knows there's something on my mind.

'When we were at the gym the other evening, well, I was going to tell you someth—'

'Actually, I'm glad you called,' Rhonda interrupts. 'Is Kieran home yet?'

'No… no, football training again.'

'You mean the school team?'

'Yes,' I say, frustrated that she's broken my flow. It's taken me half an hour to build up the courage to call her and all my strength to resist the bottle of wine in the fridge. To acknowledge the reason for my abstinence, I place my hand on my belly.

'It was cancelled,' Rhonda tells me. 'There's been no football training at all this week.'

'Really? Where the hell is Kieran, then?'

'That was actually what I was going to ask you. He wasn't in school this afternoon.'

'And no one thought to call me?' I say, standing up from the stool at the kitchen island, feeling a wave of concern sweep through me.

'The secretary did call, and left messages on your voicemail and at the surgery.'

Shit.

'Sorry, sorry… I'm a bit behind with things today.' I head to the hallway and go up to the big expanse of glass overlooking the driveway, concerned for where my son is. It was Jeremy's idea not to have any blinds or curtains up at the double-height windows when we renovated the barn. We're so private down the long drive and positioned on the edge of the village, with no houses overlooking us. More than anything, he hated the feeling of being trapped, hemmed in.

'You there, Jen?' Rhonda says.

I see my reflection staring back as I cup my hands to the glass, squinting down the drive. If Kieran has an activity after school, he'll either cycle home in the summer or otherwise I'll fetch him in the car. If I can't, he knows to call a taxi and put it on my account. I know for a fact his bike is in the garage as I saw it when I went to put something in the chest freezer out there earlier.

'Yes, yes… just checking to see if I can see him coming down the drive.' I glance at my watch. Seven thirty. I'm still rattled from encountering Scott Shaw in the supermarket earlier. Somehow, calling my best friend, telling her that I'm pregnant, that it was fate – a parting gift from Jeremy (even though I know it wasn't) – seemed the right thing to do.

'Oh, thank *Christ*,' I say, seeing a figure gradually draw closer as it lumbers down the drive in the glow of the coach lamp. I'd recognise my son's walk anywhere – shoulders forward, countering the weight of his backpack stuffed full of books, hands shoved in his pockets and head down – and if his hands aren't in his pockets then they're holding his phone, his thumbs racing over the screen. 'He's just got back,' I tell Rhonda through a flood of relief.

'Thank Christ indeed,' Rhonda repeats. 'Look, I'll let you go and give him a good grilling.' She laughs. 'Oh, and quickly, what was it you wanted to tell me?'

I watch Kieran draw up to the front door, only spotting me at the last moment. His face tells me he knows that I know.

'Nothing,' I tell Rhonda quietly. 'Nothing important at all. Chat tomorrow, bye.' And I hang up, taking a deep breath as my son lets himself inside, drawing him into my arms without the slightest intention of telling him off.

CHAPTER TEN

Jen

I'm four patients into my morning clinic when I see *his* name on my list. He's taken me at my word and booked another appointment for a referral. Good, I think. I'll happily refer him on to a physio to get him out of my hair, though I don't think he's given it enough time to heal.

'I'm sure you'll be feeling a lot better in no time, won't you, Tilly?' I say to the little girl currently sitting on her mother's lap. She's clutching her left ear and whining in pain. It's her third ear infection in the last few months.

'Thanks, Doctor,' her mother says – another of my regular patients, usually here for one of her four children.

Two patients to go before it's *him*, I see on my screen, dealing with the others as professionally as I can, even though Scott Shaw's appointment is weighing heavily on my mind. Every time I think of him, it's the same – fragments of that night at the conference.

'I'm afraid the results aren't what we were hoping for, Frank,' I tell my next patient – an elderly widower. The look on his face shows me he's resigned, that he's likely already accepted his fate. He's told me before that he's not afraid of dying, that he'll be with his wife again. 'So I'm going to transfer you back to the specialist, who will manage your cancer treatment going forward.' He's been fighting the disease for several years now. 'But you come and see me whenever you like, OK? I'm always here for you.'

He nods, giving me a little smile. 'Thank you, Doctor,' he says quietly. 'Honestly, I don't know how I'd have got through this so far without your care and kindness. And you were such a comfort to Joan in her final days.' His bottom lip quivers as he asks me a couple more questions, to which I provide the best answers I can, and then he shuffles off on his way.

I cup my head in my hands for a few moments, taking stock of everything. When I close my eyes, all I see are two naked and tangled bodies on a bed. It's not clear if they're fighting or having the most passionate sex of their lives – though I can see quite clearly that the woman is me.

My intercom buzzes. 'Yes, Peggy?' I say, grateful for the interruption.

'Your nine forty is a no-show currently. I'll send the next patient through.'

'Thank you,' I say, double-checking my list to see who hasn't arrived. Scott Shaw. Momentarily, I feel lighter inside, a sense of relief that he's not here, though I wish I knew why. Or, perhaps, I tell myself, it's because I don't *want* to know why.

'Still no sign of the nine forty?' I ask Peggy at just after 11 a.m.

'Nope. Sorry,' she says, chewing on something. 'Do you want me to call him to reschedule?'

'No,' I say quickly. 'No, no, that's OK, thanks, Peggy.'

And I continue with the rest of my day, hoping that my mind will take me back to that hotel room so I can look down on the bed again, get a good look at the person lying next to me.

'Déjà vu,' I joke to Rhonda on the phone later that evening, hoping to have the catch-up that had been cut short. 'Sorry I missed spin class earlier. Work ran late. Was it good? Actually, scratch that.

Of course it wasn't,' I say through a sarcastic laugh. Truth was, I just felt too exhausted to go. It was like that in the early stages of pregnancy with Kieran.

'Did you have a word with Kieran?' Rhonda asks. 'About the other afternoon.'

'I did,' I reply. 'A damned stern one,' I tell her for effect, though that's not how it went at all. Kieran and I had stood together in the hallway, holding each other close, crying until we had no more tears. Then we cooked, ate, and pored over old photographs of Jeremy, with my son finally revealing that he'd been feeling ill at school but hadn't wanted to come straight home. It didn't take a doctor to realise he wasn't *ill* ill at all, rather that he was suffering, still grieving. More than I'd perhaps realised since he lost his dad. They were so close, and just because he'd gone back to school, it didn't mean he was ready.

'Where did he go?' Rhonda asks.

'Just to the reservoir. He said he walked around a bit, then ran into a couple of mates when they'd finished school and went back to one of their houses for a while.'

'He should have phoned you. The last thing you need to be worrying about is his safety and whereabouts.'

'I know, I know,' I say. 'But take your teacher's hat off for a sec, Ronnie. He's struggling. I don't know how to help him. And I certainly don't feel big enough to fill the hole his father left behind.'

'You're not supposed to, Jen,' she says. 'Just be you. Just be his mum. You're still grieving too, remember? In time, the hole will heal over. It'll never go away and there'll always be a scar, but right now it's an open wound for both of you.'

'And it's my job to make sure it doesn't get infected.' I grab the just-boiled kettle and slosh some water into a mug containing a herbal teabag, resting my forehead against the wall cupboard briefly.

'Anyway, I'm glad you got to the bottom of it,' Rhonda says. 'We were worried at school. I decided not to say anything about his missing coursework to him for the very same reason. If he needs to resit some of his exams, that's an option, you know.'

'Missing coursework?' I say. 'Christ,' I add, feeling even more out of touch with my son's life. 'Thanks, Ronnie. If it's any consolation, he's at Josh's right now. He'll be back in half an hour.' I glance at the clock. 'They're meant to be studying, though they're probably on the PlayStation and—' I stop suddenly, catching sight of car headlights arcing around the driveway through the window. 'Great,' I mutter. 'Someone's here, Ron. Can I call you back in a moment?'

'Sure,' she says and hangs up.

For a moment, I wonder if it might be Josh's mum dropping Kieran home early, but in case it's not, I leave the hall light off as I creep towards the door to check. I don't want to have to see anyone or make chit-chat tonight.

Since Jeremy's accident, almost two months ago now, I've had a steady stream of well-meaning visitors. In the early days, they turned up with casseroles or home-made soup for the freezer. Flowers and sympathy cards adorned the living room, and my phone was constantly lighting up with messages of support and offers of help – for shopping, company and practical issues such as maintaining the garden and paddock.

But over the last few weeks, the offers have tapered off. And now I just want to be alone with my grief and my son, work it out our own way.

I duck back from the doorway when I see it's not Josh's mum's car, hovering out of sight in the kitchen, waiting for the doorbell to ring. I'm in two minds whether to answer it. I'd planned on chatting to Rhonda and then having a bath before fetching Kieran. A soak would have given me time to think – about being pregnant, about what to do. I know the baby inside me can't be Jeremy's – which means only one thing: that I cheated. But I also know that's simply not true; I would never have done that in a thousand years. Not willingly, anyway.

I cover my face at the thought of whatever happened that night, desperately wishing I could turn back time. Then I dare to peek through into the hallway again, hoping that whoever it is has gone. Outside on the drive, I see the light from the coach lamp above the door reflecting off the side of a car – a sleek, black vehicle that I don't recognise. Then I hear footsteps crunching across the gravel, followed by the doorbell ringing. Before I can even decide what to do, the chime sounds again. And again and again.

Please let Kieran be OK, I think, as my thoughts immediately go into overdrive. The insistence of the person outside sends me rushing to the front door. I don't see who's standing behind it until I pull it open.

'Oh!' I say, recoiling. My hand is still on the door and every fibre of my being screams at me to slam it shut, turn the deadlock and slide across the two bolts. But I just stand there, frozen.

'I hope you don't mind me calling round unannounced,' Scott says. He's wearing an army-style bomber jacket with a black crew-neck sweater underneath, jeans and tan boots, though my mind only takes in his appearance because he looks so different to when he came to my surgery or, indeed, when I encountered him in the supermarket.

Something in my stomach churns. He seems more familiar than ever.

'Mr Shaw,' I say. And then I'm silent. My mouth won't form words.

'I came to apologise,' he continues, holding up a bottle of red wine. 'I thought perhaps you might like to share this with me. If you have time, that is.'

That's when I notice the bunch of flowers he's clutching in his other hand, hanging down by his thigh.

'And I thought these might help make amends too.' He lifts the small bouquet, which turns out to be white roses.

'Apologise?' I say with a little shake of my head, frowning.

'For being an arse in the supermarket. I… I don't know what came over me. I shouldn't have got in your way like that.'

'No…' I say vaguely, unable to take my eyes off this man – my *patient* – standing in the doorway of my house with a bottle of wine and a bunch of flowers.

'So how about it, then? Let's open this and start again, shall we?'

'Start again?' I say, bewildered. But it's too late. Scott has somehow slid past me and is standing in my hallway, glancing around.

'Nice place,' he says. 'Lived here long?'

'Er… yes,' I say, only half shutting the door. I don't want to close it because I need him to leave. 'It's not actually a great time right—'

'I was in my last place nearly twenty years,' Scott says, running his hand along the edge of the hall table – the one Jeremy and I found in an antique shop in Devon. 'And ten years in the one before that. You get used to a place, right?'

'What?' I say, baffled, shaking my head. 'Look, I'm sorry, Mr Shaw, but I'm going to have to ask you to leave. I'm really busy right now, plus it's not at all ethical for us to socialise. You're my patient.'

'Mr Shaw?' he says. 'That's very formal.' He laughs. No one else would think it a particularly sinister laugh, but I do. He looks through the double doorway to the kitchen. 'Are you home alone?'

'That's irrelevant,' I tell him. 'And I really can't accept the wine or flowers, I'm afraid.' I open the front door wide again, feeling a rush of cold air. My heart thumps inside my chest as I look at him. I feel myself falling, drowning. *The hotel room… stumbling… clothes ripping… the heat of skin on skin… alcohol… a hand around my throat…*

'Nonsense,' he says. 'That would be rude.' He strides through into the breakfast area and onwards into my kitchen. 'Where do you keep the glasses?' he asks, his eyes scanning around. I glance over at my phone lying on the island unit behind him. Before I can answer, he spots them in a clear-fronted cupboard. He plonks the bottle on the granite worktop and fetches two stemmed glasses, placing them side by side. A moment later, he's handing me a drink, but I just stand there, my arms hanging limply and not even finding the resolve to pick up my phone to threaten a call to the police.

'Cheers,' he says, thrusting his drink towards me. 'To new beginnings.'

'New beginnings?' I say weakly.

'And to us,' he says, not taking his eyes off me as he takes a long, slow sip.

CHAPTER ELEVEN

Jen

'"*Us*"?' I say, using my fingers as quote marks. I take the drink off him and put it on the counter, hoping he'll put his glass down too. He doesn't. 'Really, I want you to leave now. I'm asking politely.' He's deluded. A crackpot. I should have recognised it sooner.

'Ah, come on now, Jen. There's no need for the pretence, surely?'

I shake my head and step to the other side of the kitchen island, wanting something solid between us. He must have mental health issues.

'You've got the wrong end of the stick, Mr Shaw,' I say, looking at him squarely. 'I'm your doctor, and I'd prefer it if you called me Dr Miller. In the *surgery*,' I add, knowing that after this, I won't be able to see him as a patient again. I'll be referring him to another practice.

'Bit silly to be so formal, don't you think?'

'What on earth are you talking about?'

I lean forward on the granite worktop, feeling my fingers splay out, pressing down into the cold stone as I'm back there again. *Loud music... the room spinning... firm hands round my waist supporting me... the mirrors in the lift, me wondering who the gaunt woman staring back was... the hotel room... the discarded clothes.*

Then the feeling inside me the next morning. As though I'd been invaded, stripped of my soul – even though I'd woken up alone. But oddly, I'd felt complete too. As though I'd been waiting for it all my life; as if I somehow deserved whatever had happened.

Scott says nothing. Instead, he parks himself on one of three bar stools at the island. The one Jeremy always used to sit on. He smiles, sipping his drink, looking around the kitchen appreciatively.

'I know you, don't I?' I manage to say, almost as if hearing the words will make my suspicions real. It's barely more than a whisper as I narrow my eyes at him.

Scott smiles, his shoulders shrugging in time with his silent laugh. 'That memorable, was it?' He looks away for a second, pretending he's wounded.

'*Christ.*' I stare down at the black granite. My dark reflection glares back. 'Oxford?'

He gives a quick nod. 'Look, you didn't tell me you were married. I'm sorry, OK?' He shrugs. 'I enjoyed myself that night. I thought you did too, which is why I looked you up, given that I've moved to the area. But it was a mistake, I can see that. I'll go.'

He rises from the stool and takes another large sip of his wine before putting the half-empty glass down. He turns up the collar of his jacket, his eyes sweeping up and down me. 'Don't want hubby to walk in on us now, do we?' he adds, fishing in his pocket for his car keys.

'My husband is dead,' I blurt out bitterly. I can't stand the thought of this man mocking Jeremy when he'll never be here to defend himself.

Scott freezes. 'I'm very sorry to hear that,' he says with a solemn nod. 'You didn't tell me that, either. Mind you, you were in no fit state—'

'He died a few weeks after... after we met in Oxford. On the second of January.' My nails press against the cold worktop, hating that it happened before Jeremy's accident and not after. Whatever *it* was.

Scott is thoughtful for a moment and, to my horror, he sits back down on the bar stool. 'That sounds tough,' he says, with almost a hint of compassion in his voice. His icy eyes seem to be defrosting.

I nod and make the face I usually pull when I'm trying to deflect people from my grief. It usually works, but not this time it seems.

'What happened?' His voice has lost the slightly aggressive and cocky tone it had when he arrived. The way he sits – forearms leaning on the island, hands clasped as he stares down into them – makes me wonder if he's been through something similar, as if he's also familiar with death.

'An accident,' I say, pulling out a bar stool and sliding it round the corner of the kitchen island. I don't want to sit too near him, but I also need answers about what happened that night. And then I have to decide whether to tell him I'm pregnant or not. It can't be anyone else.

'I'm sorry to hear that,' Scott says. 'Did you get a chance to say goodbye?'

'No.' I reach for the glass of wine he's poured me and, without thinking, I take a large sip. 'He was on a skiing trip in Switzerland. There was an avalanche.'

'Buried alive,' Scott says, with barely a flicker of expression. 'Or would it technically be drowning?'

I shudder, hoping he doesn't notice.

'Were you on the trip too?'

'No. It was part work and... and part pleasure,' I tell him, suddenly feeling the need to justify why my husband was away at New Year without me. I don't mention anything about Madeleine, his camerawoman. 'Jeremy made documentaries, wrote travel pieces. He was doing some preliminary filming. As well as getting some skiing in,' I add.

I'd tried to dissuade him from taking the job, pleading that surely being with his family over New Year was more important than some project that wasn't even guaranteed to go ahead, let alone get airtime or make any money.

Yes, it was a test in the hope he would choose me over her. But he didn't. A cosy trip for two, holed up in an Alpine lodge, and no doubt I'd be spun some story on his return about how conditions weren't right for filming on the mountains to explain why there wasn't any footage. *Another* story. I'd heard several over the previous twelve months about Madeleine Lacroix.

'I see,' he says, pausing while he thinks. 'I remember hearing about that avalanche on the news. A few people died, didn't they?'

'Six in total. Only three bodies were recovered. They've given up the search now.' It's as if the words fall out of my mouth automatically, I'm so used to telling people the story. If I say it in a clinical way, almost as if I'm the one reading the news report, then somehow I manage to get it out without breaking into a thousand pieces. 'They were all off-piste.'

'A rule-breaker, then,' Scott says. I swear I detect the glimmer of a smile at one corner of his mouth. It makes me want to punch him. 'We'd have got along.'

'I doubt that,' I say. 'He was an experienced skier. It was just terrible luck.'

'Very,' Scott says, taking another sip of wine. He doesn't take his eyes off me.

'Anyway, I'm not discussing my private affairs further. If it is indeed true that we've encountered each other previously, perhaps you could provide me with some… details.' I take a breath, clear my throat. 'I don't remember much about the evening.'

Scott laughs loudly, tipping back his head. For a second, he reminds me of Jeremy in one of his outrageous laughing fits, his wild hair framing his face as he guffawed at one of his own jokes. What I loved most about my husband was how he didn't care a jot what anyone thought of him. It's strange how the more subtle reasons for loving him have only come to light since his death.

'You find it amusing?'

He shakes his head, trying to quell his outburst. 'Sorry... It's just... you weren't this uptight in Eleven.'

'What the hell is Eleven?'

'The bar we were at in Oxford.'

It rings a bell, but to be honest, I didn't pay much attention when I'd followed my colleagues inside.

'What happened in the bar?'

'I noticed you come in,' Scott says. 'You looked tired. You were with a group but you somehow seemed alone.'

'I was at a conference,' I say, as if that explains everything.

'I'd been watching you for a while. A long while, actually.' Scott pauses, waiting for a reaction, but I give him none. 'Some guy bought you a drink and you chatted with a few people. Smiling politely, as one does. You didn't seem to be enjoying yourself.'

I keep my expression neutral, trying not to give away my thoughts.

'Then you went off on your own and that's when I approached you.'

'And?'

'You sat at a table, you tried to ignore me, and then you went to the toilet. You were quite rude, actually.'

There's a strange noise brewing in my head, building and buzzing as if my subconscious is firing warning signals. 'Why were you watching me?'

'Why not?' Scott says. 'You're an attractive woman. And that night you seemed... so alone.'

'What happened after I went to the toilet?' I clear my throat, about to take another sip of wine, but I push the glass away.

'You came back and quickly finished your drink. While you were gone, I'd ordered us some more, plus a few shots.'

'I sort of remember...' I say, thinking back. 'I asked you to watch my drink. But if you went to the bar—'

'No one touched it.'

'Jesus Christ,' I say. 'Someone must have put something in it. There's no way on God's earth I'd have… I'd have… *you know*, otherwise.' I stand up and go over to the huge glass doors, staring out into the blackness. The brick path leading across the lawn towards the paddock and the small lake just beyond, the low box topiary hedge surrounding the outside dining area, the pots of winter flowers I'd planted last autumn – none of it is visible in the inky darkness outside. Just the eyes of Gypsy, Jeremy's huge tabby cat, glinting back as she walks past on the terrace.

'No way you'd have had sex, you mean?' Another laugh from Scott.

Suddenly he's behind me, his breathing close. Then I feel something tugging – Scott's hands slipping loose the velvet scrunchie that's securing my ponytail.

'I prefer you with it down,' he says, spreading my hair around my shoulders so it falls forward over my cheeks. His finger reaches to my face and draws a line across my lips.

I swing round, staring up at him as I feel my throat constrict. As though someone has their hands around my neck.

My head hitting the wall… the slap… my wrists restrained… my legs forced apart. Me screaming but nothing coming out… Then blackness…

'I'm pregnant,' I tell him, looking deep into his cold blue eyes. 'And it's yours.'

CHAPTER TWELVE

Rhonda

'Busy?'

Rhonda hears a gentle knock on her open office door. She looks up from the stack of papers, peering over the rims of her black-framed glasses. It takes her a moment to focus.

'*Jen…*' she says, surprised to see her. She half stands, her eyes flicking nervously around her office as though she's ashamed of the clutter. Ashamed of *something*. She quickly stacks up the thick pile of papers she's been reading, sliding the whole lot over to one corner of her desk. 'I'm never too busy for you. Come on in.'

As an afterthought, she swipes her scarf from the back of her chair, covering the stack of papers with it.

'That's pretty,' Jen comments, reaching over and feeling the scarf fabric. When it almost falls off the papers, Rhonda quickly places it back.

'Present from Chris,' she says, not wanting to talk about the scarf or what's underneath it. Her eyes are still smarting from what she's just read. She doesn't want to believe it, hasn't taken it on board yet. Probably won't ever. It needs dealing with, quickly and without fuss, to save everyone's face. None of it needs to come out, she thinks. She can take care of it all. She's a teacher, head of her department, and has dealt with a lot worse over the years.

'Tea?' She stands up, actually glad of the interruption. 'I'm… I'm marking,' she lies. 'I could use a brain break.'

'Marking a thesis?' Jen jokes, eyeing the wodge of paper under the scarf. She slips off her jacket and drops down into the chair.

Over in the corner of her small office, beneath the large mullion window of the old Victorian building, Rhonda fills the kettle. When the drinks are made, she slides some brightly coloured student files to one side to make space for the mugs. And to further conceal the manuscript.

'Cheers,' Rhonda says, passing over a drink. 'How are you doing?'

Jen shrugs, her face expressionless. She stares at her mug, tracing her finger around the rim. 'Turns out he was in debt,' she says, looking up when Rhonda is seated opposite again. 'Jeremy.'

Rhonda closes her eyes for a moment. 'Christ. How much?'

'I'm not sure yet. A few thousand.'

'I'm so sorry to hear that, Jen.' She takes a moment to think. 'How the hell did he manage that?'

Jen shakes her head. 'I really don't know. But I just keep thinking, what else am I going to discover?'

Rhonda looks away, feels her heart skipping in her chest as she catches sight of the manuscript. She knows Jen is fighting back tears, hates seeing the utter despair written all over her face.

'You don't deserve this on top of everything else,' Rhonda says as kindly as she can. And it's true, Jen doesn't deserve what she's been served up these last couple of months. *No, this entire last year*, she thinks, knowing Jen's suspicions about Jeremy's affair. She glances at the stack of papers again.

'I'll have to speak to the bank, but I'm just not sure I've got it in me right now. I'll probably have to sell the house and—'

'Stop,' Rhonda says. 'They're not going to force a grieving widow and her son out of their home, OK?'

Jen nods, pulling a pack of tissues from her bag.

'And if it turns out you have to repay it somehow, then… then you'll figure out a way. It's not as if you don't earn m—'

'I can't get *her* out of my mind, Ronnie,' Jen says. 'The debt is the least of it really. I can't even ask him for the truth now. That died with him.'

Rhonda hadn't pressed for details when Jen had first mentioned her concerns to her last summer – rather she'd let her friend drip-feed whatever she'd felt comfortable talking about. But it turned out Jen's suspicions had begun a few months before.

The six of them had been on holiday in Devon last August: the two couples plus Kieran and Caitlin. Cream teas, surfing, beach walks and barbecues, plus a different fish restaurant every evening. All so British. All so middle-class. Not that Rhonda and Chris felt particularly middle-class – a teacher and a copper – but Jen's parents owned a beach home near Ilfracombe on the north Devon coast, and she'd invited them along.

The two families were the best of friends. The adults all got on well – though they'd often laughed about how different they all actually were – Jen the medic, the scientist; Jeremy the thinker, the explorer, the academic. But she supposed Chris's analytical mind in some way matched Jen's work as a GP – both trying to find answers and solutions from whatever evidence they had, both detectives. And perhaps in some way, too, Rhonda and Jeremy had more in common than seemed apparent – a love of literature, seeing the world slightly askew, often preferring to watch, observe and overthink absolutely everything.

Meantime, Kieran and Caitlin were a one-sided teen romance. Kieran was clearly lovesick for Caitlin, even if she wasn't giving him much encouragement in return. That summer, Jeremy had taken bets on when Kieran would make his move, commenting that Caitlin was playing hard to get and giving him a run for his money.

'Our son's not a letch like you,' Jen had joked one evening as they sat on the wooden front deck of the little west-facing cottage, watching the sun go down. They each had a cocktail, made by Jeremy, and Rhonda had baked some cheese straws.

Jen had laughed when she said it, to lighten the weight of the implication, and Jeremy had quipped back with some humorous defence, though he'd given her a sour look. Similarly, Rhonda remembered the concerned look Jen had given her earlier, recalling what the pair of them had discussed on their beach walk that afternoon.

'So what you're saying is that you don't trust him?' Rhonda had asked, kicking away a slippery rope of seaweed at the shoreline.

'Yes,' she'd replied. Her long white skirt trailed in the sand, the hem soaked a few inches with seawater.

'Have you said anything to him?' Rhonda had clenched her fists by her sides – a mix of anger and frustration. All she wanted to do was grab Jeremy by the collar, shake him and demand to know what the hell he was playing at. But for Jen's sake, she wouldn't.

'No,' Jen had answered. 'He'll tell me I'm crazy, mad, imagining things, that I'm stressed. Then he'll threaten to cancel what few paying jobs he has in his diary to prove to me that he doesn't care if he sees Madeleine or not. But of course then I'll tell him not to be silly, we need the little bit of extra money, hint that perhaps a different cameraperson would be a good compromise, and then he'll agree, but I'll feel wretched for being so suspicious, telling him he doesn't need to do that, and round and round we'll go. I'm not sure how much longer we can survive on just my salary. I'm still paying off the renovations. I've taken on a private clinic at the hospital, but I'm exhausted.'

'Madeleine,' Rhonda had repeated thoughtfully. 'And she's French, you say?'

Jen had nodded. 'French, and ten years younger than me.'

'When is this book he's writing supposed to be completely finished?' Rhonda had asked.

'Sometime never, by my estimation,' Jen replied. 'And these research trips he goes on,' she'd continued, making quotes in the air. 'Madeleine goes along too. It's the perfect opportunity for them to spend time together. Me working all hours at the practice and the hospital, looking after Kieran, the house, taking on the mental load of everything—'

'It's just so hard to believe,' Rhonda had interrupted. 'But if it's true, then he's a bastard and I hate him for you.'

'But he's not a bastard, though, is he? He's my Jeremy… Kieran's dad. I've known him since forever and I can't imagine life without him. If I'm wrong, I'm in danger of trashing a perfectly good marriage, losing all my friends and—'

'Stop,' Rhonda had said sternly. 'You won't get rid of *me* that easily, but yes, with these thoughts you are in danger of trashing your marriage. The pair of you need to sort this out.'

'Promise me you won't say anything to him?' Jen had almost begged as they'd walked back to the beach house. A spiral of smoke was visible from the front deck – someone had fired up the barbecue. 'This holiday is just what I needed. I'll put it out of my mind. For now,' she'd added.

'I promise,' Rhonda had said, linking arms with her friend as they headed up the beach towards the others. As they drew closer they soon spotted Jeremy standing in front of the Weber, tongs in hand, apron on, while Caitlin sat watching him from a swing chair, her long legs curled beneath her as she rocked gently back and forth, twirling a lock of hair around her finger.

*

'You know what makes me so sad?' Jen says now, staring into her mug of tea in Rhonda's office. 'Apart from him being dead, of course.'

Rhonda gives a slight shake of her head.

'It's that I never really felt as if I was… *enough* for Jeremy. Does that make sense?'

'Explain more,' Rhonda says, frowning and silencing her phone when it rings.

'He was so deep, so thoughtful and intricate, and he commanded such a huge presence wherever he went, attracting all kinds of attention from interesting people. He was just so… passionate about everything he did, that in comparison I felt I wasn't enough to satisfy him – intellectually and sometimes physically too,' Jen says, pausing to think. 'Sometimes I wonder how or why we even got together. But the irony is, his mind is exactly why I fell for him.'

'Stop doing yourself down, Jen,' Rhonda comments, reaching out and touching her friend's hand. 'I know grief is taking your thoughts into uncharted territory, but you were every bit a strong enough woman for him. He absolutely bloody adored you.'

Jen smiles briefly. 'I don't think it was strength he wanted. It made me feel sort of sexless in Jeremy's eyes. Just a body with a brain who had a good career and simply got on with stuff. It didn't help that for the last eighteen months or so I'd been the sole breadwinner, either. That bloody book,' Jen adds, sucking in air. 'Our sex life had dwindled to nothing before he died. *Virtually* nothing,' she adds quickly.

'Sounds to me like maybe you emasculated him a bit, Jen. Some men can't cope with competent, independent women. Perhaps you should have been more helpless,' Rhonda says through a half-hearted laugh.

'Truth is, Ron,' Jen replies, 'that's exactly how I feel right now. Helpless for the first time in my life. And he's not even here to see it, to play rescuer to me.'

Rhonda glances over Jen's shoulder, aware that someone is lurking just outside the open door to her office. She adjusts the scarf over the manuscript again.

'You're far from helpless,' Rhonda says, switching her attention back to Jen. 'You're grieving.'

Jen nods, her lips pursed, though looking as if she's about to explode. Her right leg jiggles up and down and she steeples her fingers under her chin, staring out through the huge leaded window that faces on to the quad. Ivy creeps across one of the glass panes.

'I'm pregnant,' she suddenly blurts out, each syllable a precise bullet. She continues to stare out of the window, her head held high, her chin jutting forward as the low afternoon winter sun streams in and catches her face. 'Nearly twelve weeks.'

Rhonda catches her breath, forcing down a gasp. Instinctively, she places a hand on top of the stack of papers, before glancing behind Jen to the person who has now made himself known, standing in the doorway, his lips slightly apart, his cheeks pinking up.

'Kieran,' Rhonda says, flashing a look at Jen. 'What can I do for you?' She uses her teacher's voice, rather than that of family friend.

Jen's head whips round, her eyes widening in shock as she sees her son standing there – his tie loosely knotted at his collar, the weight of his backpack pulling the shoulder of his blazer off to one side.

'Nothing,' he says quietly, staring at his mum. 'Nothing at all,' he adds, shaking his head as he turns and leaves.

CHAPTER THIRTEEN

Then

Mac's house is warm. And it smells nice – like the cleaning aisle in the supermarket. *And* it has proper carpet in the living room and two sofas in front of a television that's almost like a cinema screen. Not that Evan has been to the cinema before.

'Squash?' Mac's mum asks, lowering a tray down to him. Evan looks up at the woman's kind face. Her dark hair is pulled back in a ponytail, the strands of it falling forward as he looks at what she's offering. 'And a biscuit?' She smiles, and Evan can't help seeing straight down the V-neck of her navy uniform as she bends down, revealing a valley of flesh that, instinctively, he knows he shouldn't be looking at.

Ashamed of his thoughts, he dithers over which biscuit to choose, just so he can get a bit more of a look. It does something to him inside, as if he needs to press himself against whatever's in there, to be held and engulfed by her softness. To be somewhere safe.

'Bagsy me these,' Mac says, grabbing a couple of custard creams. He lolls back on the sofa, feet drawn up as he changes the channel.

'Go on, take what you want, Evan,' Mac's mum says.

'What we going to kill, then?' Evan whispers when Mac's mum has gone, copying Mac and pulling his feet up under him.

'Get your shoes off or Mum'll kill *you*,' Mac says, glancing towards the kitchen. Evan kicks them off.

'Shall we go up to your room, then?'

Mac leans sideways to see his mum through in the kitchen. He lowers his voice. 'Nah. Not allowed. Mum wouldn't like us being upstairs.'

'Stay downstairs, both of you,' comes a voice from the other room.

Evan nods, confused. 'Want to play outside, then?' Evan says, wondering why Mac's being boring today. Since they made Kill Club a week ago, they've spent break times trapping various insects and seeing who can make them die the slowest. Evan always wins because sometimes Mac's a sissy and can't do it.

'Or we could go on a bike ride?'

'Yeah, all right,' Mac says. He gets up and grabs a few more biscuits and finishes his squash. He calls out to his mum that they're going round the village.

'Don't be more than half an hour,' she calls back from the kitchen, plus something else about being careful, about not talking to strangers. In the hallway, as they pull on their coats, Evan smells something wafting through from the kitchen. He swallows, licking his lips.

'Come on then, dickhead,' Mac says, grinning and tugging Evan's sleeve. They run out onto the front drive, with Evan not minding being called a dickhead by Mac because right now he thinks he's pretty much the coolest boy in school.

'Go on, do it, *do* it,' Mac whispers, glancing over his shoulder. On the way in, they saw the corner shop owner busy talking to a woman at the counter. 'Now's your chance.'

Evan stares at the torches, wondering which one to slide inside his jacket.

'And nick some batteries, too,' he says, jabbing a finger at the display. He glances up at the funny round mirror at the end of the aisle, checking the shopkeeper is still distracted.

Evan nods, but then something else further along the racks catches his eye. A display of kitchen knives. The one with the short blade would be cool to have – the type his mum peels the potatoes with. He catches Mac's eye, sees the glint. Mac nods slowly, as if giving his approval, egging him on.

A moment later and Evan is striding towards the exit, while Mac takes a packet of Polo mints off the shelf near the door as a distraction and heads to the counter to pay. The woman is still talking to the owner so Mac dumps some coins on the counter, holding up the mints for the shopkeeper to see.

'Thanks, chuck,' he says and gives Mac a wave as he leaves.

'See?' Mac says to Evan as they head off down the pavement, breaking into a half-run as they wheel their bikes. 'Easy, right?'

'Peasy,' Evan replies.

Ten minutes later, when Evan's legs feel as though they might drop off from pedalling so hard up the hill, Mac slows and gets off his bike ahead of him. The road has narrowed to a single track and if a car came round the corner, Evan reckons it would skittle them both.

'You allowed up here?' Evan asks nervously, glancing back down the hill, panting. To one side is the village, with its church steeple marking the centre and all the posh houses dotted around – though somehow, they don't look quite so posh from up here. More like Lego houses. Beyond that, he sees where the village ends and the beginnings of the Westbourne estate as it bleeds into the landscape.

'No,' Mac says, ripping open the mints. He puts two in his mouth and then offers Evan the packet, who does the same. 'Mum would have a fit. But she won't know, right? I come up here all the time.'

'My mum would have a fit, too,' Evan says, thinking she probably wouldn't. Truth was, she probably hadn't even noticed he wasn't home from school yet.

'Can you keep a secret?' Mac asks, beckoning Evan to follow.

'We're Kill Club,' Evan states. ''Course I can.'

Mac drags his bike over to the hedge where there's a deep ditch, dumping it out of sight in the undergrowth. He beckons for Evan to do the same, then climbs over an old iron gate that's half hanging off its hinges. Beyond the gate is thick woodland that, to Evan, looks never-ending. The sort of place you could easily get lost in.

'This way,' Mac says, following a track between the trees. The floor of the wood is spongy – thick with rotting leaves and twigs. As they head further in, the light fades, making Evan shiver.

'Where we going?' Evan asks, glancing back over his shoulder.

Mac doesn't say anything. Rather he stops, leaning against a tree and staring all around. 'Give us that knife,' he says. Evan does as he's told, ripping the packaging off it and tearing at the plastic tie with his teeth. He drops the rubbish on the ground.

'Cool,' Mac says, running his thumb along the short blade.

Evan is silent for a moment, wondering what Mac is going to do with it, but he follows on as Mac sets off again, carving a nick in every tree he passes. 'So we don't get lost,' he says, looking back at Evan. 'I read about it in a survival book.'

Five minutes later, Mac stops. 'I need to pee,' he says, looking around.

'Yeah, me too,' Evan replies, fiddling with his zip and coming up close to Mac, who's standing next to a tree. He positions himself and looks down, waiting.

'Er, yuk,' Mac says, moving away quickly as he pulls a face. 'Weirdo,' he adds, going over to another tree a little way away. When Evan has finished and turns, zipping himself up, Mac is nowhere to be seen – but then, a few moments later, he reappears, also zipping up his flies.

They walk on a little further before Mac slows and points at something the other side of a small clearing. 'What do you think?' he says proudly. He pulls his anorak off his shoulders. 'Kill Club headquarters.'

It takes Evan a moment to see what Mac is pointing at, but when he spots the branches and sticks propped between two trees in a tent shape, he almost bursts with joy. A secret den.

CHAPTER FOURTEEN

Jen

Kieran remains mute on the journey home from school, despite my attempts at making chit-chat.

'Kier,' I say fifteen minutes later as I wrench on the handbrake in the drive. I stare up at the barn's facade – remembering how fussy Jeremy was about the builders getting the perfect shade of lime mortar for the repointing, how he demanded that all the broken corbels be restored using reclaimed bricks, how each of our windows was handmade by a local joiner. It was a labour of love, making the perfect family home. 'Kier,' I say loudly so he can hear me through his earphones.

Reluctantly, he pulls one out and turns to me.

'We need to talk about what you overheard in Rhonda's office.' I unclip my seat belt, looking across at my son. When I reach out a hand to touch his arm, he whips it away.

'No. We don't,' he says in a way that makes my heart ache. He drags his backpack out of the footwell and gets out of the car. With all the rural house calls I make, my huge black 4WD seemed justifiable when I bought it, though Jeremy turned his nose up, not understanding why I didn't invest in a classic like he had years ago.

His old Triumph Stag sits unused in the garage and I make a mental note to start it, perhaps take it out for a run to keep the battery alive. The thought of getting into something that was so cherished and personal to my husband is heartbreaking. It would almost feel like climbing inside him. And I'm still faced with the onerous task of sorting out his clothes, not to mention everything in his study – hundreds and hundreds of books, the many albums filled with stamps and coins he's collected since he was a boy, plus the boxes of militaria he has stashed in the big cupboard.

'Kieran, we definitely *do* need to talk about it,' I plead as we go into the kitchen, dumping our stuff down.

Predictably, my son heads to the fridge and does that teen thing of peering inside, his hand on the wide-open door as he scans the shelves for a quick snack so he can retreat to his bedroom.

'Why are there only ever *ingredients* in here?' he says without looking at me.

It's a start, I think, that he actually spoke. 'I'll do an online shop later,' I say. 'Get all your favourite snacks in.' If it were just me alone and I wasn't pregnant, I'd be drowning in grief and a bottle of wine, not even bothering with food. It's only because I have to care for Kieran that I eat at all. My son and my job keep me going.

Kieran looks across at me before closing the fridge door. Not slamming it, exactly, but close. 'Seriously, Mum, are you just, like, going to pretend everything's OK?' He shakes his head, making his loose curls dance around his face. His nose wrinkles up and his eyes narrow and, for a few seconds, I see a young Jeremy staring back at me – if it weren't for the freckles and soft, barely shaved hair sprouting on his face.

'No, Kier, I'm not. That's why I wanted to talk and—'

'What is there to talk about? You're pregnant and you didn't tell me.' He glares at me.

'Kier, it's not like that,' I say, reaching out and giving him a hug. 'I just needed some advice and then… well, I never expected you to find out that way. I was going to tell you tonight, I promise.' I'm kicking myself for blurting it out to Rhonda now.

My son pulls away, giving me a look that slays me before grabbing his backpack and storming off upstairs.

I stand alone for what seems like ages, unable to think about preparing dinner. I close my eyes, steadying myself on the worktop, not knowing what the hell I'm going to do. When my life rolls backwards behind my eyelids, rewinding the last few weeks and months, it's easy to pinpoint the exact moment that everything changed. *That night.*

'No,' I whisper, trying to console myself. It was before that – when I finally plucked up the courage to mention my concerns about Madeleine to Jeremy. Or rather, when I couldn't keep quiet about it any longer. It was like I was possessed. If I didn't say something, get some kind of reassurance from him, I knew it would fester and grow inside me.

Enough was enough.

'Who is "M"?' I'd asked him, trying to stay calm as I loomed over his desk, thrusting out his phone.

It was a moment before he'd looked up, finishing the sentence he was frantically typing.

'Is it Madeleine?' I'd snapped, instantly hating myself for sounding so harsh.

Frankly, I was sick of hearing about her. He mentioned her at every opportunity, weaving her into conversations she had no right to be in. It left me wondering who she was, why she felt like some ethereal creature to whom I could never match up. In my mind, Madeleine was a perfect doll – an exquisite being revered by my husband.

'Sorry, what, love?' Jeremy had pushed his fingers through his hair while reclining back in his leather captain's chair. He ran his hand over two days' worth of stubble as he refocused his attention on me and then looked down to my hand. I was jabbing his phone at him.

'You left this in the kitchen, charging. You should tell your girlfriend to be more careful.' I was boiling inside, and only just managed to keep my rage to a gentle simmer outwardly.

He took the device from me then and put it face down on the desk, with only a quick glance at what had flashed up on the screen as I'd been chopping onions. No need for real tears.

'Jen, you've got to stop this. Do you think I don't notice what you're doing? You're literally going to drive yourself insane.'

I was trembling from my core. 'A woman texts, telling you she can't wait to see you, that it's going to be even better than last time. What am I supposed to think?'

Jeremy had shaken his head then, making me feel ridiculous. He took a breath and opened his mouth to speak, but it came out as a sigh. But I noticed how his jaw tensed as he clamped his teeth together.

'And her next text said "What excuse will you give Jen this time?" followed by a kiss. How bloody thoughtful of her to consider how you'll lie to me.'

'Jen, stop.' Jeremy had picked up his phone and glanced at the screen before flopping backwards in his chair. 'How much longer are you going to keep this up? If you ever want this book to be finished, I need to focus. I had an email earlier from that editor I told you about, and they're virtually salivating about my work. You want to ruin all that for me? For *us*?'

'Who is "M"?' I said, refusing to allow him to guilt-trip and deflect me yet again.

'"M" is Mick. The production editor I worked with on that last wildlife documentary.'

I thought back. I didn't remember the name. In fact, I didn't even recall a wildlife documentary, but so many of Jeremy's projects hadn't been green-lit lately that I'd stopped asking about them in case I made him feel bad. Despite our agreement – that he would take a year off to write his book, that I would support us until it was finished – we were both acutely aware that the time limit we'd set had long since passed. My savings were virtually gone and our family was relying on me. Perhaps Rhonda was right – that my career somehow made him feel a lesser man, not the archetypal strong, breadwinning husband and father he wanted to be. But as ever, Jeremy put on a brave face and didn't complain. Then again, neither did I when I took on extra private work to make ends meet. With only one income and the renovation bridging loan with its hands around my neck, as well as school fees, the pressure had taken its toll on us both.

'Look, Jen, Mick and I played golf a few months back and he's been pestering me for another round ever since. If you must know, I've declined several times, saying it wasn't fair on you to take time out when I should be working on this.' He'd tapped his laptop. 'Mick's a bit of a bugger and suggested I lie to you about where we were going.' Jeremy folded his arms and looked up at me. 'There's nothing sinister going on.'

'Mick's the type to put a kiss on his messages to you, is he?' I was already starting to feel stupid, guilty, like a crazy woman. The type of wife I never wanted to be.

Jeremy had laughed then. 'Oh God, if you met him, you'd know he's definitely the type. One of those luvvy, over-the-top chaps. The touchy-feely sort. If I didn't know he had a wife, I'd say you had something to be worried about, yes.'

I remember feeling giddy then – though maybe it was from the glass of wine I'd had while I'd been cooking. Giddy and silly, like some immature teenager, not a GP with a family, a home, responsibilities. And it wasn't as though I had these thoughts any other time. Perhaps it was because my gut instinct had been shredded from when I was young – never knowing who to trust, always looking over my shoulder. I shuddered and, as ever, put the thought from my mind, apologising to my husband. Though I wasn't sure how much longer I could keep doing that.

*

I hear Kieran turn on his music in his room, leaving me still standing in the middle of the kitchen, feeling lost in my own home. The place feels far too big without Jeremy in it. I suddenly have an urge for a glass of wine, or a big fat spliff, like we used to do at university where Jeremy and I had met, sitting in a secluded spot down by the river on a balmy night, or leaning out of his bedroom window in his grotty lodgings. We saw each other often, but it wasn't until a couple of years after Jeremy had graduated that our relationship steadied itself into something more solid. And it wasn't long after I'd qualified as a doctor several years later that I fell pregnant with Kieran.

We were blissfully happy. Madly in love.

I slam my hands down on the kitchen counter, dropping my head. I take a deep breath, refocusing my mind.

'Right,' I say, looking up again. 'Time to get a grip.' I turn on the oven and grab a couple of chicken Kievs from the fridge, ripping open the packet before tipping them onto a baking tray. I shove them in the oven and head back to the hallway to check the mailbox outside the front door. I usually bring in any post when I get home, but after what had happened with Kieran, I'd completely forgotten.

My son's music blares even louder from his bedroom – the bass reverberating through the ceiling. I bat away the thoughts of that night as fleeting shards of memory stab at my brain. I can't deal with it right now.

I unlock the front door and then put the key in the little mailbox that Jeremy had specially commissioned – black metal with a sloping roof and a pair of swallows mid-flight painted on the front. 'Swallow Barn' is embossed underneath in a font we chose together.

There are a couple of letters inside – one a bank statement, which will go straight into my 'to be dealt with' pile because I can't face opening it right now, and the other looks to be a supermarket rewards card offer. But there's also a small packet in the mailbox – a thin padded envelope.

'Odd,' I say, knowing I didn't order anything. My next thought is that perhaps Kieran bought something online – perhaps new strings for his guitar, which he mentioned he needed the other day.

But the envelope is clearly addressed to me.

My name is neatly printed in black felt-tip pen – Dr Jennifer Miller – followed by my address. There are no identifying flourishes or slant to the characters and the postmark is illegible.

I head back inside the house, dropping the mail on the kitchen counter before taking some frozen vegetables from the freezer. They'll have to do – I really can't face preparing anything but a basic meal tonight. Once the vegetables are in a pan of water, I shove the bank statement in a drawer and then rip open the reward card envelope – £5.50 in vouchers, which I carefully detach and tuck inside my purse. With the extra debt Jeremy left behind, every penny counts right now. Then I stare at the packet for a moment, puzzled, before carefully sliding my finger under the sealed flap.

'Kieran, dinner won't be too long,' I call out, but I doubt he hears me.

At first, I don't think there's anything inside the envelope because it's so light, but when I reach in, something soft catches against my fingers. Confused, I pull out the item and stare at it for a moment, unable to make sense of what it is.

Fabric… pale-pink cotton… dirty…

'What the *hell*?' I whisper, suddenly realising how light-headed I feel. I put down the envelope and unfold the scrunched-up fabric. That's when I stumble over to a stool, steadying myself on the worktop before I sit down.

'Oh my *God*,' I whisper, my heart thundering in my chest. 'What the hell *is* this?' Or rather, I think – what the hell does it mean?

Someone has sent me a pair of girl's underpants – filthy and worn, faded and frayed. Beneath the stains are little purple flowers, screaming out the innocence of the wearer. The pants look as though they've been lying in the gutter or dropped in mud.

I place them on the worktop, peering inside the envelope to see if there's anything else. And that's when I see the Post-it note with the words 'I KNOW' printed in the same black marker as on the envelope.

The size label on the pants is faded but still just legible – 'Age 11 to 13' sends a wave of nausea through me. Quickly, I shove the pants back inside the packet, sickened by the sight of them – and that the size indicates they belonged to a young girl.

Unable to concentrate, I do my best to finish preparing dinner, grabbing a couple of plates from the cupboard, checking on the Kievs as they crisp up. I call out to Kieran again that food will be ready in ten minutes, and I think I hear him call back 'OK' above the din of his music.

The bottle of wine in the fridge signals to me as I take out the ketchup, knowing Kieran will want sauce. I put a hand on the cold glass bottle, hoping it will help to numb the thoughts swirling around my head.

Who the hell would send me such a thing? I've always thought of myself as well liked in the community, having lived here all my life, apart from during my training years. My mother was in the WI, my dad worked in the local car industry and I bake bloody cakes for the village fete, for Christ's sake. My mind scans through everyone I know, even trawling my patient list, wondering who might have a grudge against me. But I can't think of anyone – apart from Scott, of course. Despite everything that's happened, I don't see why he would send me a pair of girl's underpants. It doesn't make any sense at all.

Whoever it is, they must have made a mistake, I think, trying to convince myself it's nothing, that it doesn't mean anything.

'Probably some nutter, or a stupid joke,' I whisper, setting the table. A part of me wonders if I should tell the police, but on top of everything, I can't stand the extra layer of disruption. And it wouldn't reflect well on me either – a respected GP in a small community. Instead, I take the packet out to the garage and stash it away underneath a load of items in a storage box, before coming back inside and scrubbing my hands until they're sore.

CHAPTER FIFTEEN

Rhonda

'Right,' Rhonda says, standing in Jen's bedroom, her hands on her hips. Her blonde hair is swept up in a messy bun, held in place with a red scarf tied with a knot on top, covering her darker roots. 'Let's get stuck in.'

'I'm not sure I can, Ron,' Jen says through a voice tinged with exhaustion. 'Perhaps I should move into the spare room, just shut the door on all of this. Let me take you out for lunch instead, to say thanks for everything you've done.'

'No, it needs doing, hon,' Rhonda says, advancing further into the room slowly, picking her way through the mess as if it's a crime scene. 'You can't keep putting it off. It's time.'

'Don't judge,' Jen says as Rhonda plucks some discarded clothes from the floor, dropping them in the laundry basket. 'My head really hasn't been in a good place lately and most nights I've just fallen into bed and—'

'Stop,' Rhonda says, placing a finger over Jen's lips. 'What are mates for if not to hold your hair back and help?' God knows, Jen's been a rock for her more times than she can count. It's the least she can do to help sort out Jeremy's belongings. Besides, she wants to do it – no, *needs* to, if she's honest.

'You're an angel and I don't know what I'd do without you,' Jen replies, gripping on to Rhonda's finger when she removes it to speak. 'No one knows the mess I'm in,' she adds, sweeping her arm around the cluttered bedroom. 'Not to mention this.' She points low down on her stomach. 'I haven't told another soul apart from Kier overhearing, which didn't go down well. He's barely spoken to me since. I honestly don't know what to—'

'One thing at a time or you're going to implode in a ball of anxiety. Once we get Jeremy's belongings sorted, you'll feel a little more in control.'

Rhonda walks into the en suite bathroom, scanning around. Two toothbrushes sit side by side in the pot on the shelf above the sink, and a man's towelling robe hangs on a hook beside the shower screen. Various other men's toiletries are littered around the bathroom – Christ, it even still *smells* like Jeremy, she thinks, closing her eyes for a moment, breathing him in.

She returns to the bedroom and opens the fitted wardrobe doors. The rail on Jeremy's side is crammed with shirts, trousers and jackets, with the shelf unit to the side filled with folded jumpers and sweat tops. Rhonda unfurls a black refuse sack from the roll and tears it off.

'So it's all going in the garage for now?' she says, thinking that perhaps it would be best to donate most of it to a charity shop, perhaps keeping a couple of items for sentimental reasons.

Jen nods, her jaw tight and her teeth clenched.

Rhonda plucks out some shirts, slipping them off the hangers before folding them and placing them in the bag.

'Just stuff them in,' Jen suddenly says, ripping out a bunch of sweaters and shoving them in the sack. 'I don't give a toss any more. I just want them gone. They can go to the rubbish dump for all I care.' She lets out a half-choke and half-sob in a poor attempt at stifling her tears.

'Oh, Jen,' Rhonda says, gently taking hold of her hand. 'It's OK, it's OK...' When the tears start in earnest, she pulls her friend in for a hug, cradling her head against her shoulder as she strokes her hair. 'We'll get through this… we will. Just one moment at a time, all right?' She feels the small nod of Jen's head against her neck as she stares up at the ceiling, not sure she believes her own words.

'Thank you,' Jen says through a sniff, pulling a tissue from her pocket. 'I can't believe that only a short time ago we were all planning another trip to Devon once the kids' exams were out of the way.'

'I know…' Rhonda says, feeling herself tense up. She needs to tell Jen about Kieran, the reason he was lurking outside her office the other day. If only she'd not told him to come and see her, he wouldn't have overheard what he did. 'And we'll plan something again when you feel more up to it. Maybe we can get away in July. Jeremy will be with us in spirit.'

In reality, she can't even begin to imagine what it would be like without Jeremy there – and isn't sure she wants to find out.

'Knowing him, he bloody will be, too. Haunting us.' Jen manages a laugh.

'About those exams,' Rhonda says, turning back to the wardrobe. She continues to fold the clothes before putting them in the bag. It doesn't feel right to just shove them in without a care. Briefly, she touches a sweater to her face, closes her eyes.

'What about them?'

'I'm honestly wondering if Kieran should defer. He's had a lot to deal with the last few weeks. I don't think his mind is—'

'No,' Jen says firmly, yanking some ties off a rack. 'He would hate that. So would Jeremy.'

'It's just that he's been skipping classes quite a bit now. And when he does show up, he doesn't engage.'

Jen stares at her in disbelief, wrapping a tie around her fist until her fingers throb. 'Christ,' she says, feeling as if her son is slipping ever further from her. 'You should have told me sooner, Ronnie.'

'I'm sorry.' She looks away briefly. 'I convinced senior management that I'd deal with it. They know our relationship, that you and I are best friends. And they know how well I know Kier.'

Jen nods and closes her eyes briefly. 'Thank you. But I really don't want him to be a year behind his peers or even drop out of school aged sixteen.'

Rhonda feels the knot in her guts tighten. 'I also think he's been smoking weed, Jen. A couple of times I've smelt it on him and... well, I don't think it's helping his mood—'

Jen hurls the tie to the floor in an excessive action that doesn't have the impact required, so instead she kicks over the waste bin on the floor beside her dressing table. Tissues and cotton pads and other rubbish fly across the room. She lets out a helpless sob as she paces back and forth, trampling over discarded clothes. Then she bends down to gather up some of the spilt rubbish, but drops it again as the tears start to flow. Unable to help it, she flops down onto her bed, burying her face in the pillow.

Rhonda sits down beside her. 'I'm so sorry, Jen,' she says, reaching out for the sleeve of Jeremy's sweater lying beside them.

*

An hour later, Rhonda ties up the last bag of Jeremy's clothes. 'Shall we start taking them down?'

Jen nods, her eyes still red and puffy from tears. After her crying had subsided, Rhonda had popped downstairs and made tea. Then they'd sat on the bed together, discussing a practical plan to help Kieran – one that he wouldn't instantly run a mile from. One with an incentive.

'If you're totally sure?' Jen had asked a thousand times, punctuated by blowing her nose and profuse apologies. Rhonda knew her tears weren't just from Kieran falling behind at school. It highlighted yet another area of life where responsibility now fell on her and her alone. Gone were joint parenting plans. Gone was joint *everything*. She was completely alone, and Rhonda hoped that she'd just made one corner of Jen's life seem a little less daunting.

'Totally sure,' Rhonda had replied. 'It'll give Caitlin the boost she needs, too. And I reckon they're crazy about each other, so instead of it seeming like a chore, they'll both be dying to get stuck in. I'll give them the spare room to work in and keep them plied with drinks and snacks. Hell, I'll even throw in a pizza at the end of a session if they get through the work.'

Jen had closed her eyes, mumbling a heartfelt thank you. 'I think Kieran's crush on Caitlin is one-way, though,' she'd managed through a snotty laugh. 'It's a bad case of unrequited love, poor lad.'

'Well… Caitlin loves Kieran's company,' Rhonda had said, knowing Jen was probably right. Her daughter was certainly lovesick and dreamy-eyed over someone, but she wasn't sure it was Kieran. Truth was, she saw him more like a brother, but if studying with Caitlin gave the lad some motivation, then she wasn't about to burst his bubble.

'Can you manage?' Rhonda asks now, as they struggle across the landing with three bags each.

'Yup, but be careful on these top few steps. They're lethal. Slippery as hell, so watch out.' Jen had indicated this with a nod of her head as they padded down in socks.

'You're not wrong,' Rhonda jokes, half dropping a bag as she grabs the handrail to steady herself. 'Great idea putting polish on the treads.'

'You can thank our old cleaner for that one,' Jen replies, shoving the keys in her pocket from the hall table. 'She literally spray-polished everything out of spite after Jeremy kept telling her off for using cheap products on his beloved antique furniture.'

The two women put on their shoes and head out to the garage, waiting as the automatic door trundles open. 'Christ, it's cold out here,' Rhonda says as they duck under the automatic door.

'There is some space at the back, believe it or not,' Jen says, stopping for a moment as she stares at Jeremy's bottle-green Stag, which takes up one half of the double garage. She shakes her head. 'He loved that old thing,' she says, looking away and squeezing past the piles of boxes, bikes, old garden toys, stacked-up deckchairs, tools and everything else that had accumulated during seventeen years of family life. Her eyes flick over to a plastic tub stacked against the back wall – the place where she'd stashed the mysterious package. A shudder runs through her.

Rhonda drops a couple of the bags at the garage entrance before picking her way through all the clutter with one bag held up high. 'I'm not seeing this space you talk of.'

'Back here, look,' Jen says, pushing her weight against an old wooden garden table to shove it to one side. That's when it knocks into a huge car roof box leaning up against the wall, sending it crashing sideways and knocking over a few boxes, followed by the sound of breaking china.

'Bugger,' Jen says, dropping the bags she's holding. She picks her way through the mess to begin restacking the items. 'I think that was Mum's old vintage plates. Great – they'll be smashed and—'

'Jen…' Rhonda says, staring at the corner of the garage that the car roof box had been concealing. She frowns, waiting for Jen to look up to where she's pointing. 'Is that Jeremy's… is that his ski stuff?'

She stares at the pair of skis propped up against the brickwork with several sets of poles leaning beside them. A black helmet with a well-known ski logo on the side hangs on a hook beside the equipment, plus a chunky pair of ski boots with the same branding.

Jen stares at them for a moment. 'Yes, yes, it is,' she says finally, quietly. She glances over at the Stag, then back to Rhonda. 'It's like he's everywhere, Ron. It's not that I want to forget him, of course I don't. But I never get a respite from thinking about him. Everything triggers a memory.'

'I know… it's so hard. But what I actually meant is why is Jeremy's ski stuff… well, *here*? Didn't he take it on the trip? It's the new kit you bought him for Christmas, isn't it?'

Jen stops what she's doing and turns to Rhonda, frowning, as though it was something she hadn't even considered herself. 'Yes, you're right,' she says, as if it doesn't have an explanation.

Rhonda opens her mouth to speak, but Jen interrupts her.

'Don't think I didn't ask him the very same question when he left for the airport. In fact, it caused even more ill feeling between us when he left. Which is ghastly to think of now, given what happened.'

'Oh, Jen, I'm sorry.'

Jen shrugs. 'You weren't to know. The kit cost me a fortune, but apparently I'd got the wrong stuff, not the brand he liked. He went on and on about it, making me feel terrible.' She shakes her head and grabs one of the black sacks, virtually slinging it against the back wall so it lands near the ski equipment.

'Couldn't you have returned it for a refund?' Rhonda asks, handing Jen some more bags.

'I suppose, but it's not exactly been a priority.' Jen's expression immediately shows remorse for her sharp tone. 'He must have hired kit out there. Or maybe… maybe he borrowed some of *her* kit.'

And it's when Rhonda sees the tears welling in Jen's eyes again that she decides to change the subject.

CHAPTER SIXTEEN

Jen

'It's like Lenny's been speaking to me, Doctor,' Elsie says, patting the photograph album resting on her lap. She squints through milky eyes. 'Not in a ghostly way, I'm not into all that claptrap,' she adds in her matter-of-fact voice. 'But I can't bear it. I've not been able to look at these pictures for years, but something drove me to get them out the other day. It's like I heard his little voice, even though he was barely old enough to talk when he died.'

This is as emotional as I've ever seen Elsie. Usually, she doesn't engage when it comes to her feelings, the huge guilt she harbours for what happened to her grandson having eaten away at her over the years.

'There's no harm in remembering the good times,' I say, wondering if that's more for my own benefit than Elsie's.

'Aye,' she replies, stroking a photo of the little boy with her finger. 'There weren't time for many memories. None of us ever recovered from it. Least of all Sharon.'

'I'm so sorry to hear that, Elsie. But it wasn't your fault. The monster who did this to little Lenny took advantage of a vulnerable child. And you were a good nan, just as Sharon was a good mum. It could have happened to anyone.'

I can't imagine how hard it has been for her over the years – which is why she's ended up in this state, I think, glancing around her unkempt living room. The place is a reflection of her mind. There's more dog mess in the corner of the room, I notice, making a mental note to clean it up before I go.

'Easy for you to say that,' Elsie says, her face crumpled. 'But I should have had a proper fence put up, and I shouldn't have gone inside to answer the phone. I left Lenny playing outside.' She waves a hand towards her back garden. 'I'll never forgive myself, so why should Sharon? She hasn't contacted me in years. I used to tell myself it's because she couldn't face coming back here, to where it happened, but it's not that at all. It's because she hates me. I let her down. I let *Lenny* down.'

'Perhaps it's time to shift the blame off yourself and onto the person who did it. He was caught, he was punished. A life sentence.'

At the time, the case was all over the news for weeks and, before the trial, the murderer's identity was revealed because it was deemed in the public interest. The killer was a boy. A *child* – the same age as me and my friends – his blank face staring out from the front page of every newspaper. We talked about it at school as we tried to make sense of what had happened, how 'one of us' could do such a thing. It was a long time before we were able to move on, with special assemblies given by the head teacher, counselling offered, pupils off sick for no apparent reason.

That summer, Lenny's death had thrown an ugly spotlight on the fragility of our superficial lives. It rocked our community, stealing many other childhoods too – parents not allowing their kids out to play, children too traumatised because they knew of the killer or had sat next to him at school – *our* school – or glared at him, ridiculed him, tormented him.

We were all questioned by the police – the teachers, too. They focused on those in his class, as well as anyone who knew him – however superficially – with specially trained officers determined to eke out any snippet of information from our young minds. It seemed to go on forever. But we all sat there either crying quietly or shaking our heads, kicking our feet against the chair with no one able to provide answers.

We wondered if it was catching, like a disease, something in the local water. I remember feeling too terrified to leave the house for months, partly because I was frightened someone would be lying in wait, but also because in some way we all felt guilty, me and my friends. That we hadn't known there was evil amongst us. We wondered if it was our fault, if we had made that little boy into the monster he was.

'We're the ones left with the real life sentence,' Elsie says, her expression turning sour. 'Me and my daughter.' She shakes her head slowly and her top lip twitches. Her hands shake as they clutch the album.

Elsie is right. While she has been left suffering – will *always* suffer – the boy who killed Lenny, as a juvenile, was detained in custody for years until he gradually faded from people's minds. Though was never quite forgotten. After a decade of rehabilitation, word was that he was released and given a new identity, relocated to a different area. But his clean slate didn't last long when it was reported that he had reoffended – indecent exposure, car theft, pictures of children found on his computer and worse – and he was sent back to prison. No one really knows what happened to him after that, though his identity will always be protected. Evil seeping amongst the innocent yet again.

'He was beautiful. Look.' Elsie thrusts the album towards me. A little blond boy wearing shorts and a stripy T-shirt grins out of one of the photographs. 'I never watched the news back then. I didn't want to know anything about the person who took my grandson – what his life was like, if he'd had troubles at home. I didn't want to be able to forgive him, for there to be a reason for what he did. I didn't want him living in my head.'

'Lenny was beautiful indeed,' I reply, knowing she has no one else to talk to. His pudding-bowl cut frames his chubby, angelic face. In another picture, he's naked apart from his underpants, standing ankle-deep in an inflatable paddling pool in his grand-mother's garden. The same garden from which he was snatched only a few months later, trotting happily off to the reservoir with the temptation of sweets. It was nearly a week later when police divers found Lenny, swollen and pale, in the water.

'What kind of mother raises a boy capable of killing a toddler, Doctor?' she asks. 'What woman doesn't notice that her thirteen-year-old son has blood on his hands?'

'Elsie,' I say, taking her hand gently. The old woman is trem-bling, her leg twitching beneath her dark-blue skirt as she drums her slippered foot on the carpet. 'Let's focus on some positives, shall we? I have some good news. The care agency are able to send someone three times a week to help you. They'll provide assistance with bathing, cleaning, cooking and shopping. And it'll be company, too. How does that sound?'

Elsie stares at me, though it's as if she's looking straight through me to another place, another time. 'How does it sound?' she whispers eventually. 'It sounds as though you're sticking your nose in again, Doctor. That's how it sounds to me.'

It's dark when I turn off the lane leading out of Harbrooke and head down my drive. Kieran is staying over at Oscar's house tonight for a much-needed gaming session with his mates, and in the morning he's going straight from there to Rhonda's place to begin the extra study sessions with Caitlin. It's not as if Caitlin needs them, but Rhonda was correct in her assumption about Kieran jumping at the chance to spend time with her daughter. And if it helps get him back on track for his GCSEs this summer, then I'm all for it. I'm not sure how I'd have got through these last few weeks without Rhonda.

Instinctively, I jam on the brakes when I see an unfamiliar car parked in front of the garage – a boxy, black Mercedes. I stare at it for a moment before driving into the wide turning area, my headlights arcing over the red brick of the barn. Then the driver's door opens and a man gets out.

'Oh Christ, what the hell does *he* want?' I say under my breath. I yank on the handbrake. This is all I need on a Friday evening – especially when I'd planned on sorting through Jeremy's study while I was alone for the night. Once that job is taken care of, I'm hoping it'll be one less thing weighing on my mind.

'Jennifer,' Scott says cheerfully, opening the back door of his car and pulling out a holdall bag. 'I hope you don't mind me calling round like this. I should have phoned, but I don't have your number yet.'

I take a couple of paces across the gravel then stop, my eyes flicking from the bag then up to his face, then back to the bag again. 'Scott,' I say as politely as I can manage. 'To be honest, it's not a great time. I thought I'd made it clear the other night that it's best we don't see each other again.'

'Must have missed the memo,' he replies with a laugh, following me to the front door. I unlock it and step inside, turning to block his entrance.

'I'll have to say goodbye now, if you don't mind. I have a busy evening planned.'

'Company?' he says, his broad smile flashing in the light of the coach lamp. I go to close the door, but he puts his hand against it and wedges his foot in the doorway.

'No,' I say, trying to hide the quiver in my voice as my left hand slips inside my pocket, feeling for my phone. 'Just busy and—'

'Let me in, Jen.' His face is cold, serious, and the look in his eyes intense.

A hand around my throat… a face looming above… both of us naked… his eyes dead as he forced his way inside me… me screaming no, no, no a thousand times… but nothing coming out of my mouth…

'No!' I hear myself say now – almost a scream but not quite.

Scott recoils, taken aback. 'Jennifer, there are things we need to talk about. You're pregnant with my child, for a start and…' His eyes soften as a smile sweeps over his mouth, not just affecting his lips but his entire face. It changes him in an instant. Was it the same smile that kept me talking to him in the bar that night? The one that switched off my good judgement? I shudder at the thought. 'I need to ask you a favour.'

I stare at him, trying to overlay the man standing in front of me with the person I met in Oxford. They seem like different people – my mind telling me one thing, yet my gut screaming out another.

'Jen?' he says, slipping a hand through the gap in the door and hooking his fingers around my wrist. 'Are you OK?'

Something twinges inside me, as though his hand is gently squeezing my heart, not my arm. For a second, I'm back at the club, warming to the man who'd bought us three rounds of shots to share, eventually finding myself laughing with him, listening to his crazy stories, wrapping my arms around his sweaty neck as we danced to music I'd never even heard before. It was as though I'd become a different person that night – someone who was able to forget everything she was running away from. But I still don't know how it happened – and can hardly stand to live with myself that it did. It simply wasn't like me.

'Jennifer?'

'Sorry,' I say, snapping back to the present. I shake my head, staring directly up at Scott's face. He's undeniably attractive – but it's more than that. It's not about what I can see on the surface but more about what I can't see lurking beneath. In a strange way, he reminds me of me.

'Jennifer, do as I say and let me in.'

I stare at him, see it in his eyes – the rotten subtext that doesn't require words. 'Yes, OK, yes, come inside.' I open the door wider. 'It's cold out there,' I add by way of excuse for my actions.

As though I'd become a different person...

Scott puts his bag down on the hallway floor – something I'm aware of him doing, but as yet unaware of the implications. He slips off his coat and drapes it over the bannister rail of the open-tread staircase that winds its way up to the gallery above. On a clear day, the view from the landing through the floor-to-ceiling window in the side of the barn is stunning – a sweeping vista of the undulating countryside and woodland surrounding us.

Jeremy and I hadn't stopped talking about the place after we'd viewed what was essentially a ruin sitting in a field of mud, and had a silly low offer in with the estate agent by close of business that day. We never thought for one moment that we'd be taken seriously but the vendor had been keen to get shot of the place and it was soon ours. We were so in love, so excited about the future.

'Sorry to appear rude,' I say, beckoning Scott to follow me through to the kitchen. I justify letting him in by telling myself he's the father of my baby. Automatically, I reach for the kettle and fill it, flicking the switch. 'You're right, there are things we need to discuss.'

There's a sudden warm feeling in my belly, as if the baby growing inside senses that both its parents are present – though it's overridden by a feeling of guilt. I weigh that up with the consequences of it being Jeremy's baby, which I know it's not – the child having one dead parent. Is it somehow better this way? Or is that me trying, again, to rationalise the situation in which I find myself, making sense of whatever happened? 'But let's be clear, you are not my patient any more. Understood?'

'If that's what it takes,' Scott says, sitting on a bar stool at the island. 'You were right, by the way. My shoulder is a lot better now.'

I nod, sloshing water into two mugs with a herbal teabag in each. I didn't bother to ask him what he wanted. 'Here,' I say, handing him his drink. 'Let's sit somewhere more comfortable.'

I lead the way back through the cavernous hall and on into the equally large living room.

'Who the hell has two fireplaces in one room?' Scott says with a laugh as he walks around, inspecting everything. He runs his hands over a sheepskin draped over the back of one of two plush green velvet sofas set at ninety degrees to each other in front of the wood-burning stove. It makes me bristle inside, as though he's assessing mine and Jeremy's life together. To prevent myself from saying anything I'll regret, I open the doors to the wood burner, only taking a moment to lay and light the fire. The thing is so high-tech, it virtually gets the logs in itself.

'Someone who lives in a ridiculously huge and freezing barn, that's who,' I tell him, sitting down on the sofa nearest to the fire as it begins to take hold. 'What favour did you want to ask?' I need to get this out of the way, then we can move on to practicalities about the baby, what support he will offer and if he wishes to have a relationship of any kind with his son or daughter. I've already decided I'm keeping my baby. If he wants to help financially, that's fine by me, and I won't prevent him spending time with his child. I will deal with it unemotionally, only agreeing to necessary contact with him.

'Ah, yes,' Scott says, sipping his tea as he leans forward, his forearms resting on his legs. He's in jeans and a dark sweater today, and has a black scarf knotted around his neck. He unwinds it and places it on the sofa beside him. 'I'm getting the keys to my new place tomorrow. My new job starts soon, too. This move hasn't been without its stresses, but it's all coming together now.'

I give a quick nod, showing him I'm listening.

'Thing is, the owner of the motel where I'm staying got the dates wrong and thought I was checking out today. And I'm afraid the entire motel is booked up now, so I have to leave my room.' Scott sips his tea, waiting for me to assimilate what he's saying.

I sit there staring at him, listening to him, wondering what it is about him that terrifies me.

A hand tugging on mine, leading me on, laughter, staggering, coaxing me back to my hotel, pulling me, pushing me, shoving me… his mouth, the weight of him. It had been exciting in the bar because I was having fun, but then came the terror masked by… by something that wouldn't allow me to feel… something that stopped my screams being heard. Because all the screams were in my head…

'Actually, to be more precise, it's not a matter of *leaving* the motel any more. It's more a matter that I've already left.'

'I see,' I say, not wanting to acknowledge where this conversation is going.

'And as we have things to discuss, I thought I'd stay here with you tonight. Then we get to… to reconnect. You know, kill two birds with one stone.'

CHAPTER SEVENTEEN

Jen

'Kill two birds?' It feels as though he's just slapped me in the face.

Scott laughs. 'Don't get me wrong, I'm not going to take advantage of you.'

'Like you did in Oxford?' I huff out. 'You can't stay here.'

Scott's face turns serious – a look that tells me I've overstepped the mark. 'Jen, I think you'll agree that you were up for it that night. I did nothing wrong. I had no idea you were married or had a son, and you'd had a lot to drink.' He pauses for a second, looking smug, calm, self-satisfied. 'Don't be too hard on yourself. I get it – you don't want anyone to know what happened. Especially now that you've lost your husband. It wouldn't look good. Pillar of the community, a married GP shagging a stranger, getting pregnant.'

I stare at him, frozen, my heart trying to escape my chest. I feel a twinge down low, a dull ache like period pain. Was it my fault? Did I get blind drunk and act completely out of character – or was there more to it? One thing he's right about – it would not look good if people found out. Kieran would hate me, my friends would be horrified and I'd lose my patients' trust. Word would spread fast around here.

I open my mouth but nothing comes out.

'Jennifer, it's OK. I understand. The attraction between us was undeniable and—'

'Are you *blackmailing* me?' I ask, finally able to speak.

'If that's what you want to call it,' he says, his smirk making me want to throw up.

I cover my face, hardly able to believe this is happening.

'Why… why didn't we use a condom?' I hiss, hating I even have to ask. None of this is me or my life. I slide my hands down my face. I feel dizzy, sick, and my head is filled with unanswered questions. The only person who can answer them is sitting right in front of me, yet I don't trust him.

Scot smiles. 'You really did have a skinful, didn't you?' He shakes his head, fiddling with the string of his teabag. 'You told me that you had condoms back in your room, that you'd come prepared. I offered to use one but…' He shifts on the sofa, almost as if the memory is turning him on. 'But then you said you didn't want to, that it would ruin it. I can't believe you don't remember that?'

I shake my head. 'I… I don't remember.' All I know is that I would *never* have said those things.

'You told me that it was fine. You're a doctor, after all, so I believed you. Afterwards, as we lay there, you resting your head on my shoulder, you told me not to worry, that you were on the pill.'

I bow my head. 'I don't carry condoms. Why the hell would I?' It doesn't make sense. He must be lying.

Scott shrugs and stands up, placing his mug on the table. He goes over to the wood burner and looks down at the flames consuming the kindling, eating into the logs.

'I get that you're angry, Jennifer. You let yourself down. But what's a man supposed to do in that situation? I assure you, a baby wasn't in my game plan either.' He stares down at me. 'But look, I can't deny that a part of me is pleased. We just need to decide what to do.'

'We? *We* need to decide what to do?'

Scott nods.

'*I* need to decide what to do.'

I think back to the last six months of Jeremy's life. It's true that I was on the pill – I had been since we'd stopped trying for another baby. Though I stopped taking it when Jeremy died. Last year, our sex life had taken a nosedive, mainly because of me and the knots I'd tied myself up in. Suspicion, paranoia and accusations didn't do much for either of our libidos.

'There were a couple of times that I forgot to take the pill,' I admit. 'And I had a stomach upset for a few days in December. Just before the conference.' I cover my face again, knowing that's all it takes.

Scott sits back down, but this time right next to me. 'You'll keep the baby.'

It's not a question. I stare at him, his face only a couple of feet away from mine. His hand reaches out and touches my leg, his fingers resting on the fabric of my black work trousers. My head swims, my mind feeling bruised and battered – filled partly with the events of that night, and partly with the realisation that my husband is never coming back.

I feel a finger on my cheek.

'You're crying,' Scott says, reaching into his pocket for a tissue. I take it, dabbing at my face.

'Yes,' I say, aware that the hand on my leg has crept up to the waistband of my trousers. 'I'm keeping the baby.' He rubs the area a couple of times and his eyes almost explode in fan lines from the smile on his face.

'Good girl,' he says, leaning in and giving me a kiss on the cheek where a new tear has rolled.

*

'What do you reckon?' Scott says, holding out his phone with one hand, while the other stirs the sauce. 'Doesn't look much yet but I'll make it homely.'

I lean forward to see, putting my hand out to take the phone for a closer look, but Scott keeps a firm hold of it, swiping through a couple more pictures of the property that he's getting the keys for tomorrow.

'It looks fine,' I say flatly, not wanting to indulge in chit-chat.

'It's tiny,' Scott laughs. 'Compared to this place, anyway.' He turns back to the stove.

Earlier, I'd told him, through gritted teeth, that he could stay here for one night only. If I hadn't, he'd made it perfectly clear that he wouldn't hesitate to broadcast what had happened between us. I conned myself into thinking it would give us a chance to discuss a plan about the baby, how he would contribute and if he wanted contact after the birth. It was something that had to be addressed, and I figured I might as well get it out of the way while Kieran wasn't home.

I'd protested further, of course, about him staying the night – that he should find another hotel, but he wasn't having it. He'd given me that look again – the one where his blue eyes crystallised as if they were freezing over, somehow taking control of me, reminding me of what he knew and the consequences of that getting out.

'Tastes good,' he says, sampling the sauce. He'd insisted on cooking, despite me telling him I had little in the fridge. And it gave him an opportunity to tell me about his new job, the reason he'd relocated to the area in the first place – although I was beginning to wonder about that now.

'So you start next week?'

'Indeed,' he says, grinding more black pepper into the pan. 'Head chef at that new restaurant in Shenbury.'

'I haven't heard about a new place,' I say, though with everything that's been going on, that's not surprising. 'What's it called?'

'The restaurant?' He's silent for a moment. 'The owner is keeping it top secret until the grand opening. I'll see if I can get you an invite.'

I don't reply. Eating out is way down my list of priorities. It's taking all my mental reserves to get started on sorting out Jeremy's study. Rhonda offered to help, but I can just imagine what Jeremy would think of that – people nosing through his personal belongings.

'Right, dinner's ready,' Scott says, taking a couple of pasta bowls he's had in the oven to warm. He serves out the spaghetti and adds the sauce.

Reluctantly, I grab some cutlery, slamming it on the table harder than I'd intended, watching incredulously as Scott helps himself to a beer from the fridge. I sit down, feeling helpless as he grates parmesan over my spaghetti. I'm not in the least bit hungry, but I know I need to eat something for my baby. And with every mouthful I take, I have to keep reminding myself that it's only for one night.

'Do you like it?' he asks, watching as I take a mouthful.

Without looking at him, I give him a brief nod. The last thing I'm going to admit is that it actually tastes good.

I've not been looking after myself these last few weeks – skipping breakfast because of nausea and hardly having time for lunch. And while I've been cooking for Kieran, I've not felt like eating much myself in the evenings. Cooking reminds me too much of the routine Jeremy and I had – preparing food together, a glass of wine to hand, making plans for the weekend or our next family holiday. Sometimes he'd tell me about his book – though, looking back, he never revealed much about his progress.

'So you trained as a chef?' I ask, feeling the need to make conversation, to keep him onside. Ridiculous, given that my gut is screaming out that I did not consent to sex with this man – and certainly not from a clear head capable of making such a decision.

'Yes, I was given an opportunity to learn the trade in... in a huge kitchen in London,' Scott says, glancing up. 'I was moved around the country a few times, working in various... catering facilities.' For some reason, Scott laughs – a laugh that makes my skin crawl. 'Why did you become a doctor?' he goes on, studying me as he chews.

I think about this answer carefully, though there's no need. It's well practised, a couple of lines by rote even though it's not quite the truth.

'When I was sixteen, I was babysitting and the little girl I was looking after choked on a sweet. I saved her life and, from that moment on, I knew I had to become a doctor. It was as simple as that.' I look at Scott over the rim of my glass of water. I've never told anyone that I actually wanted to be a doctor way before that.

'I can't imagine,' Scott says, his eyes hardening again. 'Saving someone's life.'

CHAPTER EIGHTEEN

Jen

'You did *what*?' Rhonda says, tripping over the step at my front door the next day. 'Who on earth is Scott?'

'Chill,' I say, my voice wavering. 'It's fine.' But going by the look on Rhonda's face, she doesn't think it's fine at all. 'He's… he's an old friend of Jeremy's,' I say, thinking on the fly. 'He's gone now and it was only for one night.' I take the casserole dish from her, leaning down to sniff around the lid, thankful that she didn't arrive fifteen minutes ago or she and Scott would have crossed paths. 'Thanks so much for this,' I say, tapping the casserole. 'We'll have this later. Two proper meals in the same number of days.' I turn and head to the kitchen, Rhonda following me. I hadn't been expecting her to call round.

'Kier and Caitlin have their heads down studying. He arrived right on time this morning.' She goes to the kettle and fills it up. 'I've got them picking apart *An Inspector Calls*. And what do you mean, *two* proper meals?'

'Scott cooked for me last night. He's a chef.'

'Oh, did he now?' Rhonda grabs mugs, teabags, milk. She eyes me, shaking her head, her arms folded as she leans back against the kitchen worktop. 'So why haven't I heard of this Scott person before, then?'

I shrug, hesitating. 'Jeremy met him a few years ago through… um, through work. Scott was catering on set. I've met him a few times and… and he, well, he didn't know Jeremy had… you know…' I drop my eyes for a moment, hating that I'm lying to my best friend. We always tell each other everything. 'It was a huge shock for him so I invited him in for a drink. He had a few, so I said he could crash here the night. That's all.' My voice sounds choked and tight, my mouth dry as I over-explain.

I wait for Rhonda to pick up on the deceit – a hound sniffing out a fox – but she stays silent.

'By coincidence, he's starting a new job in the area, so that's why he called round.' The lies roll off my tongue.

Rhonda stares at me. 'You need to be careful, Jen.' She sloshes boiling water into the mugs.

'What?'

'You know what I mean. Attractive widow. Big house. Good career. They'll all be coming out of the woodwork now.'

'I know… but you're wrong about Scott,' I say, cupping my hands around the mug. 'Scott is… he's fine. Harmless.' I swallow some tea, burning my mouth. 'I probably won't even see him again. He gets the keys to his new place today and starts his new job in a few days.'

I kick myself inwardly, knowing that at some point I'll have to explain the inconsistency with my pregnancy dates and the birth, as well as Scott seeming more than the casual acquaintance I've portrayed if he demands to spend time with the baby. But I'll face all that when I have to.

'I've got your back, Jen, OK? But like I said, be careful.'

I nod. 'And you know I've always got yours.' But the look on Rhonda's face, the way her head hangs down over the steam of her hot drink, tells me there's something else on her mind. And it's a good chance to change the subject.

'Anyway, enough about me. What's up? You've got a face like a horse.'

It's the moment's delay before she speaks that tells me I'm right. 'It's Caitlin.'

'Is she OK?' I've been so wrapped up in my own problems these last few weeks, I've failed to notice if everything is OK in Rhonda's life.

'I don't know. She's… she's been tearful lately, though she's tried to put on a brave face. I don't know that it's boy troubles as such. Chris has noticed too.'

'That's odd. She's usually so cheerful,' I say, remembering the time we all spent together in Devon last summer. Caitlin always managed to bring a smile to everyone's faces with her carefree manner, rallying everyone for beach games or board games in the evening, baking treats each afternoon, and getting us all singing along as she strummed her guitar.

'Exactly. She's been out of sorts for a few weeks now.'

'Do you think Jeremy's death hit her harder than you realised?' It's something I'd not considered before. 'You know how teenagers overthink things, especially girls. Given Chris's job, perhaps she's anxious that something might happen to him too? I can have a word with Kier if you like, ask him to lay off talking about his dad.'

Rhonda shakes her head. 'No, if Kieran needs to talk, then he should be able to. But you're right. I shouldn't underestimate her feelings. She's known Jeremy since she was nine, and absolutely adores Chris. I'll try to reassure her that he's not going anywhere.'

We sip our tea in silence for a moment, each of us contemplating our individual ghosts. When someone dies, it's not just one hole they leave behind.

'Talking of Jeremy, weren't you going to start sorting out his study this weekend?'

I nod. 'Scott put paid to that last night by turning up, but I'm on it today.' I push up my sweatshirt sleeves to show willing, but inside I'm far from that. The thought fills me with dread.

'Then it's a good job I stopped by,' Rhonda says. 'The kids have plenty of work to be getting on with for a few hours and I've nothing better to do. Let's make a start.'

'No' isn't a word Rhonda always hears. We stand in the doorway to Jeremy's study, hands on hips, with Rhonda ready to get stuck in and neutralise the room, whereas my mind is now filled with doubt, thoughts of preserving everything just as it is. For some stupid reason, I imagine my husband might one day come back home, sit down at his desk and pick up on the chapter he was writing.

'Maybe I should leave well alone,' I say, feeling overwhelmed again. 'Just shut the door on it.'

Rhonda strides in, going up to the large oak bookcase that lines one wall. She turns her head sideways to glance at some of the titles. 'Are you ever going to read any of these?' She plucks an old edition of something off a shelf and opens the hardback, carefully leafing through the pages. 'Some of them might be worth something. This is a signed first edition. I know a dealer in Shenbury. I could get him out to take a look.'

'Maybe,' I say, going up to Jeremy's desk. I imagine him sitting there, hunched over his laptop, tapping away furiously, his expression changing to mirror every scene he was working on. Sometimes I'd bring him in a drink and he'd have a deep frown set across his brow. Other times, he'd be leaning back and typing, one leg cocked up on his thigh, a breezy, contented look on his face. I didn't have much idea of what his novel was about, and I sometimes wondered if he knew either.

'It's the personal stuff I need to go through,' I tell Rhonda. 'All his files, his papers – in case anything needs dealing with. Plus there's his bank accounts to—'

'Slow down, Jen.' Rhonda pulls a face. 'One bite at a time, OK?' She sits down in the battered leather captain's chair Jeremy found at a flea market. He never got round to fixing the wonky castor. 'You mentioned he'd gone away to make a documentary. That was the reason for the…' She bows her head briefly. 'For the ski trip?'

'Apparently.' I nod, dropping down into the chair set the other side of the desk. 'And some travel article he was writing.' I think back, but the details were all so vague. 'She was there, you know, Madeleine. On the trip.' I bite my lip, looking away.

Rhonda nods. She's listened to the story a thousand times already – me rewriting the script, speculating about what happened until I'm exhausted from it. Their history, what Jeremy saw in her that he didn't see in me; how Madeleine could bring herself to be with the husband of another woman; if they were planning a future together. And each time Rhonda has gently allowed me to spew it out, then offered an alternative that doesn't involve my husband sneaking off with a beautiful woman ten years younger than me and fucking her in the Swiss Alps.

'Jen—'

'Truth is, I don't even know if she died in the avalanche with him. I hate the thought of them lying at the bottom of a snow-filled ravine together, their love for each other frozen forever. Literally.' I shudder, worn out from it all.

'Jen… stop it. You'll drive yourself mad. Literally.'

She gets up and comes over to me, taking me by the shoulders, cradling me against her.

'I've thought about getting in touch with the Swiss authorities. Perhaps they'd tell me if Madeleine was amongst the deceased.'

Rhonda immediately shakes her head. 'No, Jen. Why torture yourself any more? I really don't think getting in touch with them is a good idea.'

I ease myself away from Rhonda. 'I've tortured myself enough as it is, stalking her online.' I let out a laugh. 'I never thought I'd be *that* woman.' *But I am*, I add in my head.

'Look, you don't even know for sure if they were having an affair. If you can hold onto that thought, it might be some consolation.'

'Yeah, you're right,' I say, though I can't help it that my guts knot. 'I don't even have Jeremy to tell me I'm being stupid or imagining things any more.' I pull my phone from my pocket, taking a breath as I open Instagram. I pass it to Rhonda. 'That's her, look. Careful you don't "like" anything by mistake.'

Rhonda stares at me, an expression of pity on her face, before taking my phone and scrolling through a few of Madeleine's pictures. 'She's travelled a lot over the years, by the looks of it. Though she's not posted anything since late December, so it's hard to tell from this if she's dead or not.' Rhonda's cheeks colour up. 'These last few show her in the mountains somewhere, perhaps on a skiing trip.'

'Exactly,' I say, relieved she agrees. 'But just *look* at her, Ronnie.' Tears prickle in my eyes. 'Do you see what I mean now?'

'She's certainly beautiful, but…' Rhonda trails off.

'What is it?' I stand up, peering over her shoulder. She's zoomed in on one particular photograph – a selfie of Madeleine somewhere in Europe from earlier last year. There's a huge, ornate church in the background, plus a bustling street scene, sunshine, tourists. It looks as though she's sitting outside a café.

Rhonda hesitates. 'There, look. Someone's clearly got their arm around her. You can just see a hand on her shoulder. But it looks as though the person beside her has been cropped out.'

I lean in closer. She's right. And it's a man's hand. I hadn't noticed before.

'But don't read too much into it. It could be anyone,' Rhonda adds.

I study the photograph intently, hugging myself, suddenly freezing cold.

'The ring,' I say, barely able to get the words out as I stare at it glinting in the sunshine. On the little finger of the mystery person is a gold signet ring – nothing flash, but it was vintage and the perfect size for my husband when I bought it. I gave it to him several Christmases ago and he hadn't taken it off since. 'It's Jeremy's,' I say, staggering backwards to lean against the wall.

CHAPTER NINETEEN

Then

'Look who it is,' the girl says, leering at Evan as she bursts through the boys' toilet door, slamming it back against the wall. The other three girls snigger as they follow in behind her, flanking her. 'If it isn't Fathead.' Her eyes dip down to his groin. 'Go on, let's see it, then.'

Evan feels his face burning beetroot as he stands beside the urinal, just about to unzip himself. The girl's hands are clamped across her chest, making her breasts show in the neck of her blouse, the first few buttons undone.

She steps closer, shoving him in the shoulder. 'I said let's see it, Fathead.' Her nose wrinkles up as she looks him up and down.

Evan shakes his head, picking his backpack up from the floor. The girl kicks it out of his hand, sending it skidding over towards one of the empty cubicles. There was no one else in here when he came in.

'Why did you shit in my locker?' she says to him. 'You gonna clear it up, idiot?'

'I never,' Evan says weakly, catching sight of a few boys gathering behind in the toilet doorway to see what's going on. 'Leave me alone.'

'Aww diddums, is Fathead gonna cry? You want your mummy, loser boy?' The girl prods him in the chest again. Ripples of laughter come from behind her.

Evan shakes his head, staring at the floor.

'You gonna pee in your little girl's pants?' she says, shoving him again. Then she reaches down for his school bag, unzipping it and tipping the contents all over the floor. That's when Evan sees his mum has put a Penguin biscuit in there. He didn't know she'd done that. The girl crushes it with her foot.

Evan doesn't move. He can't. He just stands there, his arms dangling by his sides as he wishes he was dead. No, wishing *she* was dead.

'If you don't show me your nasty little thing, I'm gonna tell on you for shitting in my locker, Fathead.'

'But I *didn't*,' Evan says weakly, feeling the tears welling up in his eyes. His entire body is shaking and he can't stop it.

'Right, I'm gonna tell the head right now what you did,' she says, turning to go. 'Come on, girls.'

'Wait,' Evan says, panicking. 'I'll show you, then,' he says, hating that he even said the words. But if his mum gets called in and finds out, then Griff will get mad as hell and he'll get a beating even worse than this.

The boys standing behind the mean girl start cheering, thrusting their arms in the air.

Get it out! Get it out!

Slowly, his head hanging down, Evan unzips his flies an inch. He stops.

'All the way, Fathead,' the girl says. A few boys whoop and jeer.

Evan undoes his zip all the way.

'And the button,' the girl demands.

He does as he's told, but before he knows what's happening, she lunges forward and yanks both his trousers and underpants down around his knees, just as the pee starts dribbling out. He can't help himself, especially not when he hears the peals of laughter from the other faces leering at him.

'What's going on in here?' a deep male voice suddenly booms.

When he looks up, Evan sees the deputy head standing there, glaring at him.

Then the girl lets out a piercing scream, covering her eyes and turning away, making a fake sobbing sound. There's a scuffle as the boys run off.

'We… we… just came in here by mistake, sir,' she pants hysterically. 'And then he… he flashed us,' she sobs, hugging her girlfriends for comfort. 'I can't believe he did it, sir. He's a pervert.' More sobs.

'No I never!' Evan pleads, pulling up his clothing.

'Go to your classrooms, girls, while I deal with this,' the deputy head says, glaring and jabbing a finger at Evan. 'Cover yourself up, boy,' he barks, before dragging Evan away by the arm.

'That's her,' Evan says at break time, pointing across the playground after he told Mac what happened. He's still shaking. 'The bitch.' He's sitting with Mac up on the mossy bank at the back of the playground, each of them irritated because the tin of snacks is empty. Someone had cut off the padlock and stolen all their stuff – three chocolate bars and a packet of chewing gum missing. Mac had kicked the old cash tin hard, scanning around to see who might be watching.

'Her? That's Gem,' Mac says, eyeing the girl. 'She's in my class. She doesn't like me either.'

As usual, she has a huddle of girls around her and a few satellite groups of boys loitering, hoping she'll notice them. Evan's heart races as she looks their way.

Earlier, in the toilets, Evan had pleaded with the deputy head, telling him over and over that the girl had made him do it. Lucky for Evan, the deputy just gave him a detention and said he wouldn't call his mum this time, but if he ever did it again, he'd be in deeper trouble.

'What kind of name is Gem anyway?' Evan asks sourly. 'She's no gem.' He remembers his mum calling him a gem once, but that was a long while ago now, and not since she got with Griff.

'She's called Jennifer Mason really. She's new and made everyone call her "Jen M" to avoid confusion. But then Mr Bradley, the PE teacher, called her "Gem", which she really liked but only 'cos all the girls have a crush on him. I reckon she's snogged him, dirty bitch.'

Evan doesn't know anything about crushing – apart from insects, of course – nor why anyone would confuse that horrid girl with anyone else, let alone want to snog her. He knows that's kissing, which means she's probably pregnant. Dirty cow.

'Reckon it was her who nicked our sweets,' Evan says, retrieving the tin from the ground. He closes the lid and tucks it inside Mac's school bag while they wait for the school bell to ring. 'You wait,' he says, staring across the playground at her. 'One day, I'm gonna get her back for what she did to me. Even if it takes the rest of my life.'

The sun beats down on the lanes, on the scorched fields, on the village, on the estate – on the whole world, Evan reckons. His mum called it an Indian summer, but he doesn't know what that is. All he knows is that he hasn't stopped sweating for three days and now, as his legs pedal until they burn, desperately trying to keep up with Mac, he realises just how dry his mouth is. He thinks he'll pass out if he doesn't get a drink soon.

'Come on,' Mac says, stopping up ahead on his bike, one foot on the ground as he twists around. Evan finally draws up alongside him, his head thrumming as if his brain has somehow got too big for his skull.

When they reach the gateway, they hide their bikes in the ditch and follow the nicks in the trees to get to the den. Over the last couple of weeks, they've secretly brought up supplies, including a tarpaulin sheet that Mac had found in his garage, along with a tiny camping stove.

Evan runs ahead to the den, tripping on a couple of roots. He's got that bottle of water on his mind, the one they didn't finish last time they were up here a week or so ago. Ducking down under the tarpaulin, he grabs it from beneath the roof of branches and leaves, twisting off the cap and gulping it down. And that's when he sees it.

'Mac, quick!' he calls out. 'This is *major*.' A strange feeling swells inside him – pressure in his chest.

Mac drops the bundle of twigs he's collecting for the fire and gallops over to the den.

'Whoa!' he says as he draws up, halting suddenly when he spots it.

'It's dead,' Evan exclaims, daring to prod its head with the toe of his shoe. '*Wicked*.'

They stare down at the foot-long creature lying prone amongst the leaves and scrubby ground of the wood. Dried blood mats its once-soft fur, making Evan want to pick it up and snuggle it against his neck.

He nudges it again with his shoe, rolling it over so its stiff front limbs stick up in the air. Mac leaps back at the sight of its eviscerated belly, which dances with something creamy and beige, like its insides are still alive.

'Yuk!' Mac squeals, cupping his hand over his mouth, making a retching sound.

Evan doesn't say a word – he can't. He's transfixed by the maggot-filled rabbit, thinking it is the most beautiful thing he's ever seen.

CHAPTER TWENTY

Rhonda

'You going to stare at that thing all night?' Chris says, shifting his position on the sofa.

'Sorry,' Rhonda replies, still scrolling on her phone, her eyes glued to the screen.

'You're missing the movie,' he adds. 'Shall I pause? Get some more beers?'

'Huh?' Rhonda says without looking up. 'Mmm…' she adds vaguely. Suddenly her head flops back against the sofa as Chris withdraws his arm from around her shoulders. 'Hey…' she grumbles, play-kicking him with her foot. Their legs are intertwined on the footstool in front of them, tangled together beneath the fleece throw. Saturday-night tradition when Chris isn't working – pizza, a few beers and a movie.

'Right, Miss Antisocial. I'll be back in five.' Chris hoists himself from the sofa, leaving Rhonda still staring at her phone, her mind whirring.

'I didn't know you had Instagram,' he says when he returns, dropping down into the nest of cushions they've made. He pops the tops off a couple of Beck's – non-alcoholic for him and a regular for Rhonda.

'I have now,' she replies, taking the bottle from him without looking up, propping it between her legs. 'Downloaded it tonight.'

'Please tell me you're not going to be broadcasting our every move to the world.'

Rhonda laughs. 'Your disgusting habits are safe with me,' she says, prodding him in the side. 'But look. Guess who this is?' She holds her phone between them and scrolls down the reel of pictures.

'Some woman who likes taking selfies?'

He's not wrong, Rhonda thinks. Though there's something else about Madeleine Lacroix – something beguiling, youthful and innocent-looking almost, though the way she looks up at the camera makes her seem anything but. Her full name is on her bio, as well as her phone number and a link to her LinkedIn profile. Her Instagram grid is that of a cool, hipster, carefree, independent and professional young woman. She's all wavy chestnut hair effortlessly styled around her slim face, and her eyes are made up in each of her photos to look sultry and smoky. With pale-pink glossy lips and highlighted cheekbones, everything about her gives the impression of being natural and un-staged, even though it must have taken huge effort.

'Living her best life,' Chris says through a snort. He swigs from his bottle, keeping one eye on Rhonda's phone screen. 'Who is she? Some influencer?'

'No. Jen showed me her profile earlier,' Rhonda admits. 'You'll think I'm crazy, but ever since I saw her face, something has… unsettled me. And I think I know why.' Rhonda thrusts the phone closer to Chris, making him recoil. 'Are you sure you don't recognise her?'

Chris takes the phone, zooming in on Madeleine's face. He shrugs. 'Hashtag vegan, hashtag eatnatural, hashtag lovemyfriends, hashtag apresski… Christ on a bike,' Chris says, pausing on a photo of Madeleine sitting at a mountainside bar, mirrored sunglasses perched on her head, her slim body wrapped up in a blue and white ski suit. Her straight, white smile is as dazzling as the snow behind her. 'Hashtag beer and pizza, I say.' He leans forward and grabs another slice of cheese and pepperoni from the box, a string of mozzarella trailing behind.

'And that, DS Christopher Prior, is why I love you.' Rhonda taps off Instagram and goes to her camera's photo stream. She quickly scrolls back through her pictures, stopping when she gets to a certain point. 'Do you think this is the same woman?' she asks, zooming in to the left of a group of people, their backs mostly turned to the camera.

'That one?' Chris asks, pointing at a woman standing almost out of shot, away from the main gathering. Her face is small and barely visible, her head shrouded by a patterned scarf. 'Isn't that Jeremy's memorial service?' he notes, recognising the large pond at Swallow Barn. All the attendees were dressed in black or grey – dark overcoats and boots against the January cold as they stood at the top of the paddock. In the photo, Jeremy's elderly parents are standing side by side at the water's edge, their heads bowed, their shoulders hunched. They barely said a word the entire day, crippled from grief.

'Mm-hmm,' Rhonda adds. 'Is it the same woman, do you think?' She zooms in further on her face. 'And why is she standing away from everyone else, amongst the trees and almost hidden?'

'Do you have any more photos with her in?'

'A couple. But even better, I have this.' Rhonda taps play on a video clip. 'It's only short as I wasn't sure if it was really the right time to be filming. When Jen came down to the lake, I switched it off. I didn't want to upset her. Take a look – just as Jen comes into shot, the woman darts back into the trees.' She presses play, starting from the beginning again. 'She doesn't appear in any of the other photos I took, and she certainly wasn't in the house afterwards for the food and drinks.'

Rhonda thinks back. It wasn't raining, but it was chilly and overcast. Since the news of Jeremy's death, she'd helped Jen plan a fitting way to say goodbye – something that would mark his passing. It was as much closure as she was going to get without a body. In the end, Jen had opted for a more private and personal gathering at home.

'Jeremy would have bloody hated a miserable send-off in a chapel, everyone weeping, morose music, some vicar who didn't even know him spouting off about what a great man he was.' Jen had said it fondly, mimicking Jeremy's tone, trying to imitate his voice – often loud and, to anyone who didn't know him, almost intimidating – though he was far from that. Beneath the posturing exterior, he was a lamb – a kind-hearted man who would do anything for anyone.

Rhonda wipes a finger under her eye.

'Play it again,' Chris says, watching intently. He taps pause when the woman comes into view. Taking the phone from Rhonda, he screenshots the video frame and then enlarges it. 'There's Caitlin, look,' he says. 'She's noticed something. See how she's turned round and is staring right at the woman?'

'Glaring at her, more like,' Rhonda says.

'Plus, look at her scarf,' Chris continues, tapping back to Madeleine's Instagram feed. 'Bingo,' he adds, pointing at a photograph of her posing on a Boris bike in a London park. The same scarf, with its unusual green and black zigzag print, is loosely wound around her neck. 'It certainly looks like the same woman, but the scarf seals it for me.'

'Nice work, Detective Sergeant,' Rhonda laughs, resting her head on his shoulder.

'Elementary,' he says with a wink. 'Why do you want to know, anyway? Who is this Madeleine person? She doesn't look much older than Caitlin.'

Rhonda hesitates, having already noticed how fresh-faced and young she seems. 'Keep it to yourself, but Jen is convinced she and

Jeremy were having an affair. They sometimes worked together, hence her being on the New Year skiing trip with him.'

'Christ on a bike again,' Chris says. He shoves the remains of the pizza slice in his mouth. 'So you think Madeleine secretly gatecrashed Jeremy's memorial?'

Rhonda nods. 'Jen certainly didn't invite her.'

'Maybe she heard about it from mutual colleagues,' Chris suggests, staring at the phone. 'It was certainly a special day. If we hadn't said goodbye in some way, it wouldn't have felt right.'

Rhonda nods pensively. She was quietly pleased with her idea for everyone to write private notes and memories of Jeremy on little pieces of biodegradable paper. The guests had gathered at the edge of the large pond – almost a small lake – on Jeremy and Jen's land and scattered the notes into the water after Jen had said a few poignant words. She'd not been keen on the idea at first, but knowing the lake was one of Jeremy's favourite places on their property, where he'd come to sit and contemplate, she had eventually agreed it would be a fitting thing to do.

'But more to the point,' Rhonda goes on, 'if Madeleine *was* at the memorial, then she clearly isn't dead, as Jen believes.'

'She thought they'd both been killed?'

'A fair assumption,' Rhonda says. 'Jen hated the idea of them being "frozen in time" together, as she put it. She's been eating herself up over it.'

'Will you tell her?' Chris asks. 'That we believe Madeleine is alive?'

'I don't know.' Rhonda flops her head back on the cushions. 'I'm worried that Jen will go and confront her.' She glances up at Chris, mirroring his concerned expression. 'As it was, I had to talk her out of contacting the Swiss authorities for information.'

Chris wipes a hand down his face, sighing through a pained expression.

'Anyway, on another note, it turns out Jen had some guy stay over with her last night.'

'A *guy* guy? Or just a friend guy?'

Rhonda shrugs. 'A friend of Jeremy's, apparently. But I've never heard of him before. I got a funny feeling about it, Chris. Something was off.' They exchange glances again, each of them considering what it means. 'When I went to the loo, I crept upstairs and poked my head around the spare bedroom door. The bed was messed up, as if it had been slept in.'

Chris nods, putting his piece of pizza back in the box. Then he prises Rhonda's beer bottle from her hand and takes a long swig.

'And on top of everything else, Caitlin's really not been herself at all lately,' Rhonda says, taking back her beer.

'She seemed unusually quiet when Kieran was here earlier, but they looked to be getting on with their work,' Chris says.

Rhonda nods. 'Something's been troubling her these last few weeks, but I can't figure out what she's think—'

Chris nudges her sharply with his elbow. 'Hey, Caitlin,' he says, looking behind his wife. 'You joining us for the movie? We can start it again. It's only been on ten minutes.'

Rhonda quickly shoves her phone under a cushion, patting the space beside her. 'Come on, love. Sit down.'

Caitlin stares at them both, her eyes narrow and suspicious. Her usual heavy black eyeliner has smudged, and the tip of her nose is slightly red. 'What were you talking about just now?' she asks, standing her ground in the doorway.

'Nothing much. Just looking at some old photos,' Rhonda replies, hoping she didn't overhear. She pats the sofa again. She hates lying to her daughter, but doesn't want anything about Madeleine to get back to Kieran or Jen. As far as she's concerned, the woman is best forgotten.

Caitlin stares at her mum for a few more seconds before eyeing the space on the sofa. Slowly, she lowers herself down, curling her legs up underneath her and leaning against her mum. She slides her hand underneath a cushion as she gets comfortable.

It's only much later, when the film has long since finished and Caitlin has gone up to bed, that Rhonda realises her phone is missing from where she'd shoved it out of sight earlier.

CHAPTER TWENTY-ONE

Jen

I head out to the garage with the last sack of Jeremy's clothes, shutting the front door on the thumping beat of Kieran's music as it blasts out from his room. I'm not about to tell him to turn it down – I know it brings him some kind of escape. He seemed pensive and withdrawn when I went to fetch him from studying with Caitlin earlier this afternoon, though he was happy enough to sit at the table with me and eat some of the reheated casserole that Rhonda had made. And he engaged with me about his school-work, agreeing that he doesn't want to miss out on the exams this summer. He even said he'd consider seeing the school counsellor to work through his grief. But after I'd cleared away the plates, I couldn't help thinking that there was something else on his mind.

I press the button on the remote and wait until the garage door curls itself up, revealing what feels like a graveyard inside. I dump the black sack alongside all the other bags that Rhonda and I already cleared out, stopping to stare at the plastic tub stashed at the back of the garage. I shudder at the thought of what's hidden in there. Rhonda and I didn't get very far with clearing Jeremy's study earlier, but managed to sort through a few books for charity.

I glance behind me, down our long drive. The coach lamps either side of the gate on the lane glow like a pair of low stars, indicating our hard-to-find entrance to visitors. I'm about to close the garage door and go back inside but, on a whim, I go over to the plastic tub and prise off the stiff lid.

I rummage through the junk that's been stashed in there for years – bric-a-brac type things that need clearing out – and pull out the padded envelope, removing the grubby pair of girl's pants along with the note. I drop down, sitting on top of another plastic storage tub.

'Who the hell would send me these?' I whisper, feeling an overwhelming sense of sadness for the young girl who would have worn them. 'And what the hell is it they claim to know?' I add, staring at the note. The plain print gives me no clue to their sender.

The pants aren't particularly remarkable – pale-pink cotton midi-briefs with little flowers on, the type a mum would buy for her daughter. And they're well worn, as though their wearer had sat on the ground in them, not caring if they got dirty. The sight of them makes me feel sick, so I shove them back in the envelope, wiping my hands down my jeans as if they're contaminated. I decided not to tell Rhonda about them earlier, knowing she'd only worry, perhaps suggesting I go to the police or, at the very least, ask Chris for advice. I just wanted to forget about them.

I'm about to go back inside, but I stop, freezing when I hear a noise. I turn to see car headlights coming down the drive, dazzling me so I can't make out who it is.

Quickly, I put the envelope back inside the plastic tub and close the lid. I head to the garage entrance and flick off the light, bringing down the automatic door. Arms folded and feet apart, I stand on the drive as the car swings in and parks. My heart sinks when the driver gets out.

'Scott,' I say, my voice giving away my disappointment. When he left, things had seemed calm, as though I'd managed to placate him, get rid of him. I certainly wasn't expecting to see him tonight.

He reaches across to the passenger side of the car and pulls out a bag – the same bag he brought into my house last night when he stayed over.

'I thought you'd be settling into your new house,' I say, fighting the wobble in my voice. Quickly, I glance up to Kieran's bedroom window, which faces over the drive. The curtains are drawn and the light is on behind it.

'So did I,' he says, walking over to me, his expression thunderous. 'There's been a problem,' he adds, wiping a hand down his tired face.

'Oh?' My heart misses a couple of beats, sensing what's coming before my brain catches up.

'When I went to pick up the keys, I was told that the landlord had already let the property privately and had failed to inform the letting agent. Which makes me officially homeless.'

'That's terrible,' I say, not wanting to acknowledge why he's here, ignoring the warning voice in my head. 'Surely you can get some kind of compensation. Had you signed all the paperwork and paid a deposit?'

Scott blusters his way through an answer, mainly by using a string of swear words and dodging my actual question. 'First thing Monday morning, they'll be hearing from my solicitor.'

'I'm sure you'll be able to claim compensation for a hotel for a few nights. They must have insurance for this kind of thing.'

Scott shakes his head and looks down, scuffing the gravel. He seems worn down, defeated, and not at all like the man I met in Oxford or, indeed, the one who was here last night. But I still can't feel sorry for him.

'What about all your stuff?' I ask. 'Did you have a removals van booked?' I shudder, clamping my arms around me as I glance behind him, half expecting a van to be following him down the drive.

'I don't have much. It's in a small storage unit. Look, can I come in?'

The last thing I want is him here when Kieran is home. 'It's not a good time,' I tell him, knowing I have to be firm this time. 'I'm sorry.'

Scott stares at me for a second, then glances up at Kieran's window, as if he's read my mind. 'I'm sorry too, Jennifer,' he says coldly. His eyes appear empty, cold, determined. 'That it's come to this.'

'It hasn't come to anything,' I say, folding my arms and stepping back towards my door. 'I let you stay one night, as agreed. You can't ask me again.'

His face breaks into a smile as he laughs. 'Oh, but I can, Jennifer. And I am. You know as well as I do that you have to let me in.'

I stare at him, my jaw tightening as I fight against every instinct not to go up and thump him. Instead, I give a small nod and turn, knowing he'll follow me inside.

In the hall, Kieran's music reverberates through my body. I wait for Scott to come in before shutting the door behind him. I close my eyes briefly, too, praying that I can get him gone soon, figure something out. He can't stay here again.

We go through to the kitchen and I reach for the kettle, but suddenly there's a hand on mine, gripping my wrist.

'Don't you have anything stronger?' he asks, standing close behind me. 'A whisky would knock the edge off a rough day.'

I turn and look up at him – his face is close. 'Sure,' I say, swallowing and prising myself from his grip.

In Jeremy's study, I take a cut-glass tumbler from the drinks cabinet and pour a small measure from the decanter. I stop, staring at my husband's empty chair, closing my eyes at the thought of what he would say. My fingers trail down the decanter after I place it back, taking the drink into the kitchen. But as I pass the living room, I see that Scott has retreated in there, sitting in Jeremy's favourite leather chair as he warms himself by the fire.

He takes the drink and I perch on the edge of the sofa. 'I'm looking forward to getting to know your son,' he says, sending shock waves through me. 'This is good stuff,' he adds, holding up the glass.

I glance at the doorway, listening out, wondering if I just heard Kieran's bedroom door open.

'That's not happening,' I say. 'You need to leave after you've had that.'

Scott stares at me, his eyes hardening. His jaw tightens and twitches. 'It's a big place for just the two of you,' he says, looking around. 'It must seem even bigger without your husband.'

'It's not really any of your business,' I snap back, hearing Rhonda's voice in my head, telling me to be careful. 'I promised I'd watch a film with Kieran this evening. You being here is not convenient tonight.'

'Not to worry,' Scott says, his expression blank. 'I'll amuse myself. Perhaps go and read in your husband's study. Or maybe your son would like me to watch the movie with you?' He takes a long, slow sip of whisky, not taking his eyes off me. 'I'll need to stay here longer than just one night, so there'll be plenty of time to get acquainted with him. All the time in the world, in fact.' He grins.

My heart thumps as I hear Kieran's music switch off and then his bedroom door opening and closing – followed by the sound of him thumping down the stairs.

'Mum?' he calls out from the hall.

Before I know what's happening, Scott is suddenly sitting beside me on the sofa. He takes my wrist again, holding it firmly, his face up close to mine. I smell the alcohol on his breath.

'I'm not giving you a choice, Jennifer,' he says, a tiny globule of spit flying from his mouth and hitting my face. 'You are carrying my baby, and I will be staying with you. We can do this the nice way or the nasty way. Up to you.'

'Mum, is there any of that casserole left? I'm starving again,' Kieran calls out from the kitchen.

My breaths are short and shallow and my chest tight as my cheeks flush.

'You *bastard*,' I whisper, my fear evident. 'Get off me…' I try to pull my hand away, but his grip is too strong.

'You don't want Sonny Jim in there to know that Mummy was a naughty girl behind Daddy's back, do you?' He flicks his eyes towards the kitchen.

I swallow, my eyes dancing around his face. My lips part but nothing comes out.

'Thought not,' Scott says with a smile. 'I won't tell if you don't.' He laughs, shoving my hand away.

'Mum? You in here?'

I hear Kieran padding across the hall, and suddenly he's standing in the doorway, eyeing up what's going on. Scott is sitting perfectly normally beside me, cradling his drink with a warm smile spread across his face.

'Kier…' I say, forcing my voice to stay even. I need to make everything seem normal. 'Kier, this is… Scott. A… a friend.'

Scott stands, extending his hand as Kieran comes further into the room. They exchange a handshake and I see my son sizing him up, giving me a quick glance.

'Your mum's an absolute star, young man. She's very kindly offered to let me stay a while. Was that vinyl you were playing just before? I'm a huge fan of that band.'

'They're my favourite,' Kieran says, his face relaxing. He shoves his hands in his front pockets, grinning. 'I saw them live last summer at Wembley. They were incredible.'

'No way,' Scott says. 'Wembley? I was there too. What a small world it is. Don't you think, Jen?' Scott looks down at me, giving me a slow wink. 'Now, what was that you said about a casserole, Kieran? I wouldn't say no to a plate of that. You can tell me what other music you're into, and all about the film your mum said we're going to watch.'

CHAPTER TWENTY-TWO

Jen

Scott Shaw is in my house…

The words haunt my mind during morning surgery, making it almost impossible to concentrate. I considered taking the morning off to deal with the situation, but I have a full clinic with patients who are relying on me. I can't possibly let them down.

The remainder of last night was unbearable – with Scott doing everything possible to ingratiate himself with my son. Whether it was discussing football or music, or the pair of them glued to the movie that Kieran and I had planned to watch, he went out of his way to weasel himself firmly into my home.

And with what he knew, the destruction he could bring to my life, I had no choice but to let him stay. I even found myself handing over a spare key this morning when he asked, making sure he did it in front of Kieran so I couldn't protest.

I don't doubt for one minute that he'll follow through with his threat if I don't comply; that he'd take delight in announcing to Kieran his mother had fallen pregnant after a night of sex with a stranger while his father was still alive – twisting the truth of what actually happened to suit himself. And neither would he hesitate in broadcasting the lies to Tim at the surgery or any of the other staff at work, and I'm sure it wouldn't take him long to find Rhonda and shame me… or inform any of my other friends or relatives. It might as well be front-page news. I wouldn't be able to live with myself if it got out, not until I've figured out the truth.

But *why*? Why would he do any of this? Did he spot me a mile off at the conference – a doctor on her own, looking troubled and with worries on her mind? There's no doubt I had my miserable and don't-mess-with-me expression on that night as I tried to overcome my paranoia about Jeremy and Madeleine, but to Scott it might as well have been a sign on my head reading 'take advantage of me'.

Perhaps he was driven by money, figuring he could target a well-off married doctor if he hung around the conference delegates – getting her drunk, slipping something in her glass, making her vulnerable. I was wearing my wedding ring, after all. And now me getting pregnant has turned into a convenient little side hustle for him, giving him permission to wring me out even more when he makes his move on my finances.

I've considered asking him how much he wants, paying him off and getting done with it – not that there's anything left to pay him off with. With Jeremy's debts to settle, I'm virtually hand to mouth at the moment, even on my decent salary. I'd have to take out another loan. One thing is for certain: I won't be naming Scott on my child's birth certificate.

I take a deep breath between patients, forcing myself to think rationally, calmly, about what I can remember from that night. Quickly, I tap flunitrazepam into Google. Commonly known as Rohypnol, or the date rape drug, I don't really need to read up about its effects, the pharmacology behind it, because I already know.

And I also know about GHB, gamma-hydroxybutyric acid, a widely available neurotransmitter and psychoactive drug, with uses ranging from medical to industrial. And it's easily obtainable, shockingly so. If my drink was tampered with that night, then it could well have been by someone who was after non-consensual sex. And with my recollection of events so poor – as though someone has slashed my memory into a thousand frustrating fragments with a razor wire – the more I read up on it, my bet is on GHB. A quick squeeze of a tiny vial and my brightly coloured cocktail would have disguised the salty taste of the liquid.

I shudder to think how close to death it would have taken me, combined with the alcohol I'd already had. There's a fine line between the so-called pleasures of chemsex and my body shutting down – literally less than a millilitre dosage. I was mistaken to believe that a random person in the club must have spiked my drink while I went to the toilet and Scott disappeared off to the bar. It wasn't random at all. It was *him*.

'Hello there, Sally,' I say as my young patient clatters her way into my office for the second time recently. I quickly switch screens on my computer. 'How's the mastitis?' I ask when she's settled herself down. Danny, her toddler, skids on his knees to the toy box in the corner.

'Getting better,' she says, leaning down into her buggy to unstrap her baby from the reclined seat. 'But it's Amber I'm worried about. There's something wrong with her eye, and she's been really grizzly and not feeding.'

The concern on Sally's face is evident, as is the exhaustion. She can't have had much of a break after giving birth to Danny before she was pregnant again. I swallow, suddenly remembering for the hundredth time this morning that *I'm* pregnant, that soon it'll be me who's feeling as though I've flown three times around the world and passed through countless time zones, not knowing what day it is, let alone having any time for myself to eat or shower or go to the gym or see friends or have a lie-in.

After washing my hands, I take the baby from her, her little legs pedalling the air. 'Hello, you gorgeous little girl,' I coo at her, giving her a beaming smile. Cradling her on my knee, I see her left eye is choked up with sticky mucus. The baby looks up at me, her one good eye trying to focus on mine. A glimmer of an accidental smile twists her rosebud mouth, her face constantly mobile as she sucks on her bottom lip. Then she jams in a fist, letting out a little howl of frustration when she misses her mouth on the first attempt. The baby smells faintly of cigarette smoke.

'It looks like a blocked tear duct,' I tell Sally. 'Has she had this since birth? Does it come and go?'

Sally nods. Danny suddenly shrieks and hurls a chunky plastic brick across my office. 'Knock it off, Danny,' Sally says in a weary voice. 'You'll hurt Amber.'

'If you pop her clothes off, I'll give her a proper going-over. There's just a little wheeze that's probably nothing, but I'd like to check it out.'

Ten minutes later and Sally is on her way again with a prescription for Amber's eye and an all-clear on her chest, plus a few words of wisdom about her partner not smoking around the baby. Sally struggles the buggy out of my door with Danny tagging along, clutching onto several plastic toys, hugging them close to his chest as he leaves. He looks up at me guiltily as I hold the door open. I force a smile, resisting the urge to tell him to take the whole sodding box.

*

As soon as clinic is over and various other matters dealt with – reviewing and writing patient reports, making referrals, some triage phone calls and a practice meeting – I leave work and head home with a heavy feeling in the pit of my stomach. Somehow, I have to get rid of Scott.

As I hurtle my car around the country lanes, jamming the brakes on and mounting the verge several times when a vehicle comes the other way, I flip between anger and fear. Of course, I'd made sure Jeremy's study door was locked and hid my jewellery and other personal items in there after Scott had gone to bed last night, and I have the key to the study safely on my fob, but the thought of him prowling about my house, opening cupboards, using my stuff, helping himself to food and tea and coffee while I'm at work makes me want to explode with rage.

The more I think about it, the more I'm certain this man raped me.

I could go to the police, I think, as I turn down my drive, though I doubt that will get very far – apart from the local paper and a whole load of shame. Despite victim anonymity, gossip would soon spread in our small community. It'd be Scott's word against mine and the case would be unlikely to progress very far, let alone result in a conviction. I've seen it too many times when I've worked alongside ISVAs, specially trained advisors who deal with those affected by abuse – our efforts for a conviction frustratingly hitting brick wall after brick wall when rape victims report their attackers. But all thoughts of the police fly out of the window when I see Rhonda's car parked squarely next to Scott's Mercedes.

Fuck.

I virtually skid to a stop on the gravel and grab my stuff before heading inside.

'Didn't *I* get an invite to the party?' I say, striding into the kitchen and dumping down my bag and keys, scowling. Breathless, I slide my coat off my shoulder and chuck it on a stool, folding my arms and involuntarily glaring at the pair of them. I try to read the atmosphere, what he might have told Rhonda already.

'Hello, Jennifer,' Scott says in that smooth way of his, the contrast in our voices instantly making me seem unhinged. He looks windblown and rosy-cheeked, as though he's been outside for hours. And his jeans have swipes of dirt up the front, and there's a bit of twig or leaf in his hair.

'I chopped some logs and brought them in for you,' he says by way of explanation as he looks down at himself. 'And while I was at it, I did a bit of clearing in the coppice down by the lake. There was an overhanging branch that was about to come down.

You don't want it rotting and fouling the water.' He stares at me, watching for my reaction. 'Do you?'

'Thank you,' I say, drawing on reserves I didn't know I had. 'And Rhonda, where are my manners? This is my… a friend, Scott. Scott, this is Rhonda.'

'Already taken care of the intros,' Rhonda replies with a glance shuttled between us. 'Scott has been telling me how good you've been to him, offering a place to stay until he gets on his feet. It's unfortunate what happened about your rental,' she adds. 'You should definitely sue for your losses, perhaps even claim money for a hotel?' she adds in a questioning tone.

As Scott busies himself with washing his hands, Rhonda takes my elbow, guiding me back into the hallway.

'Look,' she says, a concerned expression on her face. We walk through to the living room where, sure enough, there's a fresh pile of logs in the huge wicker basket beside the fire, as well as the stone nook being crammed full of them. 'Sorry for barging in. I didn't expect you to have company *still*.' She pauses, expecting me to say something, but I don't. 'Scott insisted I waited until you got home.'

I force a smile and give my head a little shake, trying to indicate it's no problem – when really, it is.

'Jen, what you told me in my office the other day… about you being pregnant. I'm so sorry we barely discussed it when I came round with the casserole. We got a bit distracted. But it's *huge* news.' Her face doesn't know whether to explode with congratulations and excitement, or crumple from pity. She's waiting for me to green-light either option.

We sit down on the sofa, each of us perching on the edge as if it's the first time we've met, and not in the least indicative of the deep, honest friendship we've forged in the five years I've known her.

I nod, unable to speak until I know where this is going.

'You know I've been concerned about Kieran, but after everything that's happened, I was wondering how he took it after overhearing about the baby. I just don't want it to affect his schoolwork even more.'

I don't say anything. *Can't* say anything.

'But… but also, I'm now wondering if it's such a good idea to have…' Rhonda trails off, her eyes flicking back to the door. 'If it's such a good idea to have company staying. You know, *male* company.'

'Ronnie, please… it's fine. Really, it's all fine,' I say, weary from everything. 'I know you're only trying to help, but I can't talk about this right now.' I also glance to the door, pushing my fingers through my hair. The roots feel slightly oily and I know the ends need a good trim.

'Thing is, Jen, Scott told me…' Rhonda leans in, lowering her voice. 'He told me you two met in a bar. And when I asked him how he knew Jeremy, he said he'd never met him.'

I try to smile, try to force an incredulous laugh to disguise the look of horror that wants to burst out of me – but it comes out as a croak. 'No, no… he's got that wrong, actually,' I say, clearing my throat. 'When Scott and I first met, it was in a bar, yes. He'd had an absolute skinful and Jeremy had to put him in a taxi. It was embarrassing, to be honest. So no wonder he doesn't remem—'

'Jen?'

I feel my cheeks burning. 'What?'

'You're shaking.'

I look down at my hands, knotted in my lap, forcing the tremble to stop. 'It's just been a long day, that's all.'

'I just don't think he should be here, that's all. Call me paranoid, but I get a… funny feeling from him. I think he's got a cheek, actually, to be imposing on you like this. I can have a word with him, if you like. Tell him to sling his—'

'Will you leave it, Ronnie, OK?' I say, snappier than intended. 'Look…' I stare at the ceiling, forcing my mind to work fast. 'It turns out that Jeremy owed Scott some money too, OK? A few thousand, apparently. Scott's had a bit of bad luck and, because of the debt, I said he could stay here for a while to make up for it a bit. It's no big deal.' My mouth is bone dry.

Rhonda stares at me, her eyes narrowing. 'I've said it before: just be careful, Jen. It seems to me he's got his feet right under your table, doing odd jobs around the place and cooking for you. He'll be getting his mail delivered here and moving his stuff into your room before you know it. When is he leaving?'

'I… I'm not sure exactly. But it's fine. Kieran really likes him. There's no problem.' My voice is flat and robotic.

Rhonda stares at me before enveloping me in a hug. 'OK, but I'm here to help get rid if you need. And Chris and his colleagues will be round in a shot if he kicks off.'

'Thank you,' I say, suddenly feeling absolutely exhausted.

'Anyway, you've got enough on your plate with this,' she says, touching my stomach. 'Do you know your dates?'

I shake my head, wishing I'd not told her about the baby. At least then Kieran wouldn't have found out the way he did. But it's not too late, I think. I can pop a couple of prescription pills, claim a miscarriage, and in a day or two it'll all be over as if none of it ever happened.

I'll deny any allegations by Scott, saying the baby was Jeremy's – the proof would be gone, after all – and it'll be my word against his, yet slightly more in my favour. No baby, no DNA test. No sleepless nights or parental rights claims or birth certificate headaches. No having to associate with him for the next eighteen years. I'll be able to put the whole sorry incident behind me and get on with my life.

Except I can't terminate this pregnancy. It goes against every fibre of my being and everything I stand for.

'I've no idea of dates,' I answer.

'Goodbye sex?' Rhonda says, counting on her fingers. 'Just before Jeremy went off to Switzerland?'

'Maybe,' I reply, glancing over to the living room door as I see a shadow slide past. 'Kieran's on the prowl for food. I'd better get some dinner on,' I say, standing and showing her to the door. 'Thanks for coming round.'

Rhonda nods, looking at me suspiciously. 'Just take care of yourself,' she says, heading for the front door. 'You know where I am.'

As she goes out to her car, she flicks me a wave and I watch the red tail lights disappear down the drive. I close the door, reluctantly locking me and my son in with the person I hate most in the world, before turning and letting out a scream that sends Scott and Kieran running to see what's wrong.

CHAPTER TWENTY-THREE

Jen

'For God's sake, Mum,' Kieran says, rolling his eyes and laughing when he sees it. He heads off to the kitchen, plugging his earphones in.

Scott studies my face for a moment – a smirk spreading across his, making me feel ridiculous for pinning myself against the wall as far away from it as possible, barely able to breathe.

'It's… it's *huge*,' I manage to say, letting out another squeal as the spider scuttles over to the carved hallway chest. 'Get the vacuum,' I beg. 'I need to get rid of it.'

Scott laughs at me. 'It must have hitched a ride in on the logs,' he says. 'There were some huge ones out in the barn when I was chopping.'

'Hurry,' I say, not daring to take my eyes off it and hating that I'm making a scene in front of him. 'The vacuum is in the cupboard over there. I… I can't stand it roaming around the house.' I sidle back towards the living room door. Living out in the country, I'm no stranger to spiders and other insects. But it was always Jeremy who dealt with them – swiftly and without fuss, almost as if he enjoyed it.

Scott gets down on his knees and crawls over to where the creature is about to disappear under the wooden chest. He cups his hands and slowly closes in, lowering his palms down until he's close enough to pounce.

'What the *hell* are you doing?' I shriek, half covering my face. 'Can't you just suck it up with the vacuum?'

He looks back at me, laughing. 'You do realise that probably won't even kill it? There are much better ways of disposing of it.'

The way he looks at me makes my skin crawl as he turns back to the spider, leaving me feeling pathetic as I watch him carefully scoop it up with his hands cupped around it.

'How can you even *do* that?' I say, opening the front door for him and standing back. 'Take it well away from the house!' I call out as he disappears across the driveway. A moment later, he's back inside, still smirking at me.

'I've had plenty of practice,' he says, shrugging and getting up close to me.

I don't know whether to laugh hysterically or thump him as I stand there, shaking. In the end, I do neither because, to my horror, Scott's mouth comes down on mine as he attempts a kiss.

Stunned, it takes me a few seconds to realise what's happening and slam my hands against his shoulders, shoving him hard. My vision blurs from another flashback – the image of his face leering down at me, hands tight around my throat and a sharp pain between my legs.

'Get *off* me!' I hiss, trying to keep my voice low, conscious of Kieran in the next room. Scott stays close for a few moments, his eyes boring into mine as I fight away the memories, feeling sick at what he's just done.

'Don't tell me you didn't enjoy it,' he whispers back, trailing a finger down my cheek. Then he turns and heads back to the kitchen, where I hear him laughing with my son as I'm left leaning against the wall wondering what the hell just happened.

*

'So tell me about your studies, Kieran,' Scott says as the three of us sit around the table, no one else appearing to notice the awkwardness of the situation, let alone the rage simmering inside me. 'What subjects are you taking?'

It's been a while since I ate in the dining room, with Kieran and I often eating at different times lately, either perched on stools at the kitchen island or, in Kieran's case, him sloping off to his room with a plate of food. But Scott suggested it – no, *insisted* on it – giving me one of his telling looks, making sure he took the chair at the head of the dining table. Jeremy and I always made a point of eating in here at weekends, leaving our phones in the kitchen so we could talk. The view down the garden through the huge glass doors is beautiful, especially with the all the outdoor lights on at night reflecting off the big pond in the paddock. But I can't look at it now, can't face the memories derailing me even more.

Kieran flashes me a look, cutting into the steak that Scott has prepared. I've barely touched mine. 'English lit, history and geography,' he says, chewing.

Scott nods. 'History, fascinating,' he says, before giving me a sly glance over the rim of his wine glass.

My glass. *Jeremy's* wine.

'Not really,' Kieran says, hunched over his plate, his knife and fork eagerly gripped as though he's not eaten in a week. 'This is really good, by the way,' he says, dunking a chip in the peppercorn sauce. 'So how did you know Dad?' he continues, not knowing what he's stirring up. 'Mum says you were old friends.' He gives me another look from beneath the loose curls of his fringe.

'Did she now?' Scott replies with a laugh. I feel his eyes boring into me, but I don't give him the satisfaction of looking up. 'Oh, we go *way* back,' he continues without missing a beat.

'Why did you become a chef?' Kieran asks, making me sigh with relief at the change of tack.

'Let's just say I kind of fell into it accidentally,' Scott replies. 'Through a sort of a training scheme.'

I listen intently. Perhaps if I can get an idea of his past, I can somehow get him out of my future.

'It was at a residential facility and there were a number of trades to specialise in,' he continues. 'I tried everything from brickwork and carpentry to landscape gardening and IT. But it was cooking that inspired me.'

'That sounds cool,' Kieran says, shovelling in more chips. 'Maybe I should go there too.' He nods, his curls bouncing about. 'Dad wanted me to go to uni but I'm like, what's the point?' My son sniffs as his eyes water.

'Degrees open doors, love,' I say. 'Your dad read philosophy, then went on to study film and journalism and—'

'Yeah, and look where that got him, right?' Kieran wipes his nose on his cuff, staring down at his food.

For a few seconds, all I can hear is the sound of my own chewing and the intermittent clatter of cutlery as I wait for the moment to pass. I've endured many of them since Jeremy died and found it best to ride them out, not to dissect them.

'Tell me about this training scheme,' I say to Scott. Maybe I can contact someone there, find out more about him.

'It was a long time ago,' he says, leering at me. 'Hey, Kieran,' he continues. 'We'll cook something together tomorrow, if you like? I can teach you a few dishes.'

'Yeah, cool,' he replies. 'Maybe I could cook for Caitlin.'

'Your girlfriend?' Scott asks.

'Not yet,' Kieran replies with a shrug.

'You didn't have to go to all this trouble, you know,' I say, indicating my plate. Anything to stop him creeping up to my son.

'It's the least I could do, seeing as you're being kind enough to let me stay for so long. Your mum's a star, isn't she, Kieran?'

I'm not letting you stay! I scream in my head, but manage to stay calm.

'Oh, and just so you know, Jennifer, I put an IOU note in the jar.' Scott reaches for the bottle of wine and sloshes more red into his glass, giving me a pitying look. 'I found some cash in a jar in the pantry,' he says. 'I'll put it back when I get my first pay cheque.'

I stare at him, seething, thankful that Kieran is now absorbed in his phone. A moment later, my son stands up, clearing his plate away, saying he has homework to do.

'You helped yourself to my money?' I retort, once Kieran is out of earshot.

'Don't be like that, Jennifer.'

I shove my knife and fork together on my plate, suddenly not in the least bit hungry. 'And you helped yourself to my late husband's wine. That's not a fiver a bottle, you know.'

'I know,' Scott replies in a way that makes me want to stab him with my steak knife. 'That's why I chose it.'

He leans closer to me, reaching out for my wrist and taking hold of it. His fingers are tight, restraining me as I try to pull away. 'I don't think it's good for the baby if you get all... worked up,' he says. 'Now, eat your steak. It's rich in iron.'

'You can't stay any longer,' I tell him, prising myself out of his grip. 'You've got tonight, then tomorrow you're leaving. There are a couple of bed and breakfasts in Shenbury until you sort out another rental property. I don't know what it is you want from me, but you're not getting it.'

He looks at me, his head tilted to one side, his jaw tight and his eyes icy.

'You know you don't mean that, Jen,' he says, sipping more wine. 'This arrangement suits us both. I was thinking, we should make it longer-term. There's no point you and Kieran rattling around in this huge place by yourselves.'

'It's not happening,' I say, standing up to clear my plate. 'I don't even know you. You're just some guy I met in a bar and—'

'Oh, Jennifer,' he says, grabbing my wrist again, this time more forcefully, dragging me back down into my chair. I hear Kieran humming to himself as he thumps back up the stairs. 'You're hurting my feelings. I'm not *some guy*. Take that back.'

I swallow drily, my mouth wanting to say something, but it can't. I'm frozen.

'We have a connection, you and me. You can't deny it. And now we have a baby on the way.' His other hand slides under the table and strokes my stomach.

I screw up my eyes, my entire body tensing. 'It was a mistake,' I tell him. 'If you're not gone by tomorrow morning before I leave for work, I'm calling the police.'

Call them now! a voice in my head screams. But I know I won't, just as I know I probably won't call them tomorrow either. I open my eyes to see him smiling, almost laughing at me. He leans forward and, to my disgust, kisses my neck – a slow, gentle kiss, making me hate my body for responding. I shoulder him away.

'Were you this cold with your husband?' he says, his breath warm against my skin. 'Is that why he's gone?'

For a few seconds, I'm back in the hotel room again, breathing the scent of him in, unaware of my body or my senses or if I should be fighting or protesting or saying no or simply going along with him. I hate my brain for keeping these details from me.

'I did not consent to sex with you that night,' I say, my words brittle and dangerous. I feel the sensation of a hand around my throat, another pinning my wrists together, the weight of him on top of me, impossible to escape. 'You put something in my drink. You *raped* me.'

'You think I roofied you?' Scott shakes his head and cups my hands between his. 'Jennifer, *Jen...* you loved every minute of it.'

'No, no I *didn't.*' I screw up my eyes again, refusing to believe him. I was drunk, yes. And I was upset and consumed by suspicion and paranoia about Jeremy. Perhaps a part of me was flirting to begin with, maybe even a part of me wanting secret payback, something for me and me alone that would cancel out whatever it was I believed Jeremy was doing behind my back. If I went home from the conference feeling as though I'd gained some kind of control over my life, got attention from a guy in a bar that Jeremy didn't know about, then it would have maybe made whatever he was getting up to slightly more bearable. Because I knew there was no way I'd be able to prove anything between him and Madeleine. Just as there was no way that I'd gone out that night with the intention of having sex with a stranger.

'See?' I hear Scott say.

When I open my eyes, he's holding out his phone, flicking through some photos.

'Now tell me you weren't enjoying yourself,' he says, shoving his phone in front of my face and scrolling through.

There are dozens of pictures of me clothed, semi-clothed, naked, posed, tied up, looking provocative, sipping from a wine glass. More of me taken from above, my head down between his legs, even a video of me moaning, begging, my words not making sense yet the tone of my voice pleading, desperate. My eyes are a dark, sunken mess from smudged make-up, but with a vacant, dead look inside, as though my soul had left my body. My lips are scarlet, almost sore, from whatever he'd done to me, my body heaving and writhing as he did things that almost convinced me this was not me in the footage – that it was someone else entirely.

Then he takes back his phone and swipes through his camera roll, showing me a completely different batch of images. I don't understand. They're blurry and the light isn't good as it's dark, but I can still make out that it's me, that this time I'm fully clothed

– and they were taken *here*, at my house. He'd been watching me, photographing me – and by the looks of it, it had been over many months.

'It was *you*,' I whisper, cupping my hand over my mouth as I retch and make a dash for the downstairs toilet.

CHAPTER TWENTY-FOUR

Rhonda

'But I thought you had a few days off for half-term?' Chris says, stretching out in bed.

Rhonda doesn't think he really minds too much if she goes into school today. It's not like they had any particular plans, and he'll no doubt just mooch around at home, exhausted from his run of shifts. Besides, Caitlin is home all day and they always enjoy spending time together.

'Hopefully we can get it all sorted in one hit,' Rhonda says, glancing away from her reflection in the bathroom mirror. She grabs a baggy sweatshirt and pulls it on over her T-shirt. She's opted for her old leggings, knowing they're likely to get filthy up in that loft. 'And then we'll have the rest of the week together.'

'You mean *you'll* have the rest of the week,' Chris says, reaching for the coffee Rhonda had brought him up. 'I've got two earlies then two lates, remember?'

'In that case, we get to spend Sunday together,' Rhonda reminds him as she ties up her hair in a band, securing it with a headscarf. She sits down on the bed, suddenly becoming pensive. 'I'm really getting concerned about Jen,' she says, biting her lip. She stares out of the window, the curtains only half pulled back. The sky is a slate grey, threatening rain. 'That guy she had to stay over for a night, he's still there and—'

Chris hoists himself up in bed, exposing his broad chest. Perhaps not quite as muscular as he was when they first met, and some of his hairs have turned silver, but Rhonda loves him even more for it. He frowns, waiting for her to continue.

'He's called Scott. Some friend of Jeremy's, apparently, though I've not heard of him before. I got a funny vibe off him. Like he was getting his feet well under the table.'

'Maybe he's providing support, Ron.' Chris shrugs, flopping back down onto his pillow. 'If having a friend stay is what she needs right now, then I don't see the problem.'

'Jen's pregnant,' Rhonda says, immediately wishing she hadn't. She fixes her stare on the wardrobe, thinking that if she doesn't look Chris in the eye then perhaps it won't feel quite so much like she's betrayed her friend. And while Jen never said *not* to tell anyone, she didn't say to tell anyone either.

Chris sits up again, blowing out through pursed lips. 'That's big news,' he says, running his hands through his hair. 'Did Jeremy know before he died?'

Rhonda shakes her head. 'I don't think so. It's early days, from what I can make out.' She swallows, wondering if she should test out her theory on Chris, or see if he arrives at the same conclusion. But then, he wasn't party to the conversations about Jen's suspicions of Jeremy having an affair and that, as a consequence, their sex life had nosedived. Though it only takes one time, and she'd not directly asked Jen about the father.

'Is she pleased?'

'Hard to tell,' Rhonda says, getting up again and putting on her trainers. 'Shocked more than anything. If we get this stuff at school sorted out in good time, I'll drop in on her later, see how she's doing.'

Chris nods. 'Don't forget your phone,' he says. 'You know what you're like with it.'

'Not true!' she says, prodding him. 'God knows how it ended up in the laundry basket on the landing the other night. I swear

I left it on the sofa after we'd watched the film.' And with that, Rhonda gives Chris a quick peck and heads off.

St Quentin's hadn't always been a private school – far from it, in fact. Up until the mid-nineties, part of it had been used as a comprehensive, with only a small section of the old early-Victorian grammar school buildings being occupied and the rest lying derelict. An ugly concrete structure had been erected in the grounds in the early eighties and was used as the main school building for the comprehensive, with satellite classrooms in prefab mobile units dotted around a tarmac playground. The council had conceded it was cheaper than renovating the crumbling Gothic ruins that had been largely out of bounds since the boys' grammar school had closed previously.

Now, St Quentin's, located on the eastern edge of Shenbury and fully restored, almost resembled a Gothic asylum with row upon row of mullioned windows, the building flanked at each end by two towers complete with stone spiral staircases. It was home to the not particularly prestigious fee-paying school that had moved there from a smaller nearby campus when the education authority sold off the property cheaply.

The concrete relics of its comprehensive years had been torn down long ago, with the ghosts of the mid-nineties events that led to its demise not quite forgotten by those still local. The murder of a local toddler by a pupil had parents pulling their children out in droves back then, until the local council had no alternative but to shut the doors on the grim reminder that had, for a while, made the area infamous.

The private school's motto was 'Sapere Aude', or 'Dare to Know', when St Quentin's opened its doors at the dawn of the new century. The charitable trust and board of governors had indeed done a good job of attracting local fee-paying pupils with its reasonable terms, as well as adhering to its mission statement of 'Education for All' by offering more scholarships than any other local private school.

And a scholarship was the only reason Caitlin was able to enrol at St Quentin's. With Rhonda taking up the head of English position when they both moved in with Chris, it seemed natural that Rhonda put her daughter in for the exam, and she and Kieran had started at the same time. It was their friendship that had brought the two sets of parents together socially.

'You've got to be kidding me,' Rhonda says as the three of them reach the top of the spiral staircase, huffing and puffing and staring into the roof void of the westernmost tower at the school. She covers her face, letting out an exasperated laugh. 'It's going to take all of half-term *and* beyond,' she groans, with the other two staff – Ellis Greene and Miranda Wells, from the history and art departments – grumbling agreement beside her.

Miranda had arrived in dungarees and trainers, looking quite the part for a day's hard graft in the loft, while Ellis had favoured a sports jacket and trousers, saying he was meeting his boyfriend for an early dinner straight afterwards. Rhonda didn't fancy his chances of not looking like a scarecrow once they'd done a day's work up here.

'Heavens above, I'll definitely have to go home for a shower before meeting Pete after dealing with this lot,' Ellis says, tapping out a text to warn his partner that he'd probably be late. 'What have we let ourselves in for?' He slips off his jacket and rolls up his shirtsleeves, shuddering at the task ahead.

'Well I'm grateful for the bonus they're paying us,' Miranda says, wading in amongst the piles of boxes and other detritus that has collected over the years.

'Me too,' Rhonda says, planning on tucking the extra money away in her and Chris's holiday fund. She gazes around the large loft space with its high, pitched roof on the inside of the tower. The air is warm and fusty, despite the cold temperature outside, and dust motes float about in the light coming from a couple of bare bulbs as they assess the task. 'I've always wondered what was up here,' she says, prising the flaps of a box open. 'And now I know. A load of crap, by the looks of it.' Rhonda stifles a sneeze.

'No wonder they asked me to help,' Ellis says. 'I bet there's loads of stuff for the school history archives here. We shouldn't be too cavalier about ditching it all.'

'I think that's why they didn't just get a clearance company in,' Rhonda says. 'They figured tackling this job now rather than waiting until the end of term was wise. The builders are booked in to replace the roof in the Easter holidays.'

'Right,' Ellis says. 'If you two want to have a root around through some boxes, give me an idea of what's in them, then I can begin ferrying stuff down to ground level and either dump it straight in the skip or put it aside for further investigation.'

Rhonda smiles and gives a salute as she and Miranda tackle a side each at the rear of the loft, stooping beneath the roof timbers and stepping over all the clutter. 'There are old textbooks from the year dot in here,' she says, lifting a box and manhandling it over to Ellis. But before he can take it, the bottom gives way and several dozen books covered in mildew drop onto the floorboards, sending a mushroom cloud of dust up their noses.

'We need masks,' Miranda says, coughing.

'And a bloody medal,' Rhonda says on her hands and knees, gathering the books and handing them over to Ellis, who begins a tireless series of trips up and down the stone spiral staircase.

Several hours later, Rhonda calls for a tea break. 'Let's take a load each down with us, save wasting a trip.' She gathers up a random box and follows the others, leaving it in the lower lobby of the tower. 'Don't chuck that one,' she says. 'Looks like old accounting records or something, but I think there are some photos in there too.'

The three of them head off to the staffroom, brushing themselves down as they cross the quad. Rhonda pulls off her headscarf and shakes out her hair, catching the same fusty smell from up in the loft in her throat, before she ties it back up again.

Over tea, they chat about various bits of school gossip, Old Hairy's contentious new policies about away sports matches, as well as the school play, which all of them are involved in somehow, as well as general plans for the Easter holidays.

Back in the lobby, Rhonda leaves the other two to head back up to the loft while she checks the contents of the last box she brought down. She smiles when she sees a file stuffed with receipts for library book orders, shaking her head at the old-fashioned ledger. It seems anything and everything had been crammed in, with no sense of order, when the comprehensive school was essentially packed up and things either stored or disposed of.

Rhonda takes the general paperwork out to the skip and delights in chucking it all in. Rooting through the remainder of the box, she finds some photographs – a number of them in albums, the glue peeling off and the pages brittle with age. But the majority of pictures are just thrown in loose, creased and yellowing, some torn and some stuck together. At the bottom of the box are a few class and whole-school photos, roughly folded to fit in the box – the extra-wide kind where the entire school would have been made to line up and stand on chairs or precariously stacked crates, the staff racked up stiffly around the edge, with senior management sitting on chairs front and centre.

'Blimey, look at these,' she says to herself, glancing up the stairs to see if the others are on their way down again to show them. 'Nineteen ninety,' she mutters, knowing from the history displays in the school's library that this wasn't long before the comprehensive shut its doors. 'Miranda,' Rhonda says as she hears her coming down. 'Come and have a look at these.'

Miranda appears from behind a stack of two boxes, dropping them onto the old quarry tiles in a cloud of dust. She blows out from exhaustion, brushing herself down. 'What have you found?' she says, peering over Rhonda's shoulder as she kneels on the hard floor. 'Old pics?'

'Yup. I think they should go to the library, let Ellis and his department decide what's fit to keep or not.'

'Agreed,' Miranda says. She takes an album out of the box, blowing on its cover, holding it carefully as she opens it. 'Blimey, look. This looks like a summer fete or something. And sports day.'

'Check out those uniforms,' Rhonda says, pointing to a girl's skirt, the hem of which barely came down to her thighs. 'Mr Meads would have a fit,' she says, joking about their strict head teacher. As Miranda flips through the pages, Rhonda does a quick double take on a couple of photos, as if something snags at the back of her mind, but then she returns to the stack of whole-school pictures. 'These are in some kind of order, look. We've got nineteen ninety, ninety-one, -two and -three here,' she says, reading out the dates printed at the bottom. 'There are no more after that because that's when the comprehensive shut down.'

'You know why, don't you?' Ellis says, jumping down the last couple of steps as he overhears the women's discussion. They both look up as he dumps another box on the floor.

'I've heard the rumours,' Rhonda says.

'Murrrder,' he replies in a silly voice, rolling out the 'r'.

'No way,' Miranda says, shocked. She's only been teaching at the school since last September.

'Some kid went to prison, right?' Rhonda says, standing up and rubbing her sore knees. It's just as she's about to shove the pictures back in the box to take over to the library that she sees a stack of individual class photos, with names printed underneath. 'I wonder where all these people are now?' she says, about to put them back in the box when one name in particular jumps out. She suddenly goes cold, barely stifling a gasp at the sight of Jeremy's young face on the back row, positioned there because he was one of the tallest boys.

'What is it?' Ellis says, just as he's on his way out to the quad.

'That's so sad,' Rhonda says, staring down at his eager face, the same trademark dark curls identifying a pubescent Jeremy. Despite his youth, his features are unmistakable. 'It's Kieran Miller's dad,' she says, knowing that neither Miranda nor Ellis teaches him. 'He died recently. We were friends.' She points to him standing proud in his blazer.

When they first met, Jen had explained that she and Jeremy went to the same school, which came as no surprise as they were both from the area and the comprehensive was where the local kids went. They'd both joked many times that they'd had nothing to do with each other in class, barely noticing each other until they were in their second year of university, having happened to end up at the same one – Jen studying medicine and Jeremy philosophy.

'Sad indeed,' Ellis comments. 'Statistically, he's probably not the only one to die out of all these faces.'

Rhonda wonders if she should take the picture home and give it to Jen, or if it would be too upsetting. Either way, she knows it can't go in the skip – none of the photographs can. How tragic, she thinks, as she puts the box aside, that the young Jeremy in the photo had no idea that his life would be cut short at the age of forty-two.

The rest of the day is filled with multiple trips up and down from the loft as they ferry the boxes and sacks of stuff down to ground level. Moving a dozen or more sacks of stage costumes, wigs and old props reveals yet another layer of saggy cardboard boxes, some too heavy to lift without removing some of the books inside.

And that's when Rhonda finds the press clippings, hidden beneath some old biology textbooks.

'I'm pooped,' Miranda says, wiping her sweaty face on her sleeve. 'Are we nearly done for the day?' She looks at her watch. 'I reckon if we come in again tomorrow, we can have it finished.'

'Mmm, sure,' Rhonda says without looking up. She flicks through the yellowing newspaper pages, some torn out and some still part of the original paper but folded open. 'You and Ellis go, if you like,' Rhonda says, glancing up. 'I'll finish this load and lock up. I've got keys.'

'If you're sure?' Ellis says, coming up behind Miranda. Rhonda glances up, confirming that she is. It's only when she's certain that she's alone that she gathers up all the clippings, shoving them in a plastic bag to take home. She wants to read all about the thirteen-year-old schoolboy found guilty of murdering a toddler back in the early nineties – the reason the comprehensive went into decline. And as she's locking up the door to the tower, she goes back into the lobby on a whim, grabbing the box containing the class photos, justifying it to herself by thinking that they might be of interest to Jen.

CHAPTER TWENTY-FIVE

Then

Evan and Mac cycle up to the den as often as they can, even when the October sunshine gives way to rain and fog and shorter days, the chillier air biting at their noses and knuckles.

'Mum says I'm not allowed out when it's dark,' Mac says gloomily.

'My mum and Griff don't care,' Evan replies, ripping open a Crunchie bar. He tosses the wrapper down by his feet, kicking it into the scrubby, leafy ground. Acrid smoke twists up from the heap of damp twigs and leaves they ignited for a campfire, which took a load of newspaper and most of the matches to get going.

'Why d'you call your dad Griff?' Mac asks, tipping the last of a bag of cheese and onion crisps into his mouth.

Evan stares across at him, watching his pink tongue dart in and out as he licks the salty remains from his lips. Evan licks chocolate from his own. 'He's not my dad,' Evan replies. 'My dad's dead. Then Mum got with Griff. He's always hitting me,' Evan says, the admission almost like a blow in itself. 'And sometimes he hits Mum.'

'Hit him back,' Mac replies, as if it's easy.

'He'd kill me if I did that. Then he'd kill Mum too, and I wouldn't be there to look after her.' Evan feels his eyes prickling and watering. 'Does your dad hit your mum?' He thinks he'll probably have to do it, too, when he's married, although he doesn't even like girls as they're all mean like Gem. He definitely wants to hit her.

''Course not,' Mac says, pulling a face. 'They love each other, Mum and Dad.'

Evan nods slowly, something catching his eye. He gets up and creeps over to a tree stump a few feet away, bent at the waist, his back hunched, suddenly, lunging at his prey, clapping and cupping his hands together around it. He makes a whooping sound and peeks between his fingers.

'Daddy-long-legs,' he says, showing it to Mac. 'Needs warming up,' he says with a throaty laugh, going over to the fire. These last few days his voice has been doing strange things, like he's got a cough even though he hasn't.

Evan releases the drowsy insect into the fire, watching as it ignites. Both kids are mesmerised as the insect crisps and curls, blackening until its legs and wings twist from the heat, before sizzling into a gooey blob. 'Coo-*ool*,' Evan says, his insides fizzing.

'It's boring just killing insects,' Mac says, opening a can of Coke.

Evan agrees. 'What would be the worst thing to kill?' he asks, staring up through the canopy of trees, spinning round a few times, his arms stretched wide. He plonks himself down on the log again, feeling dizzy. His nostrils tingle from the smoke as the wind changes and it blows in his face.

'This,' Mac says in a silly, high-pitched voice, holding up the notepad he's been doodling in. Evan looks at the page, sizing up the drawing. It's a stick person wearing a short skirt with scribbled-in hair hanging in bunches.

'Gem?' Evan says, glancing up to see Mac nodding. His voice crackles again, saliva collecting in the corners of his mouth. 'Yeah…' he says, feeling the pressure building inside. 'I'd like to throw *her* on the fire.'

*

'Ev-*an*?' Evan's mum shrieks up the stairs. He's only been home a short while, creeping past Griff, who was sprawled out in the living room, beer can in his hand, ashtray on the arm of the sofa as he growled at the football on the telly. He'd snuck up to his bedroom with the pact that he and Mac had made as they stood beside the fire still buzzing inside his head. *Kill Club secret*.

'Get down here, now. Tea!' his mum yells out.

'Where've you been all day?' she asks when he comes into the kitchen. Rosie is in her high chair, even though she can't really sit up properly yet. Usually she's attached to his mum's hip, grizzling and sucking on a slimy fist with green snot dribbling out of her nose.

'Nowhere.' Evan plonks himself down at the table and his mum puts a plate of food in front of him. 'This again?'

'I'm short this week. Eat up, it'll fill a gap,' his mum says, lighting a cigarette. She stands by the open back door, puffing smoke out into the night, her thin lips puckering up. 'Could've done with your help today, minding Rosie for me.' She holds the side of her head briefly, one finger tapping her temple, the glowing tip of the cigarette sticking out at right angles.

'Sorry, Mum,' Evan says, splitting apart the soggy bread with his fork in his right hand. He imagines the red tinned tomatoes are blood oozing out from white flesh. *Gem's* flesh.

He knows what minding Rosie means. It means that his mum had wanted to spend the day in bed fighting off another migraine. She got them a lot. They make her feel sick and she has to lie in a dark room with no sound.

'It was that brat next door again,' she says, blowing out one final time before tossing the dog end out into the garden. She glares towards the fence, making a snarling face, before slamming the back door hard. 'Screaming all the time while I was hanging out the washing. Set me head right off, he did.' She goes to the sink, plunging her hands into the soapy water.

Evan thinks he hears her mutter something about wanting to kill the little sod. Rosie gurgles in her high chair next to him.

*

Later, when Griff has gone to the pub and his mum is watching *EastEnders*, Evan feels brave. Braver than brave, in fact. It's all because Mac said they needed more cool stuff for the den. He knows Griff has some special things from when he was in the army – things he's not allowed to touch, which immediately makes him want them all the more. They're in a box under his mum and Griff's bed.

He stands at the top of the stairs, listening out – hearing the TV chattering away, Rosie making gurgling noises from her cot.

Evan slowly opens his mum and Griff's bedroom door. His heart thumps. The street light outside the window casts a glow as he goes over to the bed, careful to tread quietly because his mum is sitting right below. Kneeling down, he lifts the skirt of the nylon bedspread and shoves his hand underneath, feeling around for the box.

There. He walks his fingers along the top of the cardboard to get a grip on it, and slowly slides it out. He hears the drum of his pulse beating in his ears as he tries not to make a sound. Evan lifts the lid and stares down at the contents.

His shoulders drop. It doesn't look *that* special, he thinks, staring down at the pile of boring papers and letters. There's a photo in a frame with cracked glass – a few men in army uniform standing beside a helicopter, one of them looking like a much younger Griff. Evan pushes his hands beneath the stack of papers like he's doing a lucky dip, listening out for sounds of his mum moving. *EastEnders* will be over soon.

His fingers touch something cold near the bottom of the box. Something metal. He pulls it out, his eyes virtually exploding when he sees the tarnished cup, like the ones they give out on sports day. It's only small, no bigger than Evan's hand, but to him it's like buried treasure. Quickly, he tucks it under his hoody, trembling at the thought of what Mac is going to say when he sees it.

He freezes. A noise. His mum muttering something to herself. Then it's quiet again.

Chancing his luck, Evan scoops his hand deeper into the box, rummaging around until his feels something hard and square. He pulls it out, not caring what it is, just that it's going up his sweatshirt as well.

When he hears a bang downstairs along with Griff's voice, Evan pulls the bottom drawstring of his hoody tight before putting the lid on the box and shoving it back under the bed. His cheeks burn scarlet.

Footsteps on the stairs.

'What's all the noise up here, boy? You in bed yet? Give yer mother some peace.'

Evan virtually melts from fear. If he's caught, it won't be any normal beating. It'll be a punishment he won't get to remember. He flies out of the bedroom and runs into Rosie's tiny box room. He hears her snuffling and cooing contentedly.

'Sorry, Rosie,' he whispers, leaning over the cot, reaching down. He pinches the meaty part of her thigh as hard as he can through her towelling sleepsuit.

For a second, there's silence as Rosie stares up at him, her fist near her glistening lips, her eyes glassy and bewildered, her legs perfectly still.

And then she screams – her face puckered and her limbs thrashing as she makes a noise ten times worse than the kid next door who gives his mum the headaches. He reaches down into the cot and picks up his baby sister, holding her across his body so she conceals the items he's got stashed inside his hoody.

The door slams open behind him.

'What the—?'

Evan turns, jiggling the baby up and down as he stares at Griff's broad physique. He immediately smells the tang of beer.

'Think she had a nightmare,' Evan says, his voice suddenly high-pitched and fearful. 'I'll look after her,' he says, bouncing Rosie about.

'Get baby to sleep, and go to bed yerself, you big lunk.' Griff raises his hand high, making Evan flinch, shielding Rosie's head with his hand as he twists out of the way.

Relief surges through him when Griff leaves with only the threat lingering in the air. He puts his face down near Rosie's, smelling her sweet milky breath as he lowers her back down into her cot, his finger in the curl of her palm, her soft skin closing around him.

'Sorry, sorry, sorry,' he whispers, knowing she'll probably have a bruise tomorrow. Then he goes into his own room, jamming the door closed with the rubber wedge he nicked from school.

Sitting on the floor, his back against the door, Evan pulls the loot out from under his hoody. He sits the trophy on the thread-bare carpet, imagining Mac's face when he sees it. Carefully, he unhooks the catch on the black and gold box and opens the lid. It's only small, but looks important with its smart leather exterior.

Evan's mouth hangs open in awe when he sees the two identical badges set against the maroon velvet. Gold-coloured eagles with their wings spread wide sit on red enamel backgrounds, each one with tiny gold lettering underneath in a language that he doesn't understand.

'*Wick*ed,' he whispers. He can't wait to show Mac the treasure. He takes one of the badges out, pinning it onto his black hoody.

When he stares into his cracked mirror, he can hardly contain his excitement.

Later, in bed, with the badge pinned to his vest beneath his pyjama top and the other badge safely stashed in his school bag ready to give to Mac, Evan can't sleep; knows he won't get a wink as his fingers caress the cold metal eagle. And when sleep does eventually come, all he sees is Gem's terrified face when he finally gets the chance to teach her a lesson.

CHAPTER TWENTY-SIX

Jen

'Who's Madeleine, Mum?' Kieran asks.

I freeze momentarily as I stand at the kitchen sink, my rubber-gloved hands plunged in the hot soapy water.

'She was a colleague of your dad's, I think, love,' I say, forcing my hands to wring out the dishcloth.

'A colleague or friend?' Kieran pushes on.

I hear his leg jiggling, the heel of his trainer tap-tapping on the floor as he finishes his dinner. Thankfully, Scott is out of the house. I was hoping to spend the next hour or so with Kieran – plus have a reprieve from my thoughts, a moment of clarity to make a plan. But the note Scott left on the kitchen table – 'Back by nine' – plus Kieran's unexpected inquisition are not helping my state of mind. Scott completely ignored my threat of calling the police, not even mentioning it this morning, waving me off breezily as I went to work. And I could hardly make a scene in front of Kieran.

'A colleague. Why?' I turn, probably faster than I'd intended, and counter it with a smile.

Kieran stares at me, assessing me. He's such a young Jeremy sitting there – those loose, wayward curls, his wide-set eyes that always seem so intense. Kieran isn't as dark-haired as Jeremy was, but the high cheekbones, the angular jawbone, the way he carries himself make him seem like a living ghost, a constant reminder of the man I've lost. And it makes me love him even harder.

'Caitlin was asking,' he says.

I pull off my rubber gloves, one of them getting stuck. I just want to scream and tear it from my hand – but instead, I take a breath, keeping calm. I drag out a chair beside Kieran and sit down.

'How does Caitlin know about Madeleine?'

'She found out that her mum was stalking her on Insta. She said she went on the skiing trip with Dad.'

'What? Why… I don't think that's true.' I curse myself for sounding snappy – my son doesn't deserve that. I reach out for the note Scott left, nervously balling up the scrap of paper, praying that the gesture will somehow stop him coming back.

'Mum, did you and Dad trust each other?' Kieran asks. His leg starts jiggling again.

'What kind of question is that?' I feign a laugh.

'One that answers itself if you avoid it,' he says, those big eyes averted to the floor, the wall, the ceiling – anywhere but looking into mine.

'Of course we trusted each other,' I say. 'I just don't get why you're asking, love.'

Part of me wonders if I should just come out with it – with *everything*. My suspicions about Madeleine and Jeremy having an affair; that Scott – a random stranger – is the father of my baby, that I'm certain he drugged and raped me; how he's blackmailing me with horrific photos I didn't even know he'd taken, which is why we have a man neither of us knows staying in our house. Neutralise everything. Except it wouldn't neutralise anything. It would blow everything up beyond recognition. There would be no normal life for either of us ever again.

'What does any of this have to do with Caitlin? I'm confused.'

Kieran stares at me, opening his mouth to speak.

'By the way, how's the extra studying going?' I ask, suddenly desperate to change the subject.

'Caitlin thinks Dad and Madeleine were…' Kieran's nose wrinkles and he blinks hard several times, briefly covering his face with hands that seem too large for his skinny teenage body. 'She thinks they were having an affair. She overheard her mum talking about it to Chris, and when she checked her mum's phone, it was true. Rhonda had been stalking Madeleine so she reckons she must know something.' This time he manages to look me straight in the eye. 'I'm really sorry,' he adds, as though it's the grown-up thing to do.

Somehow, from some deep reserves within myself, I manage to answer. 'No, no, Kier, that's not true at all.' I place a hand on his. 'Don't you worry. Whatever Caitlin has overheard, she's very much mistaken. Your dad was *not* having an affair. He would never have done anything like that.' I manage a smile. 'It's unthinkable.'

'That's what I thought,' Kier says, though there's none of the relief I'd have expected. 'But Caitlin said she knows that Dad and Madeleine were on the ski trip together, and that she's checked out some of Madeleine's previous posts, and some locations matched up with where Dad was when he'd gone away. Caitlin was pretty fired up and angry about it. Maybe Madeleine knows what happened to him, how the accident happened. Is she even alive? Have you tried to contact her? She might know stuff.'

Oh, love, I want to say, while throwing my arms around him, comforting him. But I don't get a chance because suddenly there's a bang from the hallway – the front door opening and closing – and I never thought I'd actually feel grateful to Scott for anything, let alone entering my house, but I am right now.

'Hello, both,' Scott says, striding into the kitchen as if he's lived here years. My skin crawls at the sight of him, but for Kieran's sake, I smile and stand up as if he's welcome here.

'Cup of tea?' I offer – anything to keep him in the kitchen and avoid the remainder of the conversation with my son.

'You read my mind,' Scott says, placing a hand on my arm as I flick the kettle on. Kieran doesn't notice my shudder. He takes off his jacket and drapes it over the back of a chair. I catch the scent of him – something like fresh country air and aftershave. I tell myself it's unpleasant. 'How was work?' he asks.

'Fine.'

'You'll be on maternity leave before you know it,' Scott says, giving a sly look at Kieran. It makes me want to pour boiling water over him.

'Were you out property hunting?' I ask hopefully, not wanting to talk about babies or Jeremy or anything else vaguely touching on the knife edge that is my life.

'There's no point,' he replies. 'Every rental in the area gets snapped up the moment it comes on the market. With me working late most nights at the restaurant, I don't want to have to travel far. That's why staying here with you is so handy.' Again, Scott glances at Kieran. 'Thank you,' he says when I put a mug of tea in front of him, banging it down harder than I'd intended.

'I've got homework,' Kieran says in a way that yet again reminds me of his dad – an exasperated release that tells me our conversation is far from done.

'We can have a few games on the PlayStation later, if you fancy it,' Scott calls out to my son.

'Sure, cool,' Kieran says, his face brightening as he leaves the room, the sound of his footsteps heavy on the stairs.

Scott's fake smile repulses me. 'Sit,' he says to me, patting the seat beside him. 'I have another favour to ask.'

My skin goes cold. 'I'm all out of those,' I tell him, chastising myself for sounding riled. I need to keep calm, act like I'm not bothered. For now. The moment I show him I'm wavering, he gains control. Although something tells me it's too late for that.

'I won't get paid until the end of next month, so I could do with some cash. To tide me over.'

I stare at him. 'You've got a fucking nerve.'

'Don't be like that, Jennifer. Just a couple of grand until I get on my feet.'

'A couple of *thousand*? You agreed to leave this morning, for Christ's sake, and now you're asking for money?'

'I never agreed to anything, Jen. I don't know why you can't just accept that I'm here to stay, and just enjoy it. It makes perfect sense. Me, the father of your baby. You, a widow with a big house. What's the problem?'

'The fucking problem, Scott Shaw, is that you raped me.' I slam my hands down on the table, making his tea jump. I can't help myself. I'm boiling inside. 'And I'm left with this.' I jab a finger towards my stomach, flinching inwardly. It's not the baby's fault.

'Then why haven't you gone to the police? Why aren't I in an interview room being questioned and charged right now?' Scott shrugs, slowly shaking his head with a pitying look.

My hand reaches into my pocket and pulls out my phone. I don't take my eyes off him.

'Because you know it's a lie, Jennifer, that's why. You were drunk, playing away from home, and *you* wanted sex with *me* – an escape from your oh-so-less-than-perfect middle-class life – and now that you're pregnant, you're regretting it. You thought that there'd be no repercussions, that things would just pick up where you left off before the conference. Well, you're wrong, Dr Jennifer Miller. Very, *very* wrong. Life doesn't work like that.'

The slap is short, sharp and as hard as I can deliver it. Scott's head twists to the left to parry the blow. His hand comes up to his cheek, covering the smarting area. He stares at me for a moment, watching me as I'm unable to speak, my mouth hanging open.

'You're hormonal,' he says quietly. 'I forgive you. Now, go on. Call the police,' he says, eyeing my phone. 'Let's sort this out once and for all. I'll show them all the photographs and it will be done and dusted. Everything taken care of.'

I maintain my stare, my breathing tense and heavy in my chest. I've never felt so much hatred for a person. I close my eyes for a beat. 'You fucking bastard,' I spit. 'If I give you the money, will you leave?' I sound as pathetic as I feel.

'There you go,' Scott says with a satisfied smile, reaching out to take my wrists. 'That's more like the Jennifer I know. You're finally seeing sense. Let's agree on three thousand to begin with.'

Nothing around me seems real. It's as if I've woken up in my worst nightmare and there's no way out. 'And you'll really go? Leave me and my son alone? Leave the area… you could get a job somewhere else. You don't even have to pay me back.' I just need him gone from my life – my son and my baby's life. 'And I want you to delete those photos. All of them.'

'Jennifer, *Jennifer*,' he says, taking my hands again. 'Stop overcomplicating things. I'm not going anywhere. Don't you see? I'm in love with you, my darling. I have been since the moment I first set eyes on you.'

Before I get a chance to respond, I see bright car headlights sweep around the drive, briefly shining in through the window above the sink as a car swings round outside. I get up, dashing to the window to see who's here, hoping it's someone who'll save me from this hell. But the car continues to turn and, on the next go, I see its red tail lights as it speeds off down the drive towards the lane.

'That's odd,' I say, suddenly aware of Scott standing right behind me. His hand slips onto my waist. 'Whoever it is, they've gone again.'

'I don't think they arrived in the first place,' Scott says, his breath warm in my ear. 'That's my Mercedes,' he says quite calmly. 'Looks like your son has just stolen my car.'

CHAPTER TWENTY-SEVEN

Jen

The reality of Scott's words don't sink in at first.

'*Shit…*' I gasp, wriggling free from his grip. I charge through the kitchen and up the stairs. 'Kier?' I call out breathlessly, taking the steps two at a time. 'Kier, are you here?' Please let him be in his room doing his homework… *please.*

I shove open the door to my son's bedroom, my eyes scanning quickly about. Not at his desk, hunched over his laptop; not lying on his bed, tapping on his phone. Not sitting behind his drum kit, beating out a rhythm, and he's not lounging on the floor on his beanbag, listening to music. I race through to the small en suite bathroom, not caring if I'm invading his privacy.

'Kieran?' I call out, but the bathroom is empty too.

'Jesus Christ…' I pull at my hair, while my other hand goes to my stomach. Collecting myself, I go back down to the kitchen and grab my phone, dialling my son's number while Scott watches on, a smug look on his face. It rings out, going to voicemail. 'Kier, call me back? Just come home. You're not in trouble, OK? Just get back here now, love.' I try to disguise my shaking voice.

'A small drink to calm your nerves?' Scott says from across the kitchen. He's holding up one of Jeremy's prized bottles of whisky.

I stare at him, my face crumpling in disgust. 'No!' I snap. 'I don't want a bloody drink. I want my son to come back. Why the hell has he taken your car? How did he get the keys?'

Scott shrugs, seemingly unperturbed by events. 'I'd like to know myself,' he says calmly. 'Perhaps I left them on the hall table. He'd better not damage it.'

'I have to go out and look for him,' I say, grabbing my bag, incredulous that all he's concerned about is his stupid car. 'And you're coming with me,' I add, knowing he'll have to drive his car back when we find him. Thoughts of Kieran in a ditch, the car wrapped around a tree, or him speeding along the dual carriageway out of town fill my mind – or, God forbid, being pulled over by the police and being locked up in a cell for the night.

'Surely I should report my car stolen first?' Scott says, holding up his phone.

I feel the blood drain from my cheeks. 'No,' I tell him. 'Let me find him first. This isn't like him at all. He's upset about his dad… or perhaps he overheard us talking. Please don't report him… not yet.' I hate that I'm begging, my voice pleading.

Scott comes up to me and wraps his arms around me, making me tense. 'We'll get through this together,' he croons into my hair as his lips come down on my head. I force myself to play along for as long as I can stand, gritting my teeth before pushing away from him.

Then it occurs to me. '*Find My…*' I whisper, unlocking my iPhone. My mind is all over the place, my finger trembling as I log into the app. 'Please… *please…*' I say, waiting for the screen to resolve. We've always had family location sharing turned on, ever since Kieran got his first phone. Although Jeremy wasn't keen on it, often disabling his whereabouts, as he'd done just before the ski trip – though I can't stand to think what that meant now. We had far too many arguments about it, me reading one thing into his secrecy and him claiming another. Perhaps now the app will finally prove itself useful.

'His last known location…' I zoom in on the screen but it only shows me where he was heading a few minutes ago, rather than where he actually is now. 'He must have turned his phone off, or his battery has run out,' I say, jabbing my screen to refresh it.

'Let me see?' Scott says, leaning close.

'He was heading out of the village up the hill towards the reservoir,' I say, pulling on my jacket. 'Hurry,' I say, heading outside. 'It's a start at least.'

My legs are like jelly, my feet shaking on the pedals as I reverse my car, the wheels spinning in the gravel as I do a three-point turn and roar down the drive. It's fully dark now and I pull straight out onto the lane, pushing my car to its limits through the gears as I head into the village. The 'Slow Down' sign lights up, flashing my speed – forty-eight miles per hour – but I step on the accelerator even harder as I swing round the sharp bend onto the main street of Harbrooke. I barely register the lights glowing outside the pub, or the corner shop, still open, with a couple of people chatting outside, and neither do I notice the person about to step out onto the zebra crossing until they're halfway over. I jam on the brakes, just missing an old man staggering across, clearly fresh out of the pub.

'Calm down, Jennifer. You're not going to do the baby any good in this state,' Scott says, patting my thigh.

'Just look out for your car,' I tell him, wanting to add *on or off the road*, but I don't so as not to tempt fate. Kieran knows how to drive – well, as much as can be expected from trundling a quad bike around the field since the age of eight, and the old Land Rover when he could reach the pedals. Jeremy had our son learning how to drive from a young age, though the only actual on-road practice he'd gained were a couple of illicit tutorials late one evening in an empty supermarket car park. I grumbled at the time, but now I'm grateful for the limited experience he's had. It might just help keep him safe.

'Where the hell *are* you, Kier?' I say, scanning all the side turnings as we exit the other side of the village. I press a couple of buttons on my console and call Kieran's phone yet again. Nothing – this time it doesn't even ring. It goes straight to voicemail so I leave another pleading message for my son.

'Unlock my phone,' I bark at Scott, telling him the passcode. 'Refresh the Find My app. See if there's a new location showing.' *Please be OK, please be OK*, I pray silently.

Scott does as he's told. 'Nothing,' he says, gripping onto the door as I hurtle round the corner up past the entrance to the reservoir.

The lane narrows and the sky seems even darker up here as the lights of the village and the town beyond are obscured by the woodland as it closes in around us. I jam on the brakes, forced to slow down as two other cars approach from the opposite direction, pulling over onto the verge.

'Is it him?' I say, squinting out of the window to check the drivers of the other cars. 'Your registration plate?'

Scott leans forward. 'Not my car,' he says, his tone strangely flat – not angry, not concerned, not even a note of urgency. 'Pull over here,' he says before I've managed to get up any speed again. 'In this gateway.'

It's where I go into the woods for my morning runs, not that I've been on one of those lately.

'Did you see something?' I say, yanking the steering wheel sharply to the left and parking diagonally. I grab my phone off Scott. The app is still showing Kieran's last known location right about where we are now, within a couple of hundred yards or so.

'No, but look at your phone reception and 4G. It's as good as dead.' He gives me a look. 'If Kieran had driven through this black spot, it's likely his location would have updated again by now. There's a chance he's still nearby. And my guess is he's either in there…' Scott jabs a finger against the side window, gesturing to the woods. 'Or down by the reservoir.' He points with his other hand through my window, across the fields and the sharp incline to the old quarry. If I stood on the sill of my car, on tiptoe, I'd see the shimmering, inky surface of the water that, even in full sunlight, somehow always appears black and bottomless. I shudder.

'If he's in the woods, then where's your car?' I say, unclipping my seat belt and getting out. 'And what if his phone battery has died or he's turned it off? That would also explain him not showing up on the app.'

Scott pauses and I see his eyes flashing through the dark. 'My car? It's either in a ditch somewhere around here or perhaps down in the reservoir car park. Let's search for him here first.' Scott gets out and joins me by the bonnet as I contemplate the five-bar gate. 'And as for him turning off his phone, it's a possibility. But let's work on the assumption that it's poor reception for now.'

For a second, I see something akin to compassion and empathy in Scott's expression, as though he really does care – that he isn't out to destroy me and blackmail me for whatever he can get. But until I know Kieran is safe, I have to put all that out of my mind. Scott is the only help I have right now, unless I'm forced to call the police. And that fills me with dread.

'Kier-*an*…' I call out into the night, leaning over the gate. The night swallows up my voice. 'Kieran, are you out there?' My throat burns from yelling so loud.

'Kieran!' Scott yells too. 'Kieran, we're over here!' He grabs hold of the metal gate with both hands and rattles it hard, the locking chains making a clanking sound that echoes through the trees. Then the gate wobbles and squeaks again as Scott climbs over it, jumping down the other side. 'Coming?' he says, holding out his hand.

I hesitate, looking him in the eye, his features just visible by the moonlight as clouds scud past. There's something about his expression, something deep inside his eyes that makes everything seem even more terrible than it already is.

After a second, I put one foot on a bar halfway up the gate and hoist myself up, swinging my other leg over with Scott holding onto one hand firmly. I jump down the other side, careful to land lightly. I don't want to hurt my baby.

'Kieran?' I call as we walk through the woods, my feet trudging through the deep leaves still rotting down from autumn. We both have our phone torches on, illuminating a path ahead of us, making the trees appear silver in the electric light. 'Where are you, Kier?' I yell again, already knowing it's futile. There's no good reason for Kieran to be in the woods. But I follow Scott anyway, starting to think that his theory about my son being here is less and less likely.

'Don't you think we've gone far enough?' These woods have always seemed endless, as though they change every time I come up. I never seem to do the same run twice.

I stop, grabbing onto the trunk of a tree to steady myself. The ground is uneven and littered with roots, even more treacherous in the dark.

'I don't think we've gone nearly far enough,' Scott says, drawing up beside me. I feel the warmth of his body and breath on me, the light from his phone shining on the ground as it hangs down by his side.

What the hell am I doing? I think, suddenly terrified that I'm in the middle of the woods at night with the man I believe raped me.

'I'm going back to the car,' I say, shuddering. 'Kieran isn't up here.' I take one last look at my phone, refreshing the app just in case, and that's when I see it resolving – grindingly slowly – but changing locations nevertheless. Perhaps a lucky patch of reception for me and for my son at just the right time. 'Look!' I say, hating that I grab onto Scott's arm as I show him.

'Look indeed,' he says, ignoring my phone. Instead, he bends down where the torch has lit up the ground and brushes away some leaves. He retrieves something and holds it up, turning it round and round, just at the same time I see the icon on my screen indicating that Kieran is close by – down at the reservoir, by the looks of it.

'Oh, thank *God*,' I say, the relief making me feel weak. Then my eyes flash across to Scott's face and then down to what he's holding. It's a skull – small, fragile and greying from age with part of its lower jaw crumbling away. I can't help the gasp.

CHAPTER TWENTY-EIGHT

Jen

'Shall I get my *Gray's Anatomy* out to prove it?' I say when we're home. I'm exhausted. Pregnancy hormones, relief, fear and anger make for a heady cocktail. The main thing is that Kieran is safe. Remorseful and ashamed, but unscathed. One worry ticked off the ever-increasing list.

Scott examines the little skull, setting it down on the kitchen worktop. There's mud between its remaining teeth and dirt crusted between the plates of its head. 'You're the doctor,' he says, giving me a sly look.

I cup my hands around my mug of tea. 'It's some kind of rodent,' I reply dismissively. 'Or maybe a rabbit.' I check my sour tone, hating that I should feel grateful to Scott for agreeing not to call the police about Kieran stealing his car. *Oh the irony*, I think. It's me who should be calling the police about him.

Except I can't.

I pick up the skull and go to drop it in the bin. I don't want it in the house and have no idea why Scott bothered to bring it back.

'Don't,' he says, grabbing my wrist. 'Kieran might like to see it.'

'Doubtful,' I reply, pulling away from him.

'Oh, I don't know. I'm sure there's a story or two about it that he might like to hear. You know. Boys' stuff.'

I stare at Scott, trying to fathom what he's talking about, trying to gauge and read the look in his eyes, where his mind is going. I swallow, maintaining a neutral expression. I can't afford to let emotions get the better of me. 'He's not a little kid, you know,' I say, turning my back on him and heading for the sitting room.

Kieran is upstairs licking his wounds, even though I'd restrained myself from yelling at him when we found him. I was just relieved he was unharmed and, whatever reasons he had for taking the car, they didn't matter any more. Besides, I didn't want to embarrass him too much in front of Caitlin down by the reservoir, nor on the way home, with Caitlin's bike slung in the rear of my four-wheel drive and the pair of them sitting sheepishly in the back – well, not before I'd got to the bottom of what the hell he was thinking.

'Kieran?' I'd called out earlier, running down towards the water. We'd spotted the Mercedes as soon as I'd swung my vehicle into the reservoir car park. It's was tucked out of sight of the lane and the only car there, given that it had been dark for a while and all the walkers had gone home.

I'd followed the path down to the water, immediately spotting two familiar figures hunched together on the bench, looking out across the black, moonlit ripples of Bowman's Pool. Scott had gone straight over to his car to check it out, but I became aware of footsteps behind me as he followed on.

'Kieran, are you OK? What's going on?' I'd skidded to a stop on the shingled area beside the bench. 'Why did you take Scott's car?' There was a small cluster of picnic tables, along with some swings and a wooden climbing frame a few metres away. In the summer, it's a favourite haunt for the teenagers from the village to hang out, going up there on their bikes and mopeds, smoking weed, having a few beers and annoying those who've come for a quiet walk. Along with the ghosts of the past – the terrible thing that happened to Lenny Taylor years ago – the place has an eerie feel, as though the quarried land is somehow whispering its secrets.

'Kieran…?' I'd said again, watching as my son slowly turned his head towards me. Caitlin had hung hers, briefly covering her face. 'Does your mum know you're here?' I'd asked her, doubting that very much. Caitlin confirmed my fears by giving her head a brief shake. Then I saw her bike lying on the ground beside the bench.

Kieran shrugged. 'Let it go, Mum,' he'd said. I barely recognised him in that moment, especially when I saw the stump of a gone-out cigarette between his thumb and forefinger. The only positive was that it was from a packet and not a roll-up, indicating it wasn't weed. Then I spotted the glowing tip of a cigarette between Caitlin's fingers, too.

'Let it go?' I shoved my hands on my hips, trying to contain my anger. 'You stole Scott's car. You could have killed yourself, or someone else.' I took his hand, trying to make him stand up, but it was useless. My son felt heavier than ever – weighed down with grief, I'd thought, as the moon flashed out from behind a cloud briefly, lighting up his teary eyes. 'OK,' I'd said, releasing him and pacing about. 'Let's just get home. We can discuss it later. Caitlin, I'll give you a lift home too. Your bike will fit in the back. You can't be cycling alone in the dark.'

'Sorry, Dr Miller,' she'd said, reverting to the formal when usually she'd call me Jen.

Both kids were mute on the journey home, with Scott merely uttering a 'No harm done' to Kieran and patting him on the back when I ushered them into my car. *No harm done?* I wanted to yell at the top of my voice into someone's face – I just wasn't sure whose. I got in the driver's seat and ferried us all home.

'So… so you're definitely not going to report him?' I ask Scott when he sits down beside me in the living room. Arrests, a criminal record, community service, missing his exams and failed university applications all flash through my mind. I need to protect my son.

'No point,' he says, sounding far more reasonable than is warranted. A ploy by him, no doubt. Increasing the debt – real or imagined – that he seems to think I owe him. 'There's not a mark on my car. Your boy clearly knows how to drive.'

'Thank you,' I say. 'It's been tough for him lately, losing his dad. And things aren't great at school.' The pang of guilt deep inside me doesn't go unnoticed. I've not been the mother Kieran has needed these last few weeks, wrapped up in my own grief, not there to help him unravel his. I vow to change.

Scott makes a kind of rumbling in the back of his throat, but says nothing. We sit in silence for a while, listening to the sound of the fire crackling in the wood burner. Scott had stoked the embers when we got back with the logs he'd previously brought in – usually Jeremy's job. It barely seems possible that only two months ago my husband was here, working in his study, planning his trip to Switzerland, reading beside the fire, destroying me at chess, doing jobs out in the garden and paddock with Kieran, or sinking a few pints down at the local with Chris.

And now Scott is sitting beside me in his place – a stranger I met in a bar – his feet slipping so far under my lonely table that I don't ever see him leaving. With those photographs, he can do whatever he likes – only made worse by Kieran's behaviour tonight. I've gone over the newspaper headlines a hundred times already…

Respected GP shamed in sordid affair while husband plunges to his death…

Whichever way I look at it, the incriminating photographs would end my career. I'd be struck off without a backward glance, never practise again. But worse would be what Kieran would think of me, that any shred of respect he may have left for me would be gone. I know that deep down there's a simmering resentment – that if I'd worked harder at my marriage then his dad wouldn't have had to have an affair, that we'd have all gone away as a family at New Year, or stayed home together, and in some miraculous sliding-doors moment, his dad wouldn't be dead.

'Are you close to your parents?' A ridiculous question to ask Scott under the circumstances, but I need to break the silence. It's becoming bigger than the space in my head. Plus, I want to find out more about him, who this man in my house really is. What I might have on him to prise him out of my life.

'No,' he answers without looking at me. 'They're both dead. We weren't close.' His tone makes it sound rehearsed, as though it's a stock reply.

'I'm sorry to hear that,' I say. 'Kieran is so much like his dad. It almost hurts to look at him. They were very close.'

'Tell me about your husband, Jennifer,' he says. His arm is draped along the back of the sofa, his fingers toying with my hair. Something tells me not to move, to let him do it. I don't want to admit it's because I have to keep him onside.

'He was a good man,' I say, realising it sounds exactly the same as Scott's stock reply about his parents. 'Creative, loving, a good father, loyal…' I swallow the lump in my throat when I say *loyal*. 'Sometimes he was difficult to live with, but he was the love of my life. I miss him terribly.'

'I see,' Scott says flatly.

'Jeremy was a rich, deeply intelligent, complicated, ever-changing man, as though…' I pause, thinking, testing… praying that the memories of my husband aren't fading. 'As though—'

'As though there'd been a whole lot of bad in his life?' Scott finishes for me, one eyebrow raised.

I stare at him. 'No, that wasn't what I was going to say.'

'As though he was waiting for the past to catch up with him?'

I shake my head, wondering why Scott is suggesting these things. 'No. It was as though his body wasn't a big enough place for his mind to live, as though he felt trapped, frustrated, unfulfilled.'

As though he felt trapped, frustrated and unfulfilled with me, I've thought a thousand times since his death.

'Well, he doesn't have to worry about that any more, does he?' Scott adds with an infuriating smile.

CHAPTER TWENTY-NINE

Rhonda

Kieran's arrived safely, Rhonda texts to Jen, knowing this will give her friend some peace of mind. She's dished out her own kind of fury in Caitlin's direction after her and Kieran's little escapade the other night, not quite getting to the bottom of which of them thought it was a smart idea to meet after dark at the reservoir. Caitlin knew it was out of bounds at night, and Kieran, quite frankly, should have known better. And stealing a car, for heaven's sake. Poor Jen, she thinks. She has enough to deal with as it is.

When Kieran had turned up on his bike for a half-term study session with Caitlin, she'd thought he looked pale as he sheepishly came into the kitchen. Rhonda had resisted making a wisecrack about what flash car he'd nicked to get there, and Jen had begged her not to mention the incident to Chris, who might be duty-bound to report it. She'd agreed, knowing there were some things best left under a cop's radar, even off duty.

Rhonda stares at the thick wodge of Jeremy's manuscript sitting on the bed in front of her. She doesn't feel inclined to carry on reading it, and certainly not after what she discovered within its pages in her office at school the other day – the words branded in her mind forever.

Since Jeremy had given her the three hundred or so pages at the end of last year, she'd barely got round to reading even a chapter before he'd died. It wasn't that she wasn't interested, rather that work and life and then Christmas had taken over, and she'd found herself losing track of the story and had had to start again a couple of times.

She didn't tell Jeremy this, of course, but to her the book had seemed like a self-indulgent, semi-autobiographical mash-up, verging on, or pretending to be, literary, with a dash of random intrigue thrown in. It wasn't something Rhonda imagined would set the publishing world on fire – not that she knew much about that sort of thing. Jeremy had only given it to her to read because she was an English teacher… because he *trusted* me, she thinks, balling up her fists.

But then everything had changed since she'd stumbled across *those* words in her office at school the other day when she'd decided to have another read – a single page that had slipped out of the book leaving her with a sick feeling. And how awful that Jen had knocked on her office door only a few minutes after she'd set eyes on it. The irony of the timing hadn't evaded her. How could such a betrayal have happened right under her friend's nose? Poor Jen – while she was out working hard, earning a living to support her family, keeping everything going, giving Jeremy the opportunity to live out his dream – he was undeniably having an affair behind her back.

But where did that leave Rhonda now?

'In a moral bloody mess, that's where,' she mutters to herself, tapping the top of the manuscript, wondering how on earth the letter had even ended up between the pages. Had Jeremy *wanted* her find it? Is that why he'd given her his book to read? But why? It made no sense. Or maybe it ended up there accidentally. All she knows is that she doesn't know what to do. Tell Jen about it, or do nothing?

Rhonda picks up the letter again – a love letter from someone signing themselves off as 'M'.

It's written on A4 paper – thicker than the rest of the manuscript and a good-quality stock with a pale-blue tint and gold edging. Expensive paper that was once folded into thirds, most likely to fit into an envelope, with the words printed rather than handwritten.

She hears Caitlin and Kieran mumbling to each other in low voices from across the landing, hopefully discussing the essay question Rhonda has set them for the morning, before turning back to the letter.

Dearest Jeremy, it begins. Rhonda's hand shakes as she reads it again, almost knowing the words verbatim now.

You'll never know how much I cherish the rare moments we spend together. Being with you feels as natural as breathing. It's only when we're apart that I feel as though I'm suffocating, choking, that there's no oxygen in my blood. I live for the times I know I'll get to see you, especially when we can be completely alone. As rare as an eclipse. But cherished by me.

So that's why I'm writing to you again (did you get my other letter? – you didn't reply), because I want you to know how much you mean to me and how much I love you. I've loved you for so long, I can't even remember a time when I didn't. Not loving you doesn't even seem possible to me any more. I can't imagine it. And I know you love me too. I've seen it in your eyes, the way you look at me, even though you find it hard to admit it your feelings to me. When you kissed me that time when we were last away together – those beautiful few days that I'll cherish for the rest of my life – nothing else in the whole world mattered apart from your lips on mine. You make me feel special like no one else can.

I can't wait until I can see you again. I'm literally counting down the days until we go away. Are you? Do you wonder how it will feel to spend some proper time together? I only hope that one day we can be together always, shout out about how we feel and not care what anyone else thinks. We're just two people in love.

Until then and until we see each other again, my darling Jeremy, please know that I think about you every minute of every day.

All my love, M xxx

Rhonda leans back against her pillows, feeling nauseous. Self-indulgent drivel, she thinks. Almost as bad as the pages it's stuffed between. Not only would it utterly destroy Jen to know someone wrote this to her husband, but they can't even spell properly. 'Eclypse' jarred with Rhonda the first time she read it, and now the error adds an almost comical feel to the clichéd words – words that she can't help thinking were written by someone whose first language wasn't English.

'Burn it,' Rhonda says to herself. 'That's what I should do.' But she can't, not until she finds out who wrote it. *Or*, she thinks, *not until I prove that it was Madeleine.*

Rhonda rereads it, but with a French accent in her head, before putting it back between the pages of the manuscript. She wonders where the other letter that's mentioned has got to – if it's in Jeremy's study, perhaps, hidden away somewhere. It occurs to her she should find it, get rid of it in case Jen stumbles across it. The poor woman doesn't need any more pain.

Rhonda shoves the manuscript back in the carrier bag and slides it under the bed. Jeremy's book wasn't what she came up here to deal with – she'd merely been distracted by that, especially with Madeleine's Instagram account still playing on her mind. She's starting to get a handle on the woman – the woman who had seen fit to ruin her best friend's life.

Rhonda drags the cardboard boxes she'd brought back from school over to the bed. It's as she's reaching into one to take out a load of photos that there's a tap at her door, followed by a head peeking round.

'Hey, Mum,' Caitlin says. Her eyes flick to Rhonda's hands. 'Is it OK if we have some of that leftover curry for lunch?'

Rhonda smiles, rolling her eyes. 'Well, sure, you could if it was actually lunchtime.' She glances at her watch, tilting the photos away from her daughter. 'It's only half past ten. Have you written any of that essay yet?'

Caitlin makes a face. Rhonda notices that she's put on a bit more make-up than usual today, and she can't help noticing that her hair's done differently, too, how it suits her face pinned up like that.

'Some of it,' she says. 'I think Kier is struggling a bit. He seems… distracted. I've left him having a read of what I've written of my essay so far in case it helps him.'

'How about you both have a cuppa and some of those mini chocolate muffins? Maybe the sugar will give your brains a boost.' Rhonda grins but it's clear something has caught Caitlin's eye. She comes over to the bed, her head turned sideways as she stares at the pictures and other bits of paper Rhonda is clutching.

'What's all this?' she says, sitting down and reaching inside the box. She pulls out a couple of old newspaper clippings that Rhonda hasn't got round to looking at yet.

'Just some old stuff from school to sort through,' Rhonda says. 'It was going to get chucked out, but you know what I'm like with old photos and memorabilia.'

'From before St Quentin's was private?'

'Uh-huh.'

Rhonda isn't sure she wants Caitlin looking at the clippings, not with what she knows is in some of the newspaper reports about the toddler's murder.

'C'mon, you,' Rhonda says, giving Caitlin a playful tap. 'Stop procrastinating and get on with your work. I'll take you out for pizza later if you crack on.'

Caitlin's face lights up. 'And Kieran?'

Rhonda nods. 'I'll ask Jen along too.'

'Deal,' Caitlin says, leaving Rhonda to peruse the contents of the boxes.

It's moments later that her heart skips at the sight of the head and shoulders mugshot of the child killer – a pale-faced kid of around twelve or thirteen, though he barely looks it – squarely facing the camera. He has a vacant and remorseless look in his eyes, as though he doesn't give a jot that he murdered an innocent toddler. Rhonda knows the grandmother still lives in the village, and word is that she's lived her entire life alone in the shadow of her guilt.

Her eyes skim the details. *Toddler beaten and bruised… naked… strangulation… drowned…* She can't stand to read on. Another piece, written after the boy's sentencing, details how he bragged to the court about his crime, that he saw himself as a hero and the murder of the toddler as vengeance for his mother's subsequent death.

'Sounds like one seriously messed-up, personality-disordered, evil freak,' Rhonda whispers to herself, spotting his full name printed beneath his mugshot. 'Evan Locke,' she reads, almost tasting the evil in his name.

She's about to fold up the clippings but stops. She stares, wide-eyed, at the boy's clothing in the mugshot, squinting, thinking she's probably just mistaken. But to double-check, she photographs the image on her phone, like Chris did the other day, which allows her to zoom in on the distinctive badge that Evan Locke has pinned to his T-shirt.

It's grainy, but… 'But I *swear* I've seen that somewhere before,' she says, frowning and shaking her head, unable to place it.

Thinking she's probably getting freaked out and carried away by the macabre story, she shoves the clippings aside and gets on with sorting through the photographs. She wants to find all the pictures with Jeremy in so that she can give them to Jen later.

CHAPTER THIRTY

Jen

'I'm *so* glad you texted,' I tell Rhonda when the teens have gone to help themselves up at the restaurant's salad bar. 'I really needed to get out.' She doesn't know how much I mean that.

'You haven't been answering my calls,' she replies. 'I was worried I'd done something.'

I shake my head. 'Oh God, no… no. I'm so sorry. It's not you.' I tap my phone, sitting on the table beside me, thinking up an excuse. 'It keeps going onto silent mode for some reason. And my landline has been playing up.' I roll my eyes, trying to make light of it. I can't tell her that I think Scott has been trying to isolate me, prevent me from talking to family or friends. The moment she suspects I don't want him there, that I can't get rid of him, she'll tell Chris. And I know for certain he'd intervene – and I can't have that. So I smile at Rhonda, pretending everything is fine.

'Is Scott still staying with you?'

'Yes, I said he could stay a bit longer. He's had a run of bad luck.' I take a big swig of my drink to prevent myself from saying anything I'll regret.

'It's just… I'm a bit confused about why he said he didn't know Jeremy.' Rhonda snaps a breadstick in half and takes a bite. 'Doesn't that seem weird to you?'

It's the tone of her voice that tells me she's already suspicious about his presence – that, and the way she glances over at the kids to check if they're coming back to the table. She wants answers before they return.

'Oh… um… I have no idea why he told you that. Maybe you heard him wrong? I told you how they met… on set during the filming of a documentary.' I nod, even convincing myself it's true as I take another large sip of my orange juice, wishing it was something stronger.

Rhonda frowns. 'I see. And you've definitely met him before?'

'Of course. In a bar like he told you, and… and he's been to our place loads of times.'

'Jen…' She places a hand on my arm. Looks behind me to the salad bar again. 'I'm getting a really bad vibe about this. Something's not right.'

'There's no need to worry. Scott had lent Jeremy some money for… um… a film project ages ago that didn't get off the ground. He doesn't want people to know that Jeremy never paid him back.' I grab a breadstick and take a bite, instantly wishing I hadn't. My mouth goes so dry I can hardly swallow. I let out a cough, glugging down more of my drink. 'It's pure coincidence he moved to the area recently, so he decided to look me up. And he's been so kind saying I don't have to pay him the money back, which is why I'm doing him… the favour in return.'

The sudden flush in my cheeks, the way I'm fiddling with my hair, touching my nose, clearing my throat and swallowing don't help my credibility. Rhonda's expression tells me she doesn't believe me for a second.

Thankfully, a waiter comes, leaning over Kieran's chair as he delivers plates of dough balls, several pizzas and extra cutlery. We move things about to make room on the table, and then Rhonda bends down to pick up Kieran's jacket when it gets knocked onto the floor. As she's shaking it out, something falls out of the pocket, clattering and skidding under the table. She bends down to retrieve it just as the kids come back to the table, their plates piled high as they chatter between them. Probably the only two teenagers in the place discussing Arthur Miller.

'Could you fit any more food on your plate, Kier?' I nudge him as he sits down.

'Probably,' he says with a laugh as he bites into a piece of garlic bread. It's as Rhonda is sitting up again that Kieran spots something in her hand and lunges at her, swiping whatever it is that she's found, his face burning beetroot as he shoves it back in his jacket pocket behind him.

'Thanks,' is all he mutters, clearing his throat and dropping his head forward so his eyes are hidden behind his curly, wayward fringe.

I glance at Rhonda as she watches my son, her eyes boring into him. If it's anything worrying, I know she'll tell me later.

As I tuck into the pizza, Kieran's embarrassed expression reminds me of last summer, when we were all down at Croyde for those couple of weeks. I didn't expect to find the envelope of pictures under Kieran's mattress when I stripped his sheets. He's a sixteen-year-old lad, and I'm not so naive to think that he wouldn't be interested in images like those, but I'd assumed that teenagers these days got their exploratory kicks online. I figured if he was going to do it, then actual photos were probably a gentler option with nothing to click on leading him down a darker path, though I was concerned about the girls' ages.

They were posing provocatively in low-cut crop tops and shorts and, at a push, they could pass as eighteen, I supposed. While I wasn't comfortable about them being in his possession, I wasn't about to tear a strip off him on holiday. I'd planned on offering a few motherly words at a more appropriate time, when we were back home. Meantime, I decided I'd take the pictures and keep them in my room.

But then Kieran had walked in on me and caught me red-handed.

'What the fuck, Mum?' he'd said, slamming the bedroom door shut as he'd come inside. The wooden walls of the Cape Cod-style property shook.

'Sorry, love,' I'd said, smiling so he didn't feel embarrassed. 'Just thought your sheets could do with a wash.' But it hadn't come out right, and he'd snatched the pictures and the envelope from me.

'You don't understand,' he'd said tearfully. Not the reaction I'd expected. His face was a mix of teenage angst and anger as he tried to contain his emotions.

'Believe me, as a doctor and a mum, I *do* understand, love.' My voice had been calm and soothing. I didn't want to send him into a tailspin of guilt, and certainly not on holiday.

Kieran shook his head vigorously. 'No, no, you *don't*. You can't possibly. I don't look at them. It's not like that. I think… I think they're disgusting. It's sick. So fucking sick you wouldn't believe.'

And then he'd turned away and covered his face, letting out a series of frustrated sobs – something I'd not seen him do in a long while. I'd wondered if I should get Jeremy in for a chat with him, hoping father to son would feel more appropriate for Kieran. But Jeremy had taken Caitlin on a bike ride to the local fish shop to get supplies for dinner.

'The pictures aren't sick, Kier,' I'd said, going up to him and wrapping him in a hug. 'It's natural to be curious. But they're perhaps a bit inappropriate, especially if you don't know the girls' ages, or whether they properly consented to having them taken or shared.' I'd waited for a response then, but he was silent. 'Do you know them? Are they from school?' I felt him shake his head against me. The envelope was in his hand, dangling down by his side. Slowly, I reached down and teased it from him. He relinquished it without question.

'I'll look after them for now, OK?' I'd said and, after trying to lighten things up with talk of beach games later, I'd taken the envelope to my bedroom and hidden it in the lining of my suitcase. I'd not thought much more of it and, as far as I know, it's probably still there.

'Penny for them,' Rhonda says now.

'Holidays, actually,' I say, which gets the teens' attention too. 'I was just thinking back to last year, all of us in Devon.'

Rhonda gives a little nod as she takes another slice of pizza. 'Good times,' she says, knowing as well as I do that if or when we do it again, we'll be a man down.

'I think we could all use another holiday this summer. How about it, guys?' I ask, thankful the conversation has veered away from Scott. 'A trip down to the beach house?' I think I can manage that, think I can force myself to do it for Kieran's sake. It'll be something to look forward to again once his exams are over. And by then, I'll have somehow got rid of Scott.

'Sounds wonderful,' Rhonda chips in. 'I know Chris would be up for it.'

'Did you and Jeremy go away together when you were at school?' Caitlin asks me.

'We weren't actually friends at school, not like you two,' I reply, adding a laugh as I think back. 'That only happened once we got to university. And to be honest, it was a case of a familiar face in a sea of thousands. We were the only two from our year who went to Leeds, though we were on very different courses. We met at the Drama Society.'

'Sounds like you were any port in a storm, if you ask me,' Caitlin replies in a low voice. 'Ouch!' she then squeaks, as Rhonda gives her a nudge under the table.

'Think before you speak, Caitlin,' Rhonda says, rolling her eyes and mouthing *Sorry* at me.

'It's fine,' I say, though I wonder how much truth there is in what Caitlin said. Jeremy and I had never really had much to do with each other at school. But he must have known the company I kept back then, the kind of girl it turned me into. And if I'm honest, it left me with a bad taste in my mouth. If I met my younger self now, I'd be giving her a very stern talking-to about how to treat people, who to mix with, about not taking advantage of those who clearly didn't fit in. Truth is, I am ashamed of my younger self.

'So,' Rhonda says, lifting a piece of pizza high off the tray until its strings of cheese break. 'After this, how about we all go back to your place, Jen, and play a couple of games. You know, like we used to.'

It's true – it's what we did when things were right, when things were normal. A few drinks, some music on, silliness and chatter, and Rhonda would stop over the night.

'Sure, that's a great idea,' I say immediately – mainly because it diverts the conversation, but also because it's what I need. And then I remember Scott.

CHAPTER THIRTY-ONE

Rhonda

Rhonda watches Jen as she gets out of her car once they're all back at the barn, unable to decide if she looks as though she's going to implode with stress or burst from relief. Noticing that Scott's car isn't here, Rhonda suspects it's the latter. The more she thinks about it, the more uncomfortable she feels about him staying with Jen, what his intentions are. Something doesn't add up. And she wants – no, *needs* – to find out what it is.

But also preying on her mind is what fell out of Kieran's jacket pocket at the restaurant. It was only after she'd picked it up off the floor that she'd got a glimpse of it – just for a second or two before Kieran had snatched it from her. The badge looked shockingly familiar – the distinctive gold eagle, the red background – though she couldn't be totally certain. She knew Jeremy was into militaria and had a collection of items, making her wonder if Kieran had looked through them and found the badge, wanting a memento so he had something of his father's to keep close. It made sense, and was most likely why she'd recognised it earlier from the newspaper photograph. She'd perhaps seen Kieran wearing it somewhere before, but hadn't thought anything of it at the time.

But then that left the question: why was *Jeremy* in possession of a badge that she believed to be identical to the one Evan Locke was wearing in his police mugshot?

'You can have a small one, surely?' Rhonda says, bottle of wine in her hand as they gather in the kitchen.

'You're supposed to be my guilty conscience, not the devil on my shoulder,' Jen replies. But she takes another wine glass from the cupboard anyway, indicating about an inch with her fingers. 'I'm enjoying not drinking. Gives me a clearer head.'

'I've got something in the car you might like to see,' Rhonda continues. 'I didn't want to bring them in in front of Kieran, not until I've shown you first. Hang on a minute.' She puts down her glass and goes out to the drive, beeping her car unlocked and retrieving the box of photos that she'd sorted through earlier. Back in the kitchen, she dumps it on the worktop. Jen is tapping something on her phone, a frown on her face.

'All OK?' Rhonda asks.

'Yes, yes... fine.' Jen is still distracted.

'I was going through some old school archives. Well, old school crap mostly. But there were some absolute gems in there.' Rhonda pats the top of the box.

'Some *whats*?' Jen's head whips up.

'Gems. You know, treasures.'

Jen stares at her until Rhonda feels uncomfortable. It's as if she's torn between reacting to whatever she's doing on her phone and what Rhonda has just said. Perhaps bringing the photos here was a bad idea, she thinks. But it's too late now, Jen's hand is inside the box.

'Yes, yes of course,' Jen says, clearing her throat as she takes out some pictures without looking at them. Her stare is still fixed hard on Rhonda. She shakes her head. 'Sorry, I thought you meant something else.'

'I just meant the photographs, Jen, that's all. I found them at school,' Rhonda says in an uncertain voice. 'I thought you might want some – but of course, I don't want them to upset you. Look...' Rhonda takes one of the photos from Jen's fingers and points to a face in a class photograph. 'It's Jeremy.' She laughs. 'That hair,' she says. 'Unmistakable.'

Jen takes the photo again and holds it close, wiping a finger under her eye. 'Christ…' she says. 'This takes me back.'

'Good memories, I hope?' Rhonda says, wondering if she's done the wrong thing.

'Little did we all know,' she whispers, looking through more of the pictures and shaking her head. 'God, I remember him,' she says. 'He was a maths genius. And that girl was amazing at art. I wonder what happened to them all.'

'You're in a couple of the class photos somewhere,' Rhonda says. 'And one of the cross-country running team.'

But Jen isn't listening. She's pulled the newspaper clippings about the murder from the bottom of the box that now, Rhonda thinks with hindsight, she should really have left at home. Being reminded of a gruesome death from her schooldays probably isn't helpful.

'I'll take those back for the school library to deal with, I think,' Rhonda says about the cuttings.

'No… no, I want to read them,' Jen says, sitting down at the breakfast bar.

'Did you know him?' Rhonda asks, pointing to the mugshot of the child killer. 'Evan Locke?'

'Everyone knew him,' she replies flatly. Jen stares blankly at the picture, but then Rhonda sees her eyes skimming across the piece in the local paper. 'Or rather, they knew *of* him,' she adds. 'He was one of those… loner types. Didn't really have many… friends.'

Rhonda nods, thinking about it, wondering what it takes for a teacher or a parent to notice evil in a child. She wonders where he is now, if he's since been released, perhaps given a new identity, a new life, allowed to get on with his days while the dead child's family will never stop suffering.

'Look at Jeremy in this photo,' Rhonda says, hoping to distract Jen away from the gory details. She'd read through all the cuttings earlier and felt sickened. A three-year-old lured away from his gran's back garden, taken down to the reservoir where he was beaten before being dumped in the deep water. One newspaper report after the trial implied Evan Locke had had an accomplice, but that he had consistently refused to say who, almost as if he wanted to keep the 'glory' of his crime to himself.

Jen looks up when Rhonda flaps the photo about, insisting she take notice.

'Oh my *God*,' Jen says, her tone sounding brighter again. 'That was on our last sports day. They used to do a fancy dress race for the seniors' last year. Jeremy kept that kilt. It's probably still in the house somewhere, maybe the loft,' she says, pointing at him wearing it. 'Just look at his skinny legs!'

'So was Jeremy actually Scottish, then?' Rhonda asks, remembering how he'd sometimes put on a funny accent, not least when under the influence of a few drams.

'His father and grandparents were,' Jen explains. 'He had a bit of an accent at school, but it wasn't from living in Scotland. He liked to ham it up, put it on and make everyone think he was from the Highlands just to be different. Pure Jeremy,' she says fondly. 'He really should have been on the stage.'

'C'mon, hurry up you two,' comes a voice from the doorway. It's Caitlin and she's holding the lid for the Cards Against Humanity box.

'Uh-oh,' Rhonda says, sliding off her stool. She tops up her wine before following her daughter. 'Come on, Jen,' she says, turning back to her friend. 'Put that stuff aside for now. You can look at it another time.' And in her head, she makes a mental note to take the cuttings with her when she leaves tomorrow.

*

Rhonda watches her friend, a warm feeling growing inside her. Though it could be the wine she's consumed, or the heat from the fire as she sits on the rug around the coffee table with the others. But for the first time in a long time, Jen seems relaxed. Both Kieran and Caitlin are rolling around on the rug, tears streaming down their faces. It's good to see Jen forget everything, even if just for an hour or two.

'Oh… oh my God, *Mum*. I can't believe you actually just said those words. Jesus Christ, mums shouldn't… they really shouldn't speak like that.'

Jen tries to stifle another spray of laughter. 'Let me tell you, my dearest son. This game does not shock me. As a GP, I have heard and seen everything. *Absolutely* everything.'

'What, even "Grandpa's massive schlong"?' Rhonda asks, sending the kids into fits again.

'Yeah, but Mum, pairing it with "I like to spray *blank* with squirty cream" isn't something your son should ever have to hear in his lifetime.'

'You're welcome,' Jen says, standing up from the floor and stretching out. 'Anyone want anything from the kitchen?' she says, still grinning. 'I'm going to put the kettle on.' But then the smile lines on her face fall away as she hears a noise that sounds a lot like the front door opening. Suddenly she's as alert as a fox. 'I'll be back in a minute,' she adds in a serious voice before taking a deep breath and striding off.

'Right, you two,' Rhonda says. 'Let's take a quick break and then play some Pictionary, yeah?'

Kieran and Caitlin agree, before they both dive into their phones as Rhonda leaves the room. If that noise was Scott coming back, then she wants to use it to her advantage while Jen is distracted. She doesn't know if or when she'll get another chance. She feels bad for worming her way into the house tonight, engineering a gathering 'for old times' sake', yet she doesn't see she has much choice. If she doesn't do this soon, then someone is going to get hurt.

A quick glance into the kitchen tells Rhonda that Scott has indeed returned, and that Jen is embroiled in conversation with him. Briefly, she sees his hands gesturing, him pacing about. Jen recoils at something he says, but she's too engrossed to notice Rhonda. She slips away and heads to Jeremy's study, turning the handle slowly. Most doors in this old place creak and she doesn't want to draw attention to herself, though she can easily explain it away by saying she was hunting for some pens or paper for Pictionary.

'Oh great,' Rhonda mutters. The door is locked. No doubt because of Scott's presence in the house. Thinking like Jen would, that she'd want to keep the key with her, she grabs her house and car key fob off the hall table and searches the bunch for something that looks as though it would fit. On the third attempt, Rhonda has the door to Jeremy's study open. She also hears the voices from the kitchen getting louder, plus some clattering as though Jen is banging mugs about.

It's dark inside the study and as soon as Rhonda goes in, closing the door behind her, she catches the heady and evocative scent of Jeremy, almost as if he's still in there. A spicy mix of patchouli and sandalwood and something masculine yet fragrant somehow lingers, even weeks after his death. Rhonda doesn't believe in ghosts but if she was going to, now would be the time.

She swallows, her skin prickling with goosebumps. *It's almost as if he's watching me*, she thinks, feeling her way over to his leather-topped desk in the middle of the room. She flicks on the desk lamp, sitting down in Jeremy's chair. Briefly, she glances around the bookshelf-lined room, imagining him sitting here writing. Her chest fills with sadness – heavy and palpable. It would have taken nothing less than an avalanche to wipe out such a vibrant, full-of-life man like Jeremy.

She refocuses on the letter she found tucked between the manuscript pages – the reason she's come into his study. She needs to find the *other* letter, the one the sender mentioned. It must be in here somewhere, and she has to find it before Jen does. She's pretty certain it'll still be in here – there's no way Jen would have not told her about something like that if she'd found it. It would have upset her too much.

But where to start? She wonders if he's tucked it inside a book. Overall, there must be going on for a thousand of them, she thinks, tracking her eyes along the remaining spines on the shelves – not to mention the ones they stacked up for charity already. She might as well give up now if that's where it's secreted. Instead, she starts with Jeremy's desk drawers, sliding the ones to the left open and scanning through what's in there.

The contents are pretty much as she'd expected – everything from storage CDs, USB sticks, stationery, a baseball cap, files of papers that she quickly flicks through, some *National Geographic* magazines, and a dozen other random items such as a pot of foreign coins, a packet of seeds and a couple of small photograph albums. She's unsurprised to find there's nothing organised about Jeremy's desk drawers – and also no sign of a love letter.

She's about to give up, hearing Jen's voice getting louder as if she's walking through the hallway. Rhonda freezes, excuses at the ready in case she comes in – but then Scott says something that has Jen heading back into the kitchen. Rhonda holds her breath as she opens the final drawer – the shallow one in the centre of the desk. It's stiff, as though it's sticking on something, or perhaps the wood has warped. She gives it a few sharp tugs, wiggling it from side to side as she forces it open.

Suddenly it gives, but Rhonda's heart sinks when she sees a messy array of pens, rubber bands, paper clips and all manner of other miscellaneous items. She pushes the drawer closed again, but this time there's no budging it. She can't leave it open – Jen would be suspicious.

'Damn it,' she whispers, feeling silly for thinking she'd find something so easily. She leans her hip against the drawer to give it a good shove – to no avail. She gets down on her knees and peers into the back of the drawer but can't see anything that would cause the jam. As a last resort, she runs her hands over the sides of the wooden drawer and then underneath. And that's when she feels it – something stuck to the underside, preventing it from closing.

Rhonda gets down lower to see what it is. She doesn't recognise it at first – the little book taped to the underside of the drawer. And certainly doesn't immediately register what it means when she peels it away, holding the passport in her hands.

It's only when she opens it, sees Jeremy's photo staring back at her, reads that the passport is very much in date, that it slowly dawns on her what it means. Without it, Jeremy can't possibly have gone to Switzerland – making her sigh with relief that she discovered it before Jen did.

CHAPTER THIRTY-TWO

Then

It seems like an entire lifetime since Evan has been up to the den with Mac. But then it seems an entire lifetime since his mum has been in hospital, too, even though it's only been just over a week. Everything feels broken and destroyed, as though a monster has been unleashed, rampaging through his world.

'Look after the bab, boy,' Griff had said every night since the ambulance had come for his mother. He'd sauntered off down to the Crown shortly after she'd been taken to hospital, with Evan knowing he'd be back at kick-out time reeking of beer and looking for something to punch.

'Have you gone to visit her?' Mac says as he fixes the centre branch of their den back in place.

'Nah, not allowed,' Evan replies, fighting down the sick feeling. He doesn't know what three fractured vertebrae are, but he knows it means she might not walk again. Along with two broken wrists, cracked ribs and her collarbone all smashed up, he imagines her entire body must be in a plaster cast.

'You fucking say a word, boy, and I'll do the same to you, right?' Griff had told him that terrible night last week, slamming him up against the landing wall. He'd heard Rosie snuffling in her cot in the next room, smelt the sour stench of fag smoke on Griff's breath. The anger was seeping out of him.

Evan had nodded frantically.

He'd seen everything from his bedroom doorway. His mum was still down there, splayed out on the hallway floor, her neck bent at a funny angle against the skirting board because there was barely room for two people to stand side by side in the tiny space, let alone for someone to lie there after falling down the stairs.

Except she hadn't fallen. She'd been pushed. Pushed by Griff with the same hands that had him hauled up against the wall by his school sweatshirt. It was only when they heard the ambulance siren that Griff finally let go, shoving him back inside his bedroom with an order to stay put.

Evan had sat on his bed, his knees drawn up to his chin, listening to the sounds downstairs of the paramedics dealing with his mum. He heard the beep-beep of a machine that sounded as though it was measuring her heart. *His mother's heart...* He remembered the beat of it from long ago, when she held him tight and sang songs. She hadn't done that in a while.

After what seemed like ages, Evan heard his mum being clattered out on a stretcher. He watched from his bedroom window as they wheeled her into the ambulance, its blue light flashing in the summer twilight.

Then the old bag from next door came out to see what was going on, standing on her doorstep in her dirty slippers, her hands on her hips. As she turned, glancing up at him and shaking her head, Evan cried. He cried for his mum, he cried for Rosie, and he cried for himself. Because he now knew what he must do.

It was time to make a plan. A proper plan with Mac. A Kill Club plan that would make everything better, once and for all.

'I've got something for you,' Evan says, shoving his hand inside the pocket of his school trousers. Mac is sitting on the log by the den campfire, his chin in his hand as he stares down at a spider picking its way through the leaves and twigs. He looks up, frowning.

Evan holds the item out, the light filtering through the trees making it glint. 'Kill Club badges,' he says proudly, lifting up his sweatshirt to reveal an identical one pinned on his T-shirt.

'They're *way* cool,' Mac says, standing up. 'Where d'you get them?'

'Stole them from Griff,' he replies proudly. 'They're, like, real army ones,' he adds, reaching out and putting his hands on Mac's chest, aiming the pin through the fabric.

'Get off!' Mac suddenly says, batting Evan's hand away. He snatches the badge and steps back. 'I can do it myself, all right?' When it's pinned on, they stand together, their badges displayed proudly, feeling more like a real club than ever. And when Evan sees the spider scuttling along the ground again, he makes sure to stamp on it hard.

Evan knows Mac thinks he's stupid, doesn't think he's serious. They've done this loads of times before and never followed through – it's all just been plans. Gem had been first on their list, the two of them huddled round the smouldering campfire, plotting what they'd do to her.

'Cut her stupid hair off,' Mac had suggested, touching his own straggly locks. He sits down again after fixing the rabbit skull back on the branch above the entrance to the den. It had taken the boys nearly an hour to repair the damage and they couldn't be certain if it was the recent storm that had torn down half of their secret hideout, or a person.

'Then force her to eat it,' Evan had said. 'Then I'd chop her fingers off one by one… feed them to the dogs… poison her… push her head down the toilet until she can't breathe…'

He'd had enough. He hated her. If he couldn't do it now, he vowed, one day when he was bigger he would teach her a proper lesson.

'You're not serious about that little kid?' Mac says now, unwrapping a chocolate bar and touching the badge to make sure it's still there.

'Deadly serious,' Evan says as they sit side by side on the camp log. A couple of birds squawk out of the trees above them. 'It's because of that brat that my mum is in hospital. He needs teaching a lesson.' Evan's heart thumps as fast as a bird's.

Mac pulls an uncertain face, his pale skin almost see-through today. Evan wonders if he's ill or something – he always seems so... so delicate these days.

'What?' Evan says, wondering why Mac is just staring at him.

Mac doesn't reply, he just keeps on gazing at Evan with that... that *look*.

Evan grabs his pencil and begins to write. The noisy kid next door is only small and could easily be carried. Carried a long way away, he thinks, making notes. Dumped. Gone for good.

He knows the boy is about two or three years old and comes to his gran's house next door every afternoon. She looks after him while his mother works. And every afternoon, the boy is in the garden shrieking – wailing and screaming and setting the old woman's dog off yapping, which does his mum's head in even more. Migraine after migraine, she's had. Then that makes Griff angry when he comes in from the bookie's, lashing out at his mum lying in bed with a bottle of vodka in her hand when his tea's not on the table.

His poor mum.

'Will you help me do it?' Evan says. 'Get rid of that kid? He presses the sharp point of the pencil into the fleshy part of his hand until a dark globule of blood bursts out.

Mac blinks furiously as he stares at Evan. He licks his lips – as though there's something sweet on them. Then he takes a couple of breaths before leaning towards Evan and kissing him on the lips.

For a second, Evan freezes. He doesn't know what's happening. Doesn't know what the warm feeling deep inside him is – the same feeling he gets when he crushes bugs. Then he recoils, wiping the wet off his lips.

'Stop it!' he scowls. 'What d'you do that for?'

Mac shrugs and looks away. Evan thinks he looks even paler, sitting there, shivering as he stares at him. Wonders if he might dissolve in the dappled sunlight that filters through the trees above them. The leaves rustle in the breeze, almost as if they're saying *shhh*…

'Just don't tell no one you did that, right?' Evan growls, turning back to his notepad, trying to concentrate, though the feelings inside him make it almost impossible.

CHAPTER THIRTY-THREE

Jen

'You have to go. This morning.' I'm careful to keep my voice low but firm. It's early, and Rhonda, Kieran and Caitlin are still asleep upstairs.

Scott stares at me, an empty, vacant look that could mean anything – that he's about to lean in and kiss me, or grab me by the throat and throttle me. I retreat to the other side of the kitchen, near where I keep the knives.

'I've had enough,' I say. 'Things are difficult for me right now.'

'Do you *still* not understand?' Scott says. Two slices of toast suddenly pop up behind me, making me jump. He smiles. 'Nervous?'

'You can't stay because… I'm selling the barn.' It's a lie, of course, but might make him go.

'No you're not,' he says. 'And even if you were, I'd come with you.' His eyes drop down to my stomach. 'We're a family now.'

'No, Scott, we're not. Surely you have relatives to stay with? Somewhere else to go?'

'Sadly, I don't. There's no one to miss me… no parents, no siblings in contact, no uncles, aunts or even friends.' He says it as though it's something to be proud of.

'Then go back to wherever you came from, Scott. Go and get another job there.'

It was the first thing he announced to me when I came downstairs ten minutes ago, my robe wrapped tightly around me as I padded through my house barefoot – the house that doesn't feel like mine any more. 'My job at the restaurant hasn't worked out.'

'*What*?' I'd shrieked, clapping my hand over my mouth.

First his house falls through and now his job. Then he'd blustered his way through excuses about the owner of the restaurant having financial problems, delays to the renovations and opening. None of it sounded real or plausible. Made me wonder if there was even a job in the first place.

I glance behind him. Lying on the worktop is his phone. If only I could get access to it, delete all the photos… then I'd be free. But it's as if he's read my mind.

'They're all saved on a USB stick too,' he says, an annoying smile spreading wide on his face. 'So go ahead, delete them off my phone if you wish.' He reaches for it and holds it out to me, laughing now.

I turn my head away, hugging my arms around myself.

'Let me make you a coffee,' I hear him say. 'And some toast. You'll feel better then. Your blood sugar must be low, that's why you're behaving like this. I need to look after you and our little one.' When I don't take his phone, he puts it down again.

I screw up my eyes, stifling the tears. All I can see is Jeremy standing over me, large as life, his arm outstretched as he also held out his phone to me.

'You're tired, Jen,' he'd kept saying that weekend a few weeks before Christmas. Rhonda and Chris were due over at any moment and I was busy finishing off dinner. It had become his stock answer whenever I'd brought up the 'M' word – *Madeleine*. 'You're working too many hours, Jen. You're stressed. Go ahead, check my phone if it makes you feel better.'

I'd just stared at him, disbelievingly. Since the messages had come in earlier in the day, he'd been out on the quad bike in the paddock and had had several hours to delete anything incriminating.

It was yet another scene I'd caused with my 'stress', my 'madness', my 'paranoia' – me ruining what would have seemed, from the outside, like a perfect family weekend. Caitlin had come round at about eleven to see Kieran – though she'd been out in the paddock helping Jeremy since she arrived, while Kieran strummed on his guitar upstairs. And I'd been cooking. It relaxed me, helped me unwind before the week ahead. Rhonda and Chris were coming over later that afternoon to share the slow-cooked lamb I had in the oven.

All perfect. All just fine.

Then I'd had to go and ruin it by being *stressed* when I saw more texts pop up on his phone – thankfully before Caitlin had arrived, so she hadn't witnessed my meltdown. They were from 'M' again, of course.

I love you, M xxx
You OK? Miss you xxx
You there? M xxx

'Mick hassling you about golf again, is he?' I'd shoved the phone under Jeremy's nose, wanting to ram it up there.

He grabbed it, examining the message alerts on the screen. 'I don't know who the hell this is.' His voice was deep and resonant, commanding and convincing.

'Well, it's the same number that "M" texted you from before, and you seemed to know who it was then.' Whoever 'M' was clearly wasn't stored in Jeremy's contacts. But I'd remembered the last four digits of the phone number from the previous time: 6184.

Jeremy had pulled a pained face then – no, a *pitying* face as he loomed over me, as if I was the one with the problem. 'I can't stop weirdos texting me. Someone must have the wrong number.' A hand on my shoulder then, warm and comforting.

'Open it. Open your phone,' I'd demanded, refusing to be fooled yet again.

'Jen, you're embarrassing yourself. Really, it's nothing. Why would I have an affair when I've got all this to lose?' His hand swept around him then settled back on me.

Then the landline had rung, providing Jeremy with the distraction he needed as he answered it, and Kieran had appeared in the kitchen doorway, saying Caitlin had texted, asking if she could cycle over to hang out.

'Yes, yes, of course,' I'd said, touching my head, feeling frazzled and distracted. After hanging up on what was nothing more than a spam call on the landline, Jeremy had strode off then, calling out he was going outside to sort out the fencing, muttering something about me being mad as he'd left. He'd slammed the back door behind him.

Then I was alone in the kitchen. I noticed he'd taken his phone with him and, as I peeled some potatoes for later, I wondered if I'd imagined the whole thing, and whether I was indeed going mad.

'There, there,' Scott says, sitting next to me at the kitchen table. 'That's better, isn't it?' He butters me another piece of toast and spreads a thick layer of jam on it. My hands shake as I sip my coffee.

Maybe I should just succumb, I think, watching him as he brushes crumbs off my robe. Let him take care of me and the baby, have him help around the house. In time, perhaps I'll forget what he did to me, maybe the flashbacks will stop and he'll destroy the incriminating photos and videos, and one day we'll look back and laugh as we watch our little son or daughter playing happily.

'Karma…' I say, taking myself by surprise. 'Do you believe in it?'

Scott takes a moment to think. 'No,' is his decisive answer.

I try to fathom something behind his blank stare, but I'm struggling. Scott's manner is distracting and deceptive – as though he's a master illusionist. For a moment, it feels as if I've known him forever – but it's not his face that I recognise, rather something else about him. But I put it down to my mind playing tricks, processing the things my unconscious won't allow my conscious self be privy to.

'I am one hundred per cent certain there is no such thing as karma,' he adds.

'Do you take comfort in that?' I ask. 'Or is it a convenient way to deny things you don't want to face?'

Scott laughs. 'You're so serious this morning, my love,' he says. He reaches out and unties my ponytail, arranging the strands around my face. 'I love your long hair,' he says, gazing at me. 'As for karma, if it were real, then I would not be sitting here with you in this beautiful house, with our baby growing inside you, our wonderful future ahead of us.' He pauses and, for a moment, I almost see compassion inside him. I'm about to ask what he means, but he says, 'Come on, drink up. It'll do you good.'

Then I'm back there again – the noise of the bar pulsing through my head, the alcohol in my veins. *Drink up…* he'd said, holding out my glass. I'd not really wanted it but had forced it down, any shred of self-control long gone. I'd knocked it back – plus whatever he'd spiked it with.

My head swims, just like it did that night. I put down my mug, not feeling right, not feeling myself. It could be morning sickness, or it could be fear, anxiety… or all of these. I drop my head down between my knees, feeling a hand gently rub my back.

Here, drink up… remembering how I'd said the same words to Jeremy, not long before Rhonda and Chris were due to arrive that Sunday afternoon. Half an hour before, he'd come in filthy from the paddock. He'd gone straight upstairs to shower and change, and then appeared in the kitchen as though nothing had happened earlier in the day, as if those texts I'd seen from 'M' had never existed. For my own sanity, I'd gone along with it. Our friends would be arriving soon. He'd told me he was going to his study to sort some papers before the others arrived. That's when I'd taken him a glass of red wine. A peace offering.

Drink up…

He'd started, not realising I was standing right in front of his desk. I hadn't crept up on him as such, but had been careful to tread lightly. In front of him was his manuscript – open somewhere in the middle – and he was hunched over it, concentrating hard. He'd printed out a fresh copy only yesterday.

But instead of reading his own work, Jeremy appeared to be reading a letter sitting on top of the stack of papers – that's what it looked like when I held out the wine glass. But I'd only got a glimpse of it.

Drink up…

As soon as he realised I was there, he'd quickly shoved the letter inside the manuscript and stacked it all into one pile, planting both hands firmly on top. It all happened so quickly, but I spotted his nervous look, the way his jaw clamped tightly shut.

Then his trademark smile broke. 'Thank you, darling,' he'd said, taking the glass of red. 'I should be in the kitchen helping you, not sitting here.' He'd stood and come round from behind his desk then, putting a hand in the small of my back as he guided me into the kitchen. I'd glanced over my shoulder at his desk as we'd left the study, making a mental note to dig out whatever it was he'd been reading later. My mind was already in overdrive as I imagined a letter from Madeleine, perhaps something about their upcoming trip, her professing her love for him. But then Rhonda and Chris had turned up, the wine had flowed, we'd eaten my lamb stew and, by the time I remembered it the next day, the manuscript was gone from his study.

'Morning,' Rhonda says, coming into the kitchen. Her eyes dance between me and Scott, sizing up the situation. He's cut my toast into two pieces and is holding one out for me, as though he's coaxing a child to eat.

I give her a brief smile, snatching the toast from Scott.

Rhonda clears her throat. 'Right, well, Caitlin and I are heading off now. It was fun last night... pizza and games, just like old times. Let's do it again soon.' She zips up her padded jacket and heads for the hall, ignoring Scott when he says goodbye. Caitlin comes down the stairs, pulling on her hoody and stuffing her feet into her trainers.

'Is everything OK?' Rhonda says at the doorstep, once Caitlin has got in the car. She tips her head towards the kitchen. 'Things seemed a bit tense just now.'

'It's all fine,' I reply quickly, clamping my arms around my body, shivering inside my dressing gown. 'Really.'

Rhonda narrows her eyes at me before giving me a peck on each cheek. She turns to go, but stops. 'You know that Evan Locke boy?' she asks in a low voice. 'Did Jeremy know him?'

'I have... I have no idea,' I tell her, frowning. 'Why?'

'Oh, no reason...' she says, before walking over to her car. She flicks me a wave and toots her car horn as she drives off. Then I shut the front door harder than intended and lean back against it, wondering what the hell I'm going to do.

CHAPTER THIRTY-FOUR

Rhonda

Rhonda arrives at the café fifteen minutes early, having driven for over an hour to get to Reading. She'd checked it out on Google Maps before she left, so she knew exactly where she was going and where to park. It had taken a few days to build up the courage to do it in the first place.

At the counter, she orders a latte and sits down at a table near the back of the coffee shop chain, giving herself a good view of the entrance. Her heart thumps as she sips on her drink and she has to hold the cup with two hands, she's shaking so much.

Jen would kill me if she knew, she thinks. But if she's right, then ultimately she will thank her. She glances out of the large front window, eyeing her car, having parked as close as possible to the café in order to be able to drive off as quickly as possible if phase two of her plan is needed.

Phase two, she thinks, inwardly rolling her eyes. As if there's actually a phase one. She's kicking herself now for being so reckless, but something doesn't sit right and she can hardly ask Chris for help. Not yet. Reporting everything to the police would, she supposes, be phase three.

The café door opens and a young couple comes in, making Rhonda sit back in her chair again. Not her. Soon after, an old woman arrives, holding the door open behind her for someone else, but that turns out to be a delivery driver dropping something off.

Rhonda glances at her watch. Three minutes to eleven. She sips more coffee, scans the street scene outside for likely figures. She knows who to expect from the photographs, but people always look different in real life. It's as she's about to fish her phone from her bag to check the pictures again, to get her face fresh in her mind, that she feels a cold draught of air as the café door opens.

It's her, she thinks, shoving her phone away again. She stands up, knocking against the table and spilling some of her coffee. The woman is taller than she imagined and strides straight up to the counter without looking around to see if Rhonda is there. When she has ordered and paid, she calmly carries her cup over towards her table as if she'd known she was there all along.

'Rhonda?' she says as she approaches. As safe assumption given that Rhonda is the only person sitting alone. She notices the French accent.

'Madeleine, hello,' Rhonda says, being careful not to bump the table again as she leans over to shake the woman's hand – a long, slender hand with shaped and painted nails, not too long or short, with the tasteful shade of creamy pink reeking of French chic, which ties in with the rest of her understated yet immaculate outfit. 'Thank you for coming.'

Madeleine nods, her glossy chestnut waves rippling to order. As she sits, she adjusts the wide cream trousers she's wearing and, after she's removed her overcoat, she unbuttons the matching jacket to reveal a loose grey camisole top. She has a silk scarf tied around her neck, and Rhonda thinks she doesn't look as though she belongs outside of Paris. It feels as if they should have met on the Champs-Élysées.

'No problem,' Madeleine replies, though her expression is naturally suspicious because of the nature of their meeting. Her subtle accent makes Rhonda wonder if she's lived in the UK a long while. 'How is it I can help you? Your message said you wanted to speak with me urgently about a mutual friend?'

Rhonda smiles nervously and draws a breath, her mouth opening. But she can't make any words come out.

Madeleine takes a sip of her coffee, tipping her head sideways so her almond eyes appear even wider as she waits for Rhonda to speak. She offers an encouraging smile.

Rhonda feels herself sweating as she clenches her fists under the table, wishing she'd worn something other than jeans and a sweatshirt.

'Yes, that's right. We have a friend in common, I believe,' she finally manages to say, hoping Madeleine will pick up the conversational baton and say his name. She doesn't.

'And who is this friend?'

'Jeremy Miller.' Rhonda sits up squarely in her seat and manages to bring her cup to her mouth without spilling any, though it does take two hands. *Breathe*, she tells herself, forcing her shoulders down and her lungs to take in air. 'Do you know him?'

Madeleine hesitates, her eyes flicking to the ceiling and then back to Rhonda. 'Yes, I do.' Her words are clipped and precise and her expression doesn't change. There's nothing for Rhonda to read. 'How may I help you?'

'When did you last see him?'

Madeleine thinks, her eyes darting about again as she tucks a strand of hair behind her ear. Rhonda notices the large silver earrings she's wearing, wondering if they were a gift from Jeremy.

'That's a tough one,' she admits. 'A little while ago now.' She gives a small shrug.

'Can you be more specific?' All Rhonda needs is for her to say 'yesterday' or 'last week' or even 'sometime this year' to prove her theory that Jeremy is still alive and, very likely, either living with or at least involved with Madeleine – the other woman.

'Maybe some weeks, it's hard to recall exactly. Perhaps more, though perhaps less.'

'I see,' Rhonda replies slowly, though she doesn't see at all.

'Is there a problem? I do not understand why you are asking me this.'

'Are you aware… do you know what happened to Jeremy?' Rhonda was intending to delay this question, but it's clear that Madeleine is giving nothing away.

'Happened?'

Jesus Christ, Rhonda thinks. She sips her coffee, hands shaking. She hopes Madeleine doesn't notice. 'I'm afraid there was an accident.'

'Accident?' Madeleine's expression remains neutral.

'You don't know?'

Rhonda thinks Madeleine shakes her head, but she can't be sure. Whatever the gesture, it's non-committal.

'I'm so sorry to have to tell you,' Rhonda says gently, 'but Jeremy was killed a few weeks ago.' She didn't imagine for one minute that she'd have to break that news and had assumed, bluff or not, that Madeleine would admit to knowing this. *She's a good actress*, Rhonda thinks.

Silence. Madeleine does nothing but blink furiously. She tilts her head. 'Are you sure?'

'I was hoping you could tell me that.'

'You want me to tell you if you are sure that Jeremy is dead? How would I even know this?' She gives a quick shake of her head, her glossy hair rippling.

Rhonda closes her eyes for a moment. When she opens them, she places her hands face down on the table either side of her coffee cup. She leans forward.

'Look, let's not keep this pretence up, shall we? I know you've seen Jeremy recently and I know he's still alive, even though he's done the most unspeakable thing ever and allowed his wife to believe he's dead. Christ, she even had a bloody memorial service for him. His *parents* were there, for heaven's sake. She's my best friend and I'm watching her go through hell right now, so I'd appreciate you coming clean and giving the poor woman some kind of closure at least. Then the pair of you can skip off into the sunset happily ever after for all I care, because I assure you, Jen will want nothing to do with him when she finds out the truth. He's all yours.'

Madeleine sits there, saying nothing. Her fingers are laced together around her cup, but she doesn't drink from it. She maintains perfect posture, steady breathing and even her rapid blinking has ceased. But then Rhonda sees it – a swallow, her slender throat rippling.

'Jen's known you were having an affair with her husband for a long time.' Even if she denies it, Rhonda thinks, then at least she's got that off her chest on Jen's behalf, called her out on it.

'I do not know what you are talking about.'

'Oh, come on, Madeleine. I suggest we get some honesty on the table here.'

'I did not have an affair with Jeremy. Sure, we worked together sometimes. And… and I can't deny that he tried it on with me once or twice when we were away filming. In our business… that is not so uncommon. But it's not to say I enjoyed the attention.' Madeleine's accent suddenly seems more noticeable, perhaps because she's stressed. 'I am so sorry he has passed away. Please send my condolences to his wife.'

'But you already knew he was "dead". Why the pretence?' Rhonda uses her fingers as quotes, because she still doesn't believe he is.

'I… I—'

'I saw you at his memorial service, Madeleine, so don't pretend you didn't know he'd "died". Did you come along to make it seem plausible but you got cold feet? Was that it?'

Rhonda runs through the possibilities in her mind, remembering when Jen called with the news of Jeremy's death. She was in a terrible state, saying she'd just had a visit from the police, almost incoherent with grief as she spewed out what few details she knew about the accident. Rhonda had gone straight round to comfort her.

The next day, Jen said that the head of the mountain rescue team in Switzerland had contacted her. They'd updated her on progress over the next week, until finally they'd given up on recovering the remaining bodies. She'd been informed that they'd ship his few belongings back from the hotel – but then she said they'd never actually materialised. Apparently, Jeremy always had his passport, wallet and phone on him in a security belt while skiing, so it would only have been clothes left at the hotel. It had all been ghastly.

To think now that it was all staged by Jeremy and Madeleine was almost worse. How the hell could they have pulled that off? Thinking rationally, Rhonda knew they probably hadn't. But something wasn't right – especially now she'd found Jeremy's passport in his study. She can't see how he could have gone on the trip without it.

'Look, stop,' Madeleine says. 'Enough now! You do not know what you are talking about.' Her hands gesture wildly, the most animated she's been. 'But OK, yes, you are correct. I did attend Jeremy's memorial service. I'm sorry for concealing this fact.'

She bows her head for a moment.

'I was aware of the... of the tense situation between him and his wife, and I did not want to...' she trails off, thinking of the correct word, '...antagonise her with my presence. She had already warned me off the skiing trip, telling me to stay away from her husband. But he must have changed his mind at some point, because a while after I saw people posting condolences on his social media.

'A mutual colleague was attending the memorial so he gave me the details. I simply wanted to pay my last respects to the man I'd worked with for many years without a fuss, that is all. I had much respect for Jeremy, even if he wasn't always the easiest person to get along with. But I swear, we were not having an affair. *Ever*.' Madeleine mutters something in French then.

Rhonda can't deny that she seems earnest and plausible. And if she was involved in a disappearing act by Jeremy, then coming here today probably wasn't a wise move. Unless it's a double bluff, she thinks.

'Look, Jeremy used to confide in me when we were away,' Madeleine continues, her voice calmer. 'There's no denying, he was a troubled man. He told me that his wife was convinced we were having an affair. I suggested I meet with her, to give her peace of mind, but he refused.'

'Go on.'

Madeleine's glance flicks to the ceiling. 'And you are correct, I also think he was having an affair. If you can call it that,' she adds. 'And if I'm honest, the person looked a lot like…' she trails off again, her eyes narrowing as she studies Rhonda, '…like you.'

'What? *No*—' Rhonda recoils, feeling her cheeks burn scarlet.

Madeleine briefly raises a finger to her lips. 'He was a complicated soul. Never satisfied, his mind always thinking, planning, wanting some adventure.' Her hands make an exploding gesture around her head. 'He told me that he felt wretched about it, that he knew it was wrong but it had happened unexpectedly. He kept saying that he would end it, that it meant nothing to him, that he felt lured into it. I know he loved his wife, but it seemed marriage was never enough for him. I told him it was… so *very* wrong.' She turns away for a moment, looking pained.

'And *did* he end it?' Rhonda's voice is weak.

'He died, didn't he?' Madeleine shrugs.

Rhonda absorbs this, frowning. 'You mean… suicide?'

Madeleine shakes her head. '*Non, non*. I mean that by dying, the affair came to its own conclusion.'

Rhonda swallows, not knowing what to say. 'Do you know the woman's name? Jen was convinced it was you. She discovered texts from someone with the initial "M". Jeremy was always talking about you, engineering trips away with you. You can see why she was so suspicious.'

Madeleine nods. 'Indeed I can. But I do not know a name, I am sorry. It is only a coincidence that my name begins with the same initial.' Madeleine reaches into her bag and pulls out her phone. She taps and scrolls and shows Rhonda the screen. 'See? This is my husband, Gérard, and our little girl. She's nearly three. We are happy. I did not do these things you are saying. It was someone else.'

Rhonda's stomach churns as Madeleine's eyes bore into her. 'You have a lovely family. And I'm sorry, too,' she says. 'For jumping to conclusions.' She takes her own phone from her bag and shows Madeleine the photos she took at the memorial service, scrolling through them. She points to the shots of Madeleine. 'But when I saw you at the service standing away from everyone else, when I knew you hadn't also died in the accident, and then when I found Jeremy's pass—'

'*Arrêtez*… Wait, look!' Madeleine says suddenly, staring closely at Rhonda's phone. 'This person here…' She zooms in as far as she can, angling the screen so Rhonda can also see. 'This is the one Jeremy was involved with. I recognise her. I once saw him on a video call with her. He quickly cut it dead when he knew I was there, but I'd seen and overheard enough. It did not seem right to me. *Non*, not at all.' She shakes her head vigorously, scowling. 'And I told him so.'

Rhonda slowly takes the phone from Madeleine, not taking her eyes off the photo. 'Her?' she eventually says, feeling the relief wash through her.

'*Oui*… yes. She was the one having the affair with Jeremy for sure.'

And that's when Rhonda bursts out laughing. 'Oh, that would be funny if it wasn't so completely ridiculous.' She shuts down her phone and puts it away again.

'You know her?' Madeleine drains her coffee cup.

'Yes, yes I do. She's my daughter.'

'Hey, love, it's me,' Rhonda says down the line later. 'Can you talk right now? I need a bit of a favour.'

'Sure,' Chris says. 'I'm on a quick break, but then I've got someone in custody to interview. What's up?'

'Weird question, but is it possible to find out which officers went to break the news to Jen about Jeremy the night she found out he'd died? And more importantly, if it's possible to get the details of the Swiss authorities who relayed the information?' When there's silence, Rhonda thinks quickly. 'I reckon finding out more details about the accident will help Jen process things. She's struggling again.'

There's another pause on the line, then she hears Chris clear his throat. 'Why do you want to know?'

Rhonda also hesitates, hoping he doesn't think she's meddling. 'Something's not right, Chris. I found Jeremy's passport the other day. I don't see how he can have gone on the skiing trip without it.'

'Jeremy's *passport*?' he says incredulously. 'Jesus Christ.' He breathes out heavily.

'Can you just find out who broke the news to Jen? I'm concerned that they weren't really cops.'

Chris pauses again then semi-laughs – but to Rhonda it sounds forced, faked even. 'I think you've been watching too many crime dramas, Ronnie. Anyway, it's tricky,' he says. 'I can't really go looking up information unless it's for a case I'm actively working on.'

'Really?' Rhonda replies flatly.

'Not unless you want me to get in a load of trouble,' he snaps. 'I'm sorry. Look, the system is heavily monitored. But leave it with me. I can ask around, see if anyone remembers who visited. There might be a way around it.'

'OK,' Rhonda says, slightly taken aback by his tone. He's never usually short with her. 'I'd appreciate that. For Jen's sake. The night she found out was such a blur for her,' she adds, trying to force what Madeleine said about Caitlin from her mind for now. Surely it's a case of mistaken identity and nothing more. There's no way Jeremy would have done anything like that – prey upon a young girl, let alone a close family friend. And no way Rhonda wouldn't have noticed something going on between them. It's unthinkable.

'Right, better get on then, love,' Chris says. 'I'll be home a bit after eight.'

'OK, see you later,' Rhonda replies. 'I'll keep some dinner warm.'

She hangs up, her mind preoccupied with anything but dinner. To distract herself, she digs out the essays Kieran and Caitlin have emailed her to mark. They've worked hard, so she owes it to them to give prompt feedback.

It's after she's gone through Kieran's, impressed with what he's written, that she turns to Caitlin's essay, hoping he's not copied from her. But halfway through reading it, she stops, her eyes fixed on the single word. While she knows that spelling isn't Caitlin's strong point, that sometimes she forgets to spell-check, it's an unusual error to make – *eclypse*… the exact same error made by whoever wrote the letter to Jeremy.

CHAPTER THIRTY-FIVE

Jen

'Elsie?' I call out yet again. 'Are you home?' She often takes a while to get to the door, but I've been knocking for at least ten minutes now. The side gate is padlocked as usual and her front curtains are drawn, which is odd. I glance at my watch. She should be up by now; she's always been an early riser. 'Elsie, are you there?'

'Not seen her in a few days,' a voice says.

I look up. It's her neighbour – a man in his sixties wearing a white vest and smoking a cigarette.

I go over to the low fence separating the tiny front gardens. 'You don't have a key, I suppose?'

He shakes his head. 'Who are you?' He's not being rude, but comes across that way.

'I'm her doctor. I often visit and—'

'Under the mat,' the neighbour says, glancing down. He gives me a nod and stamps his cigarette butt out, going back into his house.

I check under the doormat and, sure enough, Elsie has put a spare key there. Silly, but not so silly now, I think, pushing it into the lock and turning it. Thankful the security chain isn't on, I ease the door open a crack. 'Elsie, are you home?' I call out again. 'It's Dr Miller. Just checking how you are?'

Silence. Not even Minty barking or her claws clacking on the floor as she comes to greet me. There's a faint smell of dog urine, but this time there's another smell – something slightly sweet and cloying.

'It's only me, Elsie,' I call out again as I head through to the living room, not wanting to give her a scare if she's fallen asleep by the gas fire. She always has it turned up too high. But when I go in, the gas fire is off and the room feels unusually cool. Beyond, in the small kitchen, it's the same – no sign of Elsie and everything feels cold and lifeless.

I go back to the small hallway and head up the stairs, wondering if perhaps she's taking a bath. 'Elsie? Are you home?' Or maybe she's gone down to the shops. 'Minty?' I call out in an encouraging voice, hoping the dog will appear.

Nothing.

There are three doors off the tiny landing area – one is the bathroom, which Elsie is not in. The next is a small room with a single bed and the remainder of the room crammed with boxes and general junk that's accumulated over the years. The front room is Elsie's bedroom, and it's as I draw closer that the sickly, putrid smell gets worse. I try to convince myself I don't know what it is, but as a doctor, I do.

I don't bother calling out her name before I push the door open, but I close my eyes instead, only opening them when I've taken a step or two inside.

Elsie is lying on top of her bed, clothed, peaceful-looking, despite the early stages of decomposition. I cup my hand over my mouth. It gets me every time.

'Oh, Elsie,' I whisper behind my hand, closing my eyes for another few seconds out of respect. I go up to her bed, putting my doctor's bag on the chair beside it, and pull on some gloves. I don't need to check for a pulse, listen to her heartbeat – *or lack of one* – through my stethoscope, or check the dilation of her pupils beneath her rigid eyelids in response to my light – *none* – but I do. It's my job. Her skin is cold and a purplish-grey colour, covered in darker blotches, and with a soft sheen sitting on its surface. Her clothes stretch around her already bloated body as putrefaction takes hold. My best guess is three, maybe four days since she died. I fight down another retch at the smell – I'll never get used to it.

Elsie's hands lie by her sides, and in her right one, there's a photograph. I don't touch it, but can see that it's a picture of her grandson, Lenny Taylor, looking as though it was taken the same summer he was killed – a happy, bright three-year-old boy standing ankle-deep in a paddling pool in Elsie's garden. I tilt my head sideways and make out the gap in the hedge behind him – separating the garden from the fields, beyond which is the track that leads to the quarry reservoir half a mile or so away. The hedge through which he was taken.

On Elsie's bedside table are some empty pill bottles and a glass – also empty. Again, I don't touch them but from the looks of the dates on the bottles and packets, she's been saving up the drugs I've been prescribing her for a while. Taken in these quantities, warfarin and naproxen are fatal without immediate intervention. Plus the empty half-bottle of whisky lying on the bed beside her would have numbed her passage from life. And then I see the note, just a few words on a scrap of paper, written in shaky handwriting: 'Minty at the rescue shelter.'

I swallow, fighting down years' worth of guilt that I wasn't able to help her. 'Sleep well, Elsie,' I whisper.

I'm about to head outside to make all the necessary phone calls, but I stop, my eyes fixed on Elsie's hand again. On a whim, I pluck the photograph of Lenny – his little face staring up at me – from between Elsie's fingers and stuff it in my jacket pocket before rushing outside for some fresh air.

'Some small mercy,' I mutter to myself as I head down my drive. My fingers grip the wheel tightly, my knuckles white.

Scott's car isn't here.

When I go inside, I pray that I'll find all his belongings gone too – not that he has many things here – but I find that's not the case. In fact, there are even more of his items strewn about – several pairs of men's shoes in the hallway, a pile of boxes, a radio I don't recognise on the kitchen counter, some cookery books beside it, a briefcase on the chair. Yet when I go upstairs and check in the spare room, I find it empty of his belongings.

'Another small mercy,' I say, going into my bedroom to shower and change, wondering if he's been gathering his stuff and is moving out. I need to wash the day off myself. But my heart sinks when I see it – a pile of men's clothing on my bed, my wardrobe doors open and my clothes all shoved to one side with a few men's shirts now hanging next to them. In the bathroom, it's the same – toiletries and other items I don't recognise sit beside mine.

Fuck.

He's not moving out – he's moving in *more.*

Then I hear a noise – something that sounds like crying – coming from Kieran's room across the landing. 'Kier?' I say, knocking on his door. 'Can I come in?'

There's a grunt.

'I thought you were going to Caitlin's this evening?'

Kieran shrugs. He's lying on top of his bed, staring at the ceiling. His eyes are red, his cheeks blotchy, and he has his phone in one hand with what looks like a photograph of a beach on the screen. But it's hard to tell properly.

I shudder, reminded of Elsie earlier and the photograph she held between her fingers. Once the police and ambulance arrived, I signed off the death and headed into the surgery. But my mind was on the old woman all day – the last thirty years of her life weighed down by guilt. I don't know why she chose now, after all this time, to take her own life. It's as though she wanted to give herself as much punishment as possible – a prison sentence.

'What's up, love?' I say, sitting down on the edge of his bed. He shifts his feet over to make room for me.

'Nothing,' he says, which I know from the tone means *everything*.

'Are you going to Amy's party with Caitlin? Rhonda said she'd take you. She texted me—'

'I'm not going, OK?' Kieran snaps, jerking his head up briefly to look me in the eye. Then he flops it back down onto his pillow.

'OK,' I say softly, not wanting to pressure him.

'Why has everything gone to shit?' he says, still staring at the ceiling.

I don't know how to answer that, so I rub his leg instead.

'This time last year, everything was fine. Now it feels as though there's… as if there's no point to anything.'

I force down my motherly knee-jerk reaction of wanting to lock him in his room forever to keep him safe, never let him out into a world that seems filled with pain. Not when he's saying things like that.

'I know, it's so cruel. We're still adapting, getting used to how things will feel now without your dad.'

Kieran makes a barely perceptible noise with his lips. I can't tell if it's a sad sigh or something disdainful.

'Why is Scott staying with us, Mum? I don't get it. Is he your new boyfriend?' Kieran hoists himself up onto his elbows.

'No… God, *no*. Just… a… a friend of your dad that I'm helping out. To be honest, I don't really want him here either. But… it's complicated.'

'Is he the baby's father?' He glances at my stomach.

'*Nooo*…' I say, far too defensively. I stare out of Kieran's window, across the fields, with Bowman's Woods just visible in the distance. 'Of course not.' I fight the burn in my cheeks.

'I'm not stupid, Mum.'

'I know you're not.' I reach out and take his hand and it sits stiffly within my own for a few moments. I give it a squeeze. 'Looking at old photos?' I say, spotting his screen again. I need to change the subject. 'Was that our holiday last year in Devon?'

'Yes,' Kieran says with little emotion. 'Some holiday that turned out to be.'

'What do you mean? I thought you had a nice time.'

'So did I.'

'Kier… what's going on?'

'Doesn't matter, Mum.'

As every mum knows, that means it matters. So I wait, ask him about his day at school – which turns out not to have been too bad. He got given one of the lead roles in the play and an A in his latest geography assignment.

'Don't get too excited,' he adds in a sour tone after I congratulate him. 'It was mostly Dad's work.'

'What do you mean?'

'That piece in *National Geographic* that he wrote ages ago, it fitted nicely with the topic at school.' He shrugs. 'Easy to chop it about a bit, "in my own words" and all that.'

'*Kier…*' I say slowly, trying not to be too hard on him. 'Top marks for ingenuity, though.'

He snorts out a laugh.

'Remember this day?' he says, holding up his phone and showing me a photograph.

'Vaguely,' I say, recalling our time in Devon. The two families together.

'I asked Caitlin if she had any photos of Dad on her phone as I don't have many of him.'

It's not hard to hear the bitterness in his voice, that he wants to vent something. I gently take the phone from him, looking at the picture of the virtually deserted beach.

'Looks like it was a bit windy,' I say, noticing a haze of sand blowing across the expanse of surf beach. 'Is that Dad down by the shore?' I ask, recognising Jeremy's build, his shock of curly hair and bright red windcheater.

Kieran nods.

'With Caitlin,' he says. 'I took it.' He takes back his phone and swipes through some more pictures. 'Then Caitlin sent me this one of Dad. Nice, huh?'

I look at it, a surge of sadness sweeping through the pit of my stomach as I see a close-up of my husband's face grinning out of Kieran's phone at me. 'Dad looks happy,' I say. 'It's a lovely photo.'

Kieran takes back his phone again. 'She sent me this one too.'

'Ahh, that's nice. I remember… they went on a few walks and cycle rides together that holiday, didn't they? Dad adored you, of course, but always hoped we'd one day have a little sister for you – a daddy's girl to dote on. I think Caitlin was his surrogate daughter.' I let out a fond laugh, touching my not-so-flat stomach. 'Maybe… well, maybe you'll have a little sister after all.'

But Kieran either doesn't hear me or doesn't care. 'Then Caitlin sent me a selfie of both of them together, look.' He holds out his phone briefly. Jeremy and Caitlin, almost cheek to cheek, wide grins on their faces, the choppy waves behind them. 'That's nice too. I'm glad she sent them.'

'I'm not,' Kieran snaps back.

I'm about to ask why, when he shows me another photo – similar to the last, but they are looking directly at each other as Caitlin holds out the phone, angled slightly above them, to capture the moment. It's not instantly obvious why it makes me feel uncomfortable, but it does, and when Kieran presses and holds the photo on his iPhone, I realise it's a mini video clip – one of those photo-bursts where multiple pictures are taken in rapid succession.

'Do you like it quite so much now, Mum?'

Slowly, I pull the phone from his grip, pressing and holding the photo again and again. Watching time after time as Jeremy's lips come down on Caitlin's as they share a passionate kiss.

'You know what? I think I will go to the party after all,' my son says, flopping his head back onto his pillow and shoving his earphones in.

CHAPTER THIRTY-SIX

Rhonda

'Mum?' Caitlin says, coming into the living room where Rhonda is sitting, laptop on her knee. 'You still OK to take me to Amy's party later?'

'Sorry?' Rhonda looks up, her eyes still smarting from the spelling mistake. *Surely not…* But along with what Madeleine said, she feels utterly sick.

It was a crush, she tells herself. Just a teenager having a crush on an older man. It happens often at school, with both male and female staff the target of unwanted attention from lovesick pupils. Nothing happened… *nothing happened.*

'She said I can stay over the night so you won't need to come and fetch me. Her parents will be there too. It's hardly even a party, just a few friends hanging out.'

'Is Kieran still going?'

For some reason, Caitlin pulls a sour face. She shrugs.

'I've told Jen we'll pick him up on the way.'

'No,' she says. 'He's not going.' Rhonda thinks she hears her add *I hope* under her breath.

'Yes, I'll drive you,' Rhonda says, wondering if she and Kieran have had a falling-out. She wants to ask her daughter about Jeremy, if anything happened, but she needs to ask Chris's opinion first.

Just to be sure she's not overreacting – though deep down, she knows she's not. It's more a case of she doesn't *want* to believe it.

'Can I put my black jeans in for a wash? I want to wear them with my new top but they've got a mayonnaise stain down the front.'

Rhonda rolls her eyes – it's typical for her to ask last minute about clothes she needs washing. She also knows those jeans haven't been through the wash in quite a while.

'Leave them on the landing and I'll do them. I have some other darks I can put in with them.'

'Thanks, Mum,' she says, heading off back upstairs.

Rhonda follows her up, going into her own room to gather up some other laundry items, but stops, thinking a moment before reaching down under the bed and pulling out Jeremy's manuscript. She flips through the pages and finds the letter again, double-checking to make sure she hasn't imagined the unusual spelling mistake. She hasn't.

And on rereading it in context, with Caitlin's voice in mind instead of Madeleine's, it suddenly makes perfect sense – the clunky language fitting an infatuated teenager. But if Caitlin wrote it, then why is it signed off as 'M'? She stares at the single handwritten character, supposing that it does look a little like Caitlin's oversized scrawl – something she'd never even considered when she'd first set eyes on it.

'Thanks, Mum,' she hears her daughter call out as she drops her jeans on the landing.

Shoving the manuscript away again, Rhonda grabs her own washing and heads down to the utility room. She checks the pockets of Chris's dark jeans, pulling out a tissue and a ten-pound note, then she shoves the rest of the washing in, having a quick look at the stain on Caitlin's jeans. Definitely mayonnaise. Probably from the food at Jeremy's memorial gathering, the last time she remembers Caitlin wearing them. She doesn't own any other dark trousers.

Before putting them in the machine, Rhonda checks the pockets and again, she finds an old tissue plus something else – though not money this time. It's a small piece of paper – one of the little biodegradable remembrance notes from the memorial that were scattered on the lake at the barn. A symbolic gesture in place of ashes.

She unfolds the paper, assuming it to be a blank one as she definitely remembers Caitlin adding her memory to the water. But there are some words written on it – perhaps a first attempt that she decided not to use. Rhonda turns the paper round and reads.

You'll always be alive to me… the feel of your body against mine. Love you forever. Missy xxx

Rhonda stares at it then cups her hand over her mouth as what she's reading sinks in.

Oh my God, oh my God, oh my God…

'The fucking bastard,' she says to herself, leaning back against the wall. Caitlin was only fifteen last summer. And Christ knows how long it had been going on before that.

*

Rhonda hears the beep of the washing machine as it finishes its cycle. With shaking hands, she pulls out Caitlin's jeans and throws them in the tumble dryer for twenty minutes. She's not been able to focus or think of anything else since she put the washing on, her mind concocting all kinds of horrific things about Jeremy and her daughter.

Maybe she's mistaken; maybe she's read it all wrong.

Her hands are still shaking as she sloshes boiling water into a mug with a chamomile teabag, a futile attempt at steadying her nerves. As she sits in the living room, she hears Caitlin upstairs getting ready for the party – the shower running, then her favourite music on in her bedroom, an occasional text pinging her phone.

Grooming, she thinks. That's what it was. Jeremy groomed her daughter. Right under their noses. Caitlin was in awe of him, looked up to him, had been without a father figure for much of her life until she'd met Chris, and was clearly far more susceptible and vulnerable than she'd ever realised. As a mother, as a teacher with regular safeguarding training, she curses herself for not spotting it. How *could* she have missed it? And how could Jen have not noticed either?

'But she *did* notice,' Rhonda says quietly to herself, shaking her head. She has no idea how she'll tell Jen. If she even *should* tell her. She's got enough on her plate as it is.

Kieran is looking forward to the party. See you about 7pm. Thanks for taking them xx

Rhonda stares at Jen's text. *Looking forward to the party...* The poor lad has been crazy about Caitlin for several years now, hanging around her like a puppy, hoping she'll see him as more than a friend. It's clear now why she didn't – she was coerced by the older version of Kieran, her head turned by a lecherous middle-aged man.

She sips her tea, staring at the wall in front of her, her rage building as she begins to feel the anger – not towards her daughter, but towards Jeremy, a narcissistic bully who took advantage of a young girl to boost his own ego. How he must have been laughing at them all, she thinks, her mind all over the place as she plunders her memories, trying to stitch clues and signs together. With the families being so close, she'd handed her daughter over on a plate.

In the kitchen, Rhonda chucks her empty mug into the sink, wincing as it shatters. '*Christ*,' she says, leaning forward on the worktop, her head hanging down. She screws up her eyes, unable to bear the thought of that monster doing what he did.

The feel of your body against mine…

Rhonda stifles a retch, leaning over the sink just in case.

'Hey, what's wrong?' comes a voice from behind. The hand on her shoulder makes her jump.

Rhonda turns and falls into Chris's arms, shaking her head. She sobs against his shoulder, allowing herself to be held, comforted, cocooned. Her shoulders jump up and down from crying and she knows she's getting snot and tears on Chris's jacket, but she can't help it.

'Ronnie, what on earth's wrong?' Chris holds her at arm's length, tilting up her chin with a finger. He frowns when he sees the agony written on her face.

Gasping for breath between sobs, Rhonda wipes her nose on her sleeve and opens her mouth to tell him.

'Hey, Mum, are my jeans dry yet?' Caitlin comes through the kitchen and ducks into the utility room. Rhonda hears the dryer silence and the door open as her daughter removes her jeans, grumbling that they're still damp. 'They'll have to do,' she says. 'I need to make sure my top goes OK with them and—'

She stops when she sees her mum's face. 'Oh my God, are you OK?' She glances up at Chris and then back to Rhonda. 'Mum?' She puts a hand on her shoulder.

Rhonda does her best to compose herself. She forces a laugh, wiping her nose again. 'Just me being silly,' she says through a blocked-up nose and a fake smile. 'Time of the month, I think. I broke a mug and got angry with myself.' She laughs again, burying her face in Chris's shoulder.

'Aww, Mum,' Caitlin says, joining in the group hug. 'I'm so sorry you're feeling out of sorts. You don't need to take me to the party. It's not important. I can cook dinner for you if you like?'

'It's no problem, Missy,' Chris says, giving her a kiss on the head. 'You'll still go to the ball. I'm happy to drop you off. And I'll run your mum a nice bath before we go.'

Rhonda freezes, staring up at Chris, her mouth hanging open. *Missy?* She wants to scream, but she manages to stifle her emotions. For now.

'Thank you,' she says, pulling away from her husband. 'Hurry up and finish getting ready then, Caitlin, or you'll be late.'

'Time of the month, my arse,' Chris says, when Caitlin is out of earshot. 'What's going on?'

Rhonda tears off a piece of kitchen towel and blows her nose. She drags out a chair and sits down at the table. Chris joins her. 'What the *hell* did you just call Caitlin?'

'What, Missy?' he asks, rolling his eyes.

'Yes, what did you call her that for?' Rhonda blows again before balling up the tissue, trying not to sound accusatory.

Chris looks perplexed, scratching the side of his head. 'Because she asked me to a while ago. I thought it must be a pet name you had for her. Said she liked it, but I keep forgetting to use it. She was so sweet and thoughtful to you just then, it kind of slipped out naturally.'

'She *asked* you to call her Missy?'

Chris nods. 'Yup. Shouldn't I have done?'

'When did she ask?' Rhonda rests her head in her hands, feeling drained.

Chris shakes his head, thinking. 'I don't know. Not too long ago. It was just after Jeremy's memorial, I think. Why, love? You look wrung out. What's going on?'

Rhonda shakes her head, staring at the floor. 'Just take Caitlin and Kieran to the party and I'll explain later.'

Chris nods. 'I've got some news to tell you too,' he says, standing up and rubbing his hand over his chin as he paces about. His

face is serious. 'It's probably nothing, but it turns out none of our lot went round to break the news to Jen about Jeremy's death. Don't ask me how I know,' he says, touching the side of his nose, 'but there was zilch on the system about it. And it wouldn't have been any other force, either. Are you sure Jen said it was coppers who visited?' He shifts from one foot to the other.

Rhonda nods, remaining silent as Chris goes to grab his keys and chivvy Caitlin along.

*

After they've left, Rhonda goes upstairs and empties the bath Chris has run for her. She can't face lying about, stewing in her own thoughts. She knows Chris will be gone a while – with having to fetch Kieran, drive to Amy's and then go back to Shenbury and wait for the takeaway to be prepared that he promised to pick up on the way home. Rhonda knows he's likely to bump into one of his mates in the restaurant bar, have a quick catch-up over a couple of beers – low-alcohol in Chris's case.

But she can't worry about that now. Instead, she paces about, thinking, deliberating, wondering if she would want to know if she were in Jen's shoes – if Chris had done what she believed Jeremy had. She concludes that she *would* want to know, most definitely, but decides to put it to Jen in a way that won't be accusatory, rather allowing her to put two and two together and work it out herself. And then she'll have to break it to her about the passport, that she doesn't believe Jeremy went away in the first place. Between them, they might have a chance of figuring out what's happened.

Fifteen minutes later, after snapping her laptop lid closed, her heart thumping from what she found – or rather *didn't* find – Rhonda digs out the passport from her bedroom drawer and retrieves the letter from within the pages of the manuscript. She puts them both in her handbag along with the memorial note from Caitlin's jeans and grabs her coat and keys.

CHAPTER THIRTY-SEVEN

Then

Evan hears the little brat way before he sees him. *Easy as*, he thinks, having taken the long way round the estate to the scrubby fields at the back of the gardens. He heard Griff talking to the grandmother the other day, when she popped her head over the fence to ask how his mum was. Her face was wrinkled and pinched, and Evan thought she looked like an old witch, not a grandma. His mum once said she was in her fifties, and he knows that's ancient.

The afternoon sun beats down on his neck, and he feels his cheeks glowing red. The earth is dry and cracked, with the track leading through the fields at the back of the estate looking as though mini earthquakes have split the ground. *Ant earthquakes*, he thinks, his mind drifting back to when he first met Mac, how they'd had fun killing as many beetles, ladybirds and other insects as they could catch.

But where the hell *is* Mac? He'd promised to meet him at the edge of the estate half an hour ago, but there was no sign of him. He'd not been able to wait any longer. He knew the brat's mum came to pick him up at six.

Evan can't help the grin as he creeps up to the fences and hedges at the end of the gardens. His mum would be so proud of him if she knew what he was doing – not that he can tell her. He can't tell *anyone*.

He stoops down as he walks, his trainers making crunching sounds as he moves stealthily over the dry, scrubby grass. Sometimes the fields have sheep or cows in, but now it's just some stupid plants, green and low. Easy to scoot across to disappear into the woods or somewhere the brat won't find his way back. His plan doesn't go much further than that.

Number forty-one, forty-three, forty-five… he counts in his head as he passes the end of each garden. His nostrils twitch at the smell of someone's tea cooking, making him hungry. Then he stops, knowing that this is his garden, number forty-seven. He smiles smugly as he peeks through an open knot in the fence, recognising the ancient plastic trike lying on its side, faded from the sun. His mum said she was saving it for Rosie for when she was older.

And then the hedge next door. Only one of two gardens that don't have fences up. It's thick and brambly, all apart from one spot that Evan can see from his bedroom window. Sometimes at night, he sees the jewelled eyes of a fox as it runs through the gap. It's easily big enough for a little kid to fit through.

As he waits by the hedge, hardly daring to breathe, Evan looks behind him, hoping he'll see Mac catching up. But there's no one there. And then he needs to pee. He holds himself, jiggling about, for as long as he can, desperately hoping Mac will come into view soon. But he doesn't. There's nothing to see apart from a heat mirage rippling above the baked ground. He can't hold it any longer, so he goes up against the hedge, feeling a lot better for it.

'What dat…' comes a high-pitched voice from the other side as he's zipping himself up.

The kid.

Evan's skin tingles and something swells inside him – that feeling he gets when prey is close. His palms sweat as a hand reaches inside his trouser pocket for the sweets – packets of wine gums and Love Hearts he took from the tin up at the den.

'Gra… maaa… what *dat*…?' comes the toddler's voice.

Evan can tell that the kid is just the other side of the hedge now. He reckons if he kneels down, they'll almost be face to face. Did the brat hear him peeing? See his legs through the gap?

'Let Grandma hang out the sheets to dry, darling…' Evan hears from down the garden. The old bat. He knows that when she hangs out the sheets to dry, they cut her garden clean in two across the middle – a big, white shield. This is good news, Evan thinks. She's making it easy for him. Perhaps she's fed up of the screaming brat, too. Though he's not making much noise at the moment.

Evan hears the hedge rustling. Something snuffling and snotty close by.

'You play nice for Grandma,' the voice says again, but a little more distant this time.

'Gwamma…' the kid says with a giggle, banging a toy or something on the ground. Then he lets out a high-pitched squeal and then a demonic laugh, almost giving Evan a headache, just like his mum gets. Then the kid is silent again – just gurgly breaths getting closer to the gap in the hedge. Evan dares to bend down. When he peers through the thorny opening, he's virtually face to face with the little boy – his blond pudding-bowl cut shimmering in the sun.

The toddler grins. Snuffles. Sticks his thumb in his mouth.

Evan grins back. The sweets are hot and sticky in his palm.

Then a telephone rings. Shrill and loud. Cutting through the still, humid air.

'Grandma'll just get that,' Evan hears, followed by hurried footsteps.

'Lenny pway…' the toddler says quietly, his thumb connecting a string of drool to his mouth. His cherry-red lips are parted as he crouches down at the gap in the hedge, peering through. His azure eyes search around, lighting up when they catch sight of Evan's face. The kid lets out an excited squeal.

'Shhh…' Evan whispers, placing a finger over his mouth.

The toddler mimics him, spraying spit.

'Want one?' Evan whispers, holding out the wine gum packet.

The little boy eyes it as though it's treasure, his face lighting up. He shuffles closer to the gap, waddling in a squat, his nappy hanging between his thighs as it bulges from his towelling shorts.

'Lenny want…' he says, reaching out his little fist, the fingers clenching and unclenching. Then he points to the other packet of sweets Evan is holding. 'Dat.'

'Love Heart?' Evan whispers.

The toddler nods eagerly, muttering to himself as he clambers into the thicket of hedge to get closer.

'Come on, then,' Evan says quietly. 'That's a good boy. Come and get a sweetie.' He takes a pink, powdery Love Heart from the packet and holds it out to the kid, shuffling back a pace to tempt him through.

'Lenny want…' The toddler makes little grunting sounds and drops the plastic shovel he's holding in order to use his hands to get through the remainder of the hedge. When he reaches the point where it's easier to go through than back, he lets out a little squeal as a thorn catches his arm. He rubs at it, but his eyes are still on the Love Heart sweet.

'There's a good boy,' Evan croons. 'Come and get your sweetie.' He listens out for the grandmother coming as the toddler emerges through the opening. He stands up straight and beams a smile.

'Dat…' the toddler says, pointing at Evan's hand.

'Take it, then,' Evan says, stepping back a little more.

The boy toddles forward a few small paces, his feet splayed out in his plastic jelly sandals. Evan notices his toenails. Tiny.

'Good boy,' Evan whispers, handing the sweet over. The kid pops it in his mouth, making a face when it goes in. 'Want another one?'

The toddler nods.

'Come with me, then,' Evan says, holding out his hand. The kid takes it and waddles off alongside, but it's slow progress. Evan knows he only has a few more seconds before the grandmother will come back out and realise the little boy is gone. So he bends down and scoops up the toddler onto his hip, bribing him into silence by taking another Love Heart from the packet.

Evan smells the child's sickly-sweet breath as he carries him, kicking up his pace into a jog along the rough track. It does something to him, as though all his senses have been brought to life. His entire body tingles as the pressure inside him builds. It's glorious, blissful, like nothing he's ever experienced before. The toddler's hand reaches for the sweet that Evan holds out like a carrot on a stick, and it's only when the kid starts whining that he gives it to him.

It's as he shoves it in his mouth that Evan sees 'Be Mine' written on it in powdery pink lettering – just at the same time he hears, in the far distance now, the old bat's piercing scream.

CHAPTER THIRTY-EIGHT

Jen

I leave Kieran to get ready for the party and stumble out of his bedroom in a daze.

Jeremy and Caitlin…

Somehow I make it into my room and stand there, staring at Scott's clothes dumped on my bed. It takes a moment to build – but something begins to simmer, to swell, the pressure inside me increasing with every breath I take. Instead of screaming, which is what I want to do, I lunge at the stuff on my bed and hurl it all onto the floor, the rage burning deep inside my throat as the anger comes out. *Part* of the anger. With Kieran in the house, I have to keep a lid on it. But as soon as he's out the door, God help me for what I might do.

Then I hear the front door open downstairs, but I don't care. I pull and rip at Scott's clothes, tearing shirts and jackets off their hangers and stamping on them underfoot. Then, in my bathroom, I swipe all his stuff off my shelf, sending his aftershave bottle smashing onto the tiled floor. The spicy scent fills the bathroom, invading my senses. Making me feel on fire.

I splay my hands out on the tiled wall either side of the mirror above the sink. I gasp for air, my chest heaving in and out, tears streaming down my face as I try to piece together the horror of what I just saw. No wonder Kieran has been acting strange. The girl he's been trying to build up the courage to ask out for so long has been... I shake my head, unable to hold the image in my mind any longer. It's as though I never knew my husband.

'Fucking disgusting *bastard*,' I say, looking into the mirror, spit flying out of my mouth. A woman I don't recognise stares back – drawn, hollow-eyed, thin and gaunt.

And that's when I see Scott appear behind me in the mirror, his hands coming down on my shoulders, either side of my neck... his fingers slowly reaching around my throat. I cough, feeling my pulse thrumming in my temples, staring into my own eyes in the mirror as his fingers tighten.

His hands were around my throat as my head hit the wall... We'd been drinking, laughing, staggering, drinking some more... and the lights. Blinded by the dance-floor lights. Broken memories all mixed up... One minute the bar... then the next, my hotel room, the slap... Then the bar again, the crowds, the noise... Then I was on my back, my wrists restrained... my clothes ripped off, my legs forced apart.

I didn't know where I was. Time meant nothing, as though I was everywhere at once and yet nowhere at all. I wasn't me. As much as I wanted to, I couldn't say no.

I screamed. I remember screaming, though nothing came out. I heard it in my head, but not in the room around me. I had no air in my lungs to make a sound. I just wanted someone to hear me, to save me.

I thrashed my head from side to side, frantically trying to breathe as I slapped at his shoulders. That's when he released my throat and grabbed my wrists. I sucked in a lungful of air, gasping, choking, feeling the oxygen return to my brain.

Then I saw the scar... a six-inch scar running diagonally across his chest, concealed within his sandy hair. I focused on it, making sure it was the only thing I could see, the only thing that existed while my body endured the horror of what he was doing.

God, you're handsome, *I'd thought as the pain had ripped me in two. Convincing myself that he was, that he was the most beautiful*

268   Samantha Hayes

man I'd ever seen. I told myself I wanted him, that I needed this, that it was OK for him to be forcing his way in. I told myself that I loved him. That it made it all OK.

The warmth of his skin shrouding me… the scent of his spicy cologne pervading the air.

He loomed over me, my wrists pinned either side of my head. It wasn't a grin on his face, rather some kind of twisted smile – a smile that drilled into me.

Focus… focus on the scar. Nothing else. Just the scar.

He made noises, resonating deep from within his chest, as though he'd just arrived in a place he'd always dreamt of going.

The rhythm… the steady beat of him… slow, fast, hard, soft… I hated that my body responded. I couldn't help it, the feelings growing as he knew exactly what to do.

'Your… your scar…' I'd said, my voice jumping in time with his movements – a ridiculous thing to ask as he forced himself on me. 'What happened?' I needed to know.

He stopped, his body frozen above me. He took his time answering, his lips moving in slow motion as I stared up at them. There was a delay, a time lag, before the words hit my ears. It sounded as though I was underwater, drowning, seeing his lips move through the glassy surface above me.

And then, just for a second, it became clear. As though everything was in focus, everything falling into place.

Then the blackness as I passed out… perhaps from shock, perhaps from the drugs, perhaps from self-preservation. It felt as though I'd left my body. Finally, I felt free.

I grab Scott's wrists, yanking his hands off my neck, grunting with effort. I see a woman staring out of the bathroom mirror – her eyes bulging with fear, her body shaking, veins protruding.

'Hey, *hey*…' Scott says, backing off, his hands raised. 'It's OK, it's OK. You're so jumpy. I just thought you could use a shoulder rub. Bad day?'

I swing round, staring up at him. I force my breathing to slow as my hand comes up to my throat, gently touching where his hands had been.

You tried to strangle me… I want to say, but it won't come out. I don't know if I'm talking about now or then.

'Sorry about the mess,' Scott says matter-of-factly, heading into my bedroom. 'Though…' He stands with his hands on his hips, staring at his clothes thrown everywhere. 'I didn't leave it *quite* this bad. I was going to hang them up, but I went to collect more things from the storage unit before they closed. I picked us up some nice food for dinner.' He grins.

Focus on the scar…

'I'm sorry…' I find myself saying. 'I had a shock. I shouldn't have thrown your clothes on the floor.' Then I'm on my knees, fighting back the tears as I grab shirts and trousers and jackets, hooking them back onto hangers, shoving some of them into my wardrobe. 'There's space, look,' I say, turning, grinning. I must look like a madwoman. 'Plenty of room for your things too.' I need to placate him until I figure out what to do.

'Jennifer…?' Scott says. His voice is questioning, as though he doesn't trust what I'm doing. If he saw inside my head, could read my thoughts, he'd be right.

'What did you get for dinner? I'm starving,' I tell him from the floor as I gather up underwear and socks, stuffing an armful into my lingerie drawer. It doesn't close properly so I leave it half open, overflowing. 'Kieran's off to a party tonight, so we'll… we'll have the house to ourselves.' I push my fingers through my hair, trying to straighten it out, and wipe a finger under my eye, cleaning up my smudged mascara.

Scott stands there staring at me, a doubting look on his face. His mouth opens then closes again.

'Why don't you have a shower, get freshened up?' I suggest. 'Then I'll open a bottle of wine for you, put some music on. We can cook together. It'll be lovely.'

He looks at me, his head tilted, his eyes narrowing briefly. Then he glances at the bathroom. 'Looks like it's a mess in there too.'

Within seconds, I'm on my hands and knees on the tiles, unravelling toilet paper as fast as I can to gather up the broken glass and mop up the spilt liquid.

'Ouch…' I cry, silencing myself as I grab my palm, watching the bead of blood ooze from the fleshy part. Scott is standing over me, waiting. 'It's nothing,' I say, sucking it and then gathering up the bundle of mess and dropping it into the bathroom bin. 'There.' I stand up. 'Have a nice shower. There are some clean towels on the shelf.'

Scott nods, watching as I leave the bathroom, closing the door behind me. I lean back against it for a second, taking a deep breath before heading to Kieran's room, praying he didn't hear the commotion through his music. I let out a gasp as he opens his door just as I'm about to knock, taken by surprise.

Focus on the scar…

'Sorry… sorry, love.' My voice is broken and shaky. I clutch my head.

'You OK, Mum?' my son says, pulling out his earphones.

'How dapper do *you* look?' I say, trying to sound normal. And he does. A white shirt, dark jeans, his nice tan shoes. And he's put something in his hair so his curls glisten, just like Jeremy's used to.

'Thanks, Mum,' he says, slinging on his padded jacket. 'Chris texted. He's outside. He's taking me.'

I nod. 'Right, OK. Good. You're staying over?' I follow him downstairs, wrapping my arms around my body, hugging my long cardigan around me.

'Is that OK?' He glances back over his shoulder.

'Yes, of course. I'll fetch you in the morning.'

The morning... My head, oh God my throbbing head. The wine glasses... lipstick... underwear... that feeling inside – not warm and comforting as I'd convinced myself, but rather the feeling of shame, of emptiness, of violation. I was lying alone, silently weeping... though I didn't know that by then, there were already two of us.

A car horn toots outside and Kieran turns to give me a quick peck on the cheek. He's about to head out but he stops.

'I really love her, you know. Caitlin. Stupid, right?' He hangs his head. 'How could he, Mum? How could Dad do that?' Kieran's voice wobbles and croaks, like he's thirteen again. 'Those photos of girls in my room last summer? They were Dad's. I found them in a compartment of his bag when I went to borrow his earphones.'

I drop my head, feeling another surge of pain. Then I pull him in for a hug, tight and warm and safe. 'I don't have answers, love,' I whisper in his ear. 'I don't know how he could do any of it, but we'll get through this, OK? You and I. Talk to Caitlin if you can. Be there for her.' I hold him out at arm's length. He's a good boy. My son. My beautiful son, who doesn't deserve any of this. 'But mainly, go and have fun at the party. For God's sake, have a few drinks and make a fool of yourself dancing.' I feel tears prickling in my eyes, see the same in Kieran's.

We both burst out laughing.

'Love you, Mum,' he says, wiping the corner of his eye.

'Love you too, Kier. Now, off with you,' I say, patting him on the shoulder. He turns and jogs off to Chris's waiting car. In the passenger seat, I can just make out Caitlin's face breaking into a nervous smile as Kieran gets into the car.

I shut the door, my heart thumping. And that's when I see the jacket on the floor – one of Scott's that has fallen off the oak bench in the hallway, alongside several boxes of stuff he's brought back from his storage unit.

I bend down and pick it up, resigned to my fate for now. I'm freezing, shivering, so on a whim, I put the jacket on – a navy-blue, infantry-style garment with buttons and plain epaulettes and a grey check lining. The cuffs hang down over my hands as I pad barefoot into the kitchen to open the wine, knowing what I must do. I clutch my arms around my body, trying to get warm.

I take a bottle of Chablis from the fridge, carefully peeling off the foil top, and dig the corkscrew into its neck – winding, winding until I'm deep enough. Then I lever out the cork until it makes a satisfying but dull pop. Then the creamy *glug-glug* as I pour a full glass.

I take it over to the island unit and sit down on a stool – my handbag on the one beside me. I stare at it before reaching inside, digging out the slightly crumpled medicine packet. It's not the done thing to self-prescribe, but loads of GPs do it, and the local pharmacist turned a blind eye, as ever. I open the box with shaking hands, glancing towards the door, listening. I hear the *tick-tick* of the water pipes, telling me Scott has started his shower.

Good. It gives me time.

I take out the blister pack containing the two pills. That's all it will take to end someone's life – just the two.

I feel tears filling my eyes, prickling and stinging as I press my nail against the foil ready to take out the first tablet. The glass of wine is there, all ready. Tempting and fresh, chilled and dry. My eyes blur so that I can't see anything, a tear rolling down my cheek. I put the pills down and fetch some kitchen paper to wipe my face. I've got to appear normal, as though nothing untoward is happening.

I sit down again, resting my head in my hands, screwing up my eyes. All I can see is his scar, how I focused on it that night, not allowing myself to think of anything else. I studied every fibrous strand of it, every inch of the faded keloid ridge as he raped me, the hot tears flowing from the corners of my eyes. The pain inside me is still there, almost as though the blade that had slashed across Scott's chest was now sticking into me.

I gasp, opening my eyes as the memory makes my body jolt.

They said I had it coming, someone like me…

With shaking hands, I pick up the pill packet and remove the tablet, holding it between my shaking fingers. With my other hand, I pick up the glass and take a long, slow, delicious sip of wine, swallowing it, wetting my throat. Then I put the tablet in my mouth. Mifepristone – the first of a two-step process to terminate my pregnancy. I hold the pill on my tongue, ready to wash it down. But first, I pull the collar of Scott's jacket up around my face, closing my eyes, imagining that he's here with me, telling me it's OK, that I'm doing what's right for me and Kieran. That once I've done this, he'll go away, he'll leave us alone forever.

I bury my face in the fabric, breathing in Scott's scent as though he's holding me, encouraging me to do it, telling me to swallow the pill, that the nightmare will soon be over. That once the baby is gone, then he will be too.

Something cold and hard catches on my cheek, something metal.

I open my eyes, holding the fabric of the coat away from me, staring down at the lapel. And that's when I see it. Pinned to the collar of his jacket. A badge – a shiny gold eagle against a red crescent background. I don't even need to spit out the pill because my mouth falls open and the tablet drops onto the floor.

CHAPTER THIRTY-NINE

Jen

I grab the wine glass, taking three large glugs to calm my nerves, choking them down as my eyes stay fixed on the badge – an enamel and gold military-style emblem that makes me melt with fear from the inside out. I remember this badge. I remember *him* wearing it at school, parading it around as though it meant he was special. No one would ever have guessed from the way I acted, but I was quite scared of him really.

The water pipes creak above me, and the boiler hums in the utility room, telling me Scott is still in the shower. The alcohol is already hitting me, making my thoughts fuzzy, my brain disbelieving. Mainly because I don't *want* to believe it.

Scott… *Scott?* I scream in my head. *No… no, none of this is right. It can't be…*

'Focus on the scar,' I whisper, sliding off the stool. I feel the tablet crunch under my foot as I unpin the badge from the jacket, turning it over and over in my hands. There's no mistaking it. It's so distinctive.

Knowing I don't have long before he comes downstairs – having to pretend to be normal, chatting, cooking, playing happy families – I dash into the hall to where he's dumped his belongings from the storage unit and tear open the top of one of the boxes with shaking hands.

The first is filled with a few books – a couple of cookery hardbacks, some paperback novels, a book of country walks. There are some pamphlets, too – a couple about mental health services, several about rehabilitation into the community, another about social housing and benefits. From the leaflets we have at work, I can tell they're about a year or so old.

I tear open another box – and then I hear the water stop running, the clank of the shower door opening and closing.

There are a few crumpled old T-shirts in this one, nothing like I'd imagine Scott wearing, and a watch, a pair of broken sunglasses and some tangled laptop cables. Underneath, I find more papers, including those for his car, and scan through them, keeping one ear open for Scott upstairs. I know every sound this house makes – every floorboard creak, every door opening, every wheeze and sigh.

'Oh *shit…*' I say, riffling through the prison release papers, housing documents, benefit forms and what looks like some kind of travel pass. Beneath this is a folder containing more papers… about relocation, a new identity, probation officer details.

My heart thunders as I take out a battered old notebook, some of its pages torn out, with the remaining ones covered in doodles and plans and childish scrawl – stick figures with knives stuck in them, blood flowing. It's too much for me to take in quickly, and there's no time to read through all this stuff properly. The prison release papers, along with the badge, have told me all I need to know.

Evan Locke has come back for me – just as he always swore he would.

And then I spot it, lying at the bottom of the box. A USB stick – small and black with a black cord attached to it. I grab it, chucking the papers back in the box, and scramble up off the floor, shedding the heavy coat as I run back to the kitchen where my laptop is charging. The badge is still in my hand, clutched in my sweaty palm.

'Come on, come *on*,' I whisper, waiting for my computer to boot up. Upstairs, I hear the floorboards in my bedroom creaking, my wardrobe door opening and closing. He'll be down at any moment.

'Thank God,' I whisper as the desktop screen finally appears. I shove the USB stick into the port, my fingers trembling so much it takes several attempts to get it in. My breaths are short and shallow, making me light-headed, so I take the laptop over to the stool and sit at the island worktop, clicking on the USB drive on my screen, waiting as the icons resolve.

Photos. Hundreds of them.

One by one the thumbnails appear on my screen, many of which I recognise from Scott's phone when he taunted me, showing me what had happened *that* night, threatening to blackmail me with all the pictures.

Focus on the scar…

I double-click on the first one, cupping my hand over my mouth, seeing myself lying beneath him, lipstick smeared in a red slash across my face, mascara smudged into two black eyes. My mouth is hanging open and my tongue half sticks out, and the way my head is twisted to one side, with my eyeballs rolled back in their sockets, I barely look conscious.

I cough and choke into my hand, wiping my palm on my jeans. There's no time to be sick. I go back to the thumbnail screen and scroll down, my finger wavering on the trackpad. And then I find the other batch, confirming what I saw on his phone the other night. Except this is in way more detail – as though I'm reliving the whole thing again.

I dash to the kitchen sink and hold my hair back, throwing up in the washing-up bowl. It's just the few mouthfuls of wine, but my stomach cramps and knots. I wipe my mouth on the tea towel, trying to steady my nerves. And then I hear footsteps on the stairs. Scott is coming down.

Quickly, I whip the USB stick from the port and shove it in my pocket, shutting down the window on my screen and slamming the laptop lid closed.

'That feels much better,' Scott says, striding into the kitchen, stretching. He stops dead when he sees me. 'Oh, Jennifer, my love. You look terrible.' His eyes flick to my computer and then to my hands, where I'm wringing out the tea towel, trying not to shake.

'I… I was sick,' I tell him, glancing behind me. He peers into the sink and pulls a face.

'Poor love,' he tells me, taking me by the shoulders. 'These hormones are playing havoc with you. But just think of our little baby growing inside you.'

I nod vigorously, swiping a strand of sweaty hair off my face. 'Here…' I say, easing out of his grip. 'I poured you a drink.' I grab the remains of the wine and hand it to him.

'Are we on rations?' he says, laughing as he tops up the glass.

'Sorry,' I say, moving my laptop out of the way. I don't want him asking questions.

And that's when Scott sees the badge sitting on the counter behind it – our eyes both fixing on it at the same time. He swipes it up, glaring at me. 'So you found it then,' he says, his tone suddenly hard and cold.

'It… it… was on your jacket. I was chilly so I put it on and then—'

The blow is short and sharp to the side of my head. I stagger back against the worktop, my vision blurry, raising my hand to my smarting face.

'Scott… it's OK, it's all fine,' I say, trying to sound convincing through my shaking voice. 'Why… why don't you put the badge on? For old times' sake.'

He stares at me, wondering whether to trust me. When he says nothing, I go up to him, as though I'm creeping up on a nervous animal, and take the badge from between his fingers. Then I pin it on his shirt, right about where his scar is hidden beneath the fabric.

'There,' I say, taking a look. 'You look fine.'

Scott glances down, then up again at me, his eyes boring into mine. I smile, and he offers me a small one back, gradually showing his teeth as it turns into a grin.

Then I undo a couple of his buttons and slide my hand inside his shirt, my fingers tracing across his chest until I find the scar. I stroke it gently until I hear a crooning sound at the back of his throat.

'You're safe now, Evan,' I tell him. 'No one is going to hurt you any more. Those men who did this to you in prison, they didn't understand.'

'No, no, they didn't,' Scott whispers, sweat appearing on his top lip. 'Child murderer, they called me. Said I had it coming. They tried to kill me, said next time they'd succeed.' Scott's breathing is heavy and I feel the rise and fall of his chest. 'They didn't know that I *had* to do it, Jen. That if I didn't, my mum would die.' He snorts out a half-sob. 'But that bastard killed her anyway.'

'I know, I *know*,' I say, praying I can placate him long enough to work out what to do. 'But they can't hurt you now. You're safe here with me,' I whisper, resting my head on his chest. I feel his hand on my head, his fingers gently playing with my hair.

It seems as though we stay like this forever, rocking gently as we stand in the kitchen, our heartbeats synchronising to a beat from long ago.

'Here,' I say after a while, when my shaking has subsided and I hear Scott's – *Evan's* – heart slow to a regular rhythm. 'Have some more wine.' I reach for the glass. 'Drink up,' I tell him, my mind racing at a thousand miles per hour.

CHAPTER FORTY

Jen

Drink up… I'd said the same to Jeremy the night before his trip. I couldn't stand the thought of him going to Switzerland with Madeleine. I'd convinced myself that if he did, our marriage would be over. All this – our beautiful home, the life we'd forged between us, our son, all the memories we'd made and shared together – it would be gone. Trashed for the sake of a few clichéd nights with a younger woman.

I figured if he overslept, if he missed the flight, then he'd take it as a sign and stay home with Kieran and me. He'd never get another booking at such short notice at that time of year and, even if he did, it would give me more of a chance to talk him out of it. I'd be able to convince him that we'd have the best New Year ever and he'd be glad he'd stayed home.

'I'd better not,' he'd said as I held the glass out to him. 'I have to leave here at 5 a.m. to get to the airport. You know how important this documentary is to me. I've got a good feeling about this one, Jen. I really think it's going to be big.'

I must have looked crestfallen as I dropped down into the sofa, placing the wine glass on the coffee table. I'd got one myself and had specially prepared that one for him.

'Really?' I'd said. 'We won't be able to raise a toast at New Year after all.'

I remember him eyeing the glass as the ten o'clock news came on the television – it was one of his favourite bottles of red. 'Mmm, this *is* delicious,' I'd said, sipping mine, curling up beside him on the sofa. I'd put my hand on his thigh, bringing it higher. 'Do you really have to go?' I'd tried every tactic over the last couple of weeks – from being tearful, to getting angry, to pretending I didn't care.

And still the messages from 'M' had pinged onto his phone, with him telling me I was mad, imagining it, and the latest – I was driving him away.

'*Jen…*' he'd said in a playful but chastising way as my hand had crept higher still. He'd grabbed my wrist and kissed it, making me wonder if I'd imagined everything, that things *were* fine between us and always had been, and I was just stressed and tired like he said. 'I haven't even finished packing yet. God knows where my passport has got to.'

'I'll help you,' I'd said, hoping it wouldn't come to that. I reached over to the coffee table, handing him the glass. 'Go on, you know you want to.'

'You're incorrigible,' he'd replied. 'But what the hell. Cheers.'

We'd clinked glasses, watched the news. Then I'd gone into the kitchen and refilled our drinks again. It took me a while, and by this time, Jeremy was way more relaxed, but I wanted to make sure. He was a big man.

'Not sure about this wine, actually,' he'd commented, holding up the glass. 'Is it the Rioja you opened?'

'Mmm,' I'd confirmed. 'Don't you like it? I think it's quite nice.'

Jeremy had done his usual swirling of the glass, inhaling it deeply before sipping it. He pulled a face as he drank, and we sat there watching the news then the weather, and I noticed at one point he'd dozed off.

'Love?' I'd said, flicking the television off with the remote an hour or so later. 'Are you awake? It's getting late.'

He'd mumbled something then, the empty wine glass held by the stem between two fingers propped on his lap. I took it from him and put it on the table. By then, he'd finished the whole bottle, while I'd been making sure I filled his glass out in the kitchen. Once he'd had one glass, he had no willpower.

'You look done in, Jer.'

'Mmm…' he'd said, his head lolling back on the cushion.

I'd waited a bit longer, trying to talk to him, but he was getting less and less coherent. I'd encouraged him to get into a more comfortable position, helping him put his legs up on the sofa, putting a cushion under his head, him groaning as I did so. I even covered him with a blanket. All I wanted was for him to sleep through the night, until it was too late to get to the airport. And for good measure, I'd made his passport especially hard to find. I wasn't proud of myself, but I was desperate. I wanted to save my marriage.

Breathing a little easier, I'd gone up for a shower then, wrapping myself in my silk paisley robe and tying it at the waist as I came out of the bathroom.

Then I'd let out a little scream.

Jeremy was standing there, swaying, his face red and his eyes bloodshot. He looked dreadful.

'Christ, you made me jump,' I said, smiling to hide my disappointment that he was awake so soon.

'I need to pack,' he said, opening the wardrobe doors, reaching out a hand but missing the hangers entirely. He was all over the place. 'Passport… I need to find my passport.'

'Isn't it in your study cupboard where you usually keep it?'

He'd looked at me then, as if he didn't even recognise me. 'Study… yeah…' he'd repeated and staggered off towards the stairs, leaving me to get into bed.

*

'Cheers,' Scott says to me now. 'This wine tastes good,' he comments, holding the glass up to the light. 'I'm no connoisseur, but I like it.' His mood is steadier now, less volatile, and he's still wearing his badge, occasionally touching it with his finger. He seems like a little boy again.

I smile, opening the fridge to get out the food Scott has bought for dinner. 'I have a nice bottle of Rioja you can have with dinner. Make a night of it, eh?'

'Sounds good to me,' Scott says, coming up and taking me by the waist. His face pushes against my neck, shivers running down my spine as he kisses my skin. 'Hey, you,' I giggle, squirming inside from the pretence. 'Mmm… sea bass,' I say, easing my way out of his clutches with the fish in my hand. 'My favourite.'

Scott busies himself with preparing some vegetables, while I tell him I'm popping out to the garage to fetch the wine from Jeremy's store. *I could grab my car keys and drive off*, I tell myself as I pull on my shoes and go outside, waiting for the garage door to trundle up.

'But I can't, I can't, I *can't…*' I whisper over and over as I search the garage. I can dispose of the USB stick but, even if I manage to get into his phone to delete the photographs, I can't delete his mind, erase his memory. He can still do plenty of harm.

There – on the shelves behind Jeremy's Stag. All the car maintenance stuff he used when he tinkered with the old thing. I pat its bonnet as I squeeze past, tripping over something on the floor, reaching out and grabbing the precarious metal shelving unit to steady myself. A load of bottles and cans crash to the floor, making a terrible noise.

I freeze, listening out in case Scott comes to see what's going on, but my shaky breaths are the only thing to be heard – and the soft hoot of an owl in the distance. I grab the container I need from the lowest shelf then pick my way across the cluttered garage to Jeremy's wine store. The plastic tub containing the girl's under-pants catches my eye. It's no mystery who sent them any more.

I pluck a couple of bottles of red from the rack and head back inside, slipping off my shoes and grabbing my doctor's bag. I quietly unlock Jeremy's study before Scott realises I'm inside again, flicking on the light after I gently close the door. Thankfully, Scott has put some music on in the kitchen and is clattering pots and pans about. He's up for playing happy families again now that I've appeased him, gone along with his deluded ideas. It doesn't take a doctor to see he has serious mental health issues.

I take two of the good wine glasses from the drinks cabinet, the ones Jeremy and I got as a wedding present and always used on special occasions – Christmas, birthdays, anniversaries – and grab the bottle opener from the cabinet to uncork the wine.

Like I did a few weeks ago, the night before Jeremy was due to leave, I crush up a few 10 milligram diazepam tablets with the back of a spoon, mixing just a little of the powder into one of the glasses of wine, keeping some for later. I can't have it tasting too bitter. My hand shakes as I stir the liquid, making sure all the tiny particles are dissolved. Scott isn't as large as Jeremy, so I'm praying I have enough. I'd only intended for Jeremy to fall asleep for the night, but it didn't work. Similarly, I just want Scott asleep too.

CHAPTER FORTY-ONE

Jen

'That was delicious,' I say, putting my knife and fork together. 'Are you OK?' I ask Scott as he sits opposite me. His eyelids appear droopy and he's swaying in his chair. I suggested we eat in the dining room, near the big glass doors that lead into the garden. I'd switched all the garden lights on earlier, while he was serving up. 'It looks so pretty out, especially when it's frosty. It's very romantic.'

I'd strung the lights up several summers ago, but sometimes put them on in winter too. They trail through the trees and hedge right down to the end of the garden, even reflecting on the pond in the paddock beyond. I needed him to believe everything was just as he wanted – that we were a perfect, happy family.

Scott gives me a lazy look – one that tells me his brain is sluggish and tired. 'I never stopped thinking about you, Jennifer. All the time I was in prison.'

He takes another sip of his wine, yawning. I've managed to top up his drink several more times when he's gone to the bathroom or popped into the kitchen, stirring in more of the crushed tablets. He pulled a face a couple of times, asking me what the wine was, if I'd had it before. When I asked if he didn't like it, acted offended, he smiled and drank up.

'Really?' It comes as a surprise. There was nothing that had ever suggested he felt *that* way about me at school and in fact, I'd believed the opposite was true. After everything that had happened, I'd lived in fear of ever meeting him again. He'd been a vulnerable kid with difficulties at home. I should have known better.

'The thought of you kept me going, Jennifer. Day and night, it was you who was on my mind. I'd never have got through all those years of being locked up in those wretched places without you. I was transferred several times, but you were always right there with me.' Scott yawns, drinks more wine. 'How things were at school…' He smiles at the memory. 'I had a long time to think about everything after the trial, and figured it probably meant you liked me. What do they call it – pigtail pulling?' A dreamy look comes over his face and I'm not sure if it's from what's in the wine or the memory.

I fight back the fear creeping up my throat. Whatever he thinks about me – then or now – it doesn't matter. I just need the diazepam to hurry up and kick in, for him to fall asleep.

'Why don't you sit in the armchair by the glass doors?' I suggest. I've already turned the central heating thermostat up to its highest setting in the hope that will help. 'You look done in.'

Scott nods, standing up. He grabs hold of the table as he wobbles and sways. 'Christ, did I have that much?' he says, slurring as he drains his glass. 'I feel so tired.' A sheen of sweat covers his face.

'I'll go and wash up and then we can watch a movie, or maybe get an early night.' I force myself to kiss the top of his head as he drops down into the chair. Before I gather up the plates, I drape a tartan blanket over his knees.

'The lights,' Scott says, half raising his hand and pointing down to the garden. 'Magical…' His eyes roll back in their sockets as he tries to focus, squinting then growing wide again. 'Any more wine?' he asks and, naturally, I oblige.

*

After I've cleared the plates, Scott doesn't notice that I slip back through the dining room into the hallway and back into Jeremy's study. I can't allow myself to dwell on what I'm about to do – only that, ultimately, I am *preserving* life, even if it goes against everything I trained to do. Over the years, I've become adept at blocking things out, parcelling up things in neat compartments in my mind, getting on with things in my ordered and precise way. I wouldn't have coped otherwise.

I grab my doctor's bag, thankful for the home visits I make – always keeping a supply of essential items to hand just in case. I take out two of the largest syringes I have and set them out on Jeremy's desk. Then I grab the container of antifreeze I brought in from the garage and pour a large measure of the bright-blue liquid into a whisky tumbler. On the desk, I open the first syringe packet, my hands trembling as I take off the needle cap and stick it in the fluid. Then I pull out the plunger, slowly drawing up the liquid into the barrel. I do the same with the second.

'No…' I whisper, thinking out loud. 'I need to be certain.' Knowing I won't get a second chance, I head out of the study, opening the door just a crack at first, listening out. But everything is quiet – apart from the soft classical music I'd put on at low volume in the dining room. I creep into the downstairs toilet just off the hallway and open the cabinet under the sink. I take the bottle of bleach back into the study, lock the door behind me and remove two more syringes from their packets, filling them up in the same way.

'Dear God, forgive me,' I whisper, every cell in my body shaking. I know if I don't do this, then not only is my life over, but Kieran's will be too. He's already lost one parent, and I can't allow him to lose me as well.

I touch my stomach. 'Nor you, little one,' I say quietly. 'I'm so sorry…' I add. If I hadn't discovered Scott's – *Evan's* – badge, realised who he was, then I'd have taken the tablet and then, later, the second abortion pill. My pregnancy would have terminated shortly after. I shudder at the thought, putting the needle caps back on all four of the syringes and tucking them in the large pockets of my cardigan.

I take a breath and head out of the study, trying to appear normal in case Scott is somehow still awake. Along with the diazepam, I'd added several crushed zopiclone to his food too, stirring it into the sauce after I'd served mine.

'Hey, hey, sleepyhead,' I say, walking up to Scott. I stand over the armchair, slightly angled towards the large glass doors leading out to the terrace and beyond.

Nothing.

I stare at his chest, rising and falling slowly. Breaths per minute are low. I take his wrist, floppy and heavy, and feel for his pulse. Again, it's slow and weak. Just how I need him.

'Scott, are you awake?' I say loudly, crouching down beside him.

Still nothing.

I lift one of his eyelids and see his pupil slowly react, but he stares straight through me. The drugs in combination with a large amount of alcohol have done their work – for now. But whether they mask the sting of a needle is yet to be seen.

I give him a shake, purposefully shoving his bad shoulder to see if that will rouse him. A low moan comes from his throat and his lips part, but that's it. No other movement. I do it again, prodding him harder, but not even a moan this time. He's out cold.

Before I can change my mind, I take the syringes from my pocket and place them on the side table next to the chair. His shirtsleeve is rolled up, sitting neatly above the crook of his elbow, exposing the paler flesh of his inner arm. A blue-grey vein stands out, the tight fabric of his shirt having acted like a tourniquet, saving me a job. I take the cap off the first syringe and, out of habit, I give it a tap to dislodge any air bubbles, pressing the plunger slowly until a drop of liquid dribbles out of the end. Not that it matters.

Slowly and gently, I insert the fine needle into his vein, my eyes flicking between his skin and his face to check for any reactions. I've always prided myself on giving painless injections. I bite my bottom lip, concentrating as, finally, I'm satisfied the needle is positioned correctly. Then I gently press the plunger, watching the blue liquid inside the barrel diminish as the antifreeze enters his body.

Scott doesn't make a sound, so I continue, injecting the poison into his body, watching the barrel drain. All the while, in my head, I'm telling myself I have to do this, that if I don't then my son's life, and mine, as we know it, will be over. After a few more seconds, I slowly withdraw the syringe and then do the same with the one containing bleach. Then I repeat with the other two, having delivered what will undoubtedly be lethal amounts of chemicals – especially without immediate medical treatment.

Scott will never wake up. And everything inside his head will disappear with him.

Without looking back, I scramble to my feet, gathering up the syringes and dumping them in the kitchen bin until I can dispose of them properly. Then I retrieve Scott's phone from the kitchen and go back to the dining room, taking his hand, peeling his forefinger away from his palm to imprint on the home button, unlocking the device.

Shaking, I go to his photo stream and delete the folder containing all the pictures of me – photos and videos I had absolutely no idea he was taking – both from his phone and from the cloud storage.

For a moment, I stare out at the lit-up garden, two long strings of lights trailing down towards the paddock, remembering that terrible night – the night when everything changed. How Scott could have taken those pictures, I have no idea, but he did – and all without me having a clue. My mind was elsewhere at the time.

I shudder. There's no time for regrets or memories, past or present. I must only look forward now, for Kieran and my baby's sake. And there's still work to be done.

I slip the phone into my pocket, feeling under Scott's jaw. Ever so faintly, I detect the erratic tick of a faint pulse. If he were conscious, he'd be in agony. The chemicals will destroy his blood cells and, before long, after other irreparable organ damage, his heart will stop beating. It may take a little while yet but, meantime, I'll make preparations. As a doctor, I'm no stranger to dealing with dead bodies – when, eventually, he's dead.

'You look so peaceful,' I say, standing up, hating him for everything he's done – to poor little Lenny Taylor, to Lenny's mother and Elsie, as well as to me. I'm about to fold his arms across his body, but I freeze. I heard a noise – the familiar sound snapping me back to reality.

The front door.

Opening and closing.

Then I hear a voice.

'Hell-*ooo*...?'

And when I swing round, Rhonda is standing in the doorway, her smile falling away as her eyes flick between me and Scott.

CHAPTER FORTY-TWO

Rhonda

'Jen, hi…' Rhonda stops, glancing between Scott and Jen. She tries to hide her disappointment that he's here still, but Jen knows her so well, she'll see it written all over her face.

'Ronnie…' Jen's voice is flat and broken.

'Am I interrupting?' Rhonda says, coming further into the dining room. 'Sorry, the front door was slightly open so I thought I'd let myself in.'

'It was?' Jen says, clasping her hands under her chin. She steps in front of where Scott is sitting or – taking a nap, by the looks of it. 'I… I went out to the garage earlier. I must have forgotten to lock it.'

'That's not like you.' Rhonda takes off her coat and hangs it on the back of a dining chair, keeping hold of her handbag. She feels the pressure in her chest building to an almost unbearable level. Deep breathing on the drive over hadn't helped, and she'd played out a dozen or more times in her mind how she was going to tell Jen everything she knew. Probably just spitting it out was best. After everything else, the poor woman was probably immune to shock.

'Is he asleep?' Rhonda whispers, coming up closer. If he is, she doesn't want to wake him. She needs to talk to Jen in private.

'Um… yes, yes he is,' Jen blurts out quietly. Her eyes are red and bloodshot and Rhonda can't help noticing that her entire body is shaking. And she looks pale – so thin and gaunt.

'Are you… are you OK?' Rhonda mouths, beckoning with her head towards the kitchen.

Jen shakes her head, but then nods vigorously with a look of regret sweeping over her face. Her mouth hangs open. Rhonda reaches out and takes her hand, encouraging her to follow.

'What's going on, Jen?' Rhonda says in a more normal voice, shutting the kitchen door behind them. 'Is everything OK with Mr Cocklodger in there? He looked a bit wiped out. Is he drunk? Giving you a hard time? You don't look at your best if I'm hon—'

'Shut up,' Jen spits through tight lips. She grabs hold of the worktop to steady herself, her breath heaving in and out of her chest.

Rhonda recoils. 'Jen, what the *hell's* going on? Do you want me to call Chris to come round? If Scott is giving you a hard time, he'll get rid of him. He's just picking up a takeaw—'

'No!' Jen snaps, covering her mouth. 'I… I'm sorry, Ronnie. I'm just a bit tired. You know, hormones. It's probably best if you go now.'

Rhonda looks at her, her eyes narrowing, trying to read the situation. 'No,' she says quite calmly. 'I'm not going anywhere, Jen. And if needs be, I'm stopping the night. Take it from me, you do *not* look well. Is everything OK with your pregnancy?'

'Yes, yes, the baby's fine,' Jen replies, glancing back at the door. 'Scott and I… we just had a bit of a tiff, that's all. He had a bit too much to drink, said some things he regretted and now he's sleeping it off. I've asked him to leave. He'll be gone in the morning, you'll see.'

Rhonda stares at Jen, frowning, trying to read her, trying to figure out if she's telling the truth. She wonders if now is the best time to deliver the bombshell she's about to drop, but by the looks of it, Jen could hardly feel much worse. Perhaps it's best to get it out of the way.

'Shall I put the kettle on?' Rhonda suggests, doing it anyway. 'What about one of those nice calming night-time teas you have?'

Jen doesn't say anything, rather she sits down, perching on the edge of a stool, watching Rhonda as if she's not really there. Her eyes seem vacant and frightened, as though she's empty inside.

'Here,' Rhonda says, handing her a mug a few minutes later. She sits down on the stool beside her, sliding her handbag within reach. 'While he's sleeping it off in there, there's something I need to run by you, Jen. It's a bit delicate, actually.'

Jen slowly looks across at her friend. To Rhonda's surprise, a smile forms – a lopsided one, exposing her teeth. And then she laughs – just a quiet, barely audible laugh, making her seem slightly irrational. Rhonda reaches out and touches her arm, a quizzical look on her face.

'I washed Caitlin's jeans earlier. For the party,' Rhonda begins. She sees Jen is listening, even though there's a faraway look in her eyes. 'And I found something in her back pocket.' Rhonda reaches into her bag and takes out the memorial note and lays it on the worktop between them. 'Do you remember these?' she says, sliding it over.

Jen peers down at it, giving a little nod. She wipes her nose on the cuff of her cardigan sleeve.

'Caitlin wrote this note. To Jeremy. I'm really sorry, Jen. I think…' Rhonda trails off. She has no idea what Jen is thinking as she reads the words.

'Missy?' Jen finally says, looking up at Rhonda.

'It's… it's a nickname Caitlin liked him to call her. I think… oh God, this is going to sound awful, Jen, and I don't even know how to say it, but I think Jeremy and Caitlin were… I think he…'

Jen says nothing. She takes a sip of her tea, wincing as she burns her lips, but that's it.

'I found this, too. Tucked inside Jeremy's manuscript. Do you remember, he gave it to me to read last year? To be honest, I've not had much of a chance to get stuck in, but this was between the pages and…' Rhonda silences herself, taking out the letter from her bag and also laying it out between them.

Again, Jen's eyes skim over the words and Rhonda can't be sure she's actually reading them. But her finger comes up and touches the 'M' signed off at the end.

'Is this Missy too?' Jen asks a few moments later, implying she understands exactly.

Rhonda nods, grasping Jen's hand. 'I'm so sorry,' she whispers.

Jen laughs again, hysterically this time, tipping back her head to expose her sinewy neck and protruding collarbones. 'I already knew,' she says, her voice suddenly calm. 'Kieran showed me a couple of photographs on his phone earlier… from Caitlin.'

Rhonda doesn't understand.

'He'd asked her if she had any pictures of his dad from our holiday at the beach house last summer,' Jen continues. 'I don't think Caitlin realised she'd sent one particular photo to Kieran or, if she did, she hadn't twigged that it was actually a mini video clip. It was of Jeremy and Caitlin on the beach.'

Jen falls silent for a moment, but then her sharp voice cuts through the kitchen.

'When Kieran showed me the clip, they were kissing, Ronnie. On the lips. A proper kiss, like between adults. She slides off her stool and walks over to the sink, pacing back and forth. She swings round, spit collecting in the corner of her mouth. 'Except one of them *wasn't* an adult, was she?'

Rhonda shakes her head. 'No, Jen. No, she wasn't.'

'My husband and your daughter were having an *affair*, Ronnie…' She covers her face. 'How could I have been so bloody stupid?'

'Jen—'

Suddenly Jen's fists are clenched together into tight balls and she lets out a piercing scream, her head tipped right back. She screws up her eyes and stamps her feet and then her arms flail out, swiping across the worktop, sending jars and spices and oil bottles skidding onto the floor. She kicks at them in rage.

'Hey, *hey*... come on now,' Rhonda says, reaching out and trying to stop her in case she hurts herself. 'Don't blame yourself. It wasn't Madeleine like you suspected,' Rhonda says. 'And please don't hate me, but I went to meet with her. Turns out that she also knew about Caitlin... everything she said added up. I believe her.'

Rhonda waits as Jen absorbs the news. 'Come and sit down, Jen,' she says firmly. 'I'll clean the mess up in a bit. I'm afraid I found out something else. Something that I can't actually figure out. It makes me concerned for any... well, perhaps any plans Jeremy and Caitlin may have cooked up together. And are perhaps still plotting.'

Rhonda's heart thunders in her chest. She's heard of such stories – in one case, it was a fifteen-year-old schoolgirl who'd run off with a forty-year-old teacher, fleeing to the Continent proclaiming their love. Her parents were powerless and Rhonda never found out what had happened to the girl... but she doubted it was a fairy-tale ending. She didn't want the same for her daughter.

She reaches into her bag and pulls out Jeremy's passport, laying it down on the counter. 'I'm so very sorry, Jen, but I don't believe Jeremy went to Switzerland for New Year at all.'

'*What*...?' Jen glances at Rhonda then back at the passport. She picks it up, her hands shaking, licking her chapped lips as she flips through the pages. 'Jeremy's passport?' she says, her words barely audible. 'Where the *hell* did you get this?'

'Shoot me down for snooping, Jen, but it wasn't what I was even looking for. I was searching for another letter I believed Caitlin had written to Jeremy. I figured it was hidden in his study somewhere and I didn't want you to find it and get upset.'

'You were in Jeremy's study? But I keep it locked.'

Rhonda hangs her head. 'And I know where you keep the key. Look, I was only trying to help, Jen. But I think we've got way bigger problems than that now.'

Jen pauses, thinking, then lets out another unhinged laugh. 'No, Rhonda. No. I think *you've* got a big problem. With your daughter. You leave my husband out of this. You know nothing about him. He… he had two passports. One… one of them got lost, so he applied for another, then he found the first. He must have been travelling on his other one when he left.'

Rhonda can't help but notice the tears in Jen's eyes, the unconvincing way she says it, trying to defend her husband at all costs.

'But don't you see, Jen? It means he might still be alive. Chris told me that no one from the local force even came out to see you that night to break the news. Before I came here, I looked up a few news reports about the avalanche. I couldn't find Jeremy's name anywhere on the list of those missing or dead, Jen. Could it have been fake, a set-up?'

'You… you don't *believe* me?' Jen turns pale. 'There was confusion about how many skiers had gone off-piste that day. I didn't want his name plastered everywhere, so I insisted it was kept private. Anyway, I… I never said it was the local force,' she snaps. 'I had contact from the Swiss authorities. I already told you that. Perhaps it was someone from the embassy – I can't remember, I was so upset.'

Rhonda knows for certain that she said it was a pair of coppers from the local force, but she's not about to press the point. Jen is far too upset as it is.

'You need to go now,' Jen says abruptly. 'I have to clear up from dinner. I want to get an early night.' She stands, heading to the kitchen door and waiting for Rhonda to follow, which, reluctantly, she does. As they pass the dining room, Rhonda ducks in to grab her coat, taking a last look at Scott, wondering whether to say goodbye, but he's still sleeping.

And that's when she catches sight of the badge pinned to his shirt.

'Jen?' she whispers, halting, grabbing her arm.

'Not now, Ronnie, I'm tired,' she whispers in return.

'That badge he's wearing, where did it come from?' Rhonda's eyes flick up to Scott's face. He really doesn't look well – he's a funny colour and there's foam dribbling out of his mouth. What a state to get in. But she doesn't care about that now – she's just relieved that he's zonked out from too much booze and they don't have to deal with him.

'I… I don't know. It's Scott's. He had it on his coat earlier and—'

But before Jen finishes, Rhonda dashes off to the hall and runs up the stairs as fast as she can. She hurls Kieran's bedroom door open, her eyes scanning around his room. She flings open the wardrobe doors and hunts through his clothes.

'What the hell are you doing, Ron?' Jen says, catching up behind her. 'I'm really in no mood for this right now. I just want to go to bed.'

'Where's Kieran's jacket? The one he wore when we went out for pizza?'

'Umm…' Jen looks puzzled, touching her temple. 'I don't know. On the back of his door, maybe?' She turns to look and, sure enough, hanging behind his dressing gown is Kieran's well-worn old jacket.

Rhonda pushes past and snatches it down, rummaging in the left pocket and then the right. A second later, she pulls out something, holding it up for them both to see.

'It's the same, Jen. The same badge as Scott is wearing. Don't you see?'

Jen stares at the badge for a moment, before taking it from between Rhonda's fingers. 'No, no I don't see. What's going on?' Her voice is shaky and uncertain.

'Where did Kieran get this?' Rhonda asks.

Jen blinks furiously. She opens her mouth as if she wants to say something, but nothing comes out.

Rhonda grabs Jen by the shoulders. 'Look, Jen. I know this is a lot to take in, but the child killer, Evan Locke… he had this exact same badge on him in his mugshot from way back when he was caught. No doubt about it. I've checked online and they're not at all common – some military award thing. And Scott is wearing exactly the same one, and now we find Kieran has one in his coat pocket.'

Jen stares blankly into Rhonda's eyes.

'Did Jeremy give this to Kieran?' Rhonda asks, not knowing where else it could have come from.

'Maybe. Yes… yes, possibly.' Jen frowns, looking even more flustered as the lines deepen on her forehead. 'In fact, I remember now. Yes, Jeremy did give it to Kieran.'

'Don't you see? Scott is Evan Locke, Jen. He must be. You'd never have recognised him from his childhood pictures, but look closely and I swear it's the same man. I've read all about the case online. He was released with a new identity well over a decade ago, but then quickly reoffended and ended up back inside. He's spent most of his adult life behind—'

'You're right,' Jen says calmly, as though the penny is finally dropping. 'In fact, I'd just discovered exactly the same. I knew him from school. It's what we were arguing about, which is why I've told him he must leave in the morning. He understands that I don't want… that I don't want an ex-convict in the house. It's unthinkable. He's agreed to go, and I'm certain I will never hear from him again.' She sounds almost robotic.

Rhonda sits down on the edge of Kieran's bed. She tugs on Jen's arm, indicating she should sit down too. 'I actually did lots of digging into the murder, Jen. I found old papers in the attic at school, and there's quite a lot of information online, too. As a kid yourself at the time, you perhaps didn't realise the gravity of the case, how it swept the country.'

Jen nods blankly. 'Oh, I did.'

'There was mention of an accomplice, some other kid involved in planning the toddler's murder. It was all premeditated. They had some kind of sick club, apparently. Forensic psychologists pored over the evidence, tried to get Evan to talk. Those two kids were born murderers, Jen. Born evil. It was disgusting. But Evan Locke always denied anyone else was involved, taunting the police and the court from what I've read.'

'OK,' Jen says. 'You probably ought to go now, Ron—'

'Jen, I believe the other person involved was Jeremy.'

Jen's eyes grow wide. She stares at Rhonda for a moment, her only movement a swallow.

'*What*? You really want to destroy my husband's reputation, don't you? Why? Because your daughter claims that he—'

'Jen, no, stop. That's not it. Of course, I'm upset and angry as hell if anything happened between him and Caitlin. She's a child, for Christ's sake. But this is separate. This is something different entirely. And with his passport still being here... God, none of this adds up.'

'Does it need to?' Jen says after a moment. 'Jeremy is dead. He can't hurt Caitlin any more, if that's what you're worried about. If you want to drag his reputation through the gutter, destroy Kieran's life, my life, my baby's life, even more than they already have been, then go right ahead. If you do, you are not the friend I thought—'

A noise. Coming from downstairs. A crashing sound. Then a moan.

Rhonda takes Jen by the shoulders. 'Of course I'm your friend, Jen. I always will be, whatever has happened. I just wanted to warn you about...'

More sounds from downstairs.

'I need to sort him out,' Jen says, her face suddenly deathly pale. 'He's clearly not well. I swear to God he's leaving in the morning and we will never see him again. Do you trust me on that?'

Rhonda stares into her eyes, then nods. 'OK, yes. Yes, I do, but I don't like it. Any trouble from him at all, and you call Chris. We're just at home tonight. He'll be round like a shot.'

The women head downstairs and Rhonda is ushered to the front door. 'Are you sure you don't want any help getting him to bed?' she says, peering through into the dining room. 'He's fallen onto the floor – look, for heaven's sake.'

Jen looks back over her shoulder, managing a laugh. 'And that's exactly where he'll stay until morning. By which time, I'll have all his stuff in his car and he'll be gone. I'm a doctor, Jen. Trust me on this. Let me deal with it.'

Eventually, Rhonda nods, giving her friend a kiss on the cheek before heading out of the house and driving back home to her husband.

CHAPTER FORTY-THREE

Jen

I watch the tail lights of Rhonda's car as it turns right at the end of the drive, disappearing into the night. I now have until morning to clean up this incomprehensible mess in which I find myself.

'Oh Christ,' I say when I see Scott lying on the floor, his cheek pressed against the rug. One leg convulses and several of his fingers twitch, but otherwise he doesn't move. His skin is now mottled and purple, his eyes glassy, and I can't detect any movement in his chest. Bloody foam froths from his mouth.

He is dying. Nearly dead now.

I cover my face, letting out a sob. But I have to hold it together – for Kieran's sake, for my baby's sake. For *my* sake. I never wanted any of this to happen.

'You can do this,' I mouth behind my hands. 'You *have* to.' There's work to be done and I need to move fast.

Before I head outside, I check Scott's pulse again – hardly detectable – and shine the torch from my phone into his pupils. No response. Knowing he's not going anywhere, I grab my coat and the various keys I will need, and head out to the garage again. The kit is exactly where I left it from last time – all neatly put away, cleaned and sprayed with disinfectant just in case.

I lift the rope, harness and other strapping from the hook on the wall, grabbing several carabiner clips too. The tarpaulin is still folded neatly on the shelf where I put it after I'd washed it down, so I take that before heading round the back of the garage to the large workshop where Jeremy kept the ride-on mower, other garden machinery and the all-terrain vehicle he loved buzzing around on. He bought one with such a powerful engine, I was concerned about the noise last time, but it seems the neighbours are too far away to hear.

Inside the workshop, I dump the kit in the carrying compartment on the ATV and slide open the big double doors. There's just enough light from the overhead bulb to make sure the fuel lever is switched on and the kill switch disabled. Then, getting on the vehicle, I grasp the brake safety lever and hit the power button. It takes a couple of goes but then the engine jumps into life. Jeremy was always tinkering and making sure it was in top condition.

With the two headlamps on, I slowly trundle the vehicle across the bumpy yard and round through the paddock gate, rumbling up past the pond where we held Jeremy's memorial. Briefly, I stop and stare at the water, the strings of lights up in the garden reflecting off its surface.

Shuddering, I rev the engine and continue up the paddock, opening the five-bar gate and heading up the lawn towards the house. I reverse the vehicle with its rear end facing the large glass doors leading into the dining room. Scott is still lying on the floor in the same position. I'm pretty certain he will be dead now.

I can't help bursting into tears. It feels as though I've been holding them in for decades – not just the last couple of months. I cover my face with my hands, allowing myself a few moments to get it all out – but when I open my eyes again, blurry from crying, all I see is Jeremy lying splayed out on the floor instead.

I'd been towel-drying my hair after my shower that night when I'd screamed. I'd not expected to see Jeremy standing in the bedroom, looking like death warmed up. He was swaying and his eyes were bloodshot and all I wanted was to get him into bed in the hope that he'd sleep so deeply he'd miss his flight the next day.

'Christ, you made me jump,' I'd said.

'I need to pack.' Almost tripping over his own feet, he'd gone to the wardrobe then, but he was all over the place and in no fit state to do anything. I obviously hadn't given him enough drugs. 'Passport… I need to find my passport,' he'd said.

'Isn't it in your study cupboard where you usually keep it?'

'Study… yeah…' he'd repeated, staggering off towards the stairs, leaving me to get into bed, trying to figure out what to do. I couldn't stand the thought of him going away with Madeleine.

And that's when I heard the terrible noise – crashing and thudding and yelling, the floor vibrating as I dashed onto the landing to see what had happened.

Jeremy had fallen down the stairs.

Those wretched, dangerous, over-polished stairs that I'd always hated, but never got around to sorting out.

'Jeremy!' I'd screamed, charging down after him as quickly as I could without falling myself.

Dark blood was already pooling on the hallway tiles around his head, and instantly I saw it wasn't good. The gash on his temple from hitting the sharp corner of the big wooden chest at the bottom of the stairs was deep. I hardly dared move him, given the angle at which he was lying. I was concerned about cervical vertebrae fractures, along with other possible spinal injuries.

'Oh my God, no, *Jer*…' I'd screamed, dropping to my knees beside him. If he hadn't been in his drugged-up, confused state, he'd never have fallen. He was always so careful. It was all my fault.

And that's when everything became a blur – as the consequences gradually dawned on me, submerging me in an irreversible nightmare. I don't know when, exactly, the myocardial infarction had begun – before or after he fell down the stairs. I'll never know, either, if the heart attack he suffered was triggered by the shock of the fall or the cocktail of drugs and alcohol I'd given him, or even if he already had an undiagnosed heart condition. Even several months later, my stupidity doesn't make sense to me – *a doctor, a trusted GP* – allowing jealousy, rage and obsession to make me behave in such a way towards the man I loved most in the world.

'Jeremy!' I'd screamed, thankful Kieran wasn't around to witness everything. He'd gone to stay at a mate's, having already said goodbye to his dad earlier, wishing him a good trip.

I checked Jeremy's pulse, ran for my stethoscope and listened to his heart, knowing from the unusual rhythm that things were not good. I did everything I should have done first-aid wise in those early minutes – including prolonged CPR when his heart stopped until the sweat poured off me. But it was having no effect. I ran for my phone to call an ambulance, not able to locate it at first, charging around the house like a madwoman. I don't even remember how long it took me to find it but, when I knelt down by Jeremy again just before I dialled 999, I checked his pulse, his breathing, his pupil response. I listened to his heart from every angle I could reach.

Nothing. My husband had died at the bottom of the stairs. And I knew nothing would bring him back.

Deciding what to do had not come from a rational place. Kieran would be back in the morning. If I called an ambulance, there would be enquiries into his death at the hospital, perhaps a police investigation, toxicology reports, a thorough forensic examination of my house. When they found out what I'd done, my life as a doctor, as a mother to Kieran, would be over.

Jeremy's life was already over and nothing would change that.

It took me about an hour to decide how to dispose of his body. It's the sort of thing you read about in the newspapers or crazy stories online, never believing it would ever happen to you. But everything I needed was to hand – the all-terrain vehicle to move him, ropes and tarpaulin sheeting in which to wrap him to protect the ground from contamination as I dragged him down to the large pond, using the winch on the back of the quad bike. Sliding his body through the house, avoiding doorways and moving furniture took the longest, but the winch was designed to pull weights far greater than a human body, so eventually I got him outside, temporarily tied the tarp around him and dragged him down to the pond in the dark. It seemed to take forever.

And all the while, I had absolutely no idea I was being watched.

Rain was sheeting down around me, making the ground muddy and my vision blurry as I'd got closer to the water. I'd driven the vehicle onto the jut of land sticking out into the water, getting Jeremy as near to the edge as I could. Attaching weights to him was almost the point at which I'd given up, handed myself in, but I knew that decomposition and bloating would have him floating on the surface before long and, despite all the weed, it was a risk I couldn't take.

It was about four thirty in the morning when I finally drove the ATV a few more metres and watched my husband sink into the depths – all of it captured on Scott's camera as, unbeknown to me, he lurked close by. And all I could think of as Jeremy's face disappeared out of view, shrouded by the murky water, was poor little Lenny Taylor.

Now, as I stand beside the quad bike, watching the same scene unfold, it's Evan Locke's face sinking beneath the murk as he joins my husband in the silt at the bottom of the big pond in the paddock. It's way deeper than it appears from above – at least twenty feet in parts. No one will miss him – not since he was given a new, protected identity a few years ago following his final release. And he has no relatives who'll miss him either. According to the paperwork in Scott's belongings, his probation days are in the past, and unless he were to reoffend, there's no one wondering where he is, no one out looking for him. Plus I'll lock his car up in the workshop for now, hidden under a tarpaulin. It can stay there until I decide how to get rid of it – the paperwork is in his box of stuff. From what Scott said, I believe he'd been watching me for a long time, having tracked me down early last year, but it had taken him months to build up the courage to engineer a meet when I was away in Oxford.

A couple of days after Jeremy's death, the avalanche in Zermatt had come on the news – the same place in Switzerland where my husband had booked to go. Six people missing, presumed dead, with only three bodies recovered. Of course, everyone believed that Jeremy had gone on the skiing trip – my cover until I figured out what I would tell people when he didn't return. Our marriage ending was the most obvious reason, yet wouldn't explain his absence from Kieran's life – so the avalanche, while tragic for those actually involved, provided me with the perfect story. From that moment on, Jeremy was one of the six.

After I'd cleaned up the house and packed away all the equipment, it had grown light. A new day. Jeremy should have been at the airport by now so when his mobile phone rang, I knew I had to answer it.

Madeleine.

'Jeremy is not coming on the trip,' I told her. 'And you can stay away from my husband. I know you've been having an affair and he wants nothing more to do with you. He wants to be with me, so leave us alone. If you contact either of us again, I'll be calling the police.'

After a long silence, Madeleine had said a few words. It's hard to remember what exactly, but she protested for a while, claiming her innocence, before telling me that there was no point in her going on the trip either since there would be nothing to film. And that was the last I ever heard from her.

I sat on the kitchen floor, watching the sky turn from blood red to pink streaks and then a wintry blue, a tumbler of whisky in my hand, with no idea at that point that I had a baby growing inside me. I stared at the sky through the window above, playing out what seemed like every minute of my marriage to Jeremy in my mind, fast-forwarding through the good times and the bad. Then I went upstairs and showered, put a load of washing on, and went to collect my son.

CHAPTER FORTY-FOUR

Then

Sweat pours off Evan as he lugs the kid along the edge of the field. His brisk walk has broken into a run because the grandmother is screaming her head off. There's no way he's going to get caught. When his mum comes out of hospital, he wants things to be peaceful for her. No more migraines. No more lying in bed with her vodka medicine. No more Griff beating her up. Things will get back to normal again. Life will be good.

'Shut up!' Evan snaps at the kid. 'Stop yer whining.'

Griff has said that to him a thousand times, but the kid keeps on grizzling until Evan stops and takes another sweet from the packet. Then he coos and slobbers on Evan's sleeve as he clings on, bouncing about as Evan jogs towards the woods.

Once he gets in the cover of the trees, he'll slow his pace a bit. Then it's not far to skirt around the edge to get to the reservoir. He's praying that Mac will meet him there instead, that he won't let him down. That he won't let Kill Club down.

Eventually, when his leg muscles are burning from the weight of the kid, when he's done in, dusty and exhausted, Evan reaches the entrance to the quarry. The scarred land around it is scrubby and deserted. Not a nice place. There are so many 'Keep Out' signs people rarely go there, but Evan knows a way in where they won't be spotted.

'It's your own fault,' Evan says, hitching the kid up on his hip further, the way he sees his mum do with Rosie. 'If you'd been a good boy and not made all that din, I wouldn't have to bring you out here.'

They draw up to the water's edge, with Evan pacing about at the point the land rises up to a sharp rocky outcrop. Down here, on the flat, him and Mac have paddled many times before, removing their shoes and socks, cooling their feet on hot days. They've never dared swim in the inky-black, freezing water yet, though he knows some of the older kids do. They dare each other to jump in from the top of the rocky cliff.

The kid whines and wriggles again, making Evan drop him down on the ground. He gives him another sweet and the little boy looks up at him, his blond hair glinting in the sun. He smiles, squinting his eyes. 'Dat,' he says, pointing at the packet of sweets in Evan's hand.

The last word he ever spoke.

Evan doesn't know how long he's been sitting there – could just be a few minutes, could be days. He thinks it's probably somewhere in between. The only thing he knows for sure is that the pressure inside him has gone – disappeared like a popped balloon.

He feels good. Better than good. And now the kid is gone too. Silenced.

'Evan!' he hears from behind him. 'Evan, wait!'

He swings round to see Mac running down the grassy track towards where he's sitting. He's shielded from the lane by a line of trees and a thick hedge. Only Mac would know to find him here.

'What the fuck have you done?' he says, drawing up, gasping and panting. He leans forward, hands on knees as he blows in and out.

'You were supposed to help me.' Evan scrambles to his feet.

'*What?*'

'Kill Club,' Evan says. 'You promised you'd help me get the kid and bring him here.'

'Everyone's looking for him. The village has gone crazy. The police are up at the estate. Tell me you didn't take him, Evan. Tell me it wasn't you.' Mac takes him by the shoulders, shaking him, glaring into his eyes.

'You wanted me to do it. We planned it together. You said we were a team.'

'You fucking idiot,' Mac says, spitting on the ground. 'Where is he? We'll make this right. We'll put him back. No one will know.'

Evan turns his head and looks across the water.

'You never?' Mac says, wide-eyed and red-cheeked. 'Tell me you didn't.'

'It's your fault,' Evan says, tears welling up. He hadn't thought the police would come so soon. Maybe he *had* been sitting there for hours, days even. He wasn't sure. He wasn't sure of anything any more, except the hot pee dribbling down his leg.

'Where? *Where is he?*' he hears Mac screaming.

Evan points towards the ledge he dropped the kid from. He didn't think he was alive when he went in, but couldn't be sure.

In a flash, Mac strips off his clothes – kicking off his trainers, pulling off his socks, then unbuttoning his jeans and tugging them off too, hopping about as he does so. Evan has never seen Mac in his underpants before, but it's only when Mac takes off his long T-shirt, pulling it over his head, that he sees they're pink pants with little flowers on. And it takes him a while to realise that the thing he has on under his T-shirt is… is a *bra* – like the one his mum wears, but much, much smaller and with not very much inside.

He doesn't understand.

Evan stares. He stares at Mac in those pink underpants and that matching little bra as he runs all the way down to the water. He stares as Mac charges into the shallows, his arms flailing, his eyes searching as he gets knee-deep, waist-deep, chest-deep. And then Mac's arms are doing the front crawl, cutting through the water. They're in different PE lessons at school and he had no idea that Mac was such a good swimmer… no idea about anything.

Evan looks down at Mac's discarded clothes lying in the dirt. He bends down and picks up the T-shirt, bringing it to his face and inhaling. He doesn't know what he's trying to smell, except he doesn't think it's the same person Mac was just a few minutes ago.

The pressure begins to build inside him again.

Rage.

He feels stupid. More stupid than Griff has ever made him feel. He feels disgusting and tiny, wretched and insignificant, like the ant crawling along in the dirt beside him. It only takes him a second to bring his foot up and stamp on it, and all the other stupid ants following in a line.

How could Mac have done this to him? How could he have not *realised*?

Evan shakes his head, harder and harder until his brain hurts.

He drops down onto the earth, still clutching the T-shirt, watching as Mac frantically swims back and forth in the reservoir beneath the rocky outcrop looming above. Eventually, Mac swims to the edge again and wades out of the water, dripping and exhausted. Tears are streaming down his face.

Down *her* face.

She slumps down on the ground beside Evan, her shoulders shaking as she cries. Evan touches one of them, sliding his fingers down her arm until it's level with her tiny breast. He can't take his eyes off her.

She's beautiful, like a rare butterfly. Except he doesn't want to kill her – he wants to keep her all for himself. She's the only friend he's ever had.

Mac whips her head around. 'We don't say a word, right?' she says, her teeth chattering as she bats his hand away. 'We'll get in big trouble. We keep our mouths shut. Never tell a single soul.'

Evan nods furiously.

Mac stands up again and grabs her dry clothes. 'Turn away,' she orders, and Evan does.

When she's finished dressing, when she's tying up her shoelaces, Evan reaches over to where she's discarded her wet pants. Slowly, he drags them through the dirt and clutches them in his palm, stuffing them in his pocket when she's not looking. They can go in the special tin at the den, along with everything else he's been collecting.

'Right,' Mac says, looking as though she's about to leave. 'You go home, you act normal, don't say anything about the kid, and we swear… we have to swear on our lives never *ever* to hurt another thing again. That'll eventually make all the bad go away.' She holds out her little finger for Evan to shake with his. 'Promise?'

Evan stands, staring up at her – the sight of her wet hair, the sun behind her, her pretty little freckles soothing him more than crushing any insects ever could. Whatever happens to him now, he'll never forget her, will never let her go. He'll always love her no matter what. And one day, even if they're grown-ups, he'll find her, make everything OK again, just like it always was. The two of them together forever.

'Kill Club secret,' he whispers, shaking her little finger back.

EPILOGUE

Two and a Half Years Later

Jen

Jen feels the sun on her back as she walks through the village. Despite the heat of the day, a shiver runs down her spine. But it's a good shiver – a shiver that tells her she is alive, content, and happy even. Though she hardly dares admit it.

'Hey, hey…' she says, peering forward over the hood of the buggy. 'We'll be there soon, sweetie.' She enjoys their trips to the local park on her days off. Surgery is as busy as ever, but since she's gone back to work after Millie was born, she's managed to find some kind of work–life balance.

She flicks a wave at a passing car, recognising a friend. It's amazing how many more people she speaks to now when out and about with her daughter. She can hardly believe that Millie will be turning two in a few days. Everything is set for her little party at the barn – the invites to her nursery friends sent out, the cake ordered, the decorations bought.

Kieran is almost as excited as Millie about preparations – his last summer at home before he goes off to Manchester University. Caitlin has won a place there too, and the pair never stop talking about moving away from home. They've grown inseparable this last year or two, and Caitlin's counselling has now come to an end. She's found some kind of peace after everything she's been through.

'How time passes,' Jen says, though no one hears. Millie coos and kicks her legs in the buggy, as animated and inquisitive as ever. She loves going to the park with her mum, being pushed in the swing or playing in the sandpit.

'Jennifer!' a voice rings out from across the street. 'Oh my God, is that you?'

She turns, spotting a woman about the same age on the other side of the road, also pushing a buggy. She's familiar, Jen thinks, though she can't quite place her. A patient, perhaps, though she isn't sure.

The woman checks the road and comes across.

'I can't believe it's really you,' she says, a broad grin on her face. 'And how weird is this?' She points between their two buggies – hers containing a little boy about the same age as Millie.

Jen smiles, desperately trying to remember the woman's name. She doesn't want to appear rude. Is she a mum at nursery? Has she invited her son to the party?

'Jen…' the other woman says, holding out her hand.

'Yes, yes, that's right, I'm Jen,' she replies, giving her hand a light shake. The woman is a little heavier than Jen, though she can't deny, she's also put on weight since having Millie. She hasn't been to the gym in ages.

The woman laughs. 'No, no, I mean I'm Jen too. Don't you remember?'

Jen smiles, pretending she does.

'We recently moved back to the area. Bob's got a job in Oxford so we thought we'd live near my family here in Harbrooke for the extra help with Noah. He's nearly two now. Bob commutes and…' She trails off, laughing. 'You don't have a clue who I am, do you?'

'Sorry,' Jen admits, rocking her buggy back and forth. Millie is getting tetchy now they've stopped. She turns it round so her daughter is face to face with the little boy. She hopes it will distract her while she chats.

'We were at school together,' the other woman says. 'Jennifer Mason. To be honest, I'm not surprised if you don't remember me. You've probably done your best to forget everything about me. Hand on heart, I can't say I was very nice, especially not to your… to your… *friend*.' She says the word 'friend' with a tinge of bitterness.

'To Evan,' Jen says quietly. Briefly, she remembers that terrible afternoon at the quarry lake, how, as she'd finally turned to leave, Evan had begged her not to go, sobbing as he realised the police would soon catch up with him. He'd called out to her as she walked away, swearing that one day he'd find her, that they'd be friends again, that nothing would ever come between them. Jen had blocked her ears and kept on walking.

She snaps back to the present, dropping her gaze down to the little boy. He's chubby and blond and cooing at Millie. Their feet are touching and the toddlers giggle as they bump sandals against each other.

'But I'm Jennifer Brodie now,' she goes on. 'A reformed woman.' She wiggles the fingers of her left hand about, showing off her ring.

Jen smiles, batting a fly from her face, looking down to make sure it doesn't settle on Millie. But her little girl is preoccupied with something else, gurgling and babbling newly learnt words at Noah.

'Congratulations,' Jen says. 'And yes, yes I do remember you.' She thinks Jennifer Mason – or Gem as she was known at school – looks and sounds entirely different now. Standing there in her long flowing skirt, with a printed blouse loosely tucked in, her hair tied in a messy but stylish bun, she seems anything but frosty and mean. She's the sort of mum Jen would make a beeline for at nursery – the sort of mum she'd get along with.

'So are you still Jennifer Macrory?' the other woman asks. 'Or should I say "Mac"?'

Jen laughs, rolling her eyes. 'No… no, my days of being Mac are long gone. I think there was another Jennifer in our year, too, wasn't there? It was so confusing for the staff, they had to differentiate us somehow. Being such a tomboy, the nickname for me just stuck.'

'I know what you mean,' the woman replies. 'Some people still call me Gem. It's so good to see you. Look, we should get together sometime. It would be great to catch up. You're a doctor now, I hear. I wondered if it might be you when I enrolled at the surgery. I saw your photograph on the display wall and…'

Jen listens to the woman, nodding and laughing, filling in the gaps of time in their lives, chatting about partners, and school, and the upcoming reunion… but she isn't *really* listening. Not truly.

No. Jen is focused on the two toddlers – little Millie and Noah, sitting in their buggies, the pair transfixed by a ladybird that has landed on the padded armrest of Millie's buggy.

It stretches out its wings in the heat of the sun, revealing a pretty lacy petticoat that makes Millie squeal with delight. It walks a few paces, looking as though it's about to take off and fly away, but before it has a chance, Millie brings her chubby little hand up high and, a second later, slams it down on the insect. When she takes her hand away, the ladybird is dead.

Jen watches as Millie looks across at Noah, who is captivated and clapping his hands. The two toddlers beam wide grins at each other, squealing with delight.

'So what do you think?' the other woman says. 'A play date for these two little ones?'

Jen looks up, another shiver running down her spine. She smiles too, putting her hand to her brow against the sun, praying the tear she feels forming in her eye won't roll down her cheek.

'Yes, *yes*,' she says. 'That sounds perfect. Something tells me these two are going to be the best of friends.'

A LETTER FROM SAMANTHA

Dear Reader,

I hope you loved reading *The Trapped Wife*, and that the ending left you shocked! It was such a brilliant book to write, with loads of surprises for me along the way as my characters came to life – I always think it's a good sign if an author is gripped when writing. Currently I'm busy plotting out my next novel – another twisty page-turner (I'm getting excited just thinking about it!) – so if you'd like to keep up to date with my book news, then it would be great if you could take a moment to sign up at the link below to ensure you don't miss out.

www.bookouture.com/samantha-hayes

So where did the idea for *The Trapped Wife* come from? Well… the first seed came from *way* back in my memory, my mind idly meandering through snippets that I'd filed away from long ago as I was drifting off to sleep one night, the perfect time to dream up ideas. I was aged five and had just started at my local village primary school. I was extremely shy and nervous and it wasn't long before one of the school bullies sniffed me out and made my life a misery. Every playtime, every lunch break, he was there, hounding me, chasing me, calling me names, teasing and mocking me. I was terrified – too frightened even to speak up. He had a shock of short curly hair and always had muddy knees beneath his grey school shorts, which he wore winter and summer. I felt sick at the thought of going to school each morning because I knew John would be waiting for me.

Then one day my dad asked me what was wrong, why I was always withdrawn and sad – so, reluctantly, I told him. My parents went into the school to see the teacher, demanding that the boy be spoken to about his behaviour. I'll never forget the moment when I found out that 'John' was in fact Jane – and far from feeling relief that I'd got it so wrong, it almost made the situation worse, as though I couldn't trust my own judgement in this hostile new environment. I still gave Jane a wide berth at playtimes, always keeping an eye on her in case she came after me, and I was certainly relieved when we moved away and I changed schools.

So that was the core idea for *The Trapped Wife*, and I built upon that for Evan and Mac – with loner Evan not quite aligning reality with his desperate need for a friend. But a gripping psychological thriller is multilayered, and for the present-day scenes, I was inspired by a real-life story I read online about a woman who had fallen pregnant by a man she'd only met once. They lived at opposite ends of the country and she decided to pack up her life, give up her job, leave her friends and family and move hundreds of miles to be with him. It left me wondering if it had worked out, what had happened to them – if they'd built a future together or if the pressure of a 'sudden family' had been too great.

But being an author, I couldn't help turning the story around and asking what would happen if the man had moved in with *her* instead? And more importantly, what if she didn't *want* him to – what if it was all a drunken mistake – or, way worse, what if it wasn't consensual? And on top of that, what if he was blackmailing her? That's when I started digging deeper with the questions and wondering what could be in my main characters' pasts that could link them. I've mentioned it before about my books, but challenging assumptions is a powerful tool in writing, and I think *The Trapped Wife* really illustrates this, leaving Jen backed into a corner as her past catches up with her. Desperation and fear drive her to extremes to save herself – but more importantly, to save her son and unborn child.

So that's a brief behind-the-scenes look at the ideas in this book, and a flavour of the weaving of threads that transpired over the months of writing. As ever, if you loved reading it, I'd be more than thrilled if you were able to write a quick review online. Your feedback is so helpful for other readers who might enjoy my book – and of course, I love reading your thoughts too!

I'll sign off for now. I can't wait to share my next book with you. Meantime, feel free to join me on social media or take a look at my website for more details about my books and a little bit about how I became an author – details below.

Take good care and happy reading!
Sam x

samanthahayesauthor

@samhayes

@samanthahayes.author

www.samanthahayes.co.uk

ACKNOWLEDGEMENTS

Whenever I come to write my Acknowledgements, it makes me reflect on how extremely fortunate I am to be doing a job I love as well as working with the brilliant and talented team at Bookouture. A huge thank you to my lovely editor Jessie Botterill, who has the amazing knack of making my books as good as they can be. Many thanks also to Sarah Hardy, Kim Nash and Noelle Holten in Publicity for tirelessly letting the world know about my books, to Sean and Jenny for eagle-eyed copyediting and proofreading, and Lauren for bringing everything together so seamlessly. As ever, big love to my agent Oli Munson, and everyone at AM Heath.

Thank you, too, to the dedicated bloggers and reviewers who are invaluable to authors in spreading the word about books they've read and loved. It really does make a difference, and I can't thank you enough for shouting out about my books on social media – it's so very much appreciated.

I promised I'd mention 'Café Cinq' – the impromptu lockdown garden café (when it was allowed!) that kept a group of us (semi) sane. Everyone has a story… and *none* more so than these wonderful and inspiring women. So Lynda, Jan, Nicky, Julia and Judith – I salute you with a sausage sarnie and the best coffee in town made by the indomitable Barista Brendan!

And of course, thank you to *you* for reading my book and investing in my story – I always say it, but I couldn't do it without you! I really can't wait to share my next thriller with you.

Last but not least, much love to my dear family – Ben, Polly and Lucy, Avril and Paul, Graham and Marina, and Joe. This one's for you!

Sam xx

Made in United States
North Haven, CT
03 May 2022

18825568R00193